THE GIRL NEX

THE GIRL NEXT DOOR

ELIZABETH NOBLE

WHEELER PUBLISHING
A part of Gale, Cengage Learning

GALE
CENGAGE Learning

Detroit • New York • San Francisco • New Haven, Conn • Waterville, Maine • London

Wheeler Publishing Large Print Hardcover.
The text of this Large Print edition is unabridged.
Other aspects of the book may vary from the original edition.
Set in 16 pt. Plantin.

LIBRARY OF CONGRESS CATALOGING-IN-PUBLICATION DATA

Noble, Elizabeth (Elizabeth M.)
    The girl next door / by Elizabeth Noble.
      p. cm.
    ISBN-13: 978-1-4104-2585-0 (alk. paper)
    ISBN-10: 1-4104-2585-1 (alk. paper)
    1. Apartment dwellers—Fiction. 2. Apartment houses, Cooperative—Fiction. 3. City and town life—New York (State)—New York—Fiction. 4. Home—Psychological aspects—Fiction. 5. Large type books. I. Title.
PR6114.O25G57 2010
823'.92—dc22
                          2010001999

Published in 2010 by arrangement with Simon & Schuster, Inc.

Printed in the United States of America
1 2 3 4 5 6 7 14 13 12 11 10

To the city of New York.
If I can make it there . . .

Do not go where the path may lead.
Go instead where there is no path and
leave a trail. . . .

Ralph Waldo Emerson

LIST OF CHARACTERS

Eve Gallagher New, English resident of apt. 7A. Recently relocated from Surrey.

Ed Gallagher Her husband, an ambitious banker.

Cath Thompson Eve's sister, wife of Geoff and mother to Polly and George. Eve's only family.

Violet Wallace Eighty-two-year-old resident of apt. 4B. Also English. Longest resident. Organizer of Gardening Committee.

Jason Kramer A stockbroker, and the owner of apt. 6A.

Kimberley Kramer His wife, a homemaker who used to be a tax lawyer.

Avery Kramer Their young daughter.

Esme Their Jamaican babysitter.

David Schulman A litigator, and the joint owner, with his wife, of apt. 6B.

Rachael Schulman David's wife, senior vice president of marketing at a major cosmetics company, and treasurer of the co-op board.

Jacob, Noah, and Mia Schulman Their children, aged six, four, and two.

Milena Their Polish babysitter.

Jackson Grayling III Son of Jackson Grayling Jr. and Martha Northrup Grayling, of West Palm Beach, and their tenant, apt. 5A. Currently unemployed. Aged twenty-six.

Emily Mikanowski Rents 3A and works for NBC, in production. Triathlete. Aged thirty-one. Second-generation American, born to Polish American parents in Oregon.

Charlotte Murphy Rents 2A and works at the New York Public Library. Aged 29. Of Irish descent, and born in Seattle. Lousy dresser, and romance novel addict.

Madison Cavanagh Rents 2B and works for a fashion magazine but wants to be a bride more than she wants to be an editor. High-maintenance WASP.

The Stewarts (Bobbie, Blair, Tyler, Taylor, and Ashley) Eighth floor. Just completed a renovation, having bought an adjoining apartment and knocked through for more space. Bobbie is a hedge fund manager, and Blair a lady who lunches, with unfeasibly big hair. Made themselves unpopular during construction.

Mary Their housekeeper, a stranger to job satisfaction.

The Piscatellas (Ernest and Maria) The empty nesters in 7B. Their kids, Bradley and Ariel, are away at college. Ernest works in insurance, Maria is a retired teacher. Maria is also co-op board secretary.

The Emerson-Coles (Todd and Gregory) The gay couple who own 5B. Todd is an interior architect and Gregory a pediatric anesthetist, as well as the president of the co-op board.

Dr. Hunter Stern 4A. Violet Wallace's neighbor and long-term sparring partner. A psychiatrist, practicing from an office in the apartment.

Arthur Alexander 3C. Arthur's father once owned the building. Arthur's apartment is all he has left. Homophobe and resident curmudgeon.

Che, Jesus, Raul The doormen. All Cuban. The super only hires Cubans.

The Gonzalezes (Esteban and Dolores) The superintendent and his wife. Resident caretakers of the building for the last fifteen years.

"Green lungs." Isn't that what they call parks in big cities? It isn't true in New York. In New York, Central Park — more than eight hundred acres of priceless real estate in one of the world's greatest cities — is not the lungs. It's the heart. Walk around any of the paths, away from the hullabaloo, the tourists studying maps, the omnipresent runners, the pretzel sellers, and you'll find benches everywhere. There are more than nine thousand of them. Since 1986, the Central Park Conservancy has run a program called Adopt-a-Bench, allowing residents of the city to dedicate one to someone they have loved, and love still. Here is where you feel, and hear, the heart of the city beating. There's a marriage proposal on a bench by the zoo. Statements of joy and happy memories and grateful thanks on rows of benches by playgrounds — at the Alice in Wonderland statue, facing the carousel,

13

along the water. Since 9/11, there are benches that can make you tear up, just reading the plaques. For young men and women, dead too soon, and those they left behind. "To the world you were one person. To one person you were the world."

I chose Cedar Hill for mine. It was one of your favorite places. In the winter, children toboggan there, filling the air with their laughter. In the fall, the colors are extraordinary. In the summer, it's close to the ice cream truck that parks on Fifth, and shady. But I may like spring the best of all. Full of promise and new beginnings, for the people I watch.

I wondered for a long, long time how to inscribe the plaque. Whitman, or Emerson? Puccini? A declaration of my own?

In the end, though, I chose just your name. Everything else belonged to me, and I kept it inside, written on my heart.

EIGHT A.M.

The night doorman, Jesus, was coming off his shift.

Before Raul, his replacement, arrived, he mopped the marble foyer and diligently polished the brass tread on the door threshold. The day shift doorman changed into his smart gray uniform in the staff bathroom. The porter traveled to each floor in the service elevator, collecting the black sacks of trash and sorted recycling that people left out there. In the basement, the super checked his list to see who was on, who was away, who was having things delivered or taken away. He'd done this fifty weeks of each year for more than fifteen years.

He and his wife lived in a small apartment at the back downstairs. They'd raised their boys there, though they were grown up and gone now.

In apartment 7B, Maria Piscatella kissed her husband, Ernest, goodbye chastely on the cheek, smoothing his hair down habitually as he left for work, and contemplated the breakfast dishes and another day. Her two children smiled down at her in their high school graduation outfits, from the eight-by-ten photographs that hung on the kitchen wall. She knew they'd both still be asleep, in their college beds in their college dorms far away. Up late, no doubt, last night, studying or partying.

Bradley had been gone from here two years, and Ariel since last September, and she still missed them every, every day. The apartment was still too quiet. There wasn't

15

enough mess. She had two plates, two glasses, and two mugs to load into the dishwasher. One bed to make. And no laundry today. If you'd told her ten years ago how much she would miss all of that, she'd have laughed and told you you were crazy.

Upstairs, in 8A/B, Blair Stewart's house-keeper Mary would have laughed along with Maria Piscatella. She'd been up since six, waking alone in the windowless maid's room off the laundry, as she had done for the past six months, and now she was serving waffles — each plate configured slightly differently — to the Stewarts' three kids, while Blair issued the day's instructions and Bobbie moaned that the dry cleaner's hadn't returned his gray pinstripe.

Mary didn't mind being told what to do (wrong career path, if she did), but she hated the way Mrs. Stewart did it. When she said "Clean the laundry room," she always added "really well, please, Mary," as though there were any other way to do it, or as if she ever did anything else. You'd think a woman who was so damn particular about how things were done would do some of them herself. But of course, Mrs. Stewart was perpetually busy. Today was a luncheon.

Mary had still to figure out what besides those three letters elevated a regular lunch into a luncheon, but she figured it had something to do with money. She'd go to that gym, on the corner of Madison and Eighty-fifth, the one she went to every day during the week, and then get her hair blown out and get dressed up to go out and "do good." Forget about doing any good in her own home. Mary didn't like Blair Stewart at all. God knows she needed a job, and the money wasn't bad here, but if it weren't for the kids, she'd be thinking about finding something else already. The kids were okay. A little lazy, a little spoiled maybe — but whose kids weren't, these days?

Dr. Hunter Stern, in 4A, slept on. He never had a patient until 11 a.m., and since he saw patients in the apartment, he never needed to get up before 10:30. An insomniac since his twenties, he was never asleep before three or four in the morning, and he wore earplugs so that the cacophony of a Manhattan morning didn't disturb him once he had dropped off. He couldn't take sleeping pills. He had an addictive personality, like so many of the patients he counseled. That ruled out red wine, too, which would also have worked. He read biographies avidly and usually dozed off, eventually, on the sofa, heavy tomes rising and falling on his chest.

Across the hall, Violet Wallace fried an egg and two strips of bacon, as she did every morning of the week. She carried the plate through to the dining room, where she had laid the table the night before, with a linen napkin and silver cutlery, and switched on the BBC World Service on the radio. Cat, the smoky Abyssinian cat she had resisted getting for so long, refusing to conform to the stereotype of the single old lady, and whom she still tokenly resisted loving by calling her Cat, curled her tail around Violet's chair, rubbing her back against Violet's legs, oblivious to her mistress's ambivalence.

Above her, in 5B, Gregory Cole fed Ulysses, his chocolate brown Labrador, who licked his hand appreciatively, while his partner, Todd, took a shower. Todd ate breakfast with his assistant, Gabrielle, at the office every day, so Greg made a bowl of granola with yogurt for himself and flipped open the *Times,* leaning against the granite breakfast bar in their kitchen.

"Sit down to eat," Todd called from the

bathroom.

"You can't even see me!"

"Doesn't mean I don't know what you're doing . . ."

Charlotte Murphy peered into the mirror, as she did every morning in 2A, and was, as she was every morning, disappointed to see herself peering back. Through the thin partition wall in 2B, built before building codes came into effect, Madison Cavanagh had the opposite reaction as she tossed her mane of Bergdorf blonde hair and carefully applied another coat of lengthening mascara to lashes that already almost hit her eyebrows.

Upstairs in 3A, newcomer Emily Mikanowski stretched her body into the cat on her yoga mat, trying to ignore the pile of boxes in the living room that still needed to be unpacked, while next door Arthur Alexander dreamed his troubled dreams and snored, spittle settling into the corners of his mouth.

The furnace burned, and the pipes ran. Kettles boiled on stoves, and radiators creaked. The building was waking up.

APRIL

EVE

FOUR SEASONS HOTEL, EAST FIFTY-SEVENTH STREET

"Good morning, New York!" Ed's Robin Williams impression reverberated around Eve's poor head.

Last night, celebrating their new life with dirty Grey Goose martinis in the hotel bar had seemed like the obvious — the only — thing to do. They'd had a few drinks, and a late dinner, and very sexy hotel sex, and about five hours' sleep. This morning, not so much. The dirty Grey Goose martini may be a very New York drink, but Eve was clearly still a very English girl. *Dirty* was the word. Eve's mouth felt like the proverbial bottom of the parrot's cage.

She pulled the down pillow over her head in an attempt to keep out the bright sunshine pouring in through their twelfth-floor wall of windows, but it was insistent, like Ed, who was now running through his Sinatra repertoire, oblivious to the fact that she might just have to kill him soon. Thou shalt not — not ever — drink three vodka-based cocktails. The eleventh commandment.

The doorbell rang. Ed was obviously in better shape, as usual. It took more than three drinks to fell her husband. He answered the door with a cheery "Good morning!" and admitted their breakfast, brought in by a waiter so discreet that he laid a table, arranged an orchid in a vase and silver domes on porcelain plates, then left again without ever acknowledging the groaning woman-shaped lump under the duvet.

"Come on, lightweight. Breakfast." Ed, who was, she now noticed, already showered and dressed, flipped up the bottom corner of the bedspread, exposing a foot. He squeezed her big toe.

"Ugh."

"Tea?"

"Mmm."

"Wasn't sure what you wanted, and wasn't about to risk waking you up, so I ordered pancakes, bacon, fruit salad, egg-white omelette —"

"Who would ever want to eat an egg-white anything? The yolk's the only fun part of an egg."

"And the only part that will kill you."

Eve sat up grumpily and accepted the cup of tea he proffered. "And so it begins . . ."

"So what begins?"

"You're turning American. Joining the cholesterol police."

Ed laughed. "So I guess you want the pancakes and bacon?"

"Kill or cure." Eve came to the table and peered under the silver dome on her side of the table.

"I'm hoping for cure. Busy day in prospect . . ." Ed raised his glass of orange juice in a toast, and clinked it against Eve's cup. "Here's to the new house!"

Except that it wasn't a house. Eve and Ed used to live in a house with a name, on a street with a name. In a house with a garden and a driveway and a garage for a car. Their car. Ed had a shed in the garden. Eve had a job. Eve used to live twenty-five minutes from her sister and her nieces and nephews.

That was then. This was now. She took her tea to the window and looked out at the tall gray buildings and the blue, blue sky. Steam rose from manhole covers, just like in films. She couldn't kick that feeling — like she was herself in a film. But this was real. This was it! They were here . . .

Two pancakes, three rashers of very crispy

bacon, four mugs of tea, and a fifteen-minute power shower later, Eve felt human. Ish. When she emerged from the bathroom that was bigger than her bedroom at home, Ed was on the phone and it was obviously work. She frowned at him. Today was their day.

He raised a conciliatory hand and shrugged apologetically. But he said, "Yep. Right. Yep. I'll be there in" — checking his watch — "half an hour. Forty-five minutes tops. Great." When he'd hung up he came and sat next to her on the bed and put his arm around her shoulders.

She glared at him reproachfully. "You promised."

"I know. I won't be there all day, I promise. Just a couple of hours."

Neither of them believed him.

"You'd better be there when we pick up the keys." That was three p.m.

"Definitely." Ed was pulling on his jacket. "I'll meet you there."

"Okay."

Ed took her face in his hands and kissed her deeply. "I'm going to make love to you in every room tonight."

She crinkled her nose up and sniggered. "Cheeseball. Good job it's a classic four, not a classic six."

"Get you, with your New York Realtor talk."

"Oh, I know all the lingo."

He smacked her rear. "And, FYI, I reckon I could manage a classic six or, indeed, a duplex."

Eve laughed. He probably could, actually. When they'd moved into the cottage, he'd managed every room, the patio table, and the shower, although, truthfully, things had gotten a little halfhearted by the time they'd gotten to the old larder with the freezing cold marble countertop. She'd made him promise they'd christen every house they ever had that way, even the assisted living facility she was confident they'd end up in. He remembered.

One more quick kiss, a groan of regret, and he was gone.

Back to bed then, just for a while.

She couldn't believe she was here. Everything had happened so fast. Four months ago there had been no hint of any of this. Four months ago she'd been looking out the window at her garden, at the deep beds she'd dug the year before, thinking about springtime. She'd loved that garden. And the house. Their first house. A three-bedroom cottage in a village four miles from the center of town. Top of their budget when they'd bought it, it still needed lots of work — the old couple they'd bought it from hadn't done a thing to it in twenty years — so she'd become a rabid weekend DIYer. She'd learned to strip wallpaper, and tile and grout, and over the course of a year or two she'd eradicated all the eighties décor and created a place she truly loved — all white walls and deep sofas. The garden had been the best part and the biggest revelation. She'd never taken the slightest notice of the seasons before. She'd lived in her parents' house, where the garden was somewhere to play and lounge around, in university halls and in flats, where, on hot, sunny days, Clapham Common was the only garden you needed and you ignored it for the other 360 days of the year. But after they bought the house, she drank the first cup of tea of the morning on the little patio off the kitchen, almost every day, drinking in the sights and sounds and smells of the garden all year round.

She'd been on the patio when Ed had come home that day. She was wearing his Barbour and a rainbow-striped woolly hat that she'd had forever and that Ed called "the tea cozy," drinking a mug of Earl Grey, and inspecting her beds, daydreaming of bulbs. She was always home an hour or so before Ed. He worked in London and was at the mercy of the capricious trains. Much as she loved him, that hour was often her favorite of the day. All her own. A good day's work done (mostly). Time to indulge her newfound domesticity. Marinade something. Prune something.

He'd been later than usual, that day. She'd smelled beer on his breath as he kissed her. "Evie." She loved that he called her Evie. He had, since the first day she'd met him, and he was the only person in the world who did, since her mum.

"You've been drinking!"

"Sorry, Mum. Just one."

"Who with?" She put her hands on her hips in a Lucille Ball sort of way, but she was smiling.

"The boys from work."

"The boys" were an amorphous lump of masculinity so far as Eve was concerned. She'd met them, possibly, at the Christmas party, at the Summer Family Fun Day (and the award for most misnamed day goes to . . .), but they were an indistinct lot — Ben and Dan and Tom and Dave and Tim and . . . the rest.

"Good day, then?"

"Great day."

Now her curiosity was aroused. "How so?"

"Come inside, babe. It's freezing out here. I want to talk to you." Ed pulled her by both hands, walking backward toward the door. She let him. Inside their kitchen, he went to the fridge, and pulled out a bottle of wine.

"We're celebrating." He grabbed two glasses from the dish rack and poured.

"What?"

"I've got a new job. I've been promoted."

"Ed! That's fantastic! I didn't even know you were up for something."

"Nor did I. Well, not exactly."

Eve picked up the two glasses, handing him one. "You star. Cheers."

"Cheers, Evie." They both drank.

Eve pulled out a chair and sat down, still watching him. He looked so happy. "Tell me all."

"I haven't told you the best bit."

"A raise?" A raise would be great. They could really do with reducing the mortgage. All the spare cash they'd had in the last couple of years had gone to renovations . . .

"Yes, yes, a raise. A pretty massive one. But that's not it." He widened his eyes, smirking at her.

She smacked his chest playfully. "Stop teasing me, you bugger. Wha-a-at?"

"The job is in *New York!*" Ed did jazz hands. He looked strangely comical doing jazz hands. The moment was surreal.

"What?"

"New York. The job's in the New York office. Manhattan. Two years, maybe more if we want. New frigging York, Evie! Can you believe it?"

Eve felt like all the air in her lungs had been sucked out. Her cold, garden cheeks were suddenly hot.

Ed stood in front of her, jazz hands frozen. "So talk to me. You look like a fish." He blew out his cheeks, and made ohs with his mouth. "Say something."

"Wow."

He shook her gently by the shoulders. "Say something else."

"New York."

"A whole sentence would be good."

"You took this job?"

Ed's face fell just a little. "Well . . . I told them I'd need to talk to you first, obviously, but . . ."

"But?"

"But I said I was sure you'd jump at it. You will, won't you? Jump at it? I mean, it's not like we haven't talked about something like this —"

"We talked about it once, years ago."

"But you were up for it then, weren't you?"

"Well, yes . . ."

"And nothing's changed, has it?"

"There's the house . . ."

Was that a flicker of irritation crossing his face? "And we can keep the house, Evie. Of course we can."

"I love the house." She sounded wistful, even to herself.

"I know you do. I love the house, too. We'll keep the house, Evie. They'll rent us a place, sort all of that out. It's a really sweet deal. We'll be much better off. We'll rent it out, of course. Tenants will pay the mortgage. And we'll come back."

"Will we?"

Ed knelt down by her chair and put both arms around her hips. "You don't sound happy like I thought you would, Evie."

She laid her head on top of his, in her lap. "I'm just . . . it's a bit sudden . . . it's a bit of a shock, that's all."

"Not a shock. A surprise. A wonderful, fortuitous, bloody marvelous surprise." He rubbed her hair. "Hey, Evie. We can talk about this as much as you like. We can say no."

She looked at his face, trying to figure out whether or not he meant that. His lovely face. She knew she wouldn't make him say no. Eve wasn't quite sure when it was decided that Ed had the career and she had the job. Or who had decided. But she knew that that's how it was. And so she knew that they would go to New York.

And now she just needed to figure out how to be happy about it.

And so four months later, here she was, (almost) completely happy about it. She was even (almost) a little ashamed of her initial reaction. It wasn't very intrepid of her. This was a huge adventure, wasn't it? A fantastic opportunity. The most exciting city in the world. She wanted to be the sort of woman who grabbed life. Who'd ride a bike downhill without the brakes on, and who'd sit in the front seat on the roller coaster, and who'd stand at the karaoke mike. She'd always wanted to be that sort of woman. And now she could be. This was the perfect place to be that woman. And today was a good day to start . . .

Perhaps she'd start by calling her sister. Cath had always been that woman. In some ways it made no sense that she was here and Cath was there, married to Geoff. Slightly wet Geoff. Who ever knew what alchemy was at work when two people fell in love? It made no sense, sometimes.

Cath answered on the third ring. She sounded out of breath.

"It's me. Eve."

"Eve! How are you? How's it all going?"

"Oh, you know, it's hell at the Four Seasons. What to eat? What treatment to get at the spa? Just ordering from the pillow menu is exhausting . . ."

"Shut up. I just cleaned poo out from under my fingernails."

"That's disgusting. How are the poo machines?"

"Smelly. Noisy. Adorable."

"I can hear one now."

"That's George. He wants Cheerios in the car. I've only got a minute, actually, Sis. School run, you know."

"I forgot."

"No worries. Sometimes I forget, and that's much more serious. I've got a sec. How is it, really?"

"Really? A bit weird. Ed's gone to the office, even though he's supposed to be off all day helping me, and I realize I don't know a soul. I'm totally friendless until he meets me later."

"Go shopping. No one can feel lonely in Bloomingdale's. Visa can be your best friend."

Eve laughed. "You're probably right."

"So when do you move in?"

"We get the keys this afternoon. The new

furniture should be coming tomorrow. The stuff from England is meant to have cleared customs last week, but I've got to check. So today, I suppose, officially, although we'll sleep at the hotel for another couple of nights."

"No room service in the flat, I suppose."

"In the apartment? No!"

"Listen, hon. I'd really better go. Call me later, tell me again how fabulous it is?"

"Sure. I will. Love to everyone."

"And back. We all miss you like crazy, Eve."

Eve missed her sister, too. She could picture everything about Cath at that moment. George, with his plastic beaker of Cheerios and his untamable blond cowlick; the chaotic kitchen, full of unread newspapers and sticky jars; Cath, tall and willowy and totally yummy mummy.

Suddenly a little tearful, she sniffed and reached for the remote control. Nurse Hathaway and Dr. Doug Ross were arguing again. She lost herself in the County General ER and eventually slipped back into sleep, not waking until the credits were rolling.

APARTMENT 6A

Avery Kramer was barking orders as usual. She looked like an angel but right now she was about as far from angelic as a curly blond, blue-eyed toddler could get. The blue was icy, the lash-fringed lids narrowed in cold rage. She sat in the ungainly wooden high chair, legs splayed as though to trip you on purpose, and demanded yet another breakfast option. Behind her, the kitchen sink was already piled high with dishes from rejected offerings. She'd wanted French toast but hadn't eaten it, had demanded a boiled egg but had discarded it after the first dip of a bread finger. Now, it seemed, Cheerios, no milk, were what was required.

Her mother, Kimberley, was reaching for the cereal box, talking to Avery all the while in the singsong storytime voice her husband, Jason, had grown to hate. He straightened his tie, taking in the domestic tableau, and wondered how it had all gone so wrong. His first meeting wasn't until ten a.m., but he was ready to leave already. Kissing the top of his daughter's head, he gave Kim a jaunty wave, almost a salute, but moved no closer to her.

"See you tonight!" He sounded cheerier than he felt.

"Are you going to want dinner?" she

36

asked, not looking at him.

What the hell kind of question was that? Who didn't want dinner? Why was he made to feel, should he dare answer that daily question in the affirmative, that eating an evening meal was an inconvenience? He ate breakfast at his desk. He was gone all day. His shirts and suits went to the dry cleaner's. He just wanted dinner.

"No. I've got a lunch. I'll have a sandwich."

"Good. My schedule is pretty full today."

Full of what, for Christ's sake? This question, of course, he did not ask out loud.

"Say good-bye to Daddy, Avery."

She didn't call him Jason anymore. She called him Daddy when Avery was awake and around, and when she wasn't, Kim didn't call him anything at all. The door to the Schulmans' apartment opened just as Jason closed his own behind him. The hall between the two apartments, the only homes on the sixth floor, was about ten feet wide, and he could smell Rachael's perfume before he saw her. It wasn't one of those chemical, strident fragrances; it was flowery and soft and sophisticated. Just like Rachael Schulman.

Even their children were perfect. Jacob, Noah, and Mia Schulman, bed-rumpled and sleepy, their babysitter behind them, stood in the doorway to wave good-bye to their parents. Mia looked like a bush-baby — all huge brown eyes — standing tiny between her two bigger brothers. "Love you, Mama. Love you, Daddy."

"We love you, too. See you tonight." Always the "we." Envy swelled in his throat.

David patted Jason on the top of his arm. "Morning."

"How are you?" The elevator doors opened and they got in, Rachael pressing 1 with the manicured index finger of her left hand, diamond wedding band sparkling.

"How are Kim and Avery?" Rachael asked, her wide Julia Roberts smile revealing her small, white, even teeth.

They're horrible, he wanted to say. Out loud, "Fine." A pause, a floor of silence. Rachael brushed lint from David's shoulder in a quietly proprietary way. Jason coughed. "Great weather we've been having." God, could he be any more pedestrian?

"Fabulous. Felt like a long winter, this one, hey? We're going to go out to the country this weekend. So nice to feel the sun on our skin."

Rachael's skin. Golden, even through the long winter. Smooth, even, glowing. Like the skin on the girls on the advertisements

38

for body lotion.

"You must come out for a weekend. Mia and the boys would love to have Avery to play with."

David nodded in agreement. "We'll make that happen, definitely."

Jason really, really hoped so. In the country, Rachael would wear a bathing suit. A bikini. More skin than he'd seen before. Last summer, Rachael in her short shorts had fueled his dreams for weeks. Rachael in a bikini . . . He felt his heart racing.

The elevator had reached the ground floor. Che, the doorman, was mopping the floor at the end of his night shift. Jason reached into his jacket pocket for his MetroCard and waved to Rachael and David as they climbed into the Lincoln Town Car that picked them up each morning and delivered them to their respective offices downtown.

It was a beautiful morning — classic New York blue. In their air-conditioned car, David put one hand on Rachael's knee. "Did you mean that?"

"Mean what?"

"Mean that the Kramers should come to the country with us?"

"Shouldn't I have?"

David shrugged. "I don't know. He's

always a bit . . . furtive . . . these days. And she's so uptight."

"She's protective of Avery. That's all. First baby."

"I don't remember you being like that with Jacob."

"You're biased. I think it could be fun. Besides, I feel bad for him. He always seems a bit sad to me."

"I see furtive, you see sad."

"You're just naturally suspicious."

"And you're just naturally a soft touch."

Rachael laughed. David squeezed her knee. "Fine. Invite them. I bet Kim says no. Too much danger in the country, you know. Mosquitoes. Deer ticks."

"Bears!" Rachael laughed.

"Bears. Right. Avery could get attacked by bears. She'll never come."

APARTMENT 5A

Jackson half opened his eyes in irritable protest at the bright light seeping through the blinds of his bedroom, then turned his head to read the alarm clock. Eight a.m. Jesus. He'd only been in bed for three hours.

He focused unsteadily on his left foot, sticking out from under the sheets at the end of the bed. Fuchsia pink toenails. That had seemed a good idea last night. Or this morning. His mother had left a bottle on the side of the sink when she'd invaded the apartment in a cloud of Hermès last week. He'd been watching reruns of some reality show, drinking beer, and he'd found the nail varnish, and he'd been bored . . . Not really his color, he saw now. He wondered vaguely whether she'd left remover, too. Probably not. He couldn't imagine Martha Northrup Grayling taking her own nail polish off, any more than he could imagine her making her own coffee or blow-drying her own hair. The varnish would only have been for emergency repairs. God forbid she should appear in public with a chipped nail. This was a woman who wore full makeup to the gym.

He felt too awake to roll over. He felt on the bedside table for a Marlboro and his engraved Zippo and lit up without lifting his head from the pillow, taking a deep drag.

From the hallway he heard the sound of the porter, in the service entrance, collecting the glass bottles and black sacks of trash. Too much damn noise. The building might be getting up, but he wasn't ready.

What was there to get up for, after all? No rat race for Jackson Grayling III. No job to force him into the shower and onto the subway. No mortgage, no bills. As yet, he had not woken up, either to the morning or to the realization that the absence of all the above also equaled no life.

His existence was just fine by him. His parents had sprung for this apartment a couple of years ago, anxious to remove his brooding bulk from their own pied-à-terre. Their main home, for tax purposes, was a detestable behemoth in West Palm Beach, Florida, but they had apartments in at least four other American cities, and they spent time in each, as sanctioned by their accountants, as well as a home in the Bahamas and one in the Alps. All through his childhood they'd had a town house on the Upper East Side, with a garage and a roof terrace, but they'd sold it a couple of years ago and bought one of the new apartments in the Plaza Hotel, half of which had been converted into private homes. His mother delightedly called herself "Eloise — like in the book" when she told people. He'd liked the town house and would happily be lolling around there now, had he been permitted, but he loathed the Plaza apartment and seldom went there unless summoned. His father wasn't that thrilled either, with the Plaza or with New York in general. Martha often used it alone or with her clonelike girlfriends from the South, leaving Jackson's father golfing or sailing or tax planning somewhere else. It had been years since he'd called either of them on a conventional landline. He never knew where they were, and he got tired of housekeepers telling him. Not that he called them much on their cell phones either. They had all conspired in creating a life where he really didn't need to.

Most of his money was in trust, of course. They weren't stupid enough to let him have the bulk of his fortune until he was thirty. They had bought the apartment outright. His mother and her decorator from Palm Beach had descended, reinventing the previously drab apartment into a middle-aged woman's and a gay Cuban's idea of a young man-about-town's place. It looked like a Ralph Lauren show house, but Jackson didn't really care. Girls seemed to like it. His monthly maintenance charge and utilities went directly through his father's office. He couldn't have told you how much they were, actually. He'd had to attend the board interview the co-op had required, of course. His father had demanded a blazer and tie, and his mother had hissed at him, in the elevator on the way up to the fifth floor, that he wasn't to blow it with any of his stupid jokes about late-night parties and drum kits. He wasn't an idiot — he could play along when playing along was required. The sixth generation of men in his family to attend Duke, the civic responsibility bullshit, the deciding which part of the family business to go into stuff — he could talk a good game, but the only game he actually played was basketball, once a month or so, down on the courts under the West Side Highway by the river. And by and large, he did behave himself — in the apartment. The night doormen might be able to tell a tale or two about him but the Kramers upstairs and Dr. Stern downstairs couldn't complain about him.

If the board president he met on the landing between their apartments from time to time had regrets about letting him in, they didn't show.

His father paid him an allowance for his other living expenses, and he always had the black American Express card for emergencies (he and his father had a very different definition of what constituted an emergency, but he usually got away with it). They paid for a maid who came in, with a basic grocery shop, two or three times a week and cleaned away most of the detritus left over from the last shop she'd done.

Two or three times a year he was questioned, closely and with some exasperation, about his plans for the future. Christmas, Thanksgiving, Memorial Day. He had time between these encounters to plan answers that sounded plausible, even to him. He was looking into this area, talking with people about such and such, considering another college course. Thinking about something philanthropic . . . that was always a good one.

His mother was a softer sell than his father. He was her only child, and she believed whatever he told her, staring at him, all the while, with adoration and love. Jack 2, as he insisted on calling his father, much to the old man's irritation, was not so easily mollified. He prided himself on a great bullshit antenna and it gave him no pleasure to have it twitch constantly around his only child.

The family money was old. It was Jackson's great-great-grandfather who had begun to accumulate it in serious amounts in the mid-nineteenth century. By the time of the Civil War he was already seriously rich and, despite being from the South, had somehow managed to come out the other side of that conflict even wealthier. There were definitely murky decades, morally, in the Grayling family vault, but the twentieth century had drawn a veil of respectability over them, and by the time Jackson went to college, he was taking classes in buildings bearing his family name. All his father had ever done was manage the family money, which had increased with his marriage to Martha, who came from her own fortune in horse breeding, and Jackson knew it was the expectation of both that he would one day grow up enough to be entrusted with the same. The thought bored him as only the truly privileged can be bored. And the money, which he had spent freely his entire life, perversely did not interest him in the slightest. This, he knew, incensed his father, and that was the most fun part. Last Christmas his father had lost his temper as much as he ever did and called him a "ne'er-do-well." Jackson was trying hard to rise to the challenge.

His mother had only managed, despite her family's success in breeding other animals, to produce one child — him. How he had longed for a brother or even a sister who could toe the line, take over from his father, so that they would all leave him alone.

APARTMENT 2A

Madison knocked on Charlotte's door. "Hiya, Charl!"

Charlotte pulled her chenille bathrobe tighter around her and opened each of the three locks on her door. Madison was wearing hot pink and white Lycra — a sleeveless vest and short shorts. She had been to the gym. Of course. She went five times a week.

She had that postgym glow. Madison had several glows that Charlotte had come to know well. Postgym was just one of them. She was more familiar than she might have chosen to be with postcoital, too — although that was usually on the weekends. And that big hair, with its expensive caramel highlights. And that perfectly applied makeup, the kind that looked like you didn't have any makeup on at all. She wore tinted moisturizer to the gym, because you never knew who you might meet there, she'd confided to Charlotte. Not that Madison Cavanagh needed makeup. Charlotte should know. She'd seen her without it often enough. Madison Cavanagh looked gorgeous in sweats, in rollers, in a towel. In her apartment.

Charlotte wasn't sure why Madison was in her apartment as often as she was, although she suspected that her neighbor hated being alone. In the absence of a gaggle of girlfriends, or a romantic conquest, she supposed that she was the next best thing. They'd moved in around the same time to the 650 square feet, one bedrooms on the second floor. Both apartments were owned by the management company and rented.

When they'd begun, both empty spaces were a symphony of innocuous beige and taupe. Within weeks, Madison's had been transformed, Charlotte's merely disguised a little. Madison had a big turquoise sofa and expensive-looking cushions with graphic prints on them. A wenge wood console with a dozen photo frames. Madison was in each of the photographs, smiling her big white smile. Here against a backdrop of sand dunes with her parents and her brothers, there hoisted onto the shoulders of two big men in football uniforms. Raising a cocktail glass among identical girlfriends. Center stage was given to Madison in graduation robes, her hair perfect under the mortarboard. The first time Madison had seen Charlotte's chaste single bed, dressed with a quilt and a small lace pillow, she'd twittered about how sensible it was to leave more room for storage and clothes and stuff and how, with her queen bed, she herself had barely enough room for her shoes.

She'd come borrowing milk in her gym clothes one morning in the very early days, and she'd been coming ever since. She'd wanted skim, had expressed disappointment at Charlotte's 2 percent, but had taken it anyway. Charlotte didn't think she had ever knocked on Madison's door. The pattern of their friendship — if that was, indeed, what it was — was that Madison came to her whenever she needed anything, be it milk for her cereal (and Charlotte bought skim now — how silly), a needle and thread to sew a button on, or a conversation to make her feel better about her place in the universe again.

They had never been out together, and Charlotte knew that they never would. That was not what she was for. She didn't mind. She was ambivalent about Madison in general. She supposed that Madison, if she ever stopped and thought about it, might expect Charlotte to be desperately jealous of her, envious of her looks and her ease and her place in the world. But Charlotte was smarter than that. She was curious, and sometimes mildly alarmed or vaguely amused. If Charlotte had had a pen pal back home that she wrote to about the big bad city (although she did not), her letters would have been full of the adventures of Madison Cavanagh.

Madison was the first promiscuous person

Charlotte had ever known. (And the first adult person besides herself that Charlotte had ever seen entirely naked, Madison having once stripped completely while seeking Charlotte's opinion on which short and sparkling outfit she should wear to some party or other.)

Sex was, for Madison, something completely separate from love. On one, she considered herself a talented expert. As for the other, she claimed to have had several misadventures and been left wounded and vulnerable, although Charlotte wasn't convinced. Her own virginity was a subject they never touched upon. Charlotte didn't volunteer, and Madison didn't probe. If it wasn't about Madison, it wasn't really worth discussing, and virginity hadn't been about Madison for many years.

It had been shocking to Charlotte, at first, to hear details. "Play by plays," Madison called them, laughing. But she was used to it now.

Madison had a new theme recently. Jackson Grayling III. Trip, as he was known. She'd been out with some college friends from Wall Street, who'd been joined by some guys who worked nearby. They'd been connecting the dots of their lovely lives, as young people like that did. And she'd found out that Trip, the scruffy but undeniably good-looking nocturnal guy who lived on the fifth floor, was this filthy rich trust fund guy whose parents owned half of Texas or something. Madison didn't link sex with love. But she sure as hell linked love with money. Charlotte didn't care much about money, so long as she could pay the rent and bills and buy books. She sent about 20 percent of what she earned home, where it helped cancel out the debt she owed her parents for college. And she saved, more than might be expected, from her salary at the library. She didn't crave things the way Madison seemed to.

Madison earned more than twice what she did, working at a fashion magazine. And Charlotte knew that her mother sent her checks almost every month and paid the airfare when she was going home for the holidays. But she was always claiming penury, usually because she'd spent her food money on shoes in Barneys on her lunch hour. She had what she called a "wish board" in her apartment, propped up against the kitchen cabinet next to the sink. She said she got the idea off *Oprah* once, when she'd been home with a cold and watching daytime television. Oprah had told her she should put pictures of all the things she dreamed of on a board, and that this would help her visualize them and thus come closer to attaining them. Charlotte suspected that Oprah — even if you didn't consider the idea to be hokum, as she did — had had loftier ideals for such a board and hadn't particularly meant it for an YSL Muse bag and a three-carat, princess-cut Tiffany diamond necklace. But those were the things that Madison dreamed of.

Madison talked about marriage a lot. It was inevitable, clearly, in her mind. This part of her life — the time when she dated lots of men and slept with almost all of them without ever knowing things about them — this was just now. When the time came (and Madison thought that twenty-seven was about the right time), she would get serious in her search. And the guy she found (a guy who wouldn't mind at all that she'd spent the previous five years working her way through the male population of Manhattan, apparently) would be wealthy — or, at the very least, have spectacular prospects — and be from a good family, tall, athletic, hand-some, and generous.

Fate would take care of it all. There was a little girl's heart beating far beneath the Agent Provocateur–clad bosom of Madison

Cavanagh, and it dreamed of Prince Charming.

Who may or may not currently be sporting a slightly lazy goatee and living on the fifth floor of this very building . . .

Since the story had first been told, sometime in February, Madison had been on what Charlotte called (only in her own head) "Trip watch," which was a somewhat frustrating game, since Trip rarely appeared. She'd cornered him in the elevator once or twice and talked to him about the friend of a friend they had in common, but he hadn't taken the bait. She'd commandeered a package she'd seen Raul signing for once and taken it to his door, but he'd been on the phone when she rang the doorbell, and though he'd winked and mouthed thanks at her when he'd taken the envelope, nothing more had come of it.

Charlotte wished she was so certain there was a happy ending in her future. She sat, every day, on the subway and looked at the men in the car, none of whom, it seemed, were ever looking back. Most of them, she wouldn't want. But one . . . just one, one day . . .

EVE

This apartment was beautiful, and easily the best part of their new life so far. She felt like she was living inside the pages of a magazine she used to read in the hairdresser's. Eve had found the place when she'd been over in January. The bank used a relocation company, assigning her a consultant, Francine, who was a veritable font of knowledge. She, in turn, had set up a day of appointments with real estate brokers across the city. Eve had felt impossibly glamorous, being picked up outside the hotel by a limo and driven from location to location all day.

In between appointments, Francine would talk to her about neighborhoods and budgets in the back of the car, and sip Vitamin-Water without smudging her lip gloss. She had patiently explained the difference between a co-op and a condo and a cond-op. About supers and doormen. She appeared to know the location of every Whole Foods and Dean & DeLuca and CVS pharmacy in the city, as well as every park and most Zagat-rated restaurants worth eating at. Francine lived in Brooklyn with her boyfriend, Anthony, and Anthony's two sons "from a previous relationship with a complete bi-atch." She'd left her beloved Manhattan for Anthony, a firefighter. Eve reasoned Anthony could have had no greater declaration of love from Francine.

They'd been lucky and struck gold late morning, after seeing five depressing places Eve wouldn't have lived in at any price. The last had been above a nail salon, and the smell of acetone was still in her nostrils, making her feel faintly queasy. It was probably almost time for lunch. Eve wondered if Francine ate lunch and whether, if she did, she could do that, too, without smudging her lip gloss. Francine had a call on her cell, about a place that had literally just come on the market. Eve never believed it when they said that on property shows on television, but this time it was true. On the way, Francine waxed lyrical about the location. Upper East Side. Mid seventies. Close to the Met and the Frick, and not too far from Bloomie's. Between Park and Lexington, close to the subway at Seventy-seventh and the park at Cedar Hill. Handy for the hospital, if you should be unlucky enough to need it, and close to a great gym. Ed could be at work in fifteen minutes, which seemed extraordinary. He would love that.

By the time the car stopped outside the building, Eve had allowed herself to get a little excited. No nail salon in sight, for a

55

start. Francine explained that the building was a co-op. As a tenant, renting from a management company, she could vote on board matters but never join the board. "And who in their right mind would want to, you may well ask." She raised her eyebrows cynically. Francine used shorthand, not all of which made complete sense to Eve. She didn't entirely know what a co-op board was, although Ed had explained that co-ops were like businesses, and if you owned an apartment, you owned shares in the building. She understood twenty-four-hour doormen (how cool was that?) but not why they would be called "white glove" when they weren't wearing any. She understood AC but not HVAC. Should have something to do with vacuuming. Didn't. It must be good, though, since Francine was listing it gleefully in her New York accent. This was a "reno" — a renovation, Eve realized — which received Francine's most animated response, with all stainless steel appliances and a vast Viking range (at this point Francine's cup runneth over, almost literally, since her ample chest heaved with pleasure and threatened to break free from its buttoned sweater).

The building had an awning. That was the first thing Eve noticed, apart from the absence of a nail bar. Awnings were so very New York. It was like being in an episode of *Friends*. This one was burgundy red, quite new, and attached to shiny brass poles. You could easily imagine Charlotte York coming out in a Jackie O shift dress carrying a Hermès Birkin. There was a long, thin lobby, with a marble floor, and a large circular table, on which sat an elaborate arrangement of silk flowers. There were two elevators at one end, and a small room at the other where the "white glove" gloveless doorman sat. It was full of dry cleaning, hung in plastic on racks, and parcels. He announced them and they took the elevator to the seventh floor. The elevator had a seat in the corner, and Eve sat on it, trying to suppress a giggle at the grandeur of it all. House hunting was never like this in the Surrey Hills. She tried to remember everything for when she phoned Cath, later on. A woman who looked, sounded, and even smelled like Francine, just a brunette version, greeted them and invited Eve to take a look around, explaining that the furniture was not part of the rental, but that the apartment had been "staged for viewings."

But it wasn't the furniture that interested Eve. It was the light, flooding in from the windows on three sides. She realized, standing there, that light was what had been missing from all the apartments she'd seen that morning. Even the biggest had been dark. In the light, she suddenly felt lighter herself, and for the first time all day, she began to imagine herself sitting by that window, standing at that counter. Pouring a drink for Ed and herself.

It wasn't huge. Most of the square footage appeared to be in this one room, which had the kitchen floating in the middle. You'd sit on sofas and armchairs, she guessed, at one end, and have a table and chairs at the other. The Viking range stood proudly in the middle of the run of units, looking industrial and intimidating, exactly like you might use it to cook for real Vikings. Eve couldn't imagine switching it on just to bake two potatoes for supper. There was plenty of the stainless steel that had gotten Francine so excited on the phone on the way over. Beyond, there were two bedrooms, one of which was pretty tiny, but you could probably fit a queen-size bed in it for visitors, Eve figured, so long as they didn't mind vaulting over it to get to the hallway. The master had a bathroom, with a separate shower (showerhead the size of a dinner plate, she noticed gleefully), and the only wall that would take a king-size bed faced

58

two huge windows with a great cityscape view of water towers, strangely archaic alongside the modern tall buildings. There was a helicopter hovering in the distance.

Everything was painted an inoffensive ivory, and the floor was a herringbone pattern of wood, polished shiny new and smooth.

This was unbelievably cool.

"Come see this," Francine urged animatedly, pulling Eve back away from the bedrooms. Triumphant, she opened a door, revealing a cupboard into which had been stacked a small washing machine and a tumble dryer. "Laundry." She said it like she was saying "George Clooney" or "Holy Grail." The only thing Francine apparently found more exciting than a unit with a laundry was a unit with a walk-in closet. Sadly, there wasn't one of those here, but the wardrobes in both bedrooms seemed pretty big — empty, at least. Eve wasn't entirely sure, anyway, that any of her clothes were going to work in this new life. Might take a while to fill those closets with the appropriate gear.

It felt right. Not just exactly right, like the cottage had. More right than anything else she'd seen. Different, but right. And so cool she wished she could call Cath immediately,

just to giggle on the phone. This was someone else's life. "Can we afford it?" she
whispered to Francine, although the other
real estate broker (why did you have to have
two anyway?) was down by the window,
talking into her cell phone and fiddling with
her hair.

"Yes. No third-bedroom-cum-office,
which was on your list originally. So you'll
do your paperwork in the living room and
tell anyone visiting who wants to bring their
kids that the Waldorf's about twenty blocks
that way. Yes, it's in budget. D'ya want it?"

"I want it. We do."

"Does your husband need to come see it?"

"No, he trusts me. Tell them we'll take it."

Just like that. She'd found them a home.
A light-filled, two bed, seventh-floor apartment, not a flat, with city views, in a co-op
off Park Avenue — Park Avenue! — in New
York City. It was getting more real by the
day . . .

They'd left most of their furniture in the
cottage. Renters paid more for furnished
properties, the agent said, and since she
thought the house would appeal more to
young families than to single sharers, she
told them they needn't worry too much
about things getting wrecked. Obviously,
Eve thought, the agent didn't know much

about young families. There weren't many pieces of furniture in Cath's house that didn't have scratches or dents or at the very least mysteriously sticky patches on them — except those in the front room that locked from the outside, where Cath and Geoff went to listen to classical music and read the newspapers. She didn't want to take the stuff, actually.

The cottage was pine and oak and as much retro chintz as Ed could tolerate, in a palette of duck egg blue and cream and soft pink. This apartment, their new home, called for something entirely less country and shabby chic. She'd gone shopping, armed with a Visa card that tapped into a relocation package bonus and with a new urban vision, buying a structural sectional sofa in brown suede, with sheepskin cushions, and a glass and chrome coffee table that looked like a wave.

They'd put lots of their personal things into storage in England. Ed was all for getting rid of most of it, but Eve was more sentimental, and more inclined, she thought, to tie herself to the UK, not only with family and friends but with a commercial storage unit that cost a hundred pounds a month. What they brought with them — had shipped — amounted to little more than half a container. Books (the clever, book club kind, not the really good ones with the dog-eared corners that fell open at the saucy bits), clothes (all wrong already — New York women wore dresses and heels all day and appeared to be strangers to fleeces and Barbours. Was she destined to be uncomfortable every day of her life here? she wondered), wedding pictures in silver frames (how young they looked, already), some kitchen stuff . . .

The new furniture, the things she'd ordered on that trip to America, arrived first, of course. The apartment looked like an ad when she'd arranged it all — like it, too, had been "staged for viewing" rather than living. Although she loved how it looked, she knew that she hadn't relaxed, properly relaxed, until the things from England arrived. She had worked all day to unpack and arrange everything. Ed committed the cardinal sin of not noticing until he'd been home for five minutes that evening, making an exhausted Eve tearful and resentful. She'd wanted the transformation to be a surprise. The surprise was that he was oblivious to it. Immediately contrite, he'd taken her for supper at the restaurant on the corner of the block, and ordered champagne. They'd taken, very quickly, to eating out three or four times a week. Thai, sushi, steak, Italian. Almost anything she could think of was on this block or the next one. It was quick and easy and not all that expensive and there was no washing up. Easy habit to fall into.

He was buzzing. He had been ever since they'd arrived.

Eve felt left behind. "You're really happy, aren't you?"

"I love it." He looked like a kid, and she so wanted that enthusiasm to be contagious. She wanted him to make her catch it.

"Tell me why. What is it that's making you so happy?"

Ed thought for a moment, leaning forward across the table. "I don't know. Actually, that's not true . . . I do. I'm just not sure how to say it. I feel like, for the first time, I live somewhere that moves at the same speed as me. It suits me. I love the pace, and the buzz and the tempo. I feel . . . at home here. Does that make sense?"

Eve nodded. "Yeah, I think so." She knew what he meant. Ed had always been slightly faster than everyone else, at home. She was always walking fast to keep up with him on the sidewalk. He spoke fast, he thought quickly. It did suit him, this city. He ate fast, too. He'd finished already.

"What about you?"

Eve shrugged and smiled, then looked down at her salad.

Ed took her hand under the table. "A bit different, hey?"

She was shocked to feel tears welling in her eyes. "A bit." The city didn't suit her, she realized. Not yet. It made her feel slow, and ungainly, and like she didn't know anything about anything. She wasn't used to the feeling.

Ed's face was full of concern. He put his face down to her hands on the table, squeezed them with his own, and kissed her knuckles. "I'm sorry, sweetheart. Am I being a pig?"

Eve wiped away the tear that had spilled onto her cheek. "No. Of course not. I'm really, really happy that you're happy. And I'm really, really happy with you, Ed. None of that's changed. I'm just . . . I'm just a bit lonely. That's it, I expect. I'm not used to being lonely, and it is weird and a bit awful. I can go days without talking to anyone except the doorman and people in shops. Except you."

"What about the phone?"

"Of course, the phone and the email. I have that, I know. But it isn't quite the same, you know? I don't have any friends

64

here, Ed. And talking on the phone and emailing, well, it makes me realize how far away they are."

"I know. I know, Evie. Of course I do. I want to help. What can I do?"

"It's not for you to fix, Ed." Every man she had ever known had been obsessed by fixing things. Not just in the DIY way.

"Do you want me to go back to them about you working?" They'd investigated the possibility, before they left England. A work visa wasn't so easy to get anymore; before 9/11, a wife or husband whose partner had a work visa would automatically get one, but it wasn't that straightforward or automatic now. And anyway, her qualifications wouldn't translate. It would probably be hard to teach the same way she'd done in England. They'd known, when they came, that it was unlikely. Ed had been happy enough to give up on her working, and Eve thought she had been, too. Still, there were days when she thought she wouldn't mind working behind the register at Banana Republic. At least she'd be surrounded by people all day.

"No. I don't think so. You can't fix it, I don't think. Although I adore you for wanting to. I need to shake myself by the shoulders a bit. Get out there, and do all the things you're supposed to do. Moving to New York shouldn't essentially be any different from moving to Manchester. You've got to start again, haven't you? Get involved and put yourself out there. Isn't that what they say? Join a gym," she snorted, "neighborhood watch, that kind of thing."

"Sounds good."

"Yeah." Did it? "I just need to get on with it. Now the apartment's sorted, I've run out of excuses."

"Cath's coming in a couple of weeks."

"I know. I can't wait. We're going to be tourists. And shoppers, I suspect."

"And then?"

"And then I'll sort myself out. Promise. I don't want you to worry about me. I don't want to put a downer on everything."

"Don't be daft. You're my wife. Of course I'm going to worry about you. I'll be better, I promise. I know I haven't been around that much, and that you've been left on your own a bit too much. I can fix that much, at least. We'll get some stuff going with the guys at work. They've mostly got wives and girlfriends. We'll go out."

"Sounds great." It sounded terrifying, actually, but Eve didn't want to make him feel worse than she patently already had.

"I'm sorry, Evie." He tried to squeeze her

hands again, but she pulled them out from under his and slapped them on top. He did the same, and they played a familiar game for a moment. She wanted to lighten the mood. "I feel like I've been selfish. I've been so busy and —"

"Hey." She smiled broadly at him, determined to move them past this conversation she had never really meant to start. "It's going to be fine."

She really hoped it was.

CHARLOTTE

When she watched reality television, which was often, every night, pretty much, Charlotte Murphy told herself that the problem with her was not actually with her. Away from Manhattan, she wouldn't be plain or overweight or badly dressed or dull. She'd be normal. It was only here, in this place, where she was all those things. She should move to Ohio or Kentucky or . . . to anywhere else. New York wasn't America. It was a republic unto itself. Full of beautiful, perfect, unreal people like Madison Cavanagh. Everything would be okay if she were somewhere else.

This was merely a variation on her other theory — the one she had held dear for years — that everything would be okay if she were someone else.

She forgot, or simply refused to remember, that she'd grown up outside this city, but that she had always felt this way.

Ugly Betty was her favorite show. Except that America Ferrera wasn't at all ugly. They made her look weird and geeky with those clothes, but you knew that by season three or four they were going to do a thorough makeover on her, and the swan would emerge, glamorous and attractive. When you saw the actress in *People* magazine or on *The Insider,* she really was quite lovely. Not a size zero or anything, but a pretty girl. There was no such swan lurking inside Charlotte Murphy — she was quite sure of that.

When she wasn't watching television (or listening to Madison, her neighbor), Charlotte read romance novels — everything from the literary heavyweights through Georgette Heyer to slim Silhouette Romances with Fabio on the cover. And then, when she lay in her single bed at night, she replayed the story lines, casting herself, a slimmer, prettier, easier Charlotte, in the heroine's role. The hero was sometimes Che, the doorman. Sometimes a fireman she'd seen once answering a call at the subway station at work. Mostly, it was Che. She'd known him for three years, ever since she'd moved to the city. But she'd never said more than four words to him, and they were always the same four — "Hello. How are you?" She knew nothing about him. She didn't know where he went when he wasn't working at the building. She'd sort of followed him once, last summer, as far as the subway steps, so she knew he went north, but she hadn't had the nerve to get on the train and see where he got off. He didn't wear a wedding ring, and his taste in clothes, when he wasn't in the building's uniform, was dreadful, so she didn't think there was a woman in his life. No wife or girlfriend would let him leave home dressed like that.

And sometimes, when he didn't see her approaching and was staring into space, he looked sad and full of longing to her. She made up a backstory for him. A beautiful girl back in Cuba. A broken heart. And she spent many long nights imagining mending it for him. Things always faded to black, after their first kiss.

Between them, even Madison and Georgette hadn't managed to make her imagine what might happen then . . .

He had milk, but he needed Cheerios. He had the serious munchies. The maid wasn't due until tomorrow, and he couldn't wait that long for Cheerios. Jackson looked at the clock, vaguely surprised to find himself wide awake and starving hungry at 7:30 a.m. That almost never happened. Damn.

He rolled out of bed and pulled on a pair of sweats and sneakers that were lying by the bed, covering his Bowie "Life on Mars" T-shirt with a gray sweat top. Passing the mirror he peered at himself, pulling down his bottom eyelids to inspect the redness of his eyes, and sticking out his tongue. He wasn't sure about this facial hair. Too lazy to shave, he didn't feel sufficiently testosterone-y to grow something amusingly yeti-ish. That goatee might have to go. Although his mother's aggravation at it during her last visit had been quite funny. Martha said men with facial hair had something to hide. Like weak upper lips or crooked teeth. She viewed his as unnecessary. His straight teeth had cost ten thousand dollars.

Money. Money. His wallet was empty except for credit cards. Wandering into the kitchen, he spotted a ten-dollar bill next to the receipt for last night's Thai takeout and grabbed it on his way out of the door. The elevator smelled of dog. He hated that. Early morning dog walkers. He wasn't an animal person. Leaning against the wooden paneling, he closed his eyes. When the elevator stopped at 3, he thought it had reached the ground floor, and he flung himself at the doors, straight into the girl trying to get in.

"Sorry!"

"That's okay." She looked shocked. He supposed he probably looked pretty shocking. And now that he thought of it, he hadn't brushed his teeth. Shit. He retreated to the furthest corner of the elevator and looked at his fellow passenger out of the corner of his eye.

Wow. This girl was beautiful. Really stunning. She was dressed for a run, he guessed, in those black Lycra running shorts that showed everything, and a vest with a racer back. Great body. New York was full of great bodies, though. Best reason for taking a latte to a bench in Central Park — best girl watching in the city. Ponytails swinging about, great asses that swayed, never wobbled. This girl had a face on her. A Helen of Troy face. That was much harder to find. Her eyes were so blue they were almost turquoise. She was platinum blond, and the kind that was real, too. And her skin was clear and pale, just a little pink across the cheeks. And her mouth . . . Wow. Wow.

"Going for a run?" Smooth.

She nodded, managing not to look at him like he was an idiot. "You?"

She wouldn't know he was heading to Gristedes for Cheerios, so long as she set off in a different direction.

"Think so."

He wanted to say something else. Something funny or clever. But they were on the ground floor now, and she flipped a little "See ya" over her shoulder at him and was outside straightaway, bending and stretching, which ought, he reflected, to be illegal. She didn't linger — hamstring, calves, arms — then she was off, heading west, toward the park. Jesus was watching him, an amused expression on his face.

"Who the hell is that?"

"Ms. Mikanowski. Three A."

"First name?"

"Emily."

"Emily Mikanowski. How long has she been here?"

"Three weeks or so." He laughed. "You two keep different hours, I think."

"Does she do that every day?"

Jesus nodded. "Every day. Monday through Friday. Seven thirty. Like a clock.

Doesn't get back until after I've gone. Better ask Che what time." Jackson went out onto the sidewalk and watched Ms. Mikanowski's ponytail swinging in the distance. He might have to rethink his schedule slightly.

MAY

EVE

Eve had spotted the notice pinned to the corkboard next to the mailboxes on the ground floor, among the minutes of the last board meeting, the flyer for a new Thai restaurant that had opened on Lexington, and an ad for dog walking with one of those tear-off fringes at the bottom. Eve always spent a little longer than necessary hovering around the mailboxes at this time in the afternoon. People might come and check their boxes, and they might talk to her. God, she was getting pathetic. Yesterday the mailman had talked to her, but she hadn't really understood his thick Asian accent, so that didn't count. The note was written in a neat, old-fashioned hand, in bright violet ink. The scribe had drawn tiny neat flowers in each of the corners. Doodles, really.

BUILDING BEAUTIFYING COMMITTEE
FIRST MEETING WEDNESDAY 10TH, 8

P.M. ON THE ROOF
ALL RESIDENTS INTERESTED IN
CREATING A WONDERFUL SPACE ARE
WELCOME.

Raul was putting supermarket carrier bags on the luggage rack next to the mailboxes. Someone had braved Fairway. Eve was still vaguely frightened of New York supermarkets. She'd tried them all, desperate to find the Waitrose equivalent, but it didn't exist. Whole Foods was full of ingredients she didn't recognize, and was a bit granola and wheatgrass for her. Fairway, like Zabar's, both across town on the West Side, was legendary. You needed a Valium with your morning coffee to face either of them. In Zabar's you were quite likely to be taken off at the ankle by an old lady, hunched over a shopping cart with murder in her eyes. They had something like thirty-five different types of olives at the olive bar in Zabar's. It wasn't worth it. Fairway was, to her, the grocery equivalent of the Tower of Babel. She had never come out with the ingredients she had gone in for, or without a headache. Dean & DeLuca she could handle. She and Ed might need to start selling body parts to pay for it eventually, but at least she didn't get an adrenaline rush at the door.

"Do you know what this means, Raul?" she asked him.

Raul peered at the note. "That's 4B." He always identified everybody with their apartment number. It made Eve smile — it seemed Orwellian. "Mrs. Wallace. She's English, like you."

"Really? Where's the space she's talking about?"

"On the roof." He said it as though it were obvious.

"Oh." Eve waited for Raul to expand. He usually did. Jesus, the night doorman, who usually worked the midnight to eight a.m. shift, never said a word that wasn't necessary. Che, four p.m. until midnight, said a little, but his Cuban accent was so thick Eve didn't understand much of it, although she liked his face and his ready, shy smile. Raul, she had realized, was her best bet if something needed to be explained.

"Mrs. Wallace has been trying to make a garden up on the roof for years. I don't even remember when she started. With the board, with the management company . . . These things take forever. Every year they talked about it, and nothing happened. Last year they finally decided to do it — turn the roof into a terrace. There's money, you know,

now, for seats and flowers and things. To make it nice. Now Mrs. Wallace wants to make a committee of people who live in the building, to help her."

"What a lovely idea!"

Raul smiled. "So she's gonna get one helper, I see."

"More than one, surely. It's such a nice plan. And I suppose most people would like to use it."

Now he snorted. "They'd like to use it, all right. That's not the same as wanting to do the work, though, Miss Eve."

Eve shrugged.

"I tell you who won't be helping, that's for sure." Raul leaned in conspiratorially and lowered his voice to a stage whisper. He smelled like cigars.

She leaned back. "Who?"

"The Stewarts. Eight A and B." He placed heavy emphasis on the "and," "Penthouse. Mrs. Stewart is always with the little dogs, you know?" He shrugged, making dismissive tiny dog shapes with his chubby hands, and chuckled. "Not happy, not happy at all."

Eve whispered back. "Why not?"

"They knocked through the two apart-ments, made one huge place. They have the whole floor now. That took so long, so much noise and mess, you know. They wanted the roof, too, just for themselves. They don't want nobody above them, you know?" He put one hand on top of his head, palm upward. "Nobody higher."

Eve nodded. "I understand." She thought she almost did. "And Mrs. Wallace?"

"Mrs. Wallace has lived here since before me. And I came in nineteen seventy-eight."

"She lives alone?"

Raul nodded. "Now she does."

He might have said more, but the young Chinese guy Eve had seen a few times in the elevator came in to check his post. She tried to make eye contact with him, said hi, but got little back except a distracted mumble. She got better conversation out of the doorman than she did out of her own neighbor. Nice.

Raul went to answer the phone, and Eve took one last look at the flyer, memorizing the date — Wednesday at eight.

"You should definitely do it! Sounds great! You're the green-fingered one in the family."

Ed seemed disproportionately excited about the beautifying committee; his response was affectedly animated when she told him about it over dinner. Eve felt guilty. She knew he was worried about her. That's

81

why he wanted her to go.

"Great way to meet the neighbors!"

They'd eaten pasta and drunk large beers at the Italian place on the corner, and now they were sitting on a bench in the park. Ed had changed out of his suit into shorts and deck shoes. It was nine o'clock, but it was still hot. He had his arm around her shoulders, and she was inhaling the smell of him, her face leaning against his chest.

"I know I need to meet people."

"And you will. It's much easier for me." Of course.

"It wasn't always like that. Easier for you."

"I know." He squeezed.

She'd been the noisy one, when they met. At their wedding, four years earlier, Ed had delighted in telling everyone, during his speech, that Eve had pioneered the very twenty-first-century form of mate finding: she had picked him up in a shop. Not even in a supermarket. In a dry cleaner's. He made some joke about a wedding being the traditional place to meet someone, and this being a unique variation, since she was having a bridesmaid's dress cleaned, from her sister's wedding the previous weekend, and he was picking up his gray pinstripe for a work colleague's wedding the next one.

So they'd met not at but because of a wedding. Or rather two weddings. She was already in deep discussion with the assistant when he came in. He couldn't see the face, but he didn't mind watching the bottom for a minute or two while he waited. She had a great voice, too. Deeper than her size and blondness suggested, and a bit gravelly, for a girl. He stood, amused, as she detailed each stain on the champagne satin strapless dress. Sweat, each side, nearest the armpit. Red wine, just to the left of the navel. Mud, on the hem. Something — not definitely, but very possibly profiterole filling — under the right boob. Each stain came with a little explanation.

"It was bloody hot in the marquee. Great band, though. Bopped till I dropped."

"Some idiot did that."

"They didn't have a proper wedding cake. Trust my showy sis, she had one of those profiterole tower French things. I ate about twenty-five of them."

Finished, she turned to him apologetically, and he saw green eyes. Big green eyes. And a nose that turned up at the end. It stopped her from being beautiful, relegating her for eternity to cute and appealing, but he'd always had a thing about noses like that.

"Sorry!"

"Don't be. Sounds like a hell of a wedding."

"Yep. The full monty. Still slightly hungover, actually."

It was Wednesday. She grimaced, her eyes wide and smiley. He didn't want her to go, but he couldn't think of anything else to say. She hesitated, it seemed, just for a second or two, and when he didn't say anything, he swore she almost shrugged before heading for the door.

He passed her, five minutes later. She was sitting alone in the beer garden at the front of the King's Head, a few doors down from the dry cleaner's, staring at her cell phone.

"Hello again."

"Hiya." She looked up and smiled.

"Hair of the dog?"

"What?" The ski run nose crinkled.

"Back there . . . just now . . . you said you were still hungover." Idiot.

She laughed. "Yeah."

Something stopped him from walking away from this semi-embarrassing situation. Afterward he always told her it was the nose, and the green eyes. But really, it was the commentary in the dry cleaner's. He couldn't resist.

She was waiting, she said, for friends. He was early, he said, for friends. He sat. They had a drink. And another. Her friends were late. His friends were never coming, of course. By eight thirty he had her phone number, and the rest, as he always said, was history.

They'd never met, before that day in the dry cleaner's, but it turned out that their lives had been running in close parallel, all those years. They'd been born six weeks apart, in 1978, in towns in Kent. She was from Tunbridge Wells, he was from Sevenoaks. He'd been reading politics, philosophy, and economics at Cambridge while she was down the road at Nottingham, getting her own degree in education.

They'd been living three streets apart in Chiswick for eighteen months before they met, both sharing with college mates, drinking at the same pubs, eating at the same restaurants. An old friend of his had gone out with a workmate of hers, and they'd been invited to some of the same parties, but they'd never set eyes on each other. Eve told him she loved the romanticism of that — the idea that they might have walked past each other, at the bus stop, in the aisle of Waitrose, in the cinema queue. That fate waited until they were ready before she intervened and pushed them into that same space together.

And Eve had been looking for him. She'd been looking forever, she said. In all the wrong places, wasn't that how the song went?

Ed, in contrast, had not been looking at all. He was concentrating, hard, at work. He'd joined the bank, with a golden hello of ten thousand pounds, the year he'd graduated, while his friends were slackers, bumming around. He'd never wanted to do that. He wanted to work, and to succeed. Not at any price, perhaps. But it mattered to him. He supposed, without analyzing it too much, that it was because of where he came from. He was the only child of working-class parents. He'd been to state school, from there to Cambridge — the first from his school to go. He'd definitely had a chip on his shoulder, then, at Cambridge. He'd watched all the privileged public school boys and sometimes simmered with resentment about how easy it had been for them to get to where they were. It was when he left that he realized Cambridge had leveled the playing field for him; the rest didn't matter anymore. If he worked hard, and if he did well, nothing else would matter and nothing else could stop him. So the traveling, and the endless navel contemplation — it didn't make any sense to him, when you could be getting on with it all.

Eve was different. She wasn't posh, exactly. He thought of her as being a generation ahead of him. Her grandparents may have been working-class, but her parents had both been to university, products of the same upbringing that drove him. Her father was a solicitor in Tunbridge Wells; her mother had been a teacher before she stopped work, seventies style, to raise Eve and her sister. Eve had none of the sense of entitlement he had come to despise at Cambridge, and he wouldn't call her spoiled. She was just . . . more relaxed about life. She'd done the traveling, taking a backpack around Vietnam and Cambodia and places, when she was twenty-one. She loved teaching, she said, but she didn't seem ambitious for herself. She didn't want to be a department head. Or headmistress. She wanted the kids she taught to have fun, to think she was the best teacher since Mr. Chips, and she wanted them to do well. Full stop. She slept like a baby. The first time they'd spent the night together, he'd lain awake beside her and watched her even breathing, her unlined face perfectly peaceful, and been envious. She still slept that way now. He rarely got more than five or six hours a night. His brain never really stopped.

WEDNESDAY, EIGHT P.M.

Blimey, Eve thought. I'm overdressed.

She'd showered at seven and put on a clean white linen dress and fresh makeup. Ed was working late. At seven fifty-five she took a last look at herself, making thumbs-up at herself in the mirror in their hall, then laughing at herself for doing it, and called the elevator, pushing the up button for the first time since she'd moved in.

And now she felt faintly ridiculous. She must be late. There were six or seven people — men, women, and one disgruntled-looking toddler — sitting on folding chairs placed in one corner of the roof, each one in shorts and flip-flops. Most of them held the ubiquitous water bottle all New Yorkers seemed to carry always, although she saw a small table in the corner with jugs of something colorful and a stack of paper cups. All of them were looking at her.

When, in the past, Eve had flirted with diet and exercise, she'd always been struck by the cruel and unfair way that six weeks' effort in the kitchen and the gym could be undone by six days of eating what you wanted, on a holiday or over the Christmas break. Six weeks to lose fifteen pounds and find the beginnings of a flat stomach, and six days to put half of it, and a bicycle tire at the waist, back on. It seemed to her now that her self-confidence was like that. She'd spent her entire adult life building it up, years and years, and now, in the space of weeks, it was seeping away. Nearly twenty years of cultivating the belief that strangers were friends she just hadn't met yet, and that she was interesting, and nice. And within two months, she wasn't at all sure why anyone would want to talk to her at all. That wasn't fair. She couldn't remember being so cross with herself before. She dug her fingernails into her palm, and stepped out into the sunlight.

"Hello, everyone. Sorry I'm late."

"You're not late. Come and join us." This, clearly, was Mrs. Wallace. The English accent (could be Suffolk, Norfolk?) was faint but still unmistakable. "I'm Violet, Violet Wallace."

Violet Wallace was clearly elderly but still tall and upright. She wore half-frame glasses on a chain, and a necklace of large stones that looked like turquoise, with its gray threads, but were a deep lavender color. Her hair was snow white and obviously quite long; she wore it in a French twist secured with what appeared to be lacquered chop-sticks.

"And you are?" There was something of the headmistress about her and Eve felt vaguely like a sixth former.

"Eve Gallagher. We're the new tenants in seven A."

"Hello." Violet smiled at her, not quite so scary after all. "They told me you were English. Welcome. To the building, and to our little committee. We're glad to have you."

The door behind her opened and a beautiful brunette whom Eve recognized from the park appeared. Eve had seen her a few days ago, playing near the Alice in Wonderland sculpture with three adorable dark-haired children — two boys and the sweetest little girl. They'd been having so much fun, laughing and running and climbing. At least Eve was no longer the smartest person in attendance. Rachael looked like she'd stepped out of the window of DKNY on Madison Avenue, through the Red Door of Elizabeth Arden on Fifth, onto the roof. Mind you, she looked like that in the park, too, in a sweatshirt and jeans. How did you get your hair to do that?

"Hey, Violet. Not late, am I?"

"Not a bit. Find a seat, Rachael. Still some

spare chairs — I was erring on the side of optimism. This is Eve."

Rachael smiled hi.

"In fact, why don't I do a bit of an introduction before we get started? You probably don't know most of us yet."

Eve scanned the faces. Some she recognized, but she knew no one by name. "That'd be good."

"Well, you've met me, and Rachael. This is Maria."

"We've met, actually!" Maria beamed. "We're just next door, aren't we? Hey, Eve."

Eve smiled gratefully. Maria had knocked on the door their second day with a plate of delicious homemade cannoli. She was lovely and had said Eve should ask for anything she needed. Eve hadn't, of course, but she suspected she could.

"This is Emily. Todd, and Gregory. This is Kimberley, and the temporarily tamed dervish on her lap is Avery."

The men Violet had gestured at, as she said Todd and Gregory, laughed. Eve thought the toddler's mother (Kimberley?) bristled and stiffened a little, although she continued to smile a toothy, slightly clenched smile.

"And this is Charlotte."

Eve waved. "Hello, everyone." She felt

unbelievably awkward.

They collectively waved back, and Eve took her seat gratefully.

"So, enough. Let's get on with things, shall we? As you all know, we have, at long last, managed to convince the board to let us have this space. As you can see, the fencing has gone up, so we're safe, and now, will wonders never cease, we have a budget to tart it up a bit."

Todd (or was it Gregory?) raised a fist in triumph at this point, and issued a little "Yeah!" of triumph.

"All we need to do now is spend it, and make it happen. That's where all of us come in; we need to decide what we want to do. So, suggestions gratefully received."

Everyone was quiet, but only for a moment. Then everyone started talking at once. Except Eve and Charlotte. Eve struggled to listen to all the voices.

"Well, we clearly need to paint this fence first, so the whole place feels less like a prison yard."

"And can we do something about the floor? Lay decking or something —"

"Pots, lots of pots."

"And benches. Tables, maybe. Somewhere to sit and have a cup of coffee and read the newspaper."

"Do we need board approval for everything we do? Or is the money our own?"

"Some of those soft mats so the children can play."

"But no balls."

"Of course no balls."

"I'm seeing arbors at the corners. With climbing things —"

"There are rules, right? About how the space should be used? We don't want to be inundated with complaints about noise."

Violet raised her hands and was met with almost instantaneous silence. Clearly, she carried some weight among this crowd. Again, she reminded Eve of a teacher. She'd worked with women like Violet Wallace before. They weren't all bad, but they could be terrifying when they wanted to be. She wondered if Violet had actually been a teacher.

"Okay. So no shortage of ideas, then. Let me get some of them down on paper. Hang on, hang on. One at a time . . ." She looked delighted.

An hour later, there was a list and a plan and a to-do list. The guy called Greg was obviously something important on the board; he had answered all those questions. Eve liked him. He was serious and soft-spoken. His boyfriend — she presumed that's what their relationship was — seemed like a lot of fun. He'd made extraordinary faces over some of the suggestions and giggled infectiously. Kimberley had left after about ten minutes, once she'd made sure that organizing Avery's playmats was down on the list and just as Avery had begun squirming noisily on her lap. Rachael had slipped away after half an hour or so, apologizing and saying she needed to say good night to her children. Charlotte or Emily, Eve couldn't remember which one it was, had also gone, without saying much at all. And now the others were having a drink. The colorful liquid she'd seen when she came out turned out to be frozen pomegranate margaritas. What else would Eve have expected?

And this was quite fun, she realized.

Todd and Gregory were, indeed, a couple. "I just love your dress," Todd had said. He had a real southern accent (at least, that's what she thought it was — he sounded like Bobby Ewing), and he stood a little closer to her than was strictly necessary. At one point he actually sniffed at her. "You smell delish. That's Hermès, isn't it? Un Jardin sur le Nil. Love that."

"Leave the poor girl alone, Todd," Gregory admonished him. "I'm sorry, Eve. Todd is what they call 'real friendly.' " He said the last two words in Todd's southern belle accent, though his own voice was distinctly northeastern. Undeterred by Gregory's warning, Todd began asking a thousand questions. He had the knack of appearing to be intensely interested in each of her answers, though she couldn't believe he truly was. She didn't feel interesting. These people were interesting. But her?

Violet rescued her, in the end. She'd been talking to Charlotte or Emily, but when she left, Violet came over to where they were and linked an arm through Eve's, like they'd been friends for years.

"Are you getting the third degree, sweet?"

Gregory nodded for her. "You know Todd. Not happy till he knows your shoe size."

"Tell him terrible lies. He'll never know." Violet winked at Todd, who put his arms around her and kissed her extravagantly on each cheek. Clearly he wasn't scared of her. She didn't kiss back, though.

"You're a wicked old woman, Violet Wallace. But I love you. This has been fabulous. I'm so thrilled we're going to do this. It will be stunning out here, just stunning, by the time we're done. Our own little Shangri-la."

After Greg and Todd had gone, it was just the two of them.

"Can I help to clear the chairs and things?"

"No, Eve. The porter will do that." Eve felt strange and foreign again, although Violet's voice had been kind. "We'll just clear up the drinks."

"I keep forgetting how everything works here."

"You'll get used to it, very quickly, I'm sure."

"Have you been here a long time?"

"Yes." She nodded. "A very long time."

"But you're English originally?"

"Yes. Never lost my accent, I know. Never tried, particularly. I can say *to-may-do* though, when *to-mah-do* won't do. Sometimes it's quicker!"

"Which part of England?"

"Norfolk. How about you?"

"Surrey. Though I grew up in Kent. Near Sevenoaks."

"And there's just the two of you?"

"Yes, me and Ed. He's got a job here, that's why we came."

"But not you?" She had a way of cutting through things. Eve liked it.

"No. I'm on a holiday, I suppose you could call it. A sabbatical. I used to be a teacher."

Violet didn't offer any information about

her own career, so Eve supposed she must have been wrong about her. "Much harder for you, then. To get used to things. He's too busy to think about it, I expect."

Again, she was right at the heart of it.

Eve was torn. She didn't want to seem pathetic. But she wanted to tell Violet the truth; it seemed as though she knew it already.

"It has been a bit hard. I miss my friends, my family . . ." She was piling up the plastic cups they had used for the margaritas. Violet put her hand on Eve's. It was a too-familiar gesture, like the arm linking earlier, but it didn't make Eve uncomfortable. The opposite, actually.

"Of course you do. That's perfectly natural." She smiled, and her eyes were so kind. "It's bound to take a bit of time."

For a horrible second, Eve felt her eyes fill with tears. It was this sudden intimacy. She wasn't used to it. She blinked them back, embarrassed. The kindness of strangers could be a disarming thing.

Violet busied herself with the drinks. Eve wasn't sure whether she was being kind or whether she disapproved of her tears.

"You must come out for lunch with me."

"I'd like that. Very much."

"Good. Then that's settled. Friday?"

Eve nodded eagerly. She made no pretense at having to think about whether she was free, as she might have felt compelled to do if someone else had asked. Lunch would be very nice indeed.

When she opened the door to the apartment, she saw Ed sprawled, shoeless, on the sofa, his tie loose and a bottle of Bud in his hand. The baseball game was on. He looked up and winked at her.

"How was it?"

"Good. It was fun. Or I think it will be, at least. Mrs. Wallace — Violet, the woman who's running the whole thing — she's wonderful. Fierce. She's like Anna Madrigal without the dope. And the sex change. And a bit like Joyce Grenfell."

"I know Joyce Grenfell. But who the hell is Anna Madrigal?"

"Anna Madrigal. Most memorable landlady in literature. Armistead Maupin? *Tales of the City*?"

"You've lost me."

"I forgot I was married to a man who doesn't read."

"Hey, I read."

"Newspapers."

"And the greats. Don't forget the greats. Ludlum, MacDonald Fraser, King —"

"Yeah, right, the greats. Once a year, on a sun lounger, maybe. Anyway, she was wonderful."

"Great. Now come here." Ed pulled her into his arms and hit the mute button on the television. Neither of them understood baseball anyhow. There was a lot of standing around. "You look gorgeous. Mmm." He nuzzled her neck. "Smell gorgeous, too."

"You're the second man this evening to tell me that, you know." It was ages since Ed had seen her like this — dressed up, flirtatious, light. It was a relief.

"Do I need to take someone outside and batter them?" He was butterfly-kissing the side of her face.

"No. He was totally gay. He's an interior architect, and he's called Todd." She giggled and brushed away his tickling touch. "Do you even know what an interior architect is?"

Ed began unbuttoning the small pearl buttons at the front of Eve's dress. "Haven't a clue. Listen to you. My Manhattan wife, in her white dress, on her committee, with her new gay best friend. I hardly recognize you. Oh . . . wait a second, I recognize these, at least." He'd reached her waist, pulling the linen apart, and now he was pulling the lacy cups of her bra down, exposing her nipples.

"Do you think it's the same as an interior decorator?" Eve put her hands on the back of his neck as he began kissing her skin in earnest. His hips were starting to push in to hers.

"Mmmm. Evie? I really don't give a toss what it is. I'm busy. Any chance you could stop talking now and concentrate on the matter in hand?" He moved his mouth up to hers, and she pulled him into her.

"It's not in my hand yet," she whispered, reaching for his belt.

They never made it to the bedroom. They made love fast and furiously on the sofa in the living room, in a tangle of white linen and fluffy cushions. They didn't even lower the blinds, but at least the lights weren't on.

In the shower, afterward, it surprised Eve to realize that it had been two — no, three weeks since they'd made love. Why hadn't she noticed that? She couldn't remember their ever going that long before, and she was glad they'd done it tonight.

Rolling contentedly over in their bed, grateful for the breeze that was, at last, blowing in through the wide-open window, Ed exhaled deeply. He'd known exactly how long it had been.

EMILY

Emily knocked on Charlotte's door, pulling at her skirt and smoothing her hair back behind her ears. She was on time, though she'd had to rush. Her mother had called just as she was walking out of the apartment. They hadn't spoken for a while, and she'd hated to cut her off.

Charlotte had suggested supper, after Mrs. Wallace had paired them up at the gardening committee meeting. They were supposed to come up with a plan for the containers the committee had decided to use to bring color and plants onto the terrace. She hoped Charlotte knew what she was doing; she herself hadn't a clue.

She'd gone to the meeting because it seemed a friendly thing to do, rather than out of some horticultural drive. She didn't suppose she'd use the terrace much; she wasn't one for sitting around. What free time she had, she preferred to be out on her bike or running. Still, she'd really liked Mrs. Wallace and some of the others seemed nice . . . and it was neighborly. Emily was used to being neighborly. It was how she'd been raised. Her mom had always been that way — checking on the elderly residents of their street in cold weather, making a hot stew for new mothers.

She liked Charlotte. She was quiet, but then so was Emily sometimes. It would be good to have a friend in the building. Charlotte answered the door. She was wearing a fifties-style floral apron.

"Wow — you cooked!" Emily handed her the small bunch of tulips she'd bought at the deli on her way home.

"Thanks, they're lovely. Come on in. Yes, I cooked. I'm the only person in Manhattan that does, I think."

Emily laughed. "Well, I certainly don't."

"No one does. Just me."

"I've got one of those mothers who is a brilliant cook but a rotten teacher. I'm great at eating, though."

Charlotte looked at Emily's tiny frame and wondered if that could possibly be true.

"I brought wine, too. I didn't know what color you'd drink. Here." Emily pulled the bottle out of her bag and proffered it.

Charlotte smiled shyly. "Thanks. That's really nice."

They were both a little nervous. While Charlotte uncorked the wine and poured two glasses, Emily looked around. The layout of the apartment was the same as hers. There wasn't much artifice in the room. But there were what seemed like hundreds of books, paperbacks mostly, on cheap Ikea shelves. There was a stack of hardbacks on the coffee table, too, and Emily saw that they were gardening books.

"You've been doing some homework?"

"Yeah. I like to garden. I used to do it, at home. But that was in the Pacific Northwest. I think it's different here. Colder, drier, hotter. I wanted to make good choices for plants — you know, pick things that will do well here. Do you know much about it?"

"Nothing. I never had a garden at all. I love flowers though. I think the Botanical Garden is my favorite place in the city."

"It's amazing, isn't it?"

A glass of wine loosened them both up a little. Emily had kicked off her shoes and was leaning back against Charlotte's small sofa. Charlotte, still in the apron, sat beside her. They'd made a list for Violet. Now they were talking about themselves. Charlotte was surprised how comfortable she felt. Emily was beautiful, and sort of glamorous even — the kind of woman who scared her a little. And certainly not the type she would have expected to be interested in her. But Emily was nice. And she was interested. She'd asked about Seattle, and Charlotte's family, and her job at the library. Now she was talking about herself.

"I was born in Oregon. In a town called Wilsonville. About thirty miles outside of Portland. Small-town America. My mom was born there, too. Her parents had settled there, after the war, each with their own families. There are a lot of Poles in Oregon. There are a lot of Poles everywhere, I suppose. So . . . they're good Catholics, my parents. But I was their only child. My dad left when I was three. They never got divorced. My mom wouldn't have anyway, I don't think; she was always pretty religious. But she didn't know where he was. He didn't come home one day after work. He drove a truck. We never heard from him again. He'd taken all his clothes."

"That's awful."

"Awful for her. I don't really remember him. So I've never missed him."

"But for her."

"It got worse. I think what he did to her, leaving like that, stopped her from thinking she was worth anything. He really did a number on her, you know? I mean, if you want to do that to your wife and your kid, then that's about you, right? You're screwed up somehow. But he never told her that, and you could see that she always thought it was her.

"So she had a succession of lousy boy-

104

friends. Men who didn't treat her well, because she didn't expect to be treated well. Some were worse than others. She lived with a guy for six or seven years when I was a teenager. He was the worst. He crossed the line, from neglectful to cruel. Never to me — I don't think she'd have let that happen. But to her. And I saw it. She'd gotten herself trapped — they'd moved in together, and she didn't have money of her own — he didn't want her to work. Oh, he was a pig. He wanted a maid, not a girlfriend, and she couldn't see a way out."

"Sounds awful." Charlotte couldn't help comparing Emily's experience with her own. Middle-class parents, married for thirty-five years, church on Sundays.

Emily nodded. "She was a beautiful woman, my mom. Really stunning. By the time she was thirty-five, she looked fifty."

"Is she . . . still alive?"

Emily smiled. "She is. She's single. Has been for a few years. She got herself back on her feet. I think the truly terrible boyfriend — Len, he was called — I think he did her a favor, in a way. She woke up. Decided it was better to be alone than be with someone who made you feel worthless. She has a job — a good job, in a contractor's office in Portland. She put me through college."

"She must hate you being so far away."

"Yes and no. She's always been totally determined about me. She wants all the things for me she hasn't had for herself. She wants me to be a success. To be independent. Never to need a man, or let myself be with someone who isn't good enough — who doesn't appreciate me enough. You know. Normal mother stuff, but times about ten."

Charlotte smiled.

"God. Must be the wine talking. Did we finish that bottle? I'm sorry. You invited me here to talk about plants, and I've given you my life story."

"It's fine."

"I never do this."

Charlotte giggled. "Me neither."

They smiled broadly at each other now, each recognizing in the other something that might be the beginnings of real friendship. In Emily's experience, that was rare in this city. She didn't often solicit it, and it rarely presented itself this way. She'd lived in her last apartment building for two years, and there was no one there she would still see now that she had moved.

She knew she was a product of her mother's experience. Fiercely independent, self-contained, a nightmare to date. Not that she'd done much of that. She didn't trust men. Or particularly like them. Her childhood had paraded before her a cavalcade of everything she never wanted in a man. She wasn't sure she could ever see herself married. She was too cynical.

"What about you, Charlotte? Men in your life?"

Charlotte snorted. "Only in print." She gestured to the shelves behind her. "Seems to me that we're polar opposites, Emily. You've no romance in you, and I've nothing but."

Emily laughed. "Really?"

"My whole life, I've dreamed of the big romantic scene — the big gesture . . ."

"The knight on the white horse?"

"Something like that." She laughed, too. Emily wasn't laughing at her. Not like Madison would have been.

"So, end result? Two spinsters. One wants nothing, one wants everything. And we're both alone."

"God — spinsters. What a terrible word! Does anyone still say spinster anymore?"

"I've a friend from college who married an Englishman. Their wedding certificate has her down as a 'spinster of this parish.'"

"That's terrible . . . so Victorian."

There was a sudden knock at the door, but Madison didn't wait for an answer before she burst in. She stopped in her tracks when she saw Emily and Charlotte sitting there. Her eyes narrowed a little, but she still smiled her big white Hollywood smile at them.

"Am I missing a party?"

"This is Emily. Emily just moved into the apartment upstairs. Emily, this is Madison. Madison Cavanagh. She lives next door."

"Hello."

"Hi." Madison waved. "Welcome."

"Thanks."

"So you two know each other?"

"Only from the gardening committee."

"Oh, that. How's it going?" She didn't sound particularly interested in the answer. Actually, she didn't even wait for the answer. "Charl, have you got bathroom tissue? I'm all out."

"Hang on." Charlotte disappeared into the bathroom. Madison smiled, but she looked vague and distracted. She played with her hair, flicking it back behind her shoulders. "Got a date. Got to be ready in ten. Haven't even figured out what to wear . . ."

Emily nodded. Madison looked as though she were ready to go out already. Charlotte reappeared with a roll of tissue. Madison grabbed it, air-kissed Charlotte, and headed for the door.

"Thanks a million. Gotta run. I'm seeing Tom tonight."

Charlotte had no idea who Tom was. "Have fun!"

"You know me. I always do. Good to meet you, Emily. Have fun yourselves, with your garden stuff."

Was Emily paranoid, or was Madison smirking?

Charlotte closed the door behind Madison, who had left it slightly ajar.

"Whoa! She's lively."

"She is. She's nice, though."

Emily raised an eyebrow.

"Really. She is."

Emily knew Charlotte was nice. About Madison she was not convinced.

Next door, standing in just a bra and panties as she pulled clothes from her closet, throwing rejected items onto the bed carelessly (she'd end up at Tom's tonight, she knew; he had a high floor on First Avenue and a great view of the East River), Madison reflected that Emily was just a little too good-looking for her liking. Unpolished, maybe. A natural beauty. But a beauty nonetheless. And friendly with Charlotte already. She'd have to keep an eye on her.

Madison was the type of girl who knew, within five minutes of walking into a party or a restaurant or a boardroom, whether she was the most attractive woman there or not. Normally, she was. She knew what designer you were wearing, whether your hair color was natural or enhanced, and what you weighed, to within 10 pounds or so. Emily was pure Banana Republic (this was a minus, not a plus), a natural platinum blonde, and 120 pounds wet, lots of muscle.

One to watch indeed.

EVE

Eve wasn't at all sure about this outfit. It came from the right store. It bore the right label. It was a good color for her. Hadn't the girl in the shop said so? Mind you, she'd gushed so enthusiastically about everything Eve had dared leave the changing room wearing that Eve had been tempted to come out in her underwear to see if the girl said what wonderful things the flesh tones of her bra did for her eyes. The clerk had rather lost her credibility when Eve had heard her tell the rather matronly woman in the cubicle next door that leggings were a look that worked at any age.

The perils of saleswomen on commission. They practically rushed you the minute you walked into the store: "My name's Claudia, if you need any help. Have you seen this new shipment that just came in?"

This dress was green — apple green. Not a color she would ever have worn at home. And a dress. Who wore those at home? On and on the woman had gone about how incredibly simple a dress was to wear, leaving Eve to wonder what exactly was so complicated about wearing trousers and a top. Getting them on the right way around? She said Eve "just had" to buy the dress. That the color "just popped" on her. And that it would look adorable with a cute little flat, which Eve took to mean a shoe. So literally that she'd gone straight downstairs to the shoe department and told the tall man with his hands clasped neatly behind his back that she was in desperate need of a "cute little flat" to go with the dress, pulling out a corner of it to show him the color. The term meant ballet shoes. These were cute, actually. They had a little silver cutout at the front, and all important "toe cleavage," apparently. This meant that Eve's slightly square feet were pushed into the shoes in such a way that the lines between her toes were clearly visible, and this was, she gathered, a good thing. She thought it looked a little like the foot fetishist's equivalent of builder's bum, but what did she know? She was just grateful the dress she'd chosen did not require a four-inch heel of the sort that New Yorkers appeared to be able to wear for long-distance running.

She'd let a woman at the makeup counter "do" her face, too, which was very unlike her. She remembered being goaded by Cath into having it done at the Guerlain counter in Harrods once, just before she married Ed. She'd looked ghastly — like Barbara Cartland's love child, Cath had snorted — and she'd gone straight to the one-quid-a-go washrooms to rub the stuff off.

This was much better. She looked like herself — just a slightly more polished version. The girl had been triumphant about her ability to cover all Eve's broken capillaries and rosacea. Eve hadn't known she had either, but was duly grateful that they had been camouflaged. They'd managed to un-pink her cheeks, which was nothing short of miraculous, and she'd left with a pretty heavy bag full of products and a promise that this effect was easy to re-create at home. Hm. She'd even had her hair "blown out" (apparently, this was what you called a shampoo and set).

So she was supposed to have emerged from her frumpy little English chrysalis into a beautiful New York butterfly. This was her moment. Like when Cher takes the day off in *Moonstruck* to get her gray covered before she appears in front of Lincoln Center and Nicolas Cage falls in love with her. And Julia Roberts after she gets the treatment in Beverly Hills and shows Richard Gere what a pretty woman she really is. And when the mice step back from cartoon Cinderella after they magic up a blue chiffon number.

This was not quite how it was. Kicking off the cute little flats — which were actually chafing a bit already — and rubbing her toes ruefully (oh, toes of toe cleavage), Eve dialed Cath and heard the phone ring at the other end of the line twice before she remembered that if it was five thirty here, it was ten thirty at home, and a bit late for chats of a sartorial nature. Geoff answered, with a hint of panic. Geoff panicked easily, she remembered.

"Sorry. It's me, being completely stupid about the time difference." She heard Geoff exhale. "Were you asleep?" she asked guiltily.

"Just about. But on the sofa, so it's just as well you reminded me to shift."

"Don't thank me. What about my sis?"

"Not sleepy at all. Just got in from her book club, matter of fact. Though from the smell of her, I don't know why they don't just drop the pretense and call it the tequila club."

Eve heard her sister in the background. "Oy, you cheeky sod. We do read the books, you know. Before we start the drinking part."

"If you say so, you old lush. I'll pass you over. Lots of love, Eve."

"We do read the books!" Cath's familiar voice and her English accent washed over Eve like her old polyester baby blankie. She did miss it. The other day she'd stayed up until after midnight, watching *The Vicar of Dibley* on DVD, hooked on the accents and the innuendo. The wise, measured voice of David Dimbleby, streamed through the BBC Web site, could practically reduce her to tears, and she didn't dare look for Jenni Murray.

"I know. I heard. What was it this month?"

"*The Kite Runner.* Five yeses, one no, two maybes, but not sure one of those counts, since I'm pretty sure she just watched the film and faked it. You can't ever get anyone to be really honest about a book like that anyhow. Emperor's new clothes. Afternoon chat show hosts are the new Moses, you know, handing down the rules of reading on tablets of stone. We're all just disciples."

"Haven't read it."

"Shame on you. See the film. What's up? I don't think you called to discuss the finer points of literature. And anyhow, Geoff's right. Tequila has been taken."

"I don't look right."

"You just realized? Ha ha."

"Shut up. I've got this corporate dinner thing. Well, not really. It isn't business. Ed's set it up so I can meet the girlfriends or wives, or whatever they are, of his colleagues. His idea of trying to help me assimilate. I want to look the part. Spent three hundred dollars on a dress and shoes that hurt and had my hair done and got some amazing yellow stuff for my cheeks that makes me look a bit less . . . windburned —"

"All sounds wonderful."

"But I still don't look right. Or at least I don't feel right."

"I know . . . you've forgotten to put on your attitude."

"What do you mean, you daft mare?"

"I mean no dress in the world will make you feel like you fit in there if you don't waltz in acting as if you do. Think it and it shall be so, little sis."

"You make it sound so easy."

"Because it is."

"And so nauseatingly new age."

"But you know I'm right."

"Hmm."

"Bugger off and have fun and call me in the morning."

She did.

"And . . . ?" They'd always started and ended conversations in the middle, as though the intervening minutes, hours, or days had never happened. Ed and Geoff laughed about it.

"Fun? Not sure I'd call it that."

"Tell me all. Pol's at school, George is plugged in to *Dora the Explorer*. I've just made a cup of tea. I'm all yours for at least ten minutes, which saves me from unloading the dishwasher. What was the restaurant like?"

"Gorgeous. Downtown, full of trendies. Had a round roof, like you were sitting in the bottom of a barrel, you know, and all these branches stuck everywhere, with fairy lights. Very pretty. Amazing food, though they do serve these family-of-four portions, which is ridiculous because, apparently, women don't eat in this city. I kept thinking about that scene in *Gone with the Wind* where Mammy is force-feeding Scarlett before the barbecue at the Wilkeses'. I was hearing a voice in my head saying, 'It ain't fittin', it just ain't fittin',' every time I lifted my fork to my mouth. Cocktails, of course. Those you can, apparently, drink with impunity."

"On an empty stomach?"

"So it would seem."

"What were the people like?"

"The men were nice. They're so polite. Formal, almost. Like Henry James heroes."

"Beats most blokes I ever met in London. The women?"

"Terrifying."

"How so?"

"So . . . so perfect. Tiny. I mean really, really tiny. Perfect teeth, perfect hair, perfect nails. Perfectly huge diamonds. Seriously, Cath. Each one of them had a rock on the size of Gibraltar."

"Paste. Bound to be."

"Don't think so. Real."

"Okay, so they were perfect. Were they friendly?"

"Friendly enough. But kind of stiff, too, you know? We'd nothing in common. There wasn't one of them I felt I really, you know, connected with."

"Do you need to? Connect with them, I mean?"

"No. Not really. That's not it, though. But who am I going to hang around with? I had high hopes for them. That I'd meet someone, just one woman even, that I'd feel comfortable with. It's been ages. And so far my best friends are the doorman and the old lady from downstairs who must be eighty-odd."

"She sounds great."

"She is great. But that's not enough, is it?"

It wasn't, and Cath knew it as well as she did. She and Ed had argued, a little, in the cab on the way back uptown, although Eve didn't tell Cath that part. She had a sneaking suspicion it didn't show her husband in his best light.

He had said she wasn't trying. She couldn't believe he could be that mean. She'd bought the dress, hadn't she? Had her hair done?

That didn't have anything to do with it, Ed had said. It might have helped if he'd noticed when she came in, but he hadn't. He'd been propping up the bar, and she'd been the first girl to get there (the only one not rushing in from somewhere else, the only one who'd had nothing more pressing

118

to do today than shop for a dress and have her hair done). He'd kissed her, but he hadn't said anything and she wasn't entirely sure he'd even be able to tell her what had been different about her.

She wasn't trying? How could he be so stupid? she'd retorted. Could he not see the difference between her and those women?

He'd said the only difference he could see was that they had tried to be friendly and have a nice time, and that she hadn't. The remark had snapped out of him irritably, almost shocking her.

She'd turned away from him in the cab, too tired and headachy from smiling through dinner to argue, and watched twenty, thirty, forty city blocks speed by. Even late at night, it was busy. The sidewalks were thronged with people.

Back in the apartment, she had gone straight to bed, and he'd come later, curled himself against her back, his big arm around her, saying that he was sorry, that what he had said was unforgivable. She'd patted his arm in unspoken pardon, half asleep and half panicking, her head aching.

He was right.

Early on, when they were still tourists in the city, they'd been walking in Central Park.

She was still, weeks and weeks later, exploring it. Tourists never really went into the top part. They stayed south, wandering around and staring at the maps, at the Wollman Rink, where she could never stray without thinking of *Love Story* — Ali MacGraw, facing imminent death so prettily, and Ryan O'Neal, not cold at all in the snow with just a sports jacket on. The Dairy and the carousel and the Alice in Wonderland sculpture by the boat pond. The zoo, with its huge bird nets and insane polar bears, butting each end of their tiny enclosure as they swam.

They all missed the best parts of the park. If you kept going, once you'd strolled up the Promenade, down the wide steps at the Bethesda Fountain that Mel Gibson trod in *Ransom,* and across, past the fountain where George Clooney carried Michelle Pfeiffer in *One Fine Day,* north of the Boathouse, you got to Eve's favorite parts. Turtle Pond and Belvedere Castle, the Great Lawn. The odd tourist wandered in here after a trip to the Met or the Guggenheim, but mostly you just saw New Yorkers, once you got this far. She thought the very best view to be had in the entire city was the one from the north side of the Jacqueline Kennedy Onassis Reservoir, way up at Ninety-sixth Street. So long as she stayed clear of the runners and power walkers lapping her, Eve could stand for long minutes and watch the skyline of the city from there, and it always excited her. Always amazed her that this place, this extraordinary place, was where she lived now. It was quiet enough, in this green lung, to hear yourself think. She came most days.

She and Ed had eaten a sandwich lunch, right at the beginning, at the Boathouse one Sunday afternoon. Not in the posh part with white tablecloths and out-of-work actors waiting tables. In the bar next door, where new arrivals congregated by the doorways waiting to pounce on tables as they came free, glaring at slow eaters and those who dared nurse the last half inch of lager in their glass. She'd noticed a woman two tables down, eating alone, reading the *New York Times*. She looked like Boadicea — she was tall, you could tell, and wide — not fat, but sturdy and strong. She had a waist-length silvery white plait of hair that hung across one shoulder, and she was wearing a sort of corset, in leather, that laced up the front. Behind her was one of those giant backpacks that parents buy their kids at the start of their gap years. Old and grubby, this one was stuffed full, and an extraordinary collection of items was attached by strings and chains and ropes to the outside — a small saucepan, two or three days' worth of newspapers and a David Foster Wallace paperback, a tarpaulin. The woman was clearly homeless, but she didn't seem dirty or ill fed. She was eating a sandwich, but not as though she were ravenous. What made Eve stare beyond the odd spectacle of a person like her in a place like the Boathouse was her extraordinary carriage. She held herself aloft, dignified, very still and calm. She didn't appear in the least discomfitted either by her situation or by the stares of other diners. She was reading the paper, eating her sandwich, minding her own business, utterly self-contained.

Afterward, when they'd left, Eve had mentioned her to Ed. "Did you see her?"

"Yeah. I've seen her before, actually."

"When?" New York was strange like that — eight million people here, but you saw random familiar faces almost every day.

"Out running. I think she lives in the Ramble, up there." The Ramble was the wildest part of the park, just behind the Boathouse, where the paths wandered through trees and scrub. You could get far enough into it to forget you were in the midst of the city. "I've seen her a few times, actually."

"Lives there? Actually, all the time, lives there?"

"I don't expect she's the only one. It almost seems like a bit of a shantytown in there. But yeah, I think so. Did you see the saucepan and stuff? And the newspapers? I think they use them to stuff their clothing at night, make an extra layer against the cold. She had a mat, too. Did you see it?"

Eve nodded. "That's terrible. God — I can't imagine."

"Me neither. I expect we'll find it even harder in February, when it's really brass monkeys out here."

"And they don't do anything about it? The city?"

"What can they do? Someone at work told me that when the temperature drops really low, the city's obligated to go out and try and round them up, take them to shelters or something. But they don't want to go. They hide, apparently."

"Christ, how bad must a shelter be, if you would rather be outside in the freezing cold?" Eve shuddered. "How does it happen to them, do you suppose?"

Ed shook his head. "I don't know. I think some of them choose it."

"How could you choose to be homeless?"

123

"I think we have no idea how bloody lucky we are. I think some people opt out. Can't cope. They'd rather be in here — relying on themselves, left alone — than coping with the world the rest of us live in."

"Do you think she chose it?"

"She looks pretty content with it."

The woman had looked exactly that way — content. Like she had everything she needed. Eve wondered what her story was. "I suppose." She pushed her arm through Ed's and leaned into him. "And I think I get it, in a weird sort of way. Think about how simple life is for her."

"Simple? I should think it is unimaginably hard."

"Sure, but in a survival, primeval way. Food, water, a place to sleep. She's not worrying about her tax return, is she? Or whether she's got the right stuff to wear to dinner? Or whether she'll get invited to such and such a benefit."

"You sound like a Tory."

"Well, I'm the age for it, aren't I?"

"Still think I'd rather be us."

"Still think if I chose to be her, I'd have hitched my way down south. Sleeping rough has got to be easier in Miami than here."

They'd stopped talking about it then, distracted by something or other. It was a

124

miserable subject anyway. But she hadn't forgotten about the woman in the Boathouse. She looked for her most days, if she was walking in this part of the park. She'd seen the woman once or twice, at a distance. She'd been sitting on a park bench, the backpack beside her. Not reading or talking. Just sitting, staring ahead. Eve had approached, wondering if she was brave enough to take a seat beside her; she'd learned early on that the homeless in the park usually had a bench to themselves. She didn't know why she was so interested, and when she got close enough to the bench, it turned out she wasn't brave enough to sit down. But she looked right at the woman, and the woman looked right back. When she was almost past her, the woman nodded. And went back to staring.

RACHAEL

Rachael Schulman rarely did personal email before ten in the evening. She got home by seven without fail. Everyone at work knew that the vice president in charge of marketing and PR was going to leave at six thirty, no matter what crisis might rage around her. Bedtime was sacred, and she never, ever missed it.

David wasn't so lucky. His employers were not quite so empathetic, and his work as a litigator took him away quite often — not usually for more than one or two nights at a time, but then he wasn't the fixed point in the children's day. That was her. Rachael remembered her own mother, always home from work, always in pumps and a pencil skirt, kneeling beside Rachael's own bed every night in a mist of Chanel, to kiss her good night. Once the children had been settled — in Mia's case, settled twice — Rachael had the children's lives to arrange: pediatrician, dentist, piano teacher, playdates, holiday camps, birthday parties. And their own lives: family occasions — immediate and extended — supper dates with friends, tickets to shows. There were invitations to extend and to reply to.

The house in Connecticut was a job in itself — pool guy and gardener in the summer, snowplow in the winter. She wouldn't swap the house in Connecticut for anything, though. It was their haven, their sanctuary.

They'd bought in the country long before they'd bought in the city, as soon as they had the money for it. Before, actually, they'd had quite enough money for it. Her mother had been astonished she'd chosen the country over the Hamptons. Rachael remembered the day they'd told her. She'd raised one eyebrow quizzically and asked, "What on earth will you do there?" She and David had laughed about it afterward — at the suggestion that beyond the manicured lawns and Atlantic beaches of Long Island there was no meaningful life. Each year when she went back to her mother's house, she knew how right she had been to make her family's base somewhere else. She couldn't imagine swapping it, as her mother seemed to imply she would, one day "when they could afford it." She wouldn't swap any of it. There wasn't much time to reflect on life, but if she ever did, she felt lucky to have the life she had always wanted. The life she had dreamed of.

But it took a lot of work, this perfect life. So email didn't happen until late at night. These days, it counted toward her downtime. She would change into yoga trousers and an old USC sweatshirt and take the laptop to the deepest sofa in the living room, preferably with a big glass of pinot noir, and begin to go through the messages. Yes, Jacob would love to come play Thursday after school. Sure, she'd volunteer to man a table at the school book fair. She couldn't make dinner next Tuesday, but how about the following Friday? and yes, it would be great to get together . . . It was ten thirty before she got as far as Violet's email about the roof terrace. It contained nothing particularly taxing, but it still made Rachael sigh. David, sitting on the opposite sofa, nursing his own glass, reading *The New Yorker,* heard her.

"Big sigh?"

"Oh, sorry. Didn't mean to be loud. I was just reading this note from Violet Wallace, about the 'beautifying committee.' She wants us to say when we're free to work."

"I don't know why you joined in the first place. You're never free. Especially in the summer — you'll be up at the house, won't you?" Rachael worked a three-day week in July and August, commuting down early Tuesday mornings, and returning on Thursday evenings. She'd arranged it that way, after Mia was born. It wasn't ideal, but it was the best she could do. David came on Friday nights, and went back by train on Sunday evenings. Milena, the nanny, did the rest.

"I just thought one of us should join."

"Well, I know I don't have time."

She didn't know she'd implied that he had and thus provoked the defensiveness. David did almost none of the home work. He never really had. Sometimes, just sometimes, it annoyed her. David had a great job. He was successful, capable, reliable. And there were days when you'd never guess it, watching him at home. He let her do all that stuff. All of it. And sometimes, just for a moment, she resented it.

"So you said. I didn't ask you to do it. Who has time? That's the nature of modern life. But we'll benefit, the children will benefit. Anyway, it's important, being a part of the community. And I'm on the board, and so I feel like we have to step up. And here's the kicker — you know I can't say no to Violet."

She smiled sideways at him, inviting him to tell her that she was a soft touch.

But David wasn't listening anymore. Rachael was sermonizing, as much to herself as to him, and he was already converted. She was the grand master of doing the right thing. He'd known she would join the instant he saw the notice on the board downstairs.

He knew, because he'd married a woman who was just like his mother, and now he was living his adult life just the way he had lived out his childhood and adolescence — striving for perfection, and failing. Failing every day.

Rachael hadn't looked like his mother,

and for the first few years she hadn't seemed at all like her. They'd laughed about her together, in fact. He was pretty sure he remembered his wife, at some point, making a solemn promise never to be like his mother. He hadn't found out until it was too late.

They'd met when he was a senior, in his final year at college, and Rachael was a sophomore. She was one of those effortlessly pretty, glossy girls, athletic and popular. It was obvious she came from a wealthy background. Her perfect teeth and classic, expensive jewelry gave her away. A charmed-life type. He knew the background well — it was exactly where he came from. Different coast, same deal.

David was a Californian. The indulged youngest of three sons born to a mother with old money and a father who'd made his himself. The money had surprised his father, since he was a hippie at heart and had never really wanted any. He'd written a book — part fiction, part memoir — about his experiences in San Francisco in the sixties, which had become a cult hit and then a movie. David's parents had divorced when he was seven or eight, and he and his brothers had lived with their mom in a vast house in Sausalito, mostly looking forward to weekends across the bridge in the relative squalor of their father's walk-up in San Francisco. His mother had remarried twice before he left home for college, and once more since, although she was currently single again, so far as he knew. David had sometimes thought he was fonder of each of his three stepfathers than he was of his own mother. He called them "the butcher, the baker, and the candlestick maker," although they were the Realtor, the screen-writer, and the dermatologist.

He was reasonably sure his mother had only married her last husband for the free Botox, and it had been hard to tell how emotionally damaged she had been by her fourth divorce, since by the time she rejected that husband, she'd had so many shots in her face that she could neither frown nor smile with any conviction.

She was relentlessly critical, and everyone — all her husbands and her own sons included — disappointed her constantly. She had once refused to speak to David after a piano recital in the sixth grade at school where he had missed three notes on a piece he'd been practicing for weeks. He remembered walking out of school behind her, ashamed, angry, and humiliated — hating her almost as much as he hated himself for getting the notes wrong.

He told his children every single day that he loved them and that they were wonderful. He could barely bring himself to criticize them for anything, to the point at which it was Rachael who had to correct spellings and admonish lousy table manners.

He had never really understood what had attracted his parents to each other. They were both good-looking people. At least, his mother had been — although, before Botox, her face had taken on the countenance of a woman discontented with her life. But their value systems, their beliefs, even their ideas of life's simple pleasures had been poles apart. He'd asked his father once, before he'd married Rachael, what had been between them. His father had taken a deep drag on his cigarette and thought for a moment.

Smiling ruefully, he'd answered, "Before you boys were born? Sex and drugs, mostly." Then he'd laughed. "She never did like rock and roll."

His father, his gentle, lovely dad, still vaguely surprised by life, and then by death, had died of lung cancer four years ago. He was diagnosed just after David had married Rachael and died around the same time she found out their third baby was a girl. David had whispered that news to him as he lay close to death (not quite close enough, as it turned out; he lingered in a drug-induced coma for four or five intolerable days).

David hadn't seen his mother since his father's funeral. They weren't estranged; there'd been no terrible row. But he knew she was bad for him, and he never sought her out. She, in turn, had no need of him, it seemed. His brothers and their families were both still in California — one in San Francisco and the other in the suburbs of LA, but they didn't see much of her either.

Rachael, on the other hand, was classic East Coast. If you were permitted to call your own wife a type, then Rachael was definitely a type. The beloved only daughter, born relatively late, to a successful corporate lawyer and a speech therapist, she'd been raised in Manhattan, a few blocks from where they lived now, spending summers with her babysitters and her big brothers out on Long Island, in a big house in Southampton.

While David had grown up in the shadow of his mother's disappointment, Rachael had been raised in a world where everything was wonderful. (Even if it wasn't. It had taken him a few years to work that one out. These were the type of people who'd smile and welcome a hurricane with a jaunty "What a refreshing breeze.") She'd come to USC from an Upper East Side girls' school, streetwise but naïve. It was no accident that she'd swapped East for West Coast and put five hours between herself and home. She was being suffocated by all the marvelousness, and she craved a life that was completely separate, even if only for a few years. She was spoiled, undoubtedly, and what his friends would call high-maintenance, definitely, but she was also generous and funny and real. She'd apparently fallen for his carefully cultivated surfer dude persona, laid-back and free-spirited, mimicking his father, to his mother's eternal disappointment. He'd fallen for her glossy, easy perfection and her laugh. That first year, he liked to sit at a slight distance and just watch her walking, her smooth dark hair swaying in time with her small round ass. That walk was sexy and sweet and entitled and confident, and that walk was what hooked him.

They'd flirted, as they both flirted with many others. Flirting was what passed for conversation in those days. They'd hung around in the same big, easy groups, the kind everyone else wished they could belong to. For the first year, it went no further. Neither one wanted to make the first move, although afterward they both admitted to each other that it always felt as though there was going to be one. And then one day, on the first glorious day of real spring, he'd driven them both, alone, to Santa Monica in his beaten-up old Chevy and given her a surfing lesson. He'd surfed all his life, and she'd never been on a board. She didn't know what was more attractive about him that morning — the way he looked on the board (strong and muscular and competent, like some gnarly Neptune) or the way he taught her (patiently, kindly, without laughing once, even though she could barely get onto her knees on the board before splatting sideways off into the white surf). They'd had their first kiss in that surf, after he fished her out from yet another unsuccessful attempt — a kiss cold and salty and delicious. And he'd been gone from that moment onward.

It had taken Rachael perhaps a little longer. She was torn between their romance and her ambition. He'd had to work hard to convince her that she could have both. It had started then, that feeling. That he wasn't quite good enough. He'd needed no convincing about Rachael; he'd been more sure and certain of her than of anything in his life up until that point. He felt like he'd

135

had to win her, prove himself.

They'd been married at the St. Regis in December, the year Rachael graduated. There'd seemed no point in waiting, and besides, Rachael's family would have been furious if they'd suggested living together. He was excluded totally from the planning process. Rachael's mother had gone into overdrive — Rachael surrendering as twenty years of prior experience had shown her she should. Rachael had eight bridesmaids, and he was required to produce eight matching attendants. (Two brothers, four college friends, and two slightly bemused coworkers from the law firm he'd joined in New York after they became engaged, qualified not so much by friendship as by their Jewishness, their photogenic qualities, and the fact that they were free that Sunday.) And show up. With a haircut. That was the extent of his involvement.

Snow had fallen to order (how would it dare not?) the night before, swirling around them appealingly as they left the smart rehearsal dinner at the 21 Club, obligingly stopping in time to allow a crystal blue sky and bright sunshine for the afternoon of the wedding. There had been a photograph — taken out at the Hamptons house by a photographer who shot for *Elle* and *Vogue*

— and five paragraphs (including the story of the first kiss in the surf) in the Style section of the Sunday *New York Times*. A honeymoon on St. Barts.

He'd wanted them to go to South America, but St. Barts was a gift from an aunt of Rachael's. Rachael had seemed extraordinary to him on that holiday, in a tiny white bikini and an enormous broad-brimmed straw hat. He couldn't get enough of her, in bed and out of it, and he couldn't believe how lucky he was. He watched her when she wasn't watching him, and was amazed each time all over again that she was his wife. That she had chosen him. He was so very proud of her. She would take him into her gilded world, where everything was always wonderful, and he would live there forever.

He'd been living there now for ten years. And the strain of everything always being wonderful was beginning to be terrible.

TODD AND GREG

They had their best talks in bed. The first time — the morning after the night before of their first, blind date in the East Village eight years earlier — they had begun, like an old married couple, and they were still talking now. They had their own shorthand, their own code, and they often finished each other's sentences. They talked for hours on their seven-foot pillow top mattress, read the *Times* straight through, watched CNN, ate bagels, and drank Earl Grey tea. Some of their friends were having children now, but they were wise enough to know how much they would resent giving up their talks in bed for broken nights and early starts and chocolate milk stains on the six-hundred-thread-count sheets. Most of the young parents they knew were lucky to finish a sentence, let alone a bagel with lox and the Style section. They "loved" their friends' children (like they "loved" their friends' new upholstery, and their dogs, and their new exhibition at the gallery on Chambers) — from time to time, at a healthy distance.

Mostly Todd talked and Greg listened, but Todd said that Greg's words were pearls of wisdom among the swine of his chatter. They lived great, fulfilling, independent lives, but they spent their evenings and weekends coloring them in for each other. Todd told funny stories about his clients and their homes — their weird tastes and impossible demands. Greg's stories were often more poignant; he was a pediatric anesthetist at a large children's hospital, and he spoke about patients and their families. They talked about art and film, about which they usually disagreed, and about politics, where they were always in perfect accord with one another, and about which restaurant they wanted to eat Sunday brunch at, which usually went fifty-fifty. Tonight they were talking about their neighbors. More specifically, they were talking about Charlotte Murphy and playing *Pygmalion*. Bickering, actually. Greg was Colonel Pickering, bickering.

"She's just so very uncomfortable in her skin. She wouldn't let anyone get anywhere near her at Violet's meeting. She actually stepped back when I spoke to her. I wondered if I'd forgotten to floss. And she couldn't look you in the eye."

"She's shy, she's painfully shy. Agreed. And badly dressed doesn't begin to cover it. She needs a complete makeover. But I tell you, under all that, she could be cute."

"Hmm."

"And she came to Violet's meeting. That means she's open."

"Open to planting a few containers, not to the attack of the killer queens."

"I'm telling you, we should take her under our collective wing. I don't mean attack —

nothing like that. When did you ever know me to attack?"

Greg raised an eyebrow.

"Just, maybe, corner the girl. Have a chat . . ."

"She doesn't need a makeover. She needs a great guy. That's all. Girls who wear dirndl skirts can find love, too, you know. They just have to find the guys in the stonewash denim jeans."

"You're an old romantic."

"And you're obsessed with appearances. It's really just an extension of your own vanity, you know, judging the world that way —"

"I'm not vain."

"Right. And I'm not gay."

EVE

Did making doctors' appointments as a way to fill the time count as desperate and tragic, or was she just taking full advantage of her newfound free time and seemingly unlimited insurance policy to make sure she was in great condition? Eve wondered. A New Yorker would definitely go with option two. New Yorkers could spin (and not just in the spinning room at the Equinox). She was leaning toward option one, spinning (of the stationary bicycle or the political varieties) not being a habit with her just yet. But it wasn't her fault. It was her husband who had started this particular line of dominos toppling. Ed had made the very first appointment with the first doctor, concerned (slash irritated, let's be honest) by her persistent cough, which was keeping him awake — a cough she had insisted was nothing to worry about.

He'd booked her with an internist in their neighborhood that a girl at the office had recommended. She'd told herself it was good to have a doctor, just in case, even though she hadn't been to her family doctor at home for . . . well, she couldn't remember how long. And it was something to do — get up, get dressed, hail a cab. Be going somewhere. Everyone else was, all the time.

The doctor was brisk, efficient, and not at all fun. Eve had detailed the symptoms of the cough in the calm, quasi-knowledgeable manner she had historically used with doctors, since her greatest dread was always appearing to be hysterical or hypochondriacal. The "doctor," in green pajamas, listened for a moment, in what seemed to be amused silence, before she revealed herself to be the nurse and told Eve to please put on the green gown and that Dr. Cohen would be along shortly to "work her up." Work her over, more like. Appalled by the whole gown thing — she'd worn one once, when she'd had her appendix out as a child and hadn't been quite so anxious about having her ass hanging out in the breeze (Why would she have been? In those days it didn't hang) — but ultimately obedient, she'd changed quickly and sat anxiously on the edge of the table, waiting to be "worked up" and promising herself she'd work Ed up himself that night, and not in a good way, for getting her into this.

Dr. Cohen was no more receptive than her nurse had been to Eve's self-diagnosis, bristling and pointing out that this was her job, not Eve's. She was dressed more smartly than Eve might have dressed for tea with the Queen, with a silk skirt and high heels. Enormous black pearl earrings. Before the doctor could simply listen to Eve's chest and determine whether antibiotics were required, it appeared that she needed to weigh and measure her ("You could stand to lose ten pounds, did you know?"), take her blood pressure ("That's a little high for your age. What exercise do you get?"), remove five vials of her blood ("Better look at that cholesterol"), and give her hell about having smoked ten years ago for about six months and for not having had a smear last year or a mammogram ever (at this last one, the doctor's voice was almost tremulous). By the end (oh, and PS: no antibiotics), Eve thought killing outright was probably too good for Ed — not nearly embarrassing and painful enough. Perhaps she'd book him for an early prostate exam. The insurance undoubtedly covered that.

Armed with about ten different telephone numbers, including, she noticed on her way home on the bus, ones for a dermatologist and a cosmetic dentist, along with two handouts on nutrition and exercise, her only diagnosis a severe case of indignation and humiliation, she was finally allowed to leave, vowing that only something very serious would ever bring her back here. She sniggered on the bus, fantasizing about being hit by a car and the paramedics finding, instead of the spotless underwear one should always sport in case such a catastrophic event unfolded during your day, knickers bearing the words "Do not take to American ER. Ship home to take chances with beleaguered NHS." The woman next to her, alarmed by the sniggering (and probably by all the medical literature), got up and moved to the next row. That just made the sniggering worse. Laughing to yourself had to be better than just talking to yourself, didn't it? That she did on her walks around the reservoir, content in the knowledge that everyone else was far too much in tune with their own iPod sound tracks and buy-sell cell conversations to even notice.

And yet here she was, a few weeks later, sitting in the ob-gyn's office. Cath told her she should do it.

"Why wouldn't you want to know everything was okay with you? Go. Let them check you out. Better safe than sorry." And then Cath had told her some horrible story about a mum at school who'd missed three cervical smears and been diagnosed too late to do anything about it and was dead before the Nativity play, a story which Eve suspected came in part from Cath's imagination and in part from the pages of *Good Housekeeping,* rather than from the actual school gates, but which nonetheless had the desired effect.

Cath's visit last month, gory cancer stories aside, had been brilliant. Cath was utterly euphoric, having unloaded George and Polly onto Geoff's mum for a few days. "She is so much better than Geoff," she had laughed.

"With Geoff I have to leave about a thousand notes. A Post-it on every surface. Which side of the dispenser the fabric softener goes into, who likes what on their toast, who has to be where when. He's hopeless. Actually, he isn't hopeless, he's perfectly capable, bless him. He just refuses to absorb that sort of information. He takes a certain pride in his uselessness, domestically, you know? Anyway, with his mum, you just dump 'em and run. I know they're going to eat far too many sweets and get away with blue murder, but I also know they're going to have so much fun they won't miss me, and that she won't ruin all their clothes in the wash."

They'd had an absolute ball all week. They'd done all the touristy things, Cath wearing a green foam Statue of Liberty headband for far too long. They'd cried and held hands in the harrowing and poignant museum at Ground Zero. They'd stumbled on the cobbles in the Meatpacking District, trying and failing to get a table at Pastis, after margaritas at the Gansevoort. Eve had spent more time in Century 21, the bargain store downtown, wrestling other women for cheap 7 for All Mankind jeans, in one day than she thought a person should ever have to. And Macy's, and Bloomingdale's. And

FAO Schwarz, where Cath made Eve dance barefoot with her on the giant piano, despite the crowd of glaring parents whose children had to wait. Cath shopped for England, blaming the brilliant exchange rate for the ever-increasing pile of shopping bags in the corner of the guest room. In between retail attacks, they laughed and gossiped, and ate, and talked — talked long into the night. Eve felt like she hadn't really, really talked since she'd gotten here, and it felt good.

Cath was very no-nonsense about Eve's loneliness, to which Eve confessed one evening in a Mexican restaurant. Ed wouldn't eat Mexican. He'd stayed out of the way altogether, actually, leaving her and Cath to it all week. Eve had the slightly uncomfortable feeling that he was relieved her sister was here, taking the heat off him, and glad of the opportunity to work late. She didn't want to pretend with Cath; she never had before. She admitted to how tough she was finding it.

"That'll pass. What did you expect? Everything to work perfectly from day one? You need to pull yourself together and make stuff happen for yourself. No one is going to come knocking on the door of seven A, asking if Eve can come out to play. We're not eight years old. You've got a lot to offer,

Eve. It's not like you to be wimpy like this."

"I know. I think it's just that it's all so different. They're different — Americans."

"So just be you. You'll be a novelty. Be the quirky Englishwoman. They love that stuff." Cath went cross-eyed and buck-toothed.

Eve laughed. "You make it sound so easy."

"It will be. You've always had loads of friends, right? So why would this place be any different? Pull your finger out, girlie. Plan some trips. For Christ's sake, you're in the most exciting city in the world and the whole bloody country's on your doorstep. With your hunky husband. And some dosh, for a change. No sprogs yet, cramping your style. There is absolutely no excuse whatsoever for not having the time of your life. Do you hear me?"

"I hear you. Consider me reprimanded."

"Quite right. And if you don't, you can fly home and move in with Geoff and the kids, and clean Weetabix off sisal matting, and I'll fly over here and have the time of your life for you, you ungrateful cow."

Cath sounded just like Mum when she talked like that. Looked like her, too. Eve had been missing her mother more since she'd gotten here, which was weird. Mum had been dead for such a long time. She'd missed so much — college graduation, Eve's

147

wedding. Eve had been only ten when she'd died, and she knew the loss had been harder for Cath, at fourteen. Kept being harder for Cath, too. Their dad had struggled to cope, trying to deal with his own grief, and he'd leaned on her, too hard. She'd grown up too fast.

Cath was just like Mum, though. Irreverent and funny and energetic. Mum would have loved New York. And Eve would have loved having her here. Missing someone who had been dead more, much more, than half your life was a strangely unsatisfying sensation. Half the time you didn't even really know what you were missing and wondered if it was just the idea of something that you didn't actually remember.

Thank God for Cath. Then, and now. Dad had never been much better than hopeless after Mum died, though he loved them both. And then he'd remarried, and neither she nor Cath could really stick Dawn. Not in a damaged, lost, and lonely kid way — they'd been twenty-three and twenty-seven when it happened. In a woman-to-woman, "you're not my cup of tea" kind of way. So thank God for Cath.

Friends weren't family. She felt a bit resentful about their friends, although she knew it wasn't fair. They were all still there, still meeting down at the pub and having dinner parties. She felt excluded, although she was aware that was ridiculous. She'd be there, too, if she wasn't here. She knew she couldn't expect them to be on the phone every day, or sending emails. She knew that wasn't fair. But she hadn't expected to feel so quickly forgotten. A few were planning trips, but it seemed like it was more to do with the shopping than with her. She didn't want to tell them she was low. It felt like failure. With Cath, she didn't care.

Eve wasn't sure that visiting the ob-gyn would have been the first thing on Cath's list, had she in fact been living Eve's life for her, but it was a start. The waiting room was like an illustrated book on child birth made flesh. Women with bumps of every size lined the room — from the "could just have been a big lunch" variety to the type of protuberance that looked impossible from an engineering point of view. All clearly visible behind clinging Lycra. Not a Laura Ashley smock or a forgiving maxi dress in sight. These women didn't seem to mind if their belly buttons protruded like huge third nipples. Nor did they have, apparently, baby weight elsewhere. Cath — the only pregnant woman Eve had ever seen naked, who even described herself as human contraception, before and after delivery — had been vast in pregnancy, with jellylike flesh settling indiscriminately on her hips, her bum, the backs of her knees. Not here. These women were walking ads for procreation. Glossy hair (hello, New York, how do you do that?), great nails, clear skin. And Lycra maternity wear. Not one swollen ankle that a Jimmy Choo sandal would struggle to contain.

Eve didn't know any of these women individually, but she knew them as a clan, a tribe. She knew where they'd be in a few months. She'd seen them. Actually, she'd almost been stalking them. They'd be pushing brightly colored Bugaboos down Madison Avenue, grabbing lattes at Dean & DeLuca, and shopping for size 4 dresses again in the boutiques. They'd be working out in Central Park with personal trainers. She'd watched a group of four or five the other day. They'd all had newborns in three-wheeled, all-terrain buggies. They'd been jogging, breezes blowing in the faces of their babies. And using the handles as ballet barres for squats and bends. And then, at the top of the flight of steps that led down to the Bethesda Fountain, at the boat pond, they'd abandoned the strollers at the top and run up and down, up and down, up and down, while their trainer shouted encouragement and sang to the babies, doing jumping jacks the whole time. They'd be walking down Cedar Hill with their sling-wearing husbands looking at them like they were Joan of Arc. She knew them. She knew how great their lives were, how lucky they were.

This doctor, thank God, was different from the last one. Much softer — both physically and in demeanor. She was older than the polished, kitten-heeled Dr. Cohen — Eve guessed in her mid fifties — and almost chubby, a state of being Eve realized since she had arrived in this city she had come to associate with a gentler, more relaxed persona. She was becoming a reverse fatist.

"What brings you here, Eve?"

"Well, when I first made the appointment, I wanted a — what do you guys call them?"

"A Pap?"

"Yes, a smear. Pap. And the internist I saw said I needed a mammogram, so I need a referral . . ."

"And now?" The doctor raised her glasses onto her head and peered at Eve inquisitively, a small smile playing around her lips.

"And now . . ." — this was the first time Eve had said this out loud — "now I think

I'd like to get pregnant."

She realized she was beaming, and the doctor beamed back.

That had made her sound like a flake, she realized. Like the idea had just come to her as she'd sat in the room — like the estrogen was contagious, and pregnancy an epidemic. It wasn't like that. Babies had always been in the plan. This was maybe a little bit sooner than she'd thought it would happen, but not much. And she wasn't working, was she? No time issues. No money issues, at last. No reason not to get started.

She wanted four. Two boys, two girls. Big tall boys who looked like Ed, and who would grow to be taller than her before they were teenagers. Who'd play football and cricket and break their arms and have stitches and wrestle on the rug. Pretty little girls she could cook with, and watch *Steel Magnolias* and *Sleepless in Seattle* with, take shopping. Who'd come to her and confess their crushes and ask her advice. Ed said he didn't mind how many, so long as it was more than one. He'd been one, and he didn't want that for his own child. He wanted a family, he said, not a project.

It was no surprise that family mattered so much to both of them, albeit for such different reasons. Eve wanted to re-create

152

exactly what she'd known as a young child, before her mum had died. Ed wanted to make changes to the childhood he remembered. Eve believed she'd been shown a master class in how to raise a family. Ed knew he wanted to do almost everything differently.

Babies had reared their downy, soft heads early in their lives together. Cath had had her first baby within months of Ed and Eve's getting together. Eve was obsessed with the baby and deeply in love at first sight. She'd left work in the middle of the day as soon as Cath had rung and said Polly had been born, and spent as much time with her as work, life, and a new relationship allowed. Eve had a clear, blissful memory of watching Ed taking Polly in his arms, gingerly, a tiny armful all in white, a scrunched-up face barely visible between receiving blanket and hat, and feeling her heart contract at the sight. Ed stared down at Polly, utterly absorbed. It had instantly elevated him from current love interest to something else. And did men actually realize what an aphrodisiac it was? Above his busy head, Cath had smirked and raised her eyebrows at Eve, nodding her approval.

And then, a few months after that, when they were talking about moving in together, and she knew it was getting really serious — the most serious she had ever been, certainly — she'd had a "scare." She'd missed a period, which she never did, and been sufficiently preoccupied by it to buy a test in her lunch hour. When it had been negative, and when Mother Nature had rewarded her curiosity, a day later, with heavy bleeding and agonizing cramps, he'd been almost sad, certainly contemplative, spooning her in his bed, gently rubbing her sore tummy. "One day," he had said softly. "One day it will happen to us. When we choose. When we're ready." She'd expected relief. Possibly difficult questions about how it could have happened in the first place when they were supposed to be being careful. She hadn't expected that. "When we're ready." Like they were already "we." And like their being ready was a matter of when, and not if. She'd never had a man say things like that before. Like she was staying. Forever. "When we're ready."

Eve was ready now. She was sure of it.

Dr. Jones had assured her that she was healthy and well and should have no problems conceiving, so far as she could see. The ten pounds Dr. Cohen had made sound like morbid obesity didn't seem to her to be a problem. She did the smear, putting Eve's legs in unfamiliar, uncomfortable stirrups, just to be safe, but sent her away with a wink, an instruction to "get practicing," and a bottle of folic acid.

Sure, now, of what she wanted, Eve was left with an afternoon to contemplate how to make Ed want it, too. He would be home tonight. Which was getting to be a rarer and rarer occurrence. Sometimes he just worked late. He'd ring, and tell her to go ahead and eat without him — that he'd had a lunch anyway, or that he'd be happy with a sandwich later. Sometimes he was with clients. Or colleagues. He'd asked her along a few times, but she'd come up with excuses. She didn't feel right yet. She didn't want to go until she was confident she could get it right. She didn't want to let him down — though she never said that was why. So she stayed at home alone a lot. Watching unsatisfactory American television. She couldn't figure out either the guide feature on the remote control, nor make head nor tail of the *TV Guide* magazine, so she flicked endlessly. That way, she caught the last half of a lot of great movies. Never the beginning. She'd seen Debra Winger dying in *Terms of Endearment* at least four times, but never Jack Nicholson getting drunk with Shirley MacLaine. She'd seen Julia Ormond married off to the third of three brothers in *Legends of the Fall* twice, but she'd never seen her with Brad Pitt. She kept flicking, though, in hopes.

But tonight, Ed had promised he'd be home. It would be the first night this week, and she'd thrown a tantrum — made him swear nothing would distract or delay him. She bought a bottle of champagne and a tray of peeled shrimp, on the basis that oysters were a bit obvious (and, in her opinion, a bit disgusting). She considered waiting at the table in the apartment naked but for strategically placed shrimp or a lacy apron, but only for a moment. Ed was more likely to fall down laughing than to fall into her arms. He was strictly a white cotton knickers, not a red lace guy. At least, she hoped he was, because otherwise he'd married the wrong girl. She'd been given a set of saucy underwear — with the suspender belt and everything — on her hen night. And she'd felt perfectly ridiculous in it, so she'd shoved it, balled up, in the back of the drawer before Ed came home. Tonight she shaved her legs in the shower, though.

When she heard Ed at the door, she went to him and kissed him deeply, sending him an immediate and very obvious signal. "Hello."

"Mmm." Ed kissed back. He always did. "Hell-oo-oo."

Men were quite mammalian like that — no headache or mood too bad for sex. He'd broken his leg once, when they'd been going out a few months, and she'd picked him up after it had been set. She'd been full of concern, intending to nurse him tenderly through his pain and shock. They'd been doing it on his sofa within the hour.

He looked at her face. "Something's happened. You're all . . . you're all glowy."

She smiled. He had his hands on her hips, and he poked one finger in at each side of her stomach. "Come on. What have you been up to?"

"I bought dinner. And champagne."

"Now I'm really worried. Did you crash the car?"

"We don't have a car, you idiot."

She'd uncorked the bottle and filled him a glass. She clinked her own against his. "Here's to us." Ed clinked back and loosened his tie. Eve took a deep breath. She'd planned to open the discussion with a little finesse, and maybe a little small talk, but now she just blurted out what was uppermost in her mind.

"I want us to have a baby."

If Ed was shocked, he hid it well. "Now?"

157

He sounded almost amused.

"Yes, now. Now is the perfect time." He looked skeptical.

"We just got here, Evie. We've barely settled in."

"We're settled in fine. I am, at least. And you were settled in from minute one. If you hadn't noticed, we're all unpacked."

She gestured at the picture-perfect apartment all around them, thinking as she did so that brown suede might not have been such a great choice for the sofa. Ed's eyes followed her hands, then rested back on her face.

"And it's not like we'd have a baby tomorrow. It takes nine months, you know, Ed. And it might not happen, start to happen, for months. I just want us to get started. Stop using anything. Shag like bunnies."

He grinned lasciviously. "I like the sound of that part." Then a little more seriously, "What's brought this on?"

"You make it sound like we've never talked about it before."

She had a sudden flashback to the evening in the garden when he'd told her about New York. This was the same.

"No, no — I didn't mean it to sound like that. I know we've talked about it. I know it's what we both want. I just wondered what made you want to do it now."

"I'm not working. Things are going really well for you . . . We're here."

"And you're a bit lonely. I know, Evie. I know. I'm just not sure that that makes it the right time. Don't you need a support network?"

"You can be my support network. I'm not saying I want a baby because I'm lonely. I'm not confusing an infant with a puppy, Ed. But yes, since you mention it. I am lonely. Why wouldn't I be? It takes time, getting a new life off the ground. I'm not unhappy, I promise I'm not. Lonely isn't unhappy. I love the apartment and the city and I love you. Having a baby is something I want for us, for you and me. A start on the family we always talked about having. And yes, there's no doubt in my mind that having a baby now would help with making that new life. We'd meet other people with new babies. Childbirth classes — all that. Nursery, school eventually. Cath has an entirely new set of friends since she had her kids. They're the people she spends all her time with."

"And that's what you want?"

"Of course. It's not such a half-baked idea, is it?" You'd come home more, she thought. We'd matter more than just I do.

She didn't say that.

Ed took a big gulp of champagne and put his glass down on the table.

Eve waited. She couldn't tell from his face what he was thinking. "Isn't it what you want?"

He rubbed his forehead. "I'm just settling in. Finding my feet. I knew we'd do it . . . eventually."

She was pouting, and she knew it.

"And you really want this?"

She put her arms around his neck and planted kisses all over his cheeks, his mouth, his nose. "Yes, yes, yes."

Soap opera pause. She realized she couldn't remember the last time she'd asked Ed for anything.

"Well, okay then. Let's go for it."

She pulled back, searching his face. "Do you really mean it?"

"You're right — it's going to take at least nine months. That ought to give me time to get used to the idea. Yeah. I really mean it."

She kissed him, seriously now. "I love you."

"I love you, too." Ed shook his head and drained his champagne flute. "We do get to start tonight, right?"

"Oh, yes. We do."

It felt like their first night together. That

night, all those years ago, had been a night of firsts for Eve. The first time she'd slept with Ed. The first time she hadn't been the first one to say I love you. The first time she'd had a first time with a guy completely sober, and with the lights on — deliberately, premeditatedly, consciously. She'd already known. She'd known almost straightaway, almost that first night at the pub. This was the one. She'd waited a couple of months, in case the rightness of him was a mirage, but it wasn't. He was real. And then the waiting had made it more wonderful than she could have dreamed.

There was something deliberate tonight, too. Something wonderful. Cross-legged at the end of the bed, she waited for him to come out of the bathroom. He came out in blue and white striped pajama bottoms, tied low on his hip so that she could see the start of that triangle of his shape that she loved so much and she looked at his torso, brown from weekends in the park, and muscled from mornings at the gym, almost catching her breath. He was familiar, but tonight, he was different, too. Ed stopped in the door-way, looking at her.

"You're like a little kid. You look nervous."

"I am a bit."

"Why, you daft thing? Do we have to do it

differently or something? Do you mean to tell me there is a position we haven't tried?"

"No. It's not that. You can't actually get pregnant in the only positions we haven't tried, you dirty bugger. Don't laugh at me."

"I'm not laughing at you. I promise. You're sweet."

"I was going for sexy."

"You're sweet and sexy." She thought of all the sophisticated women he was surrounded by here. Hoped sweet was still working for him.

"It's just that it's a big deal, this."

"I know. I know it is." He put a hand on her cheek, his fingers in her hair. "You do know it probably won't happen the first time?"

"Of course I do. I'm not an idiot, Ed. I know it could take months. But it *could* happen tonight."

She'd counted. And wondered how big a part her hormones had played in her decision making, and in the surge of certainty she'd had at the doctor's office. It was, bizarrely enough, exactly the right time, so far as she could work out. Tonight. So it could happen — tonight. She didn't tell Ed that. He was making fun of her enough as it was. Besides, she suspected he had only agreed because he thought it would take a bit longer. Even if he'd never admit that out loud.

"I'd better do it properly, then, hadn't I? Get it right."

Sex with her husband was always right. Eve read articles in magazines, at the hairdresser's, where journalists wrote about keeping sex fresh within marriage, and about how couples got into ruts and sex got boring, and she never understood, not really. Ed knew exactly how to get her going, but he knew how to do that in a dozen different ways, and he used them all the time, and not in the same order like she was a piece of software he was loading. He could, if he chose, make it happen in five minutes, and once in a while, that was fantastic (they called it painting by numbers, she didn't really know why), or even just necessary (hotel checkout in half an hour, late for work, friends about to arrive for Sunday lunch), but he could also make it take an hour, twice that, even, and that was better, much better. Ed loved sex, and he'd made her love it, too. Before she met him, it was something she worried about and sometimes dreaded. She'd had a sneaking suspicion she wasn't very good at it. Not with him. She was good at sex with him.

She knew he used sex as a way of getting

163

his own way, and of winning an argument, or at least diffusing one, but frankly, if it was that good, who cared? He was clever. It was impossible to sulk or to stay cross while he was doing that to her, and she'd do anything for him in those moments. He'd proposed marriage to her as she lay in a postorgasmic puddle of gratitude (not that her refusal was ever a possibility, even without the knee trembler). The night he'd told her about America, he'd made love to her to seal the deal. This time it was Eve bringing the deal to the bed.

She remembered learning, in some science class sometime, that the actual physiological point of orgasm was that the muscles involved rhythmically drew the sperm inward and made conception more likely. Tonight, as she lay under Ed waiting for the waves to stop, she concentrated on them, her eyes clenched tight. When she opened them, Ed was watching her intently, smiling.

"Still laughing at me?"

"Just enjoying the new sex face." He scrunched his own face up in mimicry.

She slapped his shoulder lazily. "Ouch."

"Does it help?"

"Don't make me really hurt you."

"I'm already hurt. How do you think it

feels, knowing that you're just being used as a stud? Like a bull. It's demeaning."

"Right."

They both dozed contentedly for a while, Eve's head on Ed's chest. He gently stroked her bare back.

"So do I get supper now? I'm starving. You've got to keep my strength up, you know!"

"You get supper. Do you want it in bed?"

"Why not? I'm far too lazy to get dressed again."

Eve slipped on her robe and went to the kitchen, collecting the shrimp, the cocktail sauce, and the glasses, which she refilled with the rest of the champagne. Ed was asleep again when she got back, his head against the pillows, although the baseball game was on in the background, and he clutched the remote control in his hand. Bloody baseball. His hair was messed up, and his five o'clock shadow was creeping. Seeing him sleep after they made love always felt like a reward to her. He was such a rotten sleeper. God, how she loved him. Putting the tray down on the chest of drawers, she pushed his hair back and kissed him gently on the forehead.

"I love you."

Without opening his eyes, he pursed his

lips into an air kiss. "And I love you, my Evie."

For the first time in a long time, Eve felt like everything was going to be all right. Lying beside her, Ed hoped that this would take a few months. The practicing was great. It wasn't that he didn't want a baby. Of course he did. Their baby. Two or three, he hoped. Eventually. He'd just rather wait a while longer.

Work was mad. Good mad, but mad. They'd take every hour he would give them. The business was more or less the same — except for the scale, which was vast, compared with the UK. But the people were different. That was the learning curve — getting the people right. It was hard bloody work. Having to worry about Eve on top of that — he was tired, all the time. Good tired, but tired. It was bound to take a few months . . . and then everything would be all right . . .

■ ■ ■ ■

JUNE

■ ■ ■

JACKSON

Jackson wasn't stupid. He'd been hearing that he was clever all his life. It was always followed by a "but" or an "if only." His teachers at school told his parents he was a smart boy but that he lacked judgment or application. His professors said he was smart but unambitious. His father said "smart, but more smart-ass." His mother said she knew he had a good brain, if only he'd use it. He was clever enough to do just enough. Just enough to get through school. Just enough to get into Duke (although without the family name, he wouldn't have). Just enough to get his bachelor's degree.

He just wasn't that interested in most stuff. But he got obsessed with things. When he was really young, it was John Deere tractors. He knew them by model number. At twelve, it was the Civil War. He'd been bitten by that particular bug on a school trip to Gettysburg. He'd been able to recite numbers of casualties, battle plans, parts of speeches Abraham Lincoln had made. He'd once spent an entire year restoring a 1978 Pontiac Firebird, working on it every night and weekend. Losing interest in it the day it was finished and once he'd driven it around the block. Right now he was obsessed again. With Emily Mikanowski. He wanted to know her. He wanted to understand her. He wanted those incredible blue eyes to look right into his, and that mouth to smile right at him.

She didn't even seem to know he was alive. Raul and Che and Jesus had helped him piece together a picture of her. Especially the fabulously indiscreet Raul. He'd always known those Spanish lessons would come in handy. He wasn't fluent, but his Spanish was better than their English. And speaking it, just making the effort, made them much more inclined to conspire with him. That, and the great holiday tips and the occasional six-pack . . .

He knew she worked at NBC. He knew she was from Oregon. Just the name told him she was Polish, somewhere down the line. He knew she was on the gardening committee they'd started. And that she was hanging out with Charlotte Murphy, the dumpy girl from the second floor. Who hung around with Madison Cavanagh — the building babe, up until the point that Emily had moved in, though not strictly his type. He knew she ran every weekday, from seven thirty until after eight a.m., and that on the weekends she cycled, on a pretty serious bike that she didn't keep in the bike room. He knew that because he'd checked. The super ran the bike room like a military operation. Everyone had to label their bike or face the consequences (no one knew what they were, but no one messed with Mr. Gonzalez's system; this was the guy who fixed blocked toilets, and it paid to stay on his good side). One bike per person. No exceptions. There was no bike labeled Emily Mikanowski.

He had no ins at NBC — nothing that would be helpful. He watched it, but that was it. He'd never been to Oregon. He'd rather poke toothpicks in his eyes than get involved in gardening of any kind; and he was pretty wary of Violet Wallace, who bore an uncanny resemblance, physically and in demeanor, to the matron of his prep school. Charlotte Murphy looked at him like a startled rabbit if they ever met in the lobby. And Madison Cavanagh like a rabbit, too, but not the startled kind.

That left the somewhat unpalatable concept of exercise. Which was a problem, since the last time he'd run for so much as a bus, Clinton had been in the White House. He tried a couple of times, during the day, when there was no danger of running into Emily. He had the stretching down; he thought he stretched like a real pro. It was when he actually started moving that the problems started. The first day, he'd been out of breath by the corner. The second time, he'd thrown up in a trash can about three hundred yards into the park. Even Good Charlotte and Blink-182 blaring through his iPod couldn't keep him going. By the end of two weeks, in which he'd given up smoking entirely, he could run a mile without stopping. But he couldn't possibly speak or look cool while doing it and he suspected that Emily could easily outrun him two to one. As much as he might enjoy watching that swinging ponytail overtaking him, running clearly was not the way to go. That left cycling.

VIOLET

Eve and Violet were in a café having lunch. Violet had driven them out to New Jersey in her ancient Buick, Joan Baez playing loudly on the stereo, to look at garden

172

furniture at a large warehouse near Elizabeth. Violet had called it a reconnaissance trip, when she'd phoned about it earlier in the week. Eve had been flattered that she had been chosen as the wingman for the outing, and excited about a day out. The feelings Eve was having were a little like those of a first date, she knew. She had something like a schoolgirl crush on Violet. This old, very English woman was her first real friend in New York. Even Eve knew that the Korean girl in the nail bar and the tall black guy in Starbucks who handed her her venti skim decaf every morning didn't count. Friends don't let friends tip them.

Eve hadn't been out of the city this way before; the Lincoln Tunnel was just somewhere she'd heard about on the TV news, always backed up. She and Ed flew in and out of JFK, through Queens. The first time she'd made the journey, last year, the first people she'd seen outside the airport had been a group of kids playing cricket on a piece of grass between the highway and the clapboard homes, and she'd felt strangely comforted by that. One weekend not long after they'd arrived, they'd taken a boat called *The Beast,* from where the Circle Line cruises left. Ed had said he couldn't bear the full three-hour cruise, that all he'd really wanted to do was see the Statue of Liberty up close (and climb into the crown, but they'd stopped that after 9/11, so you couldn't), and so they'd changed lines and bought tickets for a speedboat painted with teeth and flames, which did exactly that — drove like a bat out of hell out to Liberty Island, allowed just enough time for a photo op, and drove back again, all the while playing redneck rock and roll and aiming to get the passengers as wet as possible in the wake. It had been brilliant — exhilarating and fun. They'd steered the boat over the Lincoln Tunnel, and the captain, Crazy Horse, had said that if you looked carefully at the water, you'd see the top of the tunnel, and Eve had been the only person on the boat who'd looked, and Crazy Horse had named and shamed her for it, and made everyone laugh at her.

Going through the tunnel, as opposed to sailing over it, was neither exhilarating nor fun. They sat in traffic, being directed by cops, for nearly an hour. Eve felt almost claustrophobic once inside; it was really long, and really slow. New Jersey, this part at least, was industrial and gray and relentless. Violet said the Jersey shore was beautiful, and that inland the state was lush and green. She sounded like she knew it well.

Eve wanted to ask her about her life, but it was too soon. There was something closed off about Violet. She wasn't cold — it wasn't that — although Eve had the definite impression that she was warmer with her than with many of the residents of the building. She made Eve think of that phrase about still waters. She seemed private. Maybe that was just a period thing — a different generation. The era of the stiff upper lip.

This part of New Jersey was neither beautiful nor lush. Eve supposed it was the machinery here that kept New York working, but there was something depressing about the industrial wasteland they drove through for what seemed miles and miles. Once they got there, though, the warehouse was worth the trip. It contained a daunting variety of styles and materials, and they wandered around for a good hour without seeing everything. They both liked the teak but disagreed about whether it should be allowed to weather to a silvery gray (Violet) or oiled to retain its new, honeyed appearance (Eve). And it was very expensive. Black wrought iron was out because it would get too hot. The new wicker, plastic, was a possibility. Impossible to damage, easy to clean, and reasonably priced. They made some notes for the committee to consider, wrote

175

down costs, and Eve took some pictures with her phone, wishing she'd remembered to bring a proper camera. They looked for old-fashioned deck chairs, with primary striped canvas seats, the kind you rented for the day in Bournemouth and Weymouth, but they couldn't find them.

Now they had garden furniture fatigue, and so they'd found the diner next door and ordered panini and tea. Eve always drank tea when she was with Violet, who abhorred both coffee itself and the coffee culture of New York. She did not understand, she said, why people felt they couldn't walk a hundred yards down the street without carrying a large white paper cup full of flavored hot milk, like a city full of big babies being pacified by dairy products. When Eve did take a Starbucks back to the apartment, she always hoped the elevator doors would not open to reveal Violet, disapproving, as she smuggled her beverage in. And, actually, tea was nice. Violet gave instructions like Meg Ryan ordered sandwiches in *When Harry Met Sally,* about the temperature of the water, about the type of tea bag, the milk and the sugar. She preferred a thin porcelain cup to a thick china mug. Violet being fussy, and Eve laughing at her, had become a part of their ritual, quickly established and already comfortable.

They gossiped a little about the committee. Violet, it seemed, knew everything and everybody, and almost everything about everybody. Eve wondered how this was possible; she asked so few questions. Violet loved Todd and Greg ("just as in love as any straight married couple I've ever known; wish to God they'd make it legal in the city, save all the poor dears running off to Massachusetts to get hitched"), and Maria Piscatella, and the scarily glamorous Rachael Schulman.

She told Eve some of the history of the building's ownership. Arthur Alexander from 3C was the son of the man who'd originally owned the building. Eve knew who he was — an elderly, scruffy old man who wouldn't make eye contact in the elevator and occasionally smelled a little of stale wine. "Consider yourself lucky he'll actually get in there with you at all," Violet retorted. "If the doors open and he sees Todd or Greg or, worse still, Todd *and* Greg, he won't get in the damn thing. He's afraid being queer is catching, I think, and he'll get out on the third floor as camp as a jamboree. Silly old goat." It seemed Arthur's dad had sold the building to law firms and a bank in order for it to go co-op, in the sixties, and then squandered the money he got for it with failed deals in Atlantic City. The one-bedroom on the third floor where Arthur lived was all there was left.

"Don't know why he expected his father to make a living for both of them," Violet snorted. "Nobody left me a fortune in real estate."

Violet confessed to finding Kimberley Kramer difficult to like. "She never smiles. She's got that pinched look, and no smiles. Not with her eyes, at least, and there's nothing I like less than a smile that doesn't get to your eyes. She squints. And moans. And that child . . . that child. She's making a rod for her own back. Gives in to her at the drop of a hat. Avery is in charge and she damn well knows it. They're storing up trouble, mark my words."

"Did you have, have you got . . ." Eve didn't know how to phrase her question. She hadn't seen pictures of children in Violet's apartment, and Violet had never referred to any, but she realized she didn't know whether she had children. It was a big detail.

"Children? No." For a second, she had a far-off look, and Eve wondered if she'd crossed the line. Then Violet changed the subject back to Avery Kramer and her famous tantrums. Che had reported that Avery had once kicked her mother in the foyer because she wouldn't lift her up and let her open the mailbox. Kicking your mother in public was very high on Violet's long list of don'ts.

"I'd like some. Children. Ed and I are trying, actually."

She felt shy. She supposed that this was the way in which Violet came to know everything. You wanted to tell her things. You wanted, in some strange way, approval. "We've always said we would, and now just seems like the right time. I mean, I'm not working, we're here, just the two of us . . . It would be wonderful to be a family."

Violet smiled gently at her. "Good for you, lovely. I hope it happens for you soon. You'll be a really nice mum." She put her hand over Eve's on the table, and the two of them sat quietly for a moment while the statement, the wonderfully affirming sentence, sat in the air alongside the smell of teak and melted cheese.

Two weeks after Eve had seduced Ed with champagne, shrimp, and the ardent desire to have his seed implanted in her, on a Saturday morning, she came out of the bathroom naked, too hot from the shower

179

to pull on her bathrobe. Ed had been to a baseball game the night before with some of the guys from the office (the guys from the office having replaced the boys from the office seamlessly) and beer had been taken, so he was still in bed, which was not how things usually happened.

Ed was watching her. Not lasciviously but curiously, appraisingly. "You look different."

"Different how? I haven't changed anything."

"Different."

"That's very nonspecific. And not especially flattering."

"I can't be any more specific. You just look .... different." He cocked his head on one side against the pillow. "Did you get your period yet?"

Several years into marriage, Eve would still prefer not to discuss this with Ed. Perhaps it was the Catholic school education. She'd much rather draw a veil over the whole business.

"No."

"So is it late?"

"Yes. But only a day or two." Eve pulled on her knickers, feeling suddenly self-conscious. She didn't mind him staring lustfully at her, but this evaluative eye was disconcerting.

"You should take a test."

"I wondered that. But it's too soon."

"Are you sure?"

"No. I'm no expert. I haven't taken one since that last time. You had to wait weeks."

"And that was years ago. I bet things have changed. You can probably find out five minutes after the shag."

She made a face at him. "Well, I don't want to be obsessive."

"I'm going to go and get one." Ed jumped out of bed. "Just a hunch."

Eve laughed. "You're mad."

"Maybe. I want a coffee and a paper anyway. Be right back." He'd pulled on shorts and a T-shirt from the night before and swept his hair back from his forehead, kissing her on the cheek and slapping her butt before he left.

While he was gone, Eve looked at herself in the mirror, something she normally avoided assiduously. His assertion that she looked different made her see things she hadn't noticed before. There was a certain softness, quite distinct from the normal doughiness, that she hadn't seen. She turned sideways and stuck her stomach out. She stared at her nipples, looking for new darkness or a swelling that hadn't been there. She linked her hands under the nonexistent bump the way pregnant women do, and wondered how she'd look. Would she be like Cath, she wondered — Moby Dick, by her own admission? Or like her mother? She'd seen pictures of their mum pregnant with Cath and then, a few years later, with her, neat and small in her mini dresses, with regular-sized legs and arms, and just the one chin. Or Cath's best friend, Sheila. She remembered Cath saying she'd never wanted to kill anyone as much as she wanted to kill Sheila the time she'd gone on and on about how small she'd been when pregnant — as Cath lay somnolent on the sofa at her house, moaning about chafing on her inner thighs and Discovery Channel breasts.

"I was more of a Posh Spice," she had said, "and you're more of a . . . Fergie." She meant the duchess, not the Black Eyed Pea, and Cath had rolled her eyes and scowled at Eve. As loyal as she was to her big sister, Eve secretly hoped for her mother's pregnancy genes. Although, as she turned this way and that in the mirror, looking at her thighs and her waist, she had to acknowledge that the head-to-toe black Lycra look so in vogue in Dr. Jones's office was probably not her.

But, oh, it was lovely to be back in the

beam of Ed's attention again. It was missing too often these days.

There'd been plenty of baby making in the last couple of weeks (God, men were goal-oriented buggers), but the late evenings and early starts hadn't changed. And unless he was making love to her, it didn't often feel like he was really concentrating on her. Yesterday she'd had a manicure and pedicure at her usual place around the corner. On a whim, she'd paid the extra fifteen bucks for the ten-minute chair massage, where you knelt astride a seat and they pummelled your back, neck, and shoulders for you. This time, she'd had a man. As he had worked on her, his thumbs smoothing and resmoothing the knots in her shoulders, it had seemed so intimate that she was almost uncomfortable. His touch was so intense, and so focused on her. Loneliness was physical, too, she knew. Nobody but Ed touched her, from day to day. Her old life had been full of touch. That's why Violet's hand on hers, at the garden center, had been so comforting. Because it was rare.

Ed came back at last, with a gray cardboard tray bearing coffee and a CVS bag. He tipped its contents out onto the bed. There were four tests.

"I wasn't sure what to get. They're bloody

expensive. So I got one of everything, except the generic."

They read the boxes and she chose the one that promised it delivered the most accurate and earliest results. She looked at the other boxes, certain that they'd need them over the coming months. It wouldn't just happen so easily. It could take months. She didn't let herself think, not for a moment, about the possibility of it not happening at all. That wasn't going to happen to them. It couldn't.

"Are we really doing this?"

"Yeah. We're both thinking about it now. Either way, we should just do it."

"I don't need to pee."

"Drink this." He proffered the latte, and then sat, grinning at her.

"You look like the cat that got the cappuccino."

Maybe she did need to pee.

"You're not coming in with me."

"No, thanks. I'll pass on that particular pleasure. There'll be quite enough time spent at the business end when this all gets going."

"Not if I have anything to do with it," she called from the bathroom. "I'll be hoping labor starts while you're on a conference call, and I can let you know when it's all over."

"You wouldn't need me there? To hold your hand?"

"Do you think you'd be any good at it, then?"

"Head end, maybe."

She appeared in the bedroom again, waving the stick. Ed raised his hands in front of his face. "Do you mind?"

"Don't get squeamish on me now. Have you got a second hand on your watch?"

They sat and watched — watched the second hand, and watched the stick, nudging each other like kids. She felt giggly and giddy. And the pink line appeared, and grew pink enough to be beyond question or doubt.

Eve couldn't believe it. It couldn't be true. The first time, the very first month. This didn't happen. It happened to Catherine Cookson heroines, after they were seduced by the master, and it happened to silly girls after school dances. It didn't happen in real life. To sensible, measured grown-ups. That you should decide you wanted a baby, make love, and be pregnant. Just like that. She was flooded with delight and surprise, and, along with those emotions, with sudden, sharp fear. She felt herself clenching, as though holding herself tight was the only way to stay pregnant.

She looked at Ed, savoring the expression on his face. All the shock and joy she felt was reflected back at her in his eyes, but none of the awful fear. She latched on to the simplicity of his reaction and let it wash over her, pushing the negativity away, for now . . .

"Oh, my God. Oh, my God. We've done it. We've gone and done it." He jumped up, picked her up, and swung her around. "We're having a baby."

"We're having a baby."

He must have done a good job hiding his panic, Ed reflected, as he took Eve in his arms. So much for a few months. It must have been first go. Normally, he'd have felt rather proud of himself, but now he felt a little sick. Big gamble. He hoped that it would pay off and make Eve as happy as she had promised it would.

He wasn't used to this new, needy Eve. He was mystified by her. And, if he was totally honest with himself, a little irritated. This was all going so brilliantly. Why wasn't she making more of an effort? That night out he'd arranged, for example. They'd been nice people. It had been a nice evening. She'd blindsided him, on the way home, with her attack. She hadn't given them a chance; she'd judged on appearances, and judged harshly. That wasn't who she was. He was loving work. He'd stay longer if he could. There was always more to do, and he was desperate to attract the right attention from the right people — to quickly earn his relocation. But she would call, sometimes as early as four thirty or five, and ask when he was coming home, whether he wanted to stay in or eat out. And then that would sit there between him and his work. He would start watching the clock, feeling the pressure to get back to her.

Now, as she clung to him, he offered a silent prayer that this pregnancy would make her a little more independent again.

Not just more needy.

KIM

Avery was asleep. She lay on her back with her arms and legs splayed, one hand resting on her curls. It was hot, and she'd kicked the sheet back. Sometimes Kim just sat beside her while she slept. The nursing chair she'd bought when she was pregnant sat right beside the bed, and she would sit, and rock, and watch.

Avery was her prize. She'd never wanted

anything so much in her life, or worked so hard to get something.

Because Kim had never gotten pregnant except with Avery, she didn't have any idea how it would feel to just . . . get pregnant. For it to happen easily, quickly, without medical intervention. She told herself she would have been different, that she'd be different now. Avery was special.

The IVF had been hideous. Investigations, probes, tests, shots, months of surging hormones making her feel like someone else. The feeling of inadequacy, the awful, awful roller coaster of hope and failure and disappointment. Kim was a private person; she hated the invasiveness of it all, hated discussing those things with strangers. She never stopped feeling embarrassed, and she never really became comfortable with the conversations, or the investigations — with any of it. Every day was difficult. She couldn't do it again. She knew people did, but she didn't know how. When the sono-gram had found the first heartbeat, the first proof that something had taken, had stuck, was growing inside her, she'd crossed her fingers and prayed for a second heartbeat. New York was full of IVF twins; you couldn't walk down Park Avenue without seeing double strollers. Babies built to order. She knew there were women in the waiting room with her at the ob-gyn who didn't need IVF — who were doing it because they wanted complete control over their bodies and the timing of their pregnancies. They wanted to be pregnant only once, to take only one maternity leave, to have to regain their prepregnancy body just one time. She felt huge resentment toward them. How dare they? She couldn't control one thing about it, except by walking away and giving up. And she couldn't do that. What would become of her life? Of her marriage? She longed for them to say it was twins. Twins would mean she would never have to do it again. But there'd only been one. Just Avery. Avery would have to be enough. The guilt of her ingratitude hit her like a sledgehammer that night.

It was supposed to get better after they found the heartbeat. She meant to join the ranks of the "normal" pregnant women, the ones for whom it had been easy and instantaneous. But she couldn't. Kim couldn't relax, and she couldn't believe. She knew she'd been unbearable all the way through. Everything scared her and the whole world represented a potential threat to the baby. She was neurotic about what to eat, paranoid about strangers, terrified of public transport, wary of cell phones and rinsed salads. She'd driven Jason crazy, she knew, fussing in restaurants. When the doctors had put her on bed rest at six months, she and Jason had both been relieved. She slept more than she could ever have imagined possible, and read. The complete Henry James, F. Scott Fitzgerald, Edith Wharton. She lost herself in those other worlds and tried to fight the panic. She spent hours writing in a pregnancy journal one day intended for Avery. Except that it was full of anxiety and fear, not the simple joy of anticipation. She might never be brave enough to show it to Avery. And she moved the goalposts for herself. So she couldn't calm down during the pregnancy? She wasn't the first woman to feel that way. She would relax when the baby was born safe and healthy. Then, then she would at last be able to join the world of the normal mothers. People would see her, with the baby in the stroller, shopping, wandering in the park, watching the baby turtles in the lake in Central Park, and they wouldn't know any of it. They wouldn't be able to tell.

Avery was born by planned cesarean section. They told her that there was no reason she couldn't deliver vaginally, but that seemed too volatile to her — too much margin for error. Ironically, after hating all the intervention of the previous years, Kim wanted her delivery to be as medical as possible. The green scrubs were comforting to her, and the calm, singsong voices of the nursing staff lulled her. Jason had found it all very difficult. She knew he felt left out. All he could do was perch on the stool, up by her head, staring at the makeshift green curtain they'd erected above her stomach. Kim couldn't think about him, or even really look at him and see how he was feeling. She was concentrating too hard. This was an end and it was a beginning. Were there any other moments like this in your life?

She was still concentrating, two years later. She still couldn't deal with how Jason was feeling. She still couldn't really look at him or think about him. She knew it, but she didn't know how to change it. Wife and mother. Why was it too hard for her to be both? She read all the books. Jason had once laughed at the teetering pile of textbooks she kept in the apartment. There'd been a phase when he'd stopped laughing and eyed them hopefully, but now he didn't even do that. The books had let him down, just as she had. They didn't have the answers, and even the comfort they offered in the way of shared experience was short-lived. The solutions didn't work. She knew that men sometimes struggled to see their wives as other than mothers, after they'd watched them deliver and nurse their children. She knew that women worried about getting their figures back, about low sex drives, about being too tired to be good wives. That wasn't it. That was all true. But that wasn't it.

She didn't want it to be different. The women she read about in the books, they did want to change.

JACKSON

If you could get fit spending money, Jackson would already have been in tip-top condition. This bike had cost more than the Pontiac Firebird he'd bought when he was seventeen. And that had an engine. And a comfortable seat. This seat was so spectacularly uncomfortable that he had been forced to purchase a Tour de France-esque Lycra suit with a built-in pad that made him feel like John Wayne or a giant baby. Or a giant baby John Wayne. His legs looked ridiculously spindly in this getup. And the stuff only came in lurid colors. Or black and white. He'd gone for all black, on the basis that he looked like a giant sperm in the all-white getup, but he feared that his costume was writing checks his body would not be able to cash. The guy at the bike shop had come across as a real stoner; he'd said "cool, man" about everything. Jackson had asked for the top of the line. They worked on commission. Of course it was "cool, man." The guy had just earned his month's rent. It might have been helpful if he'd explained that the old story — the one about riding a bike — wasn't true. This was not riding a bike as Jackson knew it. And he'd had bikes. All his life. A red tricycle with a huge bell and training wheels. A chopper. A BMX. This was completely different from those.

He'd fallen first about a hundred yards from the store. A couple of kids on the sidewalk had actually laughed out loud. He must have looked like such a fool. His feet, he'd discovered, were locked into the pedals. Which meant that if he didn't begin at breakneck speed, the bicycle wobbled dangerously and he fell straight off. That time he'd skinned his elbows. By the third time he was bleeding from each limb, and he was quite sure that when he stripped later, he'd see that he'd pretty much skinned his entire left side. He'd been laughed at by kids, a homeless guy, and a middle-aged matron in a Lexus. And sworn at by two taxi drivers. He was done with the cycling thing.

"Did you label that bike, Mr. Grayling?"

"Like hell. I hope the damn thing gets stolen."

The bruises and scabs from the cycling debacle healed quickly enough, but he couldn't stop scratching the itch that was Emily Mikanowski. He hadn't pursued a girl like this since . . . since never. The girls normally did the pursuing. Trouble was, he didn't think she had the first idea he was pursuing her; most of the chasing had happened in his imagination. The doormen were really the only ones in on it. They were the cataloguers of his experiments with physical fitness, and they knew exactly what he was up to. Jesus told him to stop being such a wimp. "Ask the girl out. Just ask her." Jesus dispensed these pearls of wisdom infrequently enough, and only when he wasn't trying to secretly listen to a baseball or football game in the closet.

"I can't do that, man. For one thing, I never see her. Secondly, I am a wimp. I just don't take rejection well." Jesus gave the derisory snort of someone too familiar with rejection.

"Write her a letter then. Chicks love that."

And so, in the end, he went for conventional methods, clinging to the advice of an unmarried middle-aged doorman as though he were Deepak Chopra himself. He put a note under her door.

Dear Emily,
    You don't know me, but I'm your neighbor. I live upstairs, in 5A. My name is Jackson Grayling, but most people call me Trip. We met once — in the elevator.
    This may seem strange, but I would love to take you to dinner sometime. Any place you like. Any night is good for me. I never do this, so tread softly on my dreams.
    Call me. Please. 646 555 0172.
                                              Trip

He hadn't been sure whether or not to mention the elevator encounter. It was ages ago. It might not have left the most favorable impression. Worse still, it might have left no impression at all (hard for the ego, but a distinct possibility; Trip was well aware that Emily's apparent complete indifference toward him was a big part of her attraction). But in the end, he reasoned that referring to it made him sound less like a stalker, more like a friendly neighbor and potential love interest.

The Yeats was a stroke of genius, if he said

so himself. He'd found it printed in the order of service for a wedding he'd been to in February. Girls liked poetry. They thought it meant guys were soulful and deep and sensitive.

EMILY

Emily felt like an idiot, sitting in her own foyer dressed up like this. Raul was smiling at her as though he knew what was going on, and it was making her uncomfortable. The elevator pinged, and Todd and Greg got out with Ulysses.

"You look sweet, honey!"

"You do! Lucky guy?"

She shrugged uncomfortably.

Todd squeezed her shoulder. "Hope he's taking you somewhere nice, looking like that!"

"I just hope he's taking you somewhere with air conditioning."

"Amen to that." Eve had just come in, with two Gristedes carrier bags. She looked shiny and sweaty and hot. "It is deeply unpleasant out there."

A roof terrace conversation ensued. Emily nodded and smiled and interjected briefly where appropriate, and hoped they would all get lost before Trip came down.

The elevator doors opened, but it was Arthur. She smiled at him, but he ignored her like he always did, scowling sideways at Todd and Greg as he shuffled past — conspicuously as far from them as he could get. Raul held the door, and said, "Good evening, Mr. Alexander," but Arthur just grunted something incomprehensible at him. Eve grimaced at Todd and Greg.

"You know, that man makes me want to kiss the face off you, every time I see him!" Todd exclaimed, hands on hips.

"I'm sure he'd be thrilled to hear that." Greg rolled his eyes. "We'll invite him to Gay Pride next weekend, shall we?"

Eve giggled.

Emily felt a bit sorry for the old man. He reminded her of her grandfather, a little. Too old, maybe, and too set in his ways to accept change. This new world must be a bewildering place.

When Trip did come down, she almost didn't recognize him as the same guy who'd bumped into her in the elevator a few weeks ago. This guy was clean-shaven. And he'd had a haircut. And he was wearing a suit, not baggy sweats. Well.

Maybe Charlotte was right. She and Charlotte had been getting closer, these last weeks. They'd gone out for supper, and

watched television a couple of nights together. Charlotte cooked. She said it made
a nice change from cooking for one. She
was good, too, so Emily was a very willing
guest. Emily enjoyed her company. She'd
begun to confide in Charlotte — not something she did easily. She'd confided about
the note — showed it to her over lasagna
one night, just after she found it. Charlotte
had read it with one hand cupped over her
mouth, and her eyes, when she looked up,
sparkled more than Emily had seen before.
Maybe he did deserve a chance. Frankly,
Charlotte was gone the minute she read the
note. She'd begged Emily to call him,
threatening to do it herself, pretending to
be Emily, if she'd refused (although Emily
knew she never would).

"Don't tell Madison, though. I think she
thinks he's hers."

"Have the two of them dated then?"

"No. But that doesn't mean he isn't in her
sights."

From what Emily had seen of Madison,
there weren't many men who weren't. She'd
shrugged. "Don't you think it's weird — a
note out of the blue. I mean, I've barely
even spoken to the guy. I think it's a bit
creepy."

"I think it's romantic. How much would I

love to come home and find a note like that under my door?"

"Why don't you go out to dinner with him?"

"Yeah, right. I'm so his type."

"Don't be so down on yourself all the time, Charlotte. You're lovely."

"And you're being evasive. Are you going to call him?"

"I don't know . . ."

"When did you last go on a date, Emily?"

"I don't know. Not long ago . . . March."

"That's ridiculous. You're young, you're single, you're stunning. You should be beating them off with a stick."

"I promise I'm not."

"And he quoted Yeats, Em. Yeats. Do you know how beautiful that poem is in full?"

"I'm not a poetry kind of girl."

"Well, I am. And I'm telling you, that poem is the most romantic thing I can think of. If you say no to this guy, you're crazy." She'd had her hands on her hips. She was almost scary.

Charlotte had worn her down in the end, although she'd felt ridiculous, dialing his number. Thank God she got a machine; she was sure she'd have hung up on a real voice. She'd said she was free this Friday. That she'd meet him in the foyer, unless she heard from him that the date and time didn't work. Then she hung up, looked at Charlotte, and burst out laughing.

"I can't believe you made me do that."

"I can't believe you hesitated."

"Well, I've done it now."

Now she wondered why she had. He was good-looking; Charlotte was right. Much more, without the face fuzz. But it wasn't about that, was it? That didn't matter at all. And this felt weird.

"Hello."

"Hi." He looked almost as embarrassed as she was.

"You look stunning."

"You look . . . nice, too."

Raul was smiling even more broadly now, like a Cheshire cat, staring at them.

"Let's get out of here." Trip smiled.

"Cab, Mr. Trip, sir?"

"We'll walk up to the corner, Raul, thanks anyway."

"Have a good evening." Emily was sure he winked.

She wasn't sure what she was doing here. She didn't normally do this.

It could be a very long evening.

Emily had never been to this restaurant before. She'd heard of it, though. They'd come downtown, to West Thirteenth. They'd barely spoken in the cab. It was one of those with televisions, and they'd watched the news like they were going to be tested on it later, neither looking at the other, except from the corner of their eye.

It was like high school. Truth was, whatever Charlotte believed, Emily hadn't had many boyfriends. She was pretty enough to deter a lot of guys who simply assumed she was out of their league. And distant enough to alienate some of the others who might have chanced it. And uninterested enough to refuse a good few offers. She'd had one serious boyfriend — in her senior year at high school — but he'd gone south to college, and things had petered out quickly enough, leaving him more heartbroken than her. Sometimes she worried that she was weird. Most of the time she didn't think about it. Now, here in this cab, feeling awkward and shy, she remembered why . . .

It was incredibly hot. More like August than June. Even the slight breeze was warm, like a hair dryer. The whole neighborhood was alive, as only downtown could be, and throbbing. People spilled out of bars onto the sidewalks, and live music was coming from several places. Emily felt sort of cool, and she wasn't really used to that. Spice Market was wonderfully dark and stylish.

Trip seemed at home in a place like this. The waiter, dressed like a Buddhist monk, showed them to a rectangular table flanked by two low upholstered Balinese benches and took a drink order. Emily ordered a ginger margarita — she had no idea why. Alcohol ought to help, she reasoned. She felt awkward and shy. It seemed that he did, too, since he drank more than half the glass in one gulp when his beer arrived. At the tables all around, everyone chattered and laughed easily with each other, and Emily was self-conscious. Luckily, the menu was complicated, and deciding what to order, as well as having it all explained to them by their monk-waiter, killed the next ten minutes. They were to share food, apparently. Maybe that would help.

Trip was smiling at her. He had a sexy smile, there was no doubt about it. It definitely stirred something inside her, something usually well buried.

"You're very, very pretty."

That was no way to start a conversation. If that was his best line, he was in trouble. It might work on some girls, but it wouldn't work on her. Emily felt the blush creeping up over her cheeks.

"I'm sorry — I've made you blush."

She shrugged and smiled. "Is that why you

asked me out?"

"That's part of it."

What else could there be? "Tell me something about you. I don't know anything. It's strange, isn't it? We all live on top of each other, and most of us see each other at least once a day, but we never know anything real, do we?"

"We could start now."

The waiter arrived with satay and pot stickers. They poked at the food tentatively with chopsticks.

"So what do you want to know about me?"

"I don't know. Something. Where you come from, who your family are, what you do? How about that for a start? And how you got that name."

He laughed. "Trip. Stupid, huh? It's tradition. I'm the third Jackson Grayling. The second one is Jackson Grayling Junior. The third one is Jackson Grayling the Third, or Trip. All the 'best families' (he drew speech marks in the air with his fingers) have a Trip. Proves you've been around — that you're established. Shows a ridiculous absence of imagination, I know. I'm from New York City. I grew up here. On Fifth Avenue. Went to Regis. Then to Duke. Sixth generation male in my family to go. No brothers, no sisters. Parents still living, still married, still driving each other and me crazy. They live in West Palm Beach now, in Florida, most of the time. But they travel a lot, too. My dad retired."

Emily nodded.

"How about you?"

"I grew up in Oregon. My grandparents were Polish."

He knew that, of course, but he nodded, his eyebrows slightly raised, as if this were a revelation.

"They left Europe with their parents, after the war, and came to Portland. I was born outside the city. I'm also an only child. I went to college there, and I'm working at NBC right now, in production on the *Today* show — on the day shift, you know, researching segments for the next morning's show. I came here after I graduated, because here is the place to do what I wanted to do."

"Do you have any family in the city at all?"

"No, everyone is out West."

"Go home often?"

"Once, maybe twice a year. You — do you spend much time in Florida?"

"God, no. God's waiting room. I can't bear it there. Mom comes back to New York a lot, checking up on me."

Emily smiled. Common ground? Maybe

just a little bit. "My mom always wants to know what I'm doing. She misses me. Always on the phone. But she doesn't like the city much, and I haven't had room to put her up before, and so a trip means a hotel, and that costs such a lot, she doesn't come much. Anyway, she works."

Trip smiled, remembering his mother's last visit, and wishing cost and a day job would keep her in Florida. "What else do you want to know about me?"

Emboldened by the margarita, Emily raised an eyebrow at him. "What made you ask me out?"

"I answered that one already. Very, very pretty? Remember?"

"That's all?"

It wasn't all, not at all. "You seemed . . . interesting."

She smiled. "So . . . what do you do, Trip Grayling?"

Most of the girls Trip went out with didn't ask him that. They knew. And if it wasn't the very reason, it wasn't usually a problem either. Nothing. He didn't know how to answer the question. He felt a sudden urge to lie. But Emily wasn't a girl to lie to. That, he already knew.

"I'm not working at the moment."

"The moment?"

"No. I'm trying to figure out what I really want to do, actually."

"What did you used to do?" She wasn't going to let it go.

"Since college, nothing really specific. I went traveling a bit, after I graduated." He hoped that sounded intrepid. If she pushed, he'd have to admit to a long summer in Southern California, instead of a soul-searching, mind-expanding adventure in Nepal.

"Which was when?"

"Um. Two thousand five." Was it hot in here? Trip felt warm. His collar was itching.

"What was your major then? Safe to say it wasn't premed or law, I guess."

It felt like she was laughing at him.

Emily left the subject alone once the main courses came, but her attitude toward him had changed. She seemed suddenly wary of him. And conversation grew stilted and awkward again. Trip realized that nearly everything he wanted to say revealed things about himself that he didn't necessarily want her to know.

By contrast, everything she said made him more interested. When, at last, he steered her toward her career, she was animated, ambitious, and determined. She relaxed a little again. She loved what she did, clearly.

When she spoke about her mother, her voice was full of love and admiration. She didn't say anything about her father, except that he had left when she was very young. That had to have been tough, although she didn't say so. She was the complete opposite of him. Every word she spoke made that more obvious.

Trip wasn't used to feeling this way at the end of a date. He might expect to be kissing in a cab, instead of sitting, as he was, looking at Emily as she looked out the window. He might expect to feel good.

But he didn't. He felt terrible.

A few yards from the awning of their building, aware that Che would be waiting and listening to their every word, and sensing that the night had veered a long way from his plan, Jackson asked, "Can I take you out again?"

Emily looked at her shoes. "I don't think so. Thank you for tonight, though."

"Why not?"

She sighed, shifting from foot to foot. "We're too different, Trip. We have absolutely nothing in common except for this building. Nothing will come of it. So what's the point?"

"Does there have to be a point?"

"Of course. And I just don't think that

there is."

"Ouch. You don't pull any punches, do you?"

"Don't you want me to be honest?"

"Of course. But how can you be so sure?"

"I just am. I don't mean to hurt your feelings. I just don't want to waste your time, or mine."

"Right."

She was looking at her shoes again. He wanted to see those blue eyes. He crouched down, made her look up.

When she did, she smiled. "So — good night?"

He had no choice. He stood to the side and they walked the last few steps to the front door. Che raised an eyebrow at him, and he shrugged ruefully. When the elevator stopped at Emily's floor, she couldn't get out fast enough.

"Good night, Emily."

"Night. Thanks again."

When he got into his own apartment, the answering machine was flashing red at him. His friend Josh was shouting down the phone — from a noisy bar, by the sound of it. "Hey, Grayling? Where the hell are you? Get your ass down here . . ." He could just about hear an address. He checked his watch. The message had been left an hour ago. What the hell. He wasn't going to sit around here feeling crap about himself. He grabbed the keys he'd just dropped on the table and went back out, determined to drink away the unfamiliar feeling of inadequacy.

APARTMENT 3A

"Charlotte?"

"How was it?"

"You still up? Want some tea?"

"I'll be right up."

Charlotte pulled on her chenille bathrobe and took the stairs up to Emily's apartment. She'd been at a really good bit in *Captain Corelli's Mandolin* — Corelli and Pelagia were just about to kiss. But this was real life.

"So, tell me."

Emily handed her a mug of tea. "Not much to tell. We've nothing in common."

"I've always thought that was a highly overrated ingredient for romance. Mr. Darcy had nothing in common with Elizabeth Bennet."

"If you're going to bombard me with Jane Austen, you can go home again. She was a middle-aged virgin."

"Nothing wrong with middle-aged virgins.

Heading that way myself, remember."

"Sorry."

Charlotte waved it off with a grin. "He's cute, though, right?"

"He's cute. But he's shiftless and unsubstantial and, I suspect, unreliable. And not at all what I'm looking for."

"So! Are you going to see him again?"

Emily laughed, shaking her head. "You're hopeless. Are you even listening to me? Why would I do that?"

"I don't know. I just . . . I had a feeling about you two."

"You, Charlotte Murphy, have a feeling about all sorts of things. Che, for one thing."

Charlotte blushed. She almost wished she hadn't said anything about Che. She'd confessed, one evening, over sushi and sake. She'd never have told Madison. But it had seemed okay to tell Emily.

"Isn't it time you did something about that situation?"

"That's completely different. And you know it."

"Yes. You actually like Che!"

"You haven't given Trip a chance."

"I have, Charlotte. I gave him a whole evening. There was nothing there."

Even as she said it, Emily knew that wasn't entirely true. There'd been some-

210

thing. A glimmer. She'd been attracted to him; she couldn't deny it to herself, even if she did to Charlotte. But there was too much else besides. Too much that warned her off.

EVE

Ed had promised he'd come with her to the doctor.

And he had. She'd given him the address. Twice, actually. She'd written it down for him once, but on the morning of the appointment, he'd called and said he'd lost it, and would she email it to him.

"But we're talking right now. I can give it to you, if you give me a minute."

"Don't you know it off by heart?"

"No. I don't. Sorry. Wait a second."

"I haven't got a second, I've got a meeting, right now. Can't you just email it to me?"

How bloody ridiculous. She sent a one-liner, with no salutation or sign-off.

When they'd met, outside the doctor's offices, she was still angry. Ed shrugged. "What's the big deal?"

"I don't want to email you about stuff like this. I'm not your damn assistant. I'm your wife."

"You're being ridiculous, Eve. It doesn't matter. I'm here, aren't I? You wanted me to be here, and I'm here. I made the time to be here."

"Well, bully for you. I'm so grateful for your sacrifice." Her voice dripped with sarcasm.

His was high-pitched with exasperation. "I didn't mean it that way. Jesus, you're touchy. Is this how it's going to be?"

"Oh, shut up. Don't you dare blame this on my hormones."

"Well, I'm buggered if I'll blame it on myself. I haven't done a damn thing wrong, so far as I can see."

"You made me feel like I'm not important."

"I don't see how."

"And that's the problem."

Sure enough, the anger had quickly turned to emotion. Eve thought she might cry. This wasn't how it was supposed to be. This wasn't what she had wanted.

Ed watched her bottom lip tremble. He was genuinely confused as to why this was a problem. He'd been rushing. He'd lost the information. He'd called. He was here, for Christ's sake. In the middle of the day.

"Can we just go in? We're going to be late."

"Fine. Let's go in."

In the office, they sat side by side. There were three or four other women waiting, all further along than Eve was, but no men. Ed felt instantly vindicated. See, the other fathers weren't here.

Eve flicked through a magazine distractedly. She didn't want to fight him for every commitment over the next eight months. She wanted him to be as excited as she was. She wanted this to be as important to him as it was to her. She wanted him to be as emotionally invested at home with her as he seemed to be at work. She felt exhausted, and she hadn't even begun.

He wasn't all wrong about the hormones. She knew her fuse had shortened. She knew she was being a bit irrational. But he thought this row was about the email request. (Men — the men she knew, at least — had short memories. They carried no lessons forward. That's why you had the same rows with them over and over again. They could only think about one thing at a time.) He didn't see, or chose not to, that it was cumulative. That it was about the late evenings, and the early starts, and the conference calls to London on the weekends, and the jealousy she felt about the life he was building. He didn't apply any of that to this row, this moment.

She put a hand on his knee. He put his hand on top of it. He was like a naughty child, now. Desperate for forgiveness (even if he still didn't entirely know what he was being forgiven for). By the time the receptionist had called their names, she had granted it.

She wouldn't let it spoil this moment. This too would pass.

KIM

THE NORTH FORK, LONG ISLAND

It was Friday afternoon, and Avery was asleep. She'd be asleep for roughly another hour, and Kim was busy. Most days, while Avery slept, she lay, reading or dozing herself, on the swing seat on the veranda, in the shade, enjoying the silence and the solitude. But not on Fridays. On Friday mornings, she braved the Super Stop and Shop, which took twice as long as it should, since Avery insisted on putting every item in the cart herself. At least it tired the child out, so she slept soundly in the afternoon while Kim tidied up. For Jason's arrival. Kim dreaded summer weekends. Summer weeks were blissful, but as Fridays drew closer, she felt herself growing more and more tense. Saturdays and Sundays were awkward and uptight and uncomfortable, and by Sunday night it was all over, and she could exhale again.

Mondays were her favorite days, because they were the furthest from the weekend.

It was amazing how much mess one small girl could make. Kim stood in the doorway of the sitting room and sighed, then grabbed one of the large plastic boxes in which they kept toys, sat down cross-legged on the floor, and began sorting plastic alphabet bricks from oversized Lego pieces and tiny people.

She'd started decamping out here from June to September the year Avery had been born. The cottage had belonged to Jason's parents. It was small, and a bit ramshackle, and not in the fashionable Hamptons, but up on the North Fork, where it was quieter and more rural. You could still drive for miles through fields. You could go and buy milk in town without a full face of makeup on, and you probably wouldn't run into anyone you knew. She loved it. The house was built in a traditional shingle style; there were three bedrooms, only one truly big enough to be a double, a communal bathroom with slightly suspect plumbing, and a tiny kitchen lean-to, but there was nearly a full acre of pretty garden, and it was a ten-minute drive to the beach. Jason had talked about a pool, over the years, but now that Avery was here, Kim knew she'd have been terrified of what might happen if they'd put one in, and he didn't talk about it anymore.

Out here, she could feel herself being calmer. From Monday to Friday. She began to straighten the picture books on the shelves under the window. It was Avery's habit to pull out all of them before choosing a favorite. This week it had been *The Tale of Despereaux.* She must have read it to her five times a day, every day. Avery was obsessive that way. But still, the books all had to be looked at, before she chose.

Jason had first brought her out here the summer they'd met. His parents had been here for the summer then, and they'd come on the Friday afternoon jitney together after work. She'd never met them before, and she'd been nervous, but they'd put her at her ease quickly enough. His dad had grilled steaks on the old Weber grill on the deck. Jason was twenty-four then, she just a year younger, and his mom told Kim, in the kitchen while she dried Boston lettuce leaves for a salad, that Kim was the first girl he'd brought out to the country to meet them, and that that was how she knew he was serious about her. He hadn't told her that himself.

Order restored in the living room, Kim grabbed the laundry basket of clean sheets she'd taken off the line and headed up the narrow staircase to their bedroom. His parents took the master bedroom in those days, of course, and Jason and Kim had narrow single beds in the small rooms flanking the big bedroom. He'd crept in and climbed in beside her, very late, his hands roaming over her naked skin, and they'd tried to be as quiet as they could, although his dad had winked at her over a stack of pancakes at breakfast the next morning. There'd been a full moon, and she still remembered his face over her, in the moonlight, and his mother's kitchen confession burning in her ears as he kissed them.

It was their house now; Jason's parents had both died within a year of each other, before Avery was born. His mother succumbed to ovarian cancer, and his father had a massive stroke ten months later on a subway platform at Forty-second Street. A lay preacher on his way to scream salvation at the hordes in Times Square had taken off his sandwich board and given CPR, but he was too late. They hadn't left much — they died too young, and Jason's mother's medical bills had been big — but they left him this house, and all the memories of them it held. Now the big bed in the big bedroom was theirs. She shook the clean sheet out and arranged it across the mattress, thinking that the chaste single beds would suit them well these days.

From down the hall, she heard Avery groan and then settle again. She crept quietly down to check on her. The door was ajar. Avery had the room she'd first slept in now. She'd painted it yellow and stenciled daisies around the walls. Avery was spread-eagled, with her thumb in her mouth. One cheek was red and lined from where she had been lying on it, and her hair was damp in the heat.

Kim pulled the door to a little and went back to her task. Pillowcases, and the bedspread, an old New England quilt Jason's parents had been given as a wedding present. It suited the room. She smoothed it down neatly, reverently almost. Jason's mother had loved that quilt. She used to say that as long as they slept under it, nothing bad could happen between them. Kim sniffed. If only.

It wasn't keeping her and Jason safe. Or together. Kim came out here now, around the third week in June, in the station wagon, loaded up with clothes and Zabar's bags and toys. Esme came out from Tuesdays to Thursdays to help her with Avery and the laundry. And Jason came on Friday afternoons, lining up with the masses at Forty-fourth and Third, tuned in to his iPod and BlackBerry and clutching a Starbucks cup. They drove to Cutchogue after Avery's early supper to pick him up. Avery always demanded a milk shake from the deli opposite the stop, and drank it through a straw, leaning against the car. Mostly she was more excited about the milk shake than she was about seeing her dad after five days apart. Kim would stand there, one hand protectively around Avery, lest she should slip or slide off the car, and make promises to herself, silent, fervent promises to try harder, to make this weekend better than the last.

It usually went awry before they even got back to the house, after the dry-lipped kiss on the cheek he gave her as he tossed his bag into the back of the car. On Friday nights Jason was tired and, it seemed to her, full of brimming resentment about his work week, spent alone in the city. He never seemed pleased to be there, pleased to see them.

Before his last visit, she and Avery had

made flags from colored paper, and on the Thursday night, after Avery had fallen asleep, she'd strung them up around the living room. He didn't notice as he walked through to the stairs the next day. And when he'd come back down, having changed into a pair of pull-on cotton trousers and a T-shirt, barefoot, and she and Avery had shown him what they'd done, his smile never reached his eyes, and it barely slowed his passage to the fridge in search of a cold beer.

They seldom made love. She'd rejected him time and time again after Avery had been born. Now he never initiated sex, and on the few occasions when she did — not out of lust or desire, but out of knowing that she should, that she must — he often rejected her right back, claiming exhaustion. She wondered if it was revenge — if he turned her down to show her how it felt to be unwanted, or whether she was, simply, no longer of interest to him.

So when it did happen, which was irregularly, it was weirdly unsatisfactory for both of them. There was almost something mean-spirited about it, and she didn't know which of them was more responsible for that.

Afterward, he never held her. He rolled

off, and over and away. Here, in the country, their bed was at least a foot smaller than the one in the apartment, but he could still manage to put a lot of sheet between them, magic quilt or no magic quilt.

Kim knew they were in a terrible mess, but she didn't know how to fix it. She wondered if he would leave her. She watched *Oprah* and *Dr. Phil* and she knew they needed to talk — to each other, to someone else — but she was so, so afraid of what she would say, what he might say. And proud, and ashamed and frightened. She knew that the longer it went on, the harder it would be. The greater the distance between them, the longer the journey back.

So they didn't talk. Not about what really mattered. They spent Saturday and Sunday each longing for the short drive back to the bus stop, brittle and polite and functioning. Avery was a great distraction.

JASON

Sometimes Avery didn't even feel like his own child; she was so much Kim's that there was no room for him. He wasn't allowed, never had been, to make even the smallest decision about her. What she wore, what she ate, when she did whatever she did, and with whom — Kim was in charge. No discussion, no debate, no interest, it appeared, in his opinion about any of it. She hadn't even allowed him to change diapers, afraid that he'd get it wrong, make her sore. Nothing hurt him more (and many things hurt him these days) than walking down the steps of that damn bus on Friday nights and seeing no flicker of excitement in his daughter's eyes as she watched him walk toward her. No squeeze in her small, thin arms around his neck. What the hell was happening? Kim, too. Her whole body language suggested trepidation. Whatever hopes he allowed himself on the bus evaporated now, before he even reached the car.

He still remembered the first time he'd brought her out here. God, he'd been in love with her then. His parents had separated them, which was pretty ridiculous considering they were practically living together in Manhattan by then, and he'd told himself as they kissed good night chastely on the landing that he could go a night without her easily enough. But he couldn't, not then, and he'd crept like a teenager across the hall and into her room. He remembered her silently straddling him, arching her back so that moonlight hit her brown nipples as she rode him to an intense orgasm, made more exciting by the quiet, the cicadas and katydids the only sound track to their lovemaking. Silence between them had once meant something so different. He'd decided to marry her that night, if she would have him. He was drunk on her — and her here, at the cottage, and her with his parents, in his family.

Back then, they'd made love almost every night — in his apartment, at her place. Once, at the Botanical Garden, and, almost, in a yellow cab. They'd snuck out of a restaurant, where they'd been having dinner with ten friends to celebrate someone's birthday, after the first course to rush home and get each other into bed. One night they'd met for drinks after work at the Soho Grand, and she'd told him she was naked under her dress and pushed a room key across the bar into his hand, and they'd had unbelievable sex in the bathtub of a suite they didn't need and couldn't afford. He'd checked into a Hilton in Philadelphia on a business trip once and found her naked on the bed, having taken the train down that afternoon to surprise him.

He barely recognized this woman in the bed beside him now. Couldn't map out clearly, even in his own head, how they had got here. And he didn't know whether it was his fault. What he did know was that he couldn't go on like this much longer.

He told himself sex shouldn't matter. You could have other kinds of intimacy, couldn't you? But it did, it mattered horribly. It wasn't just the physical part, although that was tough enough. He felt ridiculously ashamed of his urges, as though they were wrong and he was base for having them. Sex had been ruined for them both by Kim's failure to get pregnant. It wasn't a leisure pursuit any longer, it was a serious mission. They didn't do it for fun anymore, they did it to make a baby, and they were getting it wrong. Jason was humiliated over and over again, in front of doctors and experts and Kim herself. She blamed him. She looked at him and in her eyes he saw her thought process — that this wouldn't be happening to her if she'd been with someone else. And from day one, it was just happening to her. Not to him. It was inconceivable (every pun intended) that their failure to get pregnant should have been just as hard for him as it undeniably was for her. He'd wanted a baby. He'd wanted babies. He sat in an office surrounded by men who had big photographs of dimpled toddlers on their desks and left early for parent-teacher conferences and built sand castles on the weekends and moaned about Disney World, and he wanted all that, too. And it hurt him, too.

He could rationalize that. He could make sense of why that process was so wretched and awful for both of them, and he could even forgive Kim for not seeing how it hurt him while she was lost in her own pain and fear. He could because he loved her, as he always had. It wouldn't have hurt so much if he didn't, after all. What man would not be hurt by not being able to give the woman he loved what she wanted more than anything else in the world? What he didn't understand was everything since.

It should have been all right after Avery came. She was the much longed-for baby. She was beautiful. She was the answer to the problem. Except that she wasn't. Avery's birth was just the beginning of the new problem. Kim hadn't given much serious indication, in the years since Avery had been born, that she needed him or wanted him, or even that she loved him.

Jason hadn't thought much about love when he was a younger man. One of the things that had made him happiest, when he was first with Kim, was that this love he felt didn't have to be analyzed and evaluated and discussed. It just was, and it was wonderful. Easy and natural and right. Now he thought about it a lot, and he wasn't sure anymore that he believed in that kind of love. Because he didn't think you could continue, indefinitely, to love someone who didn't love you back. When it seemed to be the opposite of everything it had once been — no longer easy and natural and right but actually difficult and weird and wrong. Eventually your heart gave up. And he thought his heart might be almost at that point.

He wasn't in love with Rachael Schulman. He knew that really. What he felt about Rachael Schulman was twofold. He'd certainly analyzed that, because when he'd first realized he was harboring thoughts about his neighbor, he'd been terrified. The first was lust. On one unapologetically male and mammalian level, he'd just like to get her into bed. At this point almost everything about her turned him on, so that he sometimes felt like a stupid teenager, unable to control his lustful thoughts or rebellious body parts. This first feeling wasn't too dangerous, because he understood it, as well as he understood, most of the time, that it was never, ever going to happen. Rachael Schulman might as well be Heidi Klum or Keira Knightley. The second was the one that worried him. He was in love with the idea of that kind of marriage — the kind that Rachael and David seemed to have. Not just the marriage — the family. The unit that they were. She'd become a kind of fantasy. The better she looked, the more he wanted to bask in the glow of their lives, and the worse his own situation seemed.

Saturday dawned hot and sunny. Kim was already up when he awoke. She got up with their daughter. Ostensibly, it was so that he could sleep in after a week at work. But he knew they didn't mind his not being there. He could stay there, in the bed, all morning, and no one would come for him. He stayed there until nine. Then pulled on board shorts and a T-shirt and went downstairs. After breakfast, Avery demanded a trip to the beach. Jason lay back with his sunglasses on and watched Kim assiduously applying factor 150 to Avery, paler in July, it seemed, than she had been in March.

Kim must have burned herself earlier in the week; her shoulders still looked a little sore, although she refused his offer to put sunscreen on her. He'd grown used to feeling a little like a leper — his touch, even in this most innocuous way, so often seemed repulsive to her. She was wearing an old sarong with a turtle print she'd bought on a trip to the Florida Keys they'd taken the year they were married, and her ubiquitous Crocs, the hideous rubber footwear she owned in about eight different colors and styles and which he hated with a passion he might not have thought he could summon up over women's shoes. He tried not to think of Rachael's ballerina slippers and perfectly pearl pink toenails. Kim's hair needed washing, and she'd pulled it back into a scrawny ponytail. She doesn't care how she looks to me, he realized. She doesn't want me to look at all.

All around them on this stretch of perfect white sand, perfect families reproached him. Fathers and sons in matching board shorts threw footballs endlessly. Mothers tended infants in those tiny UV tents and dispensed sunscreen and cold drinks from big plastic coolers you could wheel down onto the sand. Girls in bikinis trilled and squealed at the water's edge as their toes hit the chilly water of Long Island Sound.

Suitably shielded from the sun, Avery plonked her bottom down in the sand a few feet away and began digging with her blue spade. Kim came to sit beside him. He sensed that she was searching for something to say. Small talk.

"She digs for hours with that shovel. The other day she made a pile of sand almost as tall as she was."

She was trying. Avery was all they had in common right now.

"Does she!" He tried hard to sound as though that remark had been interesting to him.

"She's quite strong, you know."

He knew. Avery had rabbit-punched him in the kidneys in the bathroom this morning. Her charming version of "Excuse me, Daddy" as he stood trying to shave successfully in the tiny mirror fogged up by Kim's earlier shower.

"Do you see people out here much?"

"What do you mean?" Her defensive tone was a warning, but he'd embarked. Sometimes a row was better than silence. Who knew?

"I mean friends, you know. People from Manhattan, or who live around here. Do you ever do social things?"

"Of course." He didn't dare ask what. "But mostly we just enjoy the peace and quiet and the beach and each other."

This Zenlike state clearly only happened in his absence, and not for the first time this summer already, he was painfully aware that she wished he wouldn't bother to come out here and play at happy families. It was his house, damn it. His wages that paid for it all.

"Didn't Rachael say something about getting together out here?"

She looked at him sharply, and he wondered if his cheeks were red.

"Rachael spends most of her time in Connecticut. That's their house. The place they use here belongs to her parents."

"I know. But she said something about being out here for the Fourth of July weekend. I'm sure she did."

She had. In an email shortly after their conversation in the elevator, back in April. He remembered it very, very well, of course. She'd said they'd all be there. With friends and family. That they always had a big open house kind of thing. That the Kramers should definitely come, if they were out that weekend. That Kim should give her a call and they'd fix it, give her directions.

Jason couldn't admit that he didn't need directions. He knew where the house was. About a year ago, the mailman had put the Schulmans' mail in their box, back in the city, at the apartment. He'd collected it and opened the first piece before he'd realized the error. It had been a note from Rachael's mother, with a photograph of the boys she'd obviously taken and was sending to her daughter. He didn't read the note (even stalkers had their own morality, clearly), but he had read the address, embossed in pink ink at the top of the card, with a tiny delicate starfish next to it. He'd returned the mail to the doorman, with a Post-it stuck on the card on which he'd written — "Sorry! Didn't realize it wasn't ours!" All jaunty exclamation marks! And the weekend after that, he'd told Kim he was going for a drive early one morning, and he'd just driven and kept on driving, all the way to Southampton, and found the house. He didn't even really know why. It was one of the very big houses on a road just back from the beach, with private rights, no doubt. A beautifully maintained traditional gray and white colonial with a sweeping, manicured lawn and a long driveway. Down to the left-hand side you could just see a sliver of pool house and turquoise water, and beyond that the net of a tennis court.

He'd driven past it, slowly, twice, which was as much as he dared, imagining Rachael growing up there, shooting hoops in front of the garage and sunning her long limbs by that cool, clear water. Knowing that he was on the fringes of his own sanity at that moment, but not really caring.

More than anything else at this point in time, he wanted to go to that house for the Fourth of July party.

Kim hadn't replied.

Trying to keep his voice casual, he dug his fingers into the sand beside his thighs. "We could go, maybe. Sounds like it might be fun."

"Traffic would be anything but fun. It could take hours."

"Couldn't we go over via Shelter Island? Avery would love the ferry, wouldn't she? We could make a whole day of it." Low blow, Jason — using Avery like that. Low blow.

It might just work, though. Kim shrugged, which was altogether more hopeful than Kim shaking her head.

"So you'll call her?"

No answer.

"I could call, if you'd like . . ."

"I'll call."

■ ■ ■ ■ ■

JULY

■ ■ ■ ■ ■

EVE

FOURTH OF JULY

Eve wondered whether it was too soon to start eating for two. This was the best ice cream she'd ever had, and perhaps another scoop — for the baby — might be permissible. She tried to conjure up the sobering image of all the size 2 yummy mummies in the doctor's office, unafraid of Lycra, but all she could think about was the delicious combination of raspberry sorbet and chocolate brownie. And God, it was hot.

Ed had had business in Washington, D.C. on the third, and so she'd suggested that she come down with him on the train and that they stay over for the fourth and fifth. Take a look at the nation's capital on the nation's birthday. Before the baby came. She'd started saying that a lot — "before the baby comes" — even though Ed laughed and told her she was only a few weeks pregnant, no need to panic. She was working on persuading him to take a holiday in Hawaii "before the baby comes," but Washington would do for now. It was how their lives would be now, wasn't it? Forever more, life would be "before baby" and "after baby." Nothing was going to be the same. She couldn't wait. She said that often, too.

The other night, Ed had looked almost hurt. "You say that as though this bit has been okay at best — like our marriage has been the waiting room for the good bit."

She'd climbed onto his lap and pulled his head into her chest, stroking his hair. "Are you going to be one of those jealous daddies? The ones who don't want to share?"

"That depends." He rubbed his head against her breasts. "Are you going to be one of those mummies who neglects the daddy?"

She showered baby kisses all over his face. "No. No. No. No."

Eve loved trains — a love instilled during her post–A level InterRail trip around Europe at eighteen. She loved the sound of the wheels on the track, their constant, lulling rhythm. The Amtrak was everything she'd expected an American train to be — huge and high, with three steep steps up to the carriages. The journey had taken three lovely hours, and she'd leaned against Ed in the wide, comfortable seats, listening to him talk about things she didn't understand and didn't want to on his cell phone, and reading *Martha Stewart Living* magazine, wondering whether she might ever, ever be the sort of person who collected antique sugar shakers and wooden butter pats. She thought probably not. But really she was daydreaming. She'd managed not to tell anyone so far about the baby, except the doctor, of course. Cath would be the first to know. But not yet. Just for now, it was the loveliest, most wonderful secret for just her and Ed.

She kept waiting to feel sick. One or two mornings she'd lain in bed and wondered if she did, but it was really only psychosomatic. Her boobs were as sore as hell, and she felt permanently like she'd just had a three-course meal, but she wasn't sick, and for that she was grateful, if strangely disappointed.

What she was was unpredictably hormonal. Given to wild surges of soaring joy in which she felt like a wide-armed world-loving hippie. And to black moods where everything worried and frightened her. Some days the homeless guy who slept on the steps of the church on the corner reduced her to tears as she passed, and she wanted to bring home the whiskery old lady counting change for coffee at the diner by the subway station. She felt ungrateful then. She thought about an old song — "How can you tell me you're lonely?" She had everything, didn't she? She'd been into the park, looking for the woman from the Boathouse, but she hadn't found her, although she'd wandered around for an hour or so. She sat on the bench where the woman had been sitting the last time she'd seen her, thinking that she might come by, promising herself that, if she came, she'd talk to her, but she didn't come.

While Ed had gone to his meetings, she'd felt weirdly like a kid playing hooky. She wasn't used to hotels as smart as the ones they were booked into these days — the Four Seasons in New York, a Ritz-Carlton here, after thirty years of Holiday Inns and three-star Trusthouse Fortes and B&Bs — and she'd taken a long, deep bath (not too hot, the baby book said not too hot) and then curled up back in bed in a huge, heavy towelling robe to eat room service breakfast and watch reruns of *ER*. In the afternoon she'd walked the few blocks from the hotel to Georgetown, where the concierge said all the good shops were, and spent a couple of hours happily browsing in the eclectic stores that lined the main drag, picking out a tie for Ed, some pretty silver earrings for herself, and, almost guiltily, two tiny white onesies for the baby. Onesies, she'd discovered, were what Americans called babygros, and she loved the name, it being almost as cute as the garments themselves. She'd been back at the hotel, dozing on the bed, when Ed came home, business over, and though he had woken her with a gentle kiss, neither of them had the energy, suddenly, to go out exploring, and they ate dinner in the room, both in their robes this time, watching *Die Hard,* which was still dying hard long after they'd fallen asleep in a too-hot tangle of dressing gown and 400-thread-count cotton sheets.

She hadn't known how hot it would be here. Much further south, Washington, D.C. had about ten degrees on Manhattan, and no coastal breezes whatsoever. Ed had tried explaining the whole inland weather situation, but she was frankly too hot for meteorological lessons. Yesterday Ed had taken her out on a pedalboat in the Tidal Basin by the big statue of Jefferson, and she'd urged him to go faster and faster, loving the hint of movement in the air his speed generated, so that he'd been sweaty and panting by the time their half hour was up, although she was a degree cooler. It was fun, though. It was a long, long time since she and Ed had explored a new place like this together. She'd discovered New York alone, except for when Cath had been over. She'd done her exploring, before they met, and he preferred to recharge his work-flattened batteries. The holidays they took from England had always tended to be the sun-seeking type, where the most intrepid you got was choosing a lounger on the other side of the pool from where you had hung out the previous day, and the most adventure you had was in bed after three cocktails.

For this weekend, she'd bought a guidebook and a map and had a list of what they should see, if only it weren't so damn hot and she weren't so sleepy all the time. They'd already eschewed the legendary Air and Space Museum, saving it for another time. (The baby might turn out to be fascinated by Amelia Earhart and the Tiger Moth.) They had wandered, ever so slowly, from the Capitol Building up the Mall, to the incredibly tall Washington Monument and past, to the hauntingly powerful Vietnam Veterans Memorial. She had stood and cried openly, moved beyond words by the notion of all the young men whose names were carved into the black granite, all of whom were someone's baby and had once been carried in someone's womb and been daydreamed about. Ed had led her away gently, muttering to himself as much as to her that they might give the Holocaust Museum and Arlington Cemetery a pass on this particular visit. She'd sunk gratefully onto the bottom steps at the Lincoln Memorial, insinuating herself into a small corner of shade, and leaving Ed to climb to the top and admire the giant Abe alone.

And now she was thinking of that second ice cream. And she was thinking that she was happier than she'd been for months. The loneliness that had plagued her in the early months hadn't essentially been rectified at all. She had met and spent a little time with some of the women in the building, and Violet was someone she increasingly thought of as almost a friend, but really nothing was actually very different from how it had been. She could hardly claim (and still sound sane) that the fetus was her companion. But it was going to be, and she was determined to look forward. The pregnancy had brought with it lots of promises of things to come. There would be a baby, yes, and that baby could not have been more longed for, and more loved, already. But there was more, wasn't there?

The baby would bring prenatal classes, and other babies, and their mothers, and play-groups and mommy and me music classes, and membership to the club, the stroller club. Eventually she'd be holding the hand of a toddler as she climbed the Alice in Wonderland sculpture in the park, and then of a small girl, up the front steps to school, in a blue and white striped pinafore and a hair bow like the little girls who went to Marymount, the Madeline-esque copper-roofed school on Fifth Avenue opposite the Met she passed each day on her way to walk around the reservoir. She would belong, and she would have purpose, and everything would be wonderful.

Ed was back. He was smiling at her. "You look happy. Hot but happy."

"I am happy, love. So happy. In the immortal words this guidebook tells me were spoken from almost this very step, 'I have a dream.'"

They wandered up through the streets to the White House, which was surprisingly small, although it had, according to Eve's book, 132 rooms. A stranger took their picture as they stood against the black railings at the front. From there, they strolled hand in hand back to the hotel.

"I've made reservations in the restaurant

for tonight." Eric Ripert, famed chef at Le Bernardin in New York, had recently opened a place in the hotel. Eve had read the Zagat restaurant guide from cover to cover back in Manhattan and put Le Bernardin in her top ten of restaurants to try. "Before the baby comes."

"Have you? That's sweet!"

"Thought I'd treat my wife to dinner."

She squeezed his hand.

"I know I've been a bit rubbish lately."

She didn't deny it.

"And I just want to say that I'm going to try harder. We don't need to talk about it. I mean we can if you want to, but I'm saying we don't need to. I get it. And I'm going to make more of an effort."

She tried not to mind all the exertion words — he would "try" and make more "effort." This time together had been really good for them. She was so glad they'd come.

"Thank you."

He stopped and pulled her around, into his arms. "I love you, Mrs. Gallagher." Then he bent down and kissed her tummy, his hands on her hips, oblivious to the amused stares of the hotel bellboys. "And I love you, baby Gallagher."

Eve's eyes filled with tears. Ed hardly ever made gestures like that, and it moved her excessively.

RACHAEL

July Fourth was Rachael's favorite holiday,
bar none. She loved the weather, and the
inclusivity and the food and the fireworks,
and the silly, tearful sense of pride that
welled up in her when she heard "The Star-
Spangled Banner." Her family had never
been particularly religious, and so growing
up, Rosh Hashanah and Yom Kippur and
Passover were not so important to her as
these American holidays — Fourth of July
and Thanksgiving. They had never kept
Shabbat or fasted, so far as she knew, since
her great-grandparents had come from Rus-
sia in the nineteenth century. She understood and admired those who did, and she
sometimes, as a young woman, had found
the notion of becoming more observant appealing. In California as a student, she had
wondered about falling in love with someone outside the faith, unsure, despite their
lapsed state, how her parents would react.
But that hadn't happened. David hadn't
been inside a synagogue since his bar mitz-
vah, but he'd at least had one. He didn't
practice at all; he didn't believe any of it, he
said, although he was grateful that you

could be a Jew and still an atheist. They had married under the chuppah, and he had crunched the glass beneath his shoe, and it had been beautiful. And then they had settled easily enough into a fairly secular life (with brief and traumatic diversions into Judaism for a bris for both Jacob and Noah) and, when the time came, on a hybrid Christmas Hanukkah celebration for the children, which arguably would only ever work well in New York. They had a tree and a menorah and a goose and nine days of presents, went nowhere near church or temple, but sometimes to the movies on Christmas day, and if the kids were confused, they never said so (worried, perhaps, that their quota of gifts might be in some way affected).

So the American holidays were her thing — the days that celebrated pioneer spirit and the will to survive and triumph over tyranny. And since she was more a summer girl than a winter one, July Fourth was her favorite.

When she'd been a kid, that one day had lasted, it seemed, twice as long as any other day of the endless hot summer. Everything was dressed up in bunting and flags, and everyone was always in a fantastic mood. Adults forgot about children and vegetables and bedtimes, busy with their beers and their daiquiris. She remembered even as a small child marauding around in a huge gang of her cousins and the kids of her parents' friends, high on sugary root beer and s'mores roasted on the huge bonfire that was built on the beach in front of the house every year, anxious to evade the glance of anyone who might potentially send them to bed. She'd had her first kiss the Fourth of July when she was fourteen, late at night in the dunes — all marshmallow and braces, Bruce Springsteen's "Thunder Road" blaring out from the deck back at the house.

Now she stood and watched her own children rampaging, nursing her own daiquiri, along with a profound and almost smug sense of well-being. Everything was as it had always been, and as it always should be. The party had changed in only the subtlest of ways. Now she was the grown-up; among the adults at the party were her friends as well as those of her parents, older now and more sedentary, watching proceedings from deep Adirondack chairs they would later complain about heaving themselves out of. Her kids were hiding and laughing and waiting for the fireworks to start, as she had once done. She watched

David, flipping tops off beers down at the other end of the long terrace, and blew him a small kiss when his eye caught hers. It had been a fabulous day. David had moved some things around at work, come a day early to help get things ready, although her parents always hired caterers and bar staff.

That was significant. David and her mother hadn't always seen eye to eye. Truthfully, she didn't think her mother had ever really thought David was good enough for her, although whenever he'd asked, and he'd asked often in the early years, Rachael had denied it vociferously. She'd never been sure whether her mother's opinion of her husband was just the stereotype and would have been applied to any man, or whether it was specific to David. At the beginning, it had irritated him. He said her mother made him feel inadequate. She'd worked hard to negate that. It had irked her, too. Her mother was quick to criticize. It was most annoying when she amplified things that Rachael might have felt herself — making it impossible to ignore them. She'd told her mother once — one Thanksgiving when her mother had put him down at the table. She'd smiled and followed her into the kitchen and then, when no one was listening, she'd hissed at her to stop it, to get off

David's back. And her mother had smiled back, a rictus smile, and gone back out into the dining room without a word, though she had behaved impeccably for the rest of that holiday and ever since. She'd softened again when Jacob was born. David was the father of her grandchild now, and it elevated him and, to a degree, made him immune.

Now, years later, it moved her to see the two of them together, as so many things about today moved her. Friends she'd grown up with mingled with newer acquaintances. This year, for the first time, she'd invited a few people from the building. Eve and Ed because they were nice, and she thought they might be at loose ends on this most American of days. They'd gone away, though. Todd and Greg had breezed through earlier, on a tour of progressively more fabulous parties, they'd said. She'd invited them when she'd discovered they'd be out in Sag Harbor for the holiday weekend, and Todd had said he'd die for the chance to check out the house. She hoped he hadn't been disappointed — it was all very wicker and chintz, and little had changed in the last ten years — but he'd exclaimed about the proportions of the rooms and the stunning views, and if he thought the whole thing could be improved by $500,000 worth of Manuel Canovas and Philippe Starck, he at least kept it to himself. They'd just left, heading for the fireworks in Amagansett in Greg's soft-top BMW.

She'd been surprised when Kim had called and said she, Jason, and Avery would come. She'd invited them, but only in that way you invite someone when you think there is almost no chance of their accepting. She wouldn't call Kim and herself friends. Excellent neighbors. But not really friends. They'd had a few slightly awkward playdates out here last summer, trying to get Mia and Avery to find each other interesting or sympathetic, largely unsuccessfully, but they'd never had coffee on their own or lunch in the city, and she couldn't imagine that they ever would. Rachael had precious little time for the women she really enjoyed — old friends from school and from college — let alone for someone like Kim. She found Kim prickly and uptight. Rachael struggled with women who seemed to define themselves only by motherhood. She had no idea what career Kim had had before she stopped work to have Avery. She knew it was judgmental, but she disapproved, vaguely, of Kim having Esme. Why did she need a babysitter, who seemed to be almost full-time, when she wasn't working and was home herself? What did the two of them do all day? Avery was demanding, she knew — but two adults, all day? Esme and Milena had chatted, as babysitters do, on park benches and sidewalks, and Rachael knew Esme was frustrated by Kim, who was controlling and untrusting. That couldn't be easy.

She watched Mia now, in a red, white, and blue striped sundress and the small tulle wings she'd been wearing like a backpack all day, wrestling in the sand with Sadie, the next-door neighbor's granddaughter, and remembered that Mia hadn't been a natural match for Avery, any more than she felt herself to be for Kim. Avery was whiny and demanding and a lousy sharer, and Mia, the youngest of three, breezily confident and grown-up for her age, had no patience with her. They weren't stupid, kids. They were pretty good judges of character.

But they were here now, all of them. That was some commitment; their part of Long Island would have been a long schlep on a day like today. Kim actually looked prettier than Rachael had ever seen her before, in a coral pink dress that showed off her golden shoulders and a lacy white shawl. And she had a little makeup on, which was rare for her. Jason wasn't a bad-looking guy, but he could never have been Rachael's type. He was blandly good-looking — a catalogue guy — blond and relatively chiseled, with greenish eyes, she thought. But not an interesting face, and that was what she liked. She could look at David for hours — into the deep brown pools of his twinkling eyes, and at the fine lines between his eyebrows and at either side of his nose. At the million smiles he had, each one slightly different. And the small scar on his right cheek.

The Kramers were deep in conversation, it seemed, with elderly bridge friends of her parents, although Kim's eyes constantly flitted to where Avery was planted on the beach flinging an arc of sand all about her with a small blue shovel. Rachael thought that they might need to be rescued; the old man was a terrific bore and utterly Republican, and they ought to be talking to some of the younger guests. She sauntered in their direction.

Jason watched her walk toward them, his heart racing slightly. She looked so good. She was nut brown already, so early in the summer, and she had amazing shoulders, strong and muscled but still feminine and, he knew, silky soft to the touch. She was wearing a pale, short shift dress that left her arms and most of her legs bare, and little diamond disks sparkled at her ears. When she leaned in to kiss him, she smelled wonderful, and familiar.

"Jason, Kim! I'm so happy you made it! So great to see you! And hi, Avery!"

She bent down and ruffled Avery's hair. Jason saw the outline of a thong beneath the thin fabric of the dress, and felt his knees tremble just a little. He wasn't permitted to see Kim in underwear often these days, but it had been some time since he'd wanted to. She wore thongs once. But not now. She was horribly self-conscious about the little pouch created by the cesarean she'd had when Avery was born. He hadn't minded that, but she had always hated it.

"Thanks again for inviting us. We're a little late, I'm afraid." Kim was stiff and as awkward as ever.

"No such thing as late! Unless you miss the fireworks, which you clearly haven't." She gestured at the sky, where the sun was still up and beating down. "Have you found some food?"

Jason answered. "Not yet."

"You've got to get up there and grab some. My mother goes nuts on the Fourth of July, she always has. There's lobster and shrimp and filet . . ."

"Sounds delicious."

She was searching for conversation. She always had to, with these two. It could get quite exhausting. "You just missed Todd and Greg. They breezed through on their way to Amagansett."

"Ah."

Jason was standing a little too close and staring at her just a little too intently. Rachael wondered whether Kim had noticed. He did it in the apartment elevator, too, sometimes — if David wasn't there. It wasn't exactly "creepy," as Mia would say, but it did make her feel uncomfortable. She figured he was just one of those people who had a slightly different concept of personal space.

"So . . . how's your summer?"

"Avery and I are out at the house now, until Labor Day."

"And I'm back and forth on the jitney," Jason added. "You?"

"We're in the city and Connecticut mainly. I grew up out here, and so there's lots to do when we come out, but I'm not truly a Southampton girl anymore. I guess we're lucky we have the option. I mean, I couldn't imagine not being here for the Fourth of July, for example. I don't think I've ever missed one."

Jason nodded as though she had just said

something profound and he'd been the only person listening who'd understood her.

"But you're not full-time in Connecticut?"

"No." She shook her head ruefully. "That'd be great, but with work . . ." She shrugged. "I try and spend at least a part of each week up there with the kids. Milena has them, and they go to tennis camp and science camp, and all that good stuff, you know. But I gotta work."

Kim smiled tightly. When she spoke, her voice was strident. "Got to? Or want to?"

Jason and Rachael stared at her, both astounded by her rudeness. In her mind's eye, Kim moved backward from the remark, which hung in the air. In reality, it was out, and she could go nowhere but forward. Rachael was too shocked to even be angry. The full force of Kim's obvious unhappiness hit her squarely for the first time. Only someone truly miserable would be so vile. She actually felt sorry for her.

"Seems a shame, that's all, to be apart from them for so long."

Rachael sighed. How many times had she heard that tone in the voice of a nonworking mother? It didn't even make her feel defensive anymore; she'd been over that since Jacob was a toddler. It just made her feel a bit sad that women weren't as good

254

as they should be at considering other women's decisions. Or at recognizing that, for a woman, every decision (and how lucky she knew they all were to have so many choices) was a compromise. She dug a fingernail into her palm, forced a smile, and tried to remind herself that she judged Kim, too.

Jason was still glaring at Kim. He had actually moved a foot or so away from his wife. "I'm sure they have a ball."

Rachael smiled at him gratefully. "I think they do."

"I'm sure that if you went back to work, you'd do the same, Kim." Now he'd gone a little further than she'd have had him go in defense of her, and Rachael was again aware that she was caught in the barbed, bloody crossfire of a couple at odds.

"I don't think I'll even consider going back while Avery is so young."

Kim knew perfectly well that Rachael had been back at her desk when Mia was three months old. She didn't want to be having this conversation today. Today was not for squabbling. She turned her head slightly, to see if she could catch David's eye, but he was laughing at something someone had said, and he didn't see her.

Kim smiled, through only slightly gritted

teeth. "It's just that Avery was so hard-won, you know. I couldn't bear to have someone else raising her."

Jesus. The IVF card. She was really playing with a full deck today. She'd seen Kim play it before. It infuriated her. As if conceiving, carrying, and delivering a child the more conventional way was no big deal — like those babies weren't "hard-won." And the scorpion sting in the tail. "Someone else raising her." If she'd had more respect for Kim, that might have hurt. But then, if she'd had more respect for Kim, Kim would have had to be the kind of person who would never say such a thing.

Rachael smiled vaguely in Kim's direction, allowed her eyes to meet Jason's, and turned. "I've just seen someone I was at summer camp with a million years ago! You must excuse me, I have to go and say hi. Do go and find some lobster, won't you? And make sure you get a great spot for the fireworks. They're pretty amazing from here!"

More than anything, Kim wished she could take the last five minutes back. Jason was looking at her with such disgust on his face she felt like she might melt away with shame, into the sand.

"Did you have to be such a bitch?" He

spat the words at her, then turned away. And those were the last words he said directly to her at the party.

KIM

In the car on the way home, with Avery slumped in her car seat in the back fast asleep, Kim could feel Jason's disapproval. She'd felt it for the rest of the evening, sitting next to him and watching the fireworks light up the cloudless sky, wishing that he had his arm around her like so many of the other couples she could see, leaning in to each other, cozy and united. She knew she'd been cruel and vindictive, even if she'd said only a handful of words to Rachael. He had every right to be angry. To hate her, even. She didn't know why she'd done it.

That wasn't true. She did know. She'd never say so, to Jason or to Rachael. She struggled even to say it to herself. She was so far beyond jealous of Rachael Schulman that sometimes her jealousy felt like a tumor inside her. She had everything. She was beautiful, she was slim and tiny and immaculate. She looked good in everything. She had a husband who adored her, and three children it hadn't half killed her to produce, who behaved. She had a thousand friends, a career, and parents with money, and she had choices. She could say she wasn't a Hamptons girl and make Connecticut sound like such a sane, cool choice, but damn it, there she was, holding court at some Camelotlike mansion . . . in the Hamptons. Rachael had everything. She wasn't a mess. She wasn't perpetually afraid that the whole thing might collapse around her like a house of cards at any moment. She wasn't unhappy.

"I'm sorry for what I said to Rachael. It was unforgivable."

Jason was driving, staring straight ahead at the road. He didn't turn to see her face when she spoke, although she was looking directly at him. He could let it end there, or he could carry it forward into the rest of their night, their weekend, and their whole damn lives.

"It was, pretty much." Forward then.

Earlier, when she'd showered, Kim had thought about making love tonight. Even imagined a tiny jolt of lust as she'd thought about it, pulling on her underwear and thinking he might be pulling it off again later. They'd have had fun at the party, they'd have driven home companionably. He'd have noticed she'd made an effort to look nice. He might even have told her. It might have happened that way. They might have ended the night lying together under his mother's magic quilt.

It seemed ridiculous now, even to have thought it. It hadn't happened that way, and they wouldn't. Again. She remembered how it used to be. Always. But out here, she remembered more. The way it used to be haunted her, especially here. Did he remember it, too?

Silence. Treacle thick, dark, and impenetrable.

Then, "Why would you feel the need to do it?"

Answers bubbled in her throat. Defensive, petty, unjustifiable reasons. Small answers. "I don't know." Her voice broke.

"Are you so fucking miserable that you need to spread it wherever you go?" The same tone of voice he'd used on the beach. It was so new and so hard. It frightened her.

Jason viewed the prospect of Kim's tears with impatience and distaste. What did she have to cry about? She'd ruined the afternoon and evening for him. Rachael hadn't come near either of them again, until right at the end as they were leaving. Avery had grown irritable and loud, although the other children had lain silently on the cool sand, in the laps of their parents, watching the fireworks, enraptured.

They were toxic — all three of them. They were toxic and he didn't know why, or when it had happened. And he hated it.

Kim slept in the single bed next to Avery's that night, in self-imposed exile, although he raised no objection as she collected her pillows and a blanket from the end of their bed, but he couldn't doze off. The air was still and his mind was racing. At around three a.m. he got up in search of cold water. Coming back upstairs, he stopped at the door to Avery's room. His daughter had climbed in with his wife at some point, and the two of them lay, their faces together, entwined in the narrow bed. Kim had one arm across Avery protectively, and Avery in turn had one tiny hand on Kim's neck. He felt a jolt of tenderness, so unfamiliar it was almost shocking. He stood and watched them for a while, bathed in the same moon-light of a lifetime ago.

Back in his own bed, Jason sat with his head in his hands and wept — something he hadn't done, so far as he could remember, since the day Avery had been born.

RACHAEL

In Southampton, the caterers had just finished clearing up. Leftovers that would feed a small village were wrapped and stacked in the two enormous Sub-Zero refrigerators in the chef's kitchen. Rachael's parents had gone to bed. So had the kids, utterly exhausted. Mia and Jacob had been asleep already, barely stirring when David had hoisted them one on each shoulder and carried them upstairs to bed. Rachael was lying on the enormous wicker sofa on the terrace, her feet up on David's lap. The ocean beyond the house was their sound track. This was always the best part of the party, Rachael realized with a smile. When everyone had gone home happy, and it was quiet again. She was almost asleep herself. She and the kids had been up, sailing, by seven a.m., while David had played golf at the Salisbury with some friends from work. He'd burned his nose. He always burned his nose. Long, lovely day. It had been golden. That's what they called those days when you wouldn't change a second. Their first one had been the day in the surf, all those years ago. They'd had more than their fair share, she reasoned. And this had been another one. Lucky, lucky them. She thought of Jason and Kimberley, just for a moment, the image of them and the way they looked at each other passing over her golden mood like a black rain cloud.

This had been fun, but she was also eager to get to Connecticut. They'd drive up tomorrow, take the two ferries required. If they left after breakfast, the kids could be in the pool by early afternoon. She'd taken the rest of the week off, and Milena was taking some holiday time, so it would just be the five of them for the next four days. Bliss.

"So we'll head off in the morning?"

David was rubbing her feet. His hands slowed, and the pressure of his touch lessened. "Aah."

"What?"

"I meant to tell you earlier, only it's been a crazy day."

"Tell me what?"

"I've got to go in to work tomorrow. Next two days, most likely. Got a call this morning, while I was on the golf course. Some new information on a biggish case we've got pending . . ."

"Which absolutely has to be dealt with this week?"

"I'm afraid so."

"Fourth of July week?"

"They go to trial at the beginning of next

week, so yes, I'm afraid so."

"Well, that stinks! I was looking forward to the rest of the week — just us."

He leaned down and kissed the big toe on each of her feet. "Me, too. Of course. And I will be there on Friday night without fail, even if I incur the wrath of the senior partner. I swear. We'll have the weekend. Promise."

Rachael stuck her bottom lip out petulantly. "I suppose I have to live with it," she said sulkily.

He mimicked her tone. "Yes, you do."

"Well, all right then. But you have to make it up to me."

"Anything! Your wish is my command, m'lady."

"Mmm. So let's start with the foot rub. Pick up the pace a little, will you? I've had better from Mia."

David picked up her left foot and chewed on her little toe playfully. "You have, have you?"

She squirmed and squealed, trying to free her foot from his tight grip. He held her down with one hand and moved his lips up her calf, across her knee, and on to her bare, brown thigh. The mood changed in a heartbeat. "Anything else?"

Not so giggly now, Rachael moved her

hands to the back of his head, pulling him a little northward on his delicious journey, and ran her fingers into his hair, across his earlobes. "I can probably think of something . . . We should go inside . . ."

"Why? When did you get so prudish? Your parents are in bed. The kids are dead to the world . . ."

"Mmm . . . prudish. How dare you!"

"I want you now, Rach. Right here and right now . . ."

DAVID

Early the next morning, when Rachael had dropped him at the jitney stop, David's heart sank slightly when he recognized Jason Kramer in the fifth row. The bus was very quiet — most people must be staying out to make a long weekend of it — and he couldn't avoid his gaze. Jason looked up from his book and waved, and David slumped into the double seat across from his neighbor.

"You got to work, too?"

"I'm afraid so."

"Stings to leave, hey?"

"Absolutely."

This verbal badminton was a stretch for him at this time in the morning. He wanted to drink his coffee and doze and watch the rural landscape turn urban. He didn't want to chew the fat with Jason Kramer.

"Great party last night. Those fireworks were spectacular."

"Rachael's parents throw a great Fourth of July party."

"It must have been thousands of dollars, just for the pyrotechnics."

David had lived in New York for a lot of years now, but he'd never quite got used to the money conversation. He never really wanted to discuss how much he'd paid for his car or his apartment or his kids' tuition or his wife's engagement ring — all areas completely within bounds for a New Yorker, it seemed.

"Suppose. They don't consult me on their party budget." He knew he sounded testy, and Jason looked a little discomfitted. Good. So he should.

"No, no, of course. I just meant that they were amazing."

"They were." David nodded and half smiled, letting Jason off the hook.

"And Rachael looked wonderful. You're a lucky man, David."

"That, I *do* know."

He knew, too, that this was an appropriate opportunity to reciprocate, but he didn't feel entirely comfortable complimenting Jason on Kim. She didn't do much for him, to be honest. Sour-faced, and a bit of a mess, most of the time, though she hadn't looked bad last night, from a distance, which was as close as he'd gotten. Still . . .

"You, too! Avery's grown. She's going to be a tall one, that girl."

"Eighty-fifth percentile for her age." God, Jason didn't believe he'd said that. Kim recited these numbers at him after every visit to the pediatrician (and there seemed to be a disproportionate number of visits to the pediatrician). He wasn't even sure what that meant, to be honest. But he knew it was good, as far as Kim was concerned.

David looked vaguely puzzled too. Guess he didn't know what it meant either. Jason tried to look busy with his BlackBerry for a few minutes, sending emails and listening to voice mails. There weren't that many. He could probably have stayed out on Long Island for the next day or two. If he'd wanted to. He looked at David, who was dozing now, his head lolling back against the headrest of the seat. Jason didn't give much thought to other men's good looks, but he took a long hard stare at David now that he had the chance. He was handsome, but not conventionally so. And not especially so. His suit was expensive, Jason could see that, but his whole look was less Wall Street, more Venice Beach. The Californian in him would not be constrained by a navy, light wool single-breasted suit and a Ferragamo tie. Curls escaped from where they had been brushed back, and his hair was definitely a little too long at the back. His nose was red from too much sun. He'd hung his suit jacket on the hook beside the seat, and the top two buttons of his shirt were undone beneath the loose tie. Jason could see thick, dark hair. And good muscle definition underneath the shirt. David must be a regular at the gym.

This was the man who slept beside Rachael Schulman every night. The man who got to touch her whenever he wanted, to hold that smooth, brown, taut little body in his arms and have those chocolate brown eyes look into his with love and desire and happiness.

What the hell was he doing on the first jitney on July fifth?

He'd watched them say good-bye. Rachael had been leaning against their car. She had to have just tumbled out of bed into it. Her hair wasn't as tamed as he was used to seeing it, although he liked it like that — big and wild. She was wearing voluminous floral trousers, the waistband too big, so that they sat low on her hips, and he could see her flat stomach. And a white vest, with thin straps.

David had kissed her, open-mouthed, one hand holding her head, the other pulling her ass in toward his hips, possessively. It was a kiss other people were not meant to see, but Jason had watched every second of it.

And he knew for certain that he would not be on the 7:30 a.m. jitney if he had that at home. Traffic was light. David opened his eyes and they were already in Queens. Twenty-five minutes later he said good-bye to Jason and was standing on the sidewalk in midtown. It was going to be another relentlessly hot day. Already the oppressive, heavy dampness of midsummer midtown hung in the air.

He flipped open his cell and dialed a number, simultaneously hailing a cab. Uptown.

"It's me."

"Where are you?"

"Forties and Third."

"Already? You must be eager."

"I'm eager, all right? That's what you want to hear, isn't it?"

"I'm waiting."

He hung up and climbed into the yellow cab that had stopped next to him. He gave his destination, then sat back and wiped the sweat beads that had already formed on his brow.

Jason watched the cab pull away, wondering why David would be heading north when his office was at Grand Central, about a block or so west.

EMILY

Emily had begun doing mini triathlons in her first year at high school. She'd always been athletic. At first she'd done them in teams. She could swim or cycle, although she preferred to run. She'd been a senior when she'd done her first solo event — a half triathlon. And a freshman at college when she'd completed her first full one. This would be her fourth, and her first in New York City.

At home, her mom would have come to cheer her on, but here she kept it pretty quiet. No one at work knew she did it. It wasn't about support, for Emily. It was about being alone. She'd never cared much for team sports. She liked to compete against herself, not other people; her satisfaction came from shaving seconds off her time, not from beating the competitor next to her. She'd told Charlotte, who'd said she was her hero and that she was in awe of her. But Charlotte was going home to Seattle that weekend for a cousin's wedding, so she wouldn't be around. Which was fine. She'd make a fuss, Emily knew, because she was sweet and kind, but Emily didn't like a fuss.

Her mom had given her her bike for her twenty-first birthday. She knew it had cost a fortune; Mom must have saved for ages. It was a Kestrel Talon carbon road bike, with a frame weight of less than seven and a half kilograms. There'd never been a lot of money for extras. Enough for what she needed, always, but her mom must have gone without to buy the bike. There was a bike room in the building, but there was no way Emily would leave it there among the rusty ladies' bikes and kids' bikes with training wheels. It lived up on a hook on her living room wall, which was fine with her because she thought it was more beautiful than art. Actually, to her, it was art.

The run was still her favorite. Ten kilometers. A breeze if you hadn't swum and cycled first. You used your legs as economically as you could during the swim, but your thighs were still like jelly after 40 km on the bike. It was the Hudson swim that made her most nervous this time. Not the swimming so much as the water. She didn't like the human soup part of the race — even though they were in groups, split into amateurs and professionals, and then, as amateurs, again, into age and gender packs. That first part, when everyone charged in and jockeyed for position in the water, that part could make her feel panicky.

She'd spent three months' spare cash on a new wet suit — specifically designed for this event. It meant you didn't have to change, and that would save minutes. Coming out of the water was the worst.

The adrenaline was coursing around her. She loved that feeling. She could get addicted. Last summer she'd gone paragliding, back in Oregon. Same feeling — hot and breathless and excited. You couldn't explain the rush to someone — they had to feel it.

She'd just finished registering in the tent. They'd written her race number on her arm and leg — 1232 — with a Sharpie marker and put a timing band around her wrist. She would set off in twenty minutes. The weather was pretty much perfect. It was early, so it wasn't too hot yet. The forecast promised relatively low humidity for this time of year, although the sun would be hot by the time she got to the run. She wondered if she needed the bathroom, and decided that it was just nerves. She jogged on the spot for a minute or two and swung her arms from side to side. This was the worst part. She just wanted to get on with it.

The swim took twenty-eight minutes. She'd been right; the first part, until things spread out a bit, was grim. Too many bodies, too many flailing arms and kicking legs. Someone had kicked her, hard, in the right hip. She'd have a bruise tomorrow. She'd been worried too about swallowing too much dirty water, but in the splashing, it was impossible not to. Good time, though. Not her personal best, but good enough. She'd been working hard on the bike. It was there she was hoping to shave off minutes. She'd done the last 40 km in fifty-nine minutes. But last week, in training, she'd managed fifty-four. She ran out of the water, ignoring the shaking in her thighs and oblivious to the large group of cheering supporters gathered behind the tapes at Seventy-ninth and Riverside, found her bicycle, and climbed on, slipping her feet into the special shoes attached to the pedals.

So she didn't see Jackson.

It was Raul who'd told him she was doing it. The New York City Triathlon. He'd sidled up to Jackson in the lobby a few days ago and delivered the information in an elaborate stage whisper, like some bumbling spy.

Jackson had googled the event, not daring to ask her directly. He could guess what she might say, if he asked if he could come and support her. He knew what a triathlon was, but until he read about it on Wikipedia, he'd had no idea of the distances involved. Now he was seriously impressed, and embarrassed at the memory of his own attempts on the racing bike. And thinking, not for the first time, that he was really fighting above his weight when it came to Emily Mikanowski.

He didn't know who'd be there for her. Legions of Emily fans, he presumed. But he had to try.

She came out of the water sooner than he'd thought. It had to have been less than half an hour, he reckoned. Wow. She emerged like Ursula Andress in a wet suit, and he saw her straightaway, pulling her swimming cap off, her platinum ponytail tumbling to her shoulders. And ran right past him. Shit. That hadn't been the plan.

Next leg then.

Except that spectators and supporters

weren't allowed on the West Side Highway; it was deemed by the organizers to be dangerous. So he couldn't catch the end of the cycle ride. He would have to wait for ninety minutes or more, until the end of the third leg, the run. He headed over right away, determined to bag a place at the front. The road race would wind its way through the park, ending up near the Seventy-second Street transverse, at the band shell. There was already quite a crowd, and a festival atmosphere. A steel band was playing. He wondered if he'd been stupid to come. There had to be hundreds of people here, if not thousands. And she wasn't expecting to see him. She wouldn't be looking for him.

The organizers had set up a zone for finishers. There was a water station and someone handing out silver blankets. Medical-looking people. A long row of people in triathlon T-shirts held hundreds of medals on ribbons. Once you'd passed the finish line, had your number taken, picked up what you needed, and collected your medal, you filtered out of that zone and you were loose in the park. That was where Jackson waited. He'd miss her actual finish, but he stood a better chance of spotting her here, where the crowd was thinner.

And then, there she was. Looking pretty and fresh and strong. She chatted for a moment with the guy who put the medal around her neck, laughing at something he said and the triumph of the moment. She didn't look around at the crowd. Maybe there wasn't anyone there for her. Except for him. She didn't seem to be expecting anyone or anything. She looked so beautiful. Like an Amazon.

And then she saw him. At that point he was hard to miss. Because he was wearing a neon yellow T-shirt, on which he had had printed, in huge pink letters, GO EMILY! It clashed beautifully with the red baseball cap bearing the same legend. He'd had them made up in one of those dodgy-looking printing shops near Times Square.

Now he stood with his arms wide and his chest out, smiling.

And Emily smiled back, a smile especially for him. And he felt rewarded. She walked toward him, and her blue eyes sparkled.

"You're an idiot."

"You're my hero."

She laughed. Charlotte was going to swoon when she got back. Actually swoon. It was pretty nice. It probably constituted fuss. But it was pretty nice.

"I thought about balloons."

"I hate balloons."

"Or flowers."

"They'd have wilted. It's hot out here."

"Exactly. I've wilted, too, but it isn't so obvious."

They stood about two feet apart and looked at each other.

"Are you okay? I mean, how do you feel? I can't imagine —"

"I'm great. Feel fantastic. I'll be sore later. And I'll sleep like the dead. But right now, I'm golden."

"You look golden." She did. "Can I walk you home?" She surely couldn't object to that, could she?

"That'd be nice."

It was lovely to be with her. Strangers congratulated her, a few kids raising their palms for a high five. New Yorkers loved an athlete. People probably thought they were a couple, Jackson thought, and he liked how it felt.

She was quiet, but it was comfortable quiet. Not like dinner had been. Maybe she was just exhausted. But either way, he liked how it felt. When they got back to the apartment, she turned to him and gave a funny little bow. "Thank you, Trip. That was very sweet."

"You're very welcome."

She nodded shyly. "Now I'm going to go upstairs and get in a bath."

"Okay."

"So I'll see you sometime, hey?"

What was that? He'd hoped for a bit more. But something told him not to push. Let her think about it for a while. Think about him. He was in no hurry, he realized. Emily Mikanowski was worth waiting for.

The following Sunday afternoon Jackson's elevator and his heart stopped on Emily's floor. He crossed his fingers and prayed to someone that it would be Emily, not grumpy Arthur, waiting to get in, and someone rewarded him. Emily was wearing a cobalt blue strapless jersey sundress and carrying a laundry basket, on top of which were bottles of laundry detergent and fabric softener.

"Hi." She smiled warmly at him, then tilted her head downward, toward the plastic basket. "Laundry."

"Let me help?" He took the basket before she could argue.

"Thanks."

"You're welcome. How are the muscles?"

"Fine!"

On the ground floor, she tried to take the laundry from him, but he kept going, walking to the back of the building, where the service elevator took them down the last floor into the basement.

"You really don't need to."

"It's nothing. Listen. No more grand gestures. I promise. I can see that isn't your kind of thing. But how about a coffee? Just while you wait for your laundry? What is that, anyway? Twenty minutes, half an hour tops. Don't tell me you had anything better to do."

She reached into the basket and pulled out *People* magazine. "Just this!"

"I rest my case."

He bought them two iced lattes and carried them into the park, where they sat on a bench near the Seventy-second Street entrance. The park was crowded with people already. New York out to enjoy the stunning weekend weather.

"I think we got off to a rotten start, Emily."

"Jackson —" she tried to interrupt him.

"No, no, please just listen to me, for a minute." He raised a hand, and she sat back.

"I haven't been honest with you, not entirely. About who I am. I admit, I don't have a job. I live off my parents, effectively, who are either patient enough or stupid enough to let me, while they wait to see if I'm going to turn out to be any good at all.

I drink too much, I smoke the occasional joint. I keep late hours, and I never make my own bed. I have been to bed with more girls than I should have, and most of them I didn't really care for. I'm not fit — can't run for a bus. I'm all of that. I'm almost certainly not good enough for you, and I don't claim to be.

"You're beautiful and smart and an athlete and everything. You're . . . you're lovely. I was trying to play it cool and handing you a line, simply because I felt less cool than I ever had in my life before when I was around you. Still do. But here's the thing, Emily. I felt something. I felt something I'm pretty sure I never have before. You've made me think about things differently, and that has really, really shaken me.

"And the other thing is, I think you felt it, too. Just a bit, maybe. But I think you did. And so, I just wanted to bring you out here, and buy you a coffee, and . . . and tell you. Just in case you think it might be possible for you not to judge me on who you think I am or who I was, maybe. But maybe a little more on who I could be. Who I want to be.

"And if that doesn't sound like an outrageous suggestion, whether you might consider possibly going out with me for dinner again. Starting over."

He was a funny one, this one. He was right. About a couple of things. She had judged him. She knew she had. And she had felt something, in spite of him, and in spite of herself. And now this diatribe.

"Dinner?"

"Just dinner." He nodded emphatically. "Or lunch. Or brunch. Breakfast, even."

"So long as there's food, right?"

"There doesn't have to be food. We can go bowling if you like."

Now she laughed. "I hate bowling."

"Thank God. I'm crap at bowling. And cycling."

"Okay, so lunch."

"Lunch. Lunch sounds great. Lunch sounds epic. When?"

"One day. Soon. Maybe."

"So I make my big speech, and you're still playing it cool."

She smiled. "Have to make the most of my advantage, don't I?"

Eve

At 6:30 p.m. on a Tuesday afternoon in mid-July, the power went out all over Manhattan. The subways stopped in their tracks. The air-conditioning units that had been cooling apartments and offices and stores across the city went quiet. The televisions, blaring out the early evening news, were suddenly silent. It was the first major power blackout of the summer. The 1.6 million or so residents of the small island had brought the ancient, complicated system to its knees, and it had protested, faltered, and given up. Con Edison, the power company that handled most of the grid in New York, swung into action, but the spokesman who gave interviews to the radio reporters said it would take at least eight hours to restore power to most people, and that residents should expect to be in darkness well into the night. People were supposed to have kits ready; at least one of the five boroughs had a blackout each summer. The last great city-wide blackout had been in 2003. People still told stories about it. Eve had gotten talking to a jolly woman in a shop on Amsterdam only the week before, who'd told her that she'd walked from Amsterdam in the eighties all the way home to Queens that day, with her toddler in a stroller. Somewhere in the sixties they'd met a woman carrying her own toddler, and so they'd shared the stroller, all the way back. Been great friends ever since. The woman said New Yorkers had been changed overnight on 9/11, and that they'd been changed again that night.

A common enemy, she said — that was all you needed. Al Qaeda or Con Ed — it made no difference, really.

Ed was in Chicago with work. Eve busied herself while it was still light, feeling a little excited — and a little irritated. *Grey's Anatomy* was on tonight. Television in general, and her favorite programs in particular, had taken on a disproportionate importance in her life over the recent months. Sometimes she talked to Ed about characters as though they were real (because she almost thought of them that way), and he shook his head at her, smiling that half laugh. She found the flashlight she'd bought at Bed Bath & Beyond only a couple of weeks earlier, after she'd heard the blackout stories. She put tiny votive candles intended for intimate dinners and romantic seductions along the windowsill in the living room and in the kitchen. She filled the kettle and a couple of saucepans. She wasn't sure why, but it seemed like a good idea. She wondered about the contents of the fridge freezer and realized there was nothing she could do about them. Bugger — she regretted the big shop she'd done over the weekend. She'd bought as many bags of frozen fruit as she thought she could fit in — raspberries and strawberries and mangoes, vowing to juice and smoothie herself and the baby daily. She had no idea how long it would take for stuff to thaw and get ruined, but she hoped the power wouldn't be off all night. She was a bit of a scaredy-cat. She usually kept the telly or the radio on all night when Ed was away, and it was going to get awfully dark and awfully quiet later on, without power. Her cell phone rang, and Ed's name flashed on the screen.

"Hello, power cut central here."

"Oh, God. No, really?"

"Really. Trust you to miss the first one."

He was instantly defensive. "It isn't like I planned it this way."

"I wasn't serious." This was happening too much lately. They seemed to get three sentences into a conversation before it turned sour. She knew she was touchy. But he was crabby, too.

"You sounded serious." There was an uncomfortable silence.

"I just hate that you aren't here."

All she wanted was comfort. To be verbally stroked over the phone. For him to commiserate with her, just for a moment. He was right — it was no big deal. If he'd done that, she'd have been fine.

He didn't.

"God, Eve, it's just a power cut, for

Christ's sake. Light a damn candle. Go to bed. You're asleep the whole time anyway."

"That's not fair." He left by seven a.m. every morning — who the hell wasn't asleep then? And if she dozed off on the sofa in the evening, waiting for him to come home, then so what? She was pregnant.

"I just don't understand why you're making so much fuss."

She threw the phone down. She'd never done that to him, ended a call in anger, not in all the years they'd been together. Her hand shook, and tears sprang into her eyes.

The phone rang again, and Ed's name flashed up. She let it go to voice mail.

When she checked, he hadn't left a message.

She thought he might have rung to apologize, but she'd forgotten how stubborn he could be. There would be no appeasement tonight.

CHARLOTTE

Charlotte was the happiest woman in the city at this moment. She couldn't wait to tell Emily. This was the kind of thing that happened in her novels. And in her dreams. Not in real life. But here she was. The elevator had stopped. Somewhere between the first and second floors. To think she'd contemplated taking the stairs; she'd been reading an article at lunchtime on ways to get fitter in your everyday life, and it said you should climb more stairs, but it was so damn hot, and she was tired. So she'd taken the elevator for one floor. And now it was stuck. She wasn't in the least bit scared. Not, at least, about the elevator. There was an emergency light; it had flickered on almost as soon as the elevator had juddered to a stop. The alarm had been sounded, so people — the right people — knew what had happened, but the power outage was citywide, and it might take the firemen hours to get to the building. Firemen would be coming. To rescue her. But she hoped it took them all night to get here. Let them rescue every other person in the city first.

Che was in here with her. Che. Was. In. Here. With. Her. He was delivering pizza to the penthouse.

Ordinarily, he'd ride up with the delivery guy, and there'd be three of them in here, but the guy must have been in a rush. Maybe the Stewarts didn't tip. It wouldn't surprise her. They didn't smile or say thank you much, that she'd observed, and tips were the same sort of thing, weren't they? Her heart had almost stopped when he stepped into the elevator with her. This had never happened.

She was just back from work. She'd let two subways go at the station; the cars had been really crowded, and she couldn't face squeezing in. Then she'd stopped for Tasti D-Lite, the zero-fat "frozen treat" that she'd read somewhere was really just gas and chemicals, but who cared when it had seventy calories and cooled you down? New York, New York. And eaten it in, for the air conditioning in the store. It was humid as hell. She marveled at how those tiny decisions (taste chocolate cookie dough; wait for sprinkles; eat at the bar) had led to this. A minute earlier or a minute later, and she wouldn't be here now. Thank God she'd been to the bathroom before she left work. She'd followed Arthur Anderson up the block, overtaking him at the lights. Thank God he was so slow, and so mean that she'd felt no compulsion to walk with him, pass the time of day. He'd be sitting in the foyer, no doubt swearing and muttering. But he wasn't in here with them.

Che shifted nervously from foot to foot. Both of them studied the wood paneling and tiled floor of the small space. When he inadvertently caught Charlotte's eye, he nodded toward the pizza box with a slight smile. "At least we won't be hungry, if we're stuck too long in here."

She smiled. "That's true."

Now he nodded toward the book bag she was carrying. "A lot of books."

Charlotte nodded. "I work at the library. You know the big library?"

"Midtown? With the steps, and the skating rink in the winter. The one in the movie?"

"That one." She nodded. Everyone said that. The beautiful, historic library had stood and functioned since 1911, but the world at large had no idea it was there until Hollywood filmed *The Day After Tomorrow* there.

"They burned all the books in that movie, right?" He raised one eyebrow at her.

Charlotte made a face of mock horror. "Yeah."

"What do you do? At that library?"

"I work in the main area. With the public."

Che nodded. "You like to read a lot, hey?"

"I love to read." It's the only thing I have in my life, she thought. Silence. "And you, Che?" It was the first time that she'd ever used his name. "Do you like to read?"

"In English, not so much. My English, it isn't so good. For speaking, it's okay. For reading, not so much."

"But in Spanish?" Charlotte panicked as soon as she said it. God, it *was* Spanish, right?

Che shrugged. The reading conversation was clearly exhausted. Charlotte wondered what to say next.

"You're Cuban, is that right?"

"Yes, Cuban. All the doormen in this building are Cuban. The super is Cuban, the doormen are Cuban, the porter is Cuban. The staff of the whole building is Cuban. Little Havana, right here, on the Upper East Side." He smiled broadly at his own joke.

"Have you lived in America always?"

"No, no. Fifteen years. Citizen since two thousand three."

"And have you family back in Cuba?"

"My mother, my sisters."

"And do you get home, back to Cuba, to see them often?"

"I was there in two thousand five. Before that, two thousand one."

"And here — do you have family here?"

"No. No one."

Charlotte searched his face for signs of the heartbreak she'd invented for him but saw only embarrassment. This was more conversation than was normal for a doorman and a resident, she supposed. She worried that she'd been too nosy — invasive. They fell silent for a moment. Charlotte realized it was very hot in the elevator. She leaned back against the wood of its interior and hoped she wasn't getting too shiny. Or, God forbid, that she smelled.

When she leaned back, Che did, too. They smiled awkwardly at each other.

"It's hot."

She nodded agreement.

"And you? You are not from New York?"

"Not originally, no."

"Where, then?"

"From Seattle."

"All the way across on the other side." He cocked his head westward.

"Exactly."

"Is that why you came to New York. To get far away?"

She supposed it was, although no one had ever put it to her that way before. Trouble was, she'd come with her, so to speak. She was the same Charlotte Murphy she'd been in Seattle. It was funny how a language barrier made some things crystal clear.

"But Murphy. It's an Irish name, isn't it?"

"Yes. We're all from somewhere else, aren't we, really? My great-grandparents came over from Cork, right at the beginning of the last century, to make a new life

— a better life."

"And me, too. From Cuba."

"Will you ever go back, do you think, to Cuba? To live?"

"Not to live. I'm American now. To see family. But not for good."

He had the loveliest face. Charlotte supposed most people might not swoon over him; he wasn't matinee-idol material. His dark hair was thinning, and he was a little skinny — slight, almost. He always had a heavy five o'clock shadow, the line of his beard sharp against his skin, like a cartoon character. But he had the biggest, darkest, almond-shaped eyes, with long black eyelashes. She loved his eyes.

"We should sit down. We could be in here a while." Charlotte sat, tucking her voluminous skirt decorously under her. She looked up at him. "Sit. Please."

He did, drawing his knees in to his chest, laying the pizza box on the floor between them. She made herself look into those eyes and smile, and the eyes smiled back.

JACKSON

In 5a, Trip wasn't expecting the knock on the door. He knew Todd and Greg weren't home next door; he'd knocked, himself, when the power had first gone out, to see if they had a spare flashlight. Resigned to a dull evening without his Xbox or Pay Per View, he'd smoked a joint, and until the knock on the door, he was thinking that sleeping was the ideal way to pass the blackout. He thought about checking on Emily, but she was probably with Charlotte. Besides, he wasn't sure he could take much more rejection. He was still smarting from the triathlon.

"Want some company?" Madison was leaning against the door-frame, waving a bottle of wine, a little breathless from the three flights of stairs. "I get scared, you see."

She didn't look like much scared her. She was wearing the very shortest of denim shorts and a white top with thin spaghetti straps. The white cotton really showed off the tan he just bet she'd gotten in May and June at a Southampton house share full of good-looking young people. He'd seen her once or twice, waiting for the jitney. There was a sexy sheen of sweat on her brown skin. Funny how some people could sweat sexily. Her blond hair was twisted into a knot on her head, but strands had escaped, and they curled damply around her long, slender neck. Madison Cavanagh was hot, in every sense of the word. Trip stood back without saying a word and let the door open wide. Madison sloped in, smiling slyly, and kicked it shut behind her. Trip had found a couple of candles in a kitchen drawer and set them next to the sofa, but it was pretty dark. It was surreal to look out of the window and see . . . nothing. The sounds were different, too. Lots of sirens, and sporadic shouting. Not riot-level, scary shouting, but an alien sound nonetheless. And underneath it all, an almost eerie quiet rolled through. The buzz of the city had been stilled.

"Have you got glasses?"

He found two, and Madison poured and drank.

"Cheers. Here's to energy." She made everything sound dirty.

She threw herself down on the sofa, tossing one long leg across its arm, and patted the cushion next to her. "Come sit by me, Jackson Grayling the Third."

"That's pretty formal, don't you think?" But he sat down.

"Isn't it strange? We've been neighbors for, what is it, two years now, and we've never really done this."

"Sat in the dark together?"

"Spent time together. That's New York for you, isn't it? We all live on top of each other, but we never really get close." He had a flashback to something Emily had said on their first date. Madison was moving closer right now. He guessed she might get on top next. She wasn't exactly disguising her intentions for the evening. Madison was stepping things up a notch or two. She'd always been flirty but, to be honest, their schedules weren't all that compatible, and he rarely saw her around.

"New York's a crazy place."

"I know some stuff about you, though. By osmosis."

"What do you know, Madison?"

"Enough." She emptied her glass. "Candles are sexy, aren't they? Everyone looks gorgeous in candlelight." The way she said it implied that she looked gorgeous in everything from fluorescent down, and that it was kind of candlelight to bestow the same favor on the rest of the population just for the evening.

Trip knew what was on her mind, and it amused him. It also, he had to admit, revved him up a little, though his responses were a little dulled by the grass. And it was going to be a long night . . . He wasn't going to make it too easy for her, though. He wasn't going to tell her she was gorgeous, which was clearly exactly what she wanted. She was — in a kind of obvious, very Manhattan way. He knew enough about women to know she worked at it and that, to look that good all the time, she had to be a bit obsessed. He bet she went to the gym almost every day. He knew without looking that she'd be waxed and plucked and trimmed and painted in all the right places. She was the kind of girl who'd get up straight after sex to rush to the bathroom, and the kind of girl who liked to do it in front of mirrors. Not entirely his type except, loosely, by virtue of gender.

"Did you know that there is always a spike in the birthrate nine months after a blackout?"

He laughed. "I read that somewhere, too. What else are you going to do without *Deal or No Deal,* right? Although I never figured out why people can't find a condom with a flashlight."

"I don't think it's just boredom. I think the darkness brings something out in people. Something sort of primitive."

"Is that right?" This was bullshit, but he was, by now, mildly interested in where he thought it might be going.

"Don't you feel it, Trip?" She put her hand on his thigh, brazenly.

He laughed. "You're a real piece of work,

you know that?"

"I do know that, as a matter of fact." She shook her hair out, pushed her chest forward. Of course she did. She'd been hearing it for years. Trip didn't know why him, why tonight? Maybe it didn't matter. He hadn't historically put a lot of thought into much about his life; why overthink this? Just go with the flow.

"You never heard of the subtle art of seduction, Madison?"

"Hey — I can do subtle. I can practically do tantric, thanks very much. You just seemed like more of an obvious kind of a guy to me."

"You mean I'm too lazy for the more elaborate stuff?"

Madison didn't answer. She smiled. A little cat-that-got-the-cream smile. "Am I right?"

Once maybe. Definitely. Jackson was a little confused by his own reaction. This was the stuff of male magazine fantasy. Christ, this was the stuff of his own fantasies. Good-looking girl — great-looking girl, actually — power outage, sex on a plate, without even leaving the apartment or having to spin a line. He should be peeling the straps down on that top right now. Unwrapping the package that had been delivered right into his lap.

But he was still sitting here. The grass slowed him down, for sure, but there was something else, too. He was a bit too stoned to know what it was.

Madison put her glass down on the coffee table and in one stealthy movement, swung her leg around so that she was sitting across him. She took his glass from him and, leaning back, set it down next to hers. She did everything slowly and deliberately. She took his hands and put them on her tiny ass, grinding herself into his groin. "Question is, are you so lazy that you're going to make me do all the work myself?" She nipped at his bottom lip with her perfect white teeth, daring him, and arched her back so that her breasts brushed against him.

Okay, so he was only human. Trip thrust his hips upward, groaning softly, and pulled her into him, kissing her mouth, her face, her neck. He pulled the front of her top down with both hands. She wore no bra, and her rosy pink nipples grazed his cheeks. He sucked first one, then the other, into his mouth greedily. Madison pulled her top off, and he grabbed for her small round breasts as she fumbled with the buttons on his shirt, moaning lustfully as her fingers felt the soft hairs on his chest.

The weirdest thing happened. It had to be the weed. Trip was suddenly watching himself, from somewhere in the corner. He was minutes away, seconds away, from entering the babe who was Madison Cavanagh, thrusting himself into her wet, willing body. It would be fantastic, he knew. Madison knew what she was doing. She wasn't the first girl to throw herself at him, and she probably wouldn't be the last. He was good-looking, he was rich, he was easygoing. It had never been tough for him.

His first lover had been a counselor at a summer camp in Montana. He'd been fifteen and she'd been twenty-two. She'd led him into the seventh-grade bunk while everyone else was rehearsing the team cheer and given him something to really cheer about, and for the longest time afterward the smell of mildew and sunscreen gave him a hard-on. There had been an indecently long parade of willing partners ever since. Girls at college, of course. He had never gotten a bad reputation among the sororities, despite the roll call he notched up, because he always treated women kindly. He liked women, and that was the key. He was always pretty honest, and he was good. He knew he was because they told him. And they told each other. The girls weren't his favorites, though. Over the years there'd been a piano teacher, a professor, and once, because he could, his mother's shrink. Those older women had been the best. They were fantastic lovers, grateful and experienced. And they didn't want to hang out with him afterward; they never wanted to go to the movies or to dinner. They didn't want to tame him, hook him, or change him. They just wanted to fuck him.

Which was exactly what Madison Cavanagh apparently wanted to do right now, here in the darkness. And he didn't want it. What's more, he didn't think he actually could do it. He couldn't quite believe it. The point was . . . that there was no point. No point to this. It would just be sex. He didn't care about her at all. For the first time, that actually seemed to matter.

He stopped moving, and waited for Madison to realize that he had. She opened her eyes and looked at him quizzically. Her cheeks were grazed red by his stubble and her breathing was heavy.

"What's wrong?" She pushed her blond hair back from her face.

"I'm sorry." Was he really saying it? "I don't want this."

"What?"

"You're gorgeous, Madison. I just . . . I'm

not into this right now."

"Whoa! You seemed pretty damn into it about twenty seconds ago."

He didn't know what to say, so he shrugged, but he put one hand on her shoulder.

Madison, it seemed, thought it was worth one more try. She leaned forward and licked his ear. The whole gesture turned him off, and he pushed her away, a little less gently this time, with his hand.

Madison shook it off. "I did something wrong?"

"No. No. It's not that. Not at all."

"It's not about me, right?" Her voice was suddenly bitter. Wow — that was fast.

"Right. It really isn't."

She pulled her shirt across her chest, held it there with one arm, and pushed her hair back again. She laughed a small, sardonic laugh. "Well, that's a new one on me."

"I am really sorry. I should have said right away. Except I didn't know, right away."

Madison pulled herself off his lap and turned her back on him to pull her shirt on.

He watched her.

"Don't bother to explain. It's no big deal. It was a way to pass the time, that's all. Your loss, Trip."

"I don't doubt it."

She wasn't as tough as she was trying to sound, he knew that. But he also knew there was no way of salvaging the situation, making it less humiliating for her.

Was it Emily? It had to be Emily. These were uncharted waters for Trip, and he was more confused than anything else. He wished he were sober. And he was sorry. He shouldn't have let Madison get started on him. He'd known from the start, if he was honest with himself, what she was here for.

Madison was standing by the door now, tidying her hair self-consciously.

He went to her. "I really am sorry, Madison."

"Yeah. You should be. I'll see you around, Trip." She didn't want to make eye contact with him. He opened the door for her.

Emily was standing in the corridor with a small flashlight. Her blue eyes took in the scene in the faint light — Madison, disheveled, red-cheeked and half-naked, the buttons undone on Trip's shirt — and she looked at him with such a look.

"Hey, Emily." Madison made her voice sound light. "See you, Trip." She passed Emily and headed for the stairwell without looking at him, grateful for the interruption and desperate to get away. Emily stood still and stared at him, but he couldn't read her face.

"Emily?" His voice pleaded with her.

"Sorry." Why was she apologizing to him? She turned to follow Madison.

"Emily, please . . . Nothing happened."

She stopped and turned. "You don't answer to me for what you do."

But I want to, he thought. I want to.

And then she was gone, with her tiny beam of light, and he was left in the darkness.

VIOLET

Down on the fourth floor, Eve knocked on Violet's door, hoping she would find her home, and alone. Violet opened her door and pulled her in, closing the door behind her quickly.

"Thank God it's you, Eve. Come in at once. I was terrified you were going to be Hunter Stern, 'rescuing me' — he's a terrible chauvinist, at heart — and I'd have to spend an intolerable night talking psycho rubbish."

"I hope you don't mind. Ed's in Chicago."

"Mind? I'm delighted to have the company, lovely. Come on in."

Violet's apartment looked pretty; her

301

furnishings and artwork lent themselves to candlelight, somehow. There was, Eve had decided, something entirely Victorian about Violet in general, and this was her lighting. It wasn't that she was old-fashioned; in many ways, she seemed to Eve more with it than she was herself, despite her age. It was something more subtle than that. About a gentleness, a calm that was decidedly not twenty-first-century. Violet had candles burning on almost every surface — tall pillars in hurricane lamps, small votives in lacy white cups, elegant dinner candles in her silver candelabra.

Once Violet could see her more clearly, it was obvious that Eve had been crying. Her eyes were red-rimmed, and there was a flush on her chest.

"What's wrong? You've been crying. Are you all right?"

Eve nodded, embarrassed. "Ed and me . . . we had a stupid fight. On the phone."

"Sweetheart." Violet put an arm around Eve's shoulders, and Eve dropped her head into the crook of her friend's arm, grateful for the hug, and for the absence of questions. Violet gave her one gentle squeeze, then moved into the room.

"Looks like the set of *The Phantom of the Opera* in here, doesn't it?"

"I think it looks beautiful," Eve protested.

"Me, too. I'm drinking sloe gin. Can I tempt you?"

"God — sloe gin. Haven't had that in years . . . Do you know, Violet, sloe gin was the first thing I ever got drunk on."

"Fancy. Cider — that was me. Harvest Festival. Fell off a stack of hay and broke my wrist. My father nearly killed me."

"Well, that sounds very bucolic. Sloe gin was me, had no idea how strong it was, and I behaved very badly at a friend's twenty-first."

"And I behaved less than well at a church social." They both laughed. "So how about it? No one to behave badly with here, so we're perfectly safe. You'll take a glass?"

"I can't, Violet." She may as well tell her. She was nowhere near twelve weeks, of course. But Ed had said she wouldn't be able to keep the secret that long. And anyway, Violet wouldn't tell. She shrugged her shoulders and an excited grin broke out on her face.

"I'm actually pregnant."

"Darling girl. How wonderful! Come here!" Violet gave her a hug, and a kiss on both cheeks. "That was quick."

"Wasn't it? Ed's terribly proud of himself."

"I daresay he is!" She was pouring herself

303

a large glass, and she raised it in tribute to her friend. "I'll find you some barley water in a minute, but first I must toast this momentous news. To Ed and Eve, and their extraordinary fecundity. So how pregnant? When is this baby coming?"

"Beginning of March."

"Ages away."

"Yes, I know. It seems it, doesn't it? I'm only about five minutes pregnant, really."

"It's all happening in there, though, isn't it?" She pointed to Eve's tummy. "All that magic."

What a lovely way to put it. It was exactly how Eve saw it, she realized. Magical things were happening inside her. Magical, inexplicable, wonderful things.

Violet raised her own glass in a toast. "Congrats. Lovely. Come and sit down. No wonder Ed is worried about you." Violet took Eve's hand and held it in her lap briefly. "Just promise me something, Eve. Don't just have one, will you? Have more than one baby. Have lots of babies."

"I hope we will."

"Good, good. You do that." She squeezed Eve's hand once and released it.

Violet changed the subject then. She talked about the last big blackout. Hunter Stern had come in to rescue her, and they'd drunk a bottle of red wine each, and then had a fantastic row about psychology versus the stiff upper lip ("silly, pompous old fart") that got so loud Arthur downstairs had started banging on the ceiling with a broom handle and scared them half to death.

"I slept so soundly, I didn't even know the power was back on." She laughed. She told great stories — there was something almost theatrical in her performances — and Eve loved to listen. This one had taken her mind off Ed and the stupid argument.

Then they were both quiet for a while.

"You're a mysterious old bird, aren't you, Violet Wallace?"

"That I am. Imagine if I told you everything, all at once. Why would you bother to keep coming to see me?"

"Are you joking? I'd come because you're wonderful." Eve laughed. I'd come because you're the best friend I have in this place, she thought, and because I need you, but she was too shy to say it out loud.

"Wonderful and mysterious, you see. Deadly combination . . ."

Eve lay her head back on the sofa and closed her eyes for a moment. Violet felt a wave of tenderness for the girl — and a wave, straight after that, of surprise. It wasn't like her.

"Tell me how you came to be here, Violet."

"You don't want to hear all that. It's a very long story."

"Listen to me." She sat forward earnestly. "I'm missing *Grey's Anatomy.* I need to be entertained. Please tell me. I'd really love to hear it."

Violet rubbed her eyes, and Eve worried that she'd overstepped the mark.

"I mean, you don't have to, if you don't want to . . ."

Now Violet smiled kindly at Eve. "Are you kidding me? We oldies live for this. We just like to make you work for it. And since you're a captive of the blackout, I'm starting at the very, very beginning."

Violet put her glass down and folded her hands in her lap. Eve leaned back against the sofa cushions and curled her feet under her, ready to listen to Violet's story. The sound of her deep voice, with its familiar lilting accent, largely unchanged by her time in America, was comforting.

"So in true Dickensian style, let me get started. How is it you're supposed to do it? Ah yes! I was born. I was born during a thunderstorm in November nineteen twenty-nine, in the front bedroom of my parents' farm in Norfolk. Another difficult labor for my mother, a third disappointment

306

for my dad. My two sisters, Iris and Daisy, were four and two. I was supposed to be a boy, as they also ought to have been. A boy to help on the farm.

"Being helped on the farm was my father's obsession, you see. He'd been one of four sons, the youngest, born in nineteen hundred, just as the century turned. His father was the fourth generation of the Hill family at the farm. They could trace Hills in the village back to, oh, I don't know — forever. My grandmother had been a good wife and produced four strapping sons — Matthew, Paul, John, and Adam, my dad. She'd assured the farm for the next generation and died in the process — giving birth to my father. It wasn't uncommon in those days. No doctors, no drugs, no hospital for most people. I don't know much about how my father was raised — not much beyond a few dates and the odd story — and I can't imagine what it must have been like for my grandfather. Four young boys and forty acres. I know he drank — and that how much he drank and what he did when he was drinking made my father a lifelong teetotaler. That's why he was so cross when I got drunk on the cider at the Harvest Festival when I was twelve. I know there was a second wife — Mabel — but I have no idea what happened to her. They were both dead before I was born. She didn't ever sound like a stepmother — of the wicked or any other kind. More like a drinking companion for my grandfather. They pretty much drank themselves to death, I reckon. I think the boys — my dad included — had a bloody tough life, doing the lion's share of the work on the farm. Until the war.

"Matthew and Paul joined up straightaway. John was conscripted eventually. My dad was too young to fight. He'd been born in nineteen hundred, you remember, and the war was over before lads his age were conscripted. Too young for the first one, too old for the second. Lucky devils, that lot. Except that I think not going to war had a legacy of its own. He stayed behind and ran the farm — first with John, and then pretty much alone. Waiting. For his brothers to come home, or to be called to join them himself, if the war lasted long enough. He was just a child — thirteen years old when war broke out. Not much of a childhood up until then, and by the time the fighting started, what little there had been must have come to an abrupt end. None of them were very old, mind you. Matthew was nineteen, I think; Paul eighteen. Not much more than

kids. Full of bravado, no doubt. That whole
'We'll be back before Christmas' nonsense,
I expect. Well, they weren't back before
Christmas — none of them. Matthew was
killed in early nineteen fifteen. They never
got a body for burial, or full details of what
happened, but it was Gallipoli. Paul was
home by the end of nineteen sixteen, burned
and blinded at the Somme, just as John was
called up. John lost a leg immediately after
the Armistice was signed, and died of blood
poisoning somewhere along the way home.
A whole family almost wiped out."

"My God — that's awful."

"You can't imagine it now, can you? It
wasn't just them. It would have been almost
every farm in the valley, every village in the
county . . . a generation, pretty much. The
numbers were huge. Nearly a quarter of a
million killed at Gallipoli. Not far off half a
million at the Somme. Bloody terrible."

Violet stopped talking. Eve didn't know
what to say.

"I think I'll have another glass of gin, actually." Violet went to the sideboard and filled
her glass.

"Do you know, it really is unimaginable,
isn't it? Pointless. Such a waste."

"Utterly."

"How did your father take it, do you

think? I mean, did he talk about it much?"

Violet snorted. "Never. Talking about it is a bit of a modern phenomenon, I think. Men like my father didn't talk about much on that level."

Eve thought of her own father and his inability to talk about their mother after she died — how she and Cath had talked and cried alone while he sat downstairs, not watching the television and smoking cigarettes.

"But I think it was Matthew's death that hit him hardest. Matthew was the oldest, and I think he'd been a father figure of sorts. He was the luckiest one, in a way. What killed Matthew killed him fast. The war killed John and Paul as well, it just took longer. And it changed my father forever. I always think it was like he got his heart so badly broken by all of that, he never recovered. I don't think he was capable, after the war took or changed everyone he loved, of being kind, or gentle — or of really loving properly. No mother at all, no father to speak of. He was just . . . He was hard.

"I remember my uncle Paul. He died when I was about seven years old. I never stopped being scared of him. His eyes were terrifying — milky white and opaque. They moved constantly — flickering and unseeing. The burns were bad — huge, ugly pink and shiny welts across one side of his face and neck, disappearing into his shirt collar. He had no whiskers. I knew they went all the way down his left side, those horrid marks. His lungs had been burned, too, and he coughed and spluttered and wheezed. You could hear him at night. But his eyes were the worst part. He wasn't much older than my dad, but he was always an ancient old man to me — hideous and frightening. I can remember my mum trying to get me to talk to him. He sat, always, in the corner of the big kitchen we had, in a rocking chair. He must have sat there for fifteen years, coughing and not seeing and waiting to die. 'Show your uncle Paul your doll,' she'd say, or, 'Why don't you read your book to your uncle Paul, tell him what the pictures are?' He'd nod his head and put his hands out towards the sound of my voice. But those eyes never stopped still, and I couldn't go near him."

Eve looked at Violet, more than eighty years old, sitting across from her, and tried to imagine the little girl, frightened of her invalid uncle.

"I think his brother Paul was pretty much the only person my dad showed kindness to. At least in front of me. He cared for Paul like he was a child. My dad was gruff and matter-of-fact about it, but if you watched him, watched the two of them together, he could be tender, too, with his brother. It was like Paul was all he had left. Even though we were there. If I sound like I feel sorry for him, then that's what fifty years of reflection will do for you. Believe me, I didn't always feel that way. For years, I hated him. You'd be amazed at what I found a way to blame on him."

"When did he die?"

"Not until nineteen seventy-six. But I hadn't seen him for years before that. He sold the farm in the sixties and went into a nursing home. He had emphysema at the end, I think."

"I'm sorry. Did you and he have a falling out?"

Violet snorted. "We never fell in." She shook her head, as though she realized she'd missed a big chunk of the story and was re-arranging her thoughts. "So, at the end of the war, there he was, left with a farm, drunken parents, an invalid brother, and this obsession with having help on the farm. I honestly think that's the only reason he married my mother. Why she married him, I've never understood. He was a good-looking bugger, I'll say that for him. Perhaps she had a fatal attraction for tough nuts or thought she could change him. I don't know. We never talked about it. You didn't, then. You just got on with it. Not like today, when we feel compelled to talk about everything and keep Hunter Stern and his like in red wine.

"Oh, but he was a mean bastard. I don't remember him ever giving any of us, my mother included, a cuddle or a kiss. God knows how three of us were conceived. I never saw one single moment of affection pass between them. I never saw him hold her hand or stroke her hair or even touch her. He never hit her. But he never showed her any love either."

"What happened to your mum?"

"She died when I was about fifteen. Her death certificate said cancer, but I always think of it as death by shrinking. She shrank and shrank, the whole way through my childhood. She got smaller and thinner and paler and weaker, in front of our eyes. Like a plant, you know? She was never tended, and she died. At the end, she was lying in her bed, the bed we'd all been conceived in, born in, where she'd lain beside my father for years and years, and it was like there was a doll tucked under the covers. It may have been cancer that finally did it, but I'm convinced the process had begun years earlier. She died of neglect, and a broken heart." Violet's voice had become small, and she was staring into the fireplace.

"And so that's what you blamed your dad for?"

"My dad. My sisters. Myself."

"But it wasn't your fault."

"I always felt I should have saved her. I loved her like nothing on earth. It wasn't enough."

"That's a terrible pressure to put on yourself, Violet. Especially as a young girl. She was ill. People get ill. Clearly, from what you say, she wasn't happy. But that wasn't down to you. Any more than the cancer was. And that doesn't kill you."

Violet shook her head. "You're right, I suppose." And then she was quiet for a moment.

Eve wondered whether Violet had had enough, whether she should say something else — lighten the mood. Or tell her about her own mother, dead at forty-two. But she wanted Violet to tell her more.

"So. Exit mother stage right. Enter husband stage left." Violet laughed. "I'm more of a cliché than I'd like to be, I'm afraid. Classic escape strategy. We couldn't get out fast enough. Daisy was already married by the time mum died, to some dough-faced boy she'd met at school, who couldn't go to war because he'd had a club foot or some such. And Iris went off to be a nurse, down to London, first chance she got. Everyone was after deserting the farm and my father again, which did nothing to improve the lousy mood he'd been in for twenty years. I honestly think he thought they shot the bloody archduke in Sarajevo in nineteen fourteen and that Hitler invaded Poland in 'thirty-nine just to mess up his sodding farm and leave him with all the work. One big worldwide conspiracy to keep him up to his neck in barley and beets."

"And you? Were you his land girl?"

"Only until I could get the hell out of there, too."

"And how did you do that?"

"I married a Yank, my darling. I married a Yank. That, lovely girl, is the very, very long-winded account of how I ended up on the boat that brought me here in 'forty-seven."

"Wow! You were a war bride."

"See? I told you I was a cliché. One hundred thousand odd of us from England alone, I think. Thousands more from Australia, all over . . ."

"That's not a cliché. That's utterly fascinating."

"Do you think so?"

"Absolutely. And incredibly romantic."

"You're getting ahead of yourself. Not so sure I'd go that far."

"So tell me then. Who was he?"

Violet smiled. It crossed her mind briefly that Eve was just humoring her, but then she watched the girl stretch her legs and re-curl them into a new position, her head comfortable against a pillow. She seemed to really want to know.

"His name was Gus Campbell. Gus. Could he have sounded more American?"

Eve laughed.

"He was from Elizabeth, New Jersey. Twenty-four years old when I met him, twenty-five when we were married. Six foot two inches, built like a brick outhouse. He had so much hair. American men do, have you noticed? Big thick shocks of hair. Must be the diet. Gus's was strawberry blond, and his eyebrows were so blond they were practically invisible. He was pale and freckly. He could get a sunburn on a cloudy day, that man. He always had these extraordinary lines on him, in the summer — angry red meets translucent white. On his neck, his arms. Even where his socks went. Like a human zebra."

"How did you two meet?"

"We all found a way, during the war. It's true what they say — it was different then. It was actually wonderfully exciting. Not if you were in the thick of it, I don't suppose, and getting the bombs and all that, but to be truthful, we didn't have any of that. We had rationing and shortages and GIs. The 'overpaid, oversexed, and over here' kind. With their big shoulders and their big voices and their big country back home, where they weren't so severely rationed or sand-bagged or bombed. Sounded like bloody Oz to us. You always hear about the silk stockings and the chocolate and things, and that was true, they did have that sort of thing. But what they also had, which was far more exciting than a square of Hershey's or a block of mascara, was this . . . this at-titude. Invincibility. Like all Englishmen were in black-and-white and these guys burst in in glorious Technicolor, you know? They were gorgeous, and we were pretty shamelessly moths to the flame. And there was this kind of . . . frisson in the air, all the time. I suppose it was the carpe diem stuff. You never knew what was coming. It gave us all a bit of recklessness. A now-or-never attitude. And after umpteen years of being stuck on that farm, I was more than ripe for a bit of recklessness."

"I understand." Eve nodded.

"So they would come into town. To the pub and the tea shop and the newsagent. It was funny how people reacted to them. The older ones were pretty much against. Everyone under twenty-five was wildly excited. Girls in particular, of course."

"Was it love at first sight?"

"Oh, my God, Eve, you are a soppy blighter. Not at all. Lust maybe. He was huge. I liked that first of all. Huge and strong. And so blond. Like a big Viking or something!" She laughed at herself.

Eve joined in. "A Viking!"

"Yeah. Not quite the rape-and-pillage type. A slap-and-tickle Viking!"

"So was it quick?"

"By standards then, yes. Everything went a bit faster in the war. By today's, not so much. People seem to get married so quickly now. Before they can even begin to really, really know each other. I think that's because they know now how easy it is for them to walk away. You don't need to be sure anymore, because nothing is meant to be forever."

"But you were sure?"

"Is anyone ever completely sure?"

"I think I was. I couldn't imagine not marrying Ed. Not being with him. He felt like . . . the person I was meant to be with. On my wedding day, I was definitely sure. I don't think I could have done it if I wasn't. It's such a big thing — a church wedding. All those people, and the vicar, and . . . God."

"Well, that's one difference. I didn't have to be sure in front of a congregation. I only had to be sure in front of two witnesses. And I don't believe God was there. Not then, not now, and never in between either. I was sure of something — that he was my ticket out. I was sure of that. Did I love him? I wanted to. I loved what he stood for. I think I thought I loved him. I fancied him, for sure. He was the first boy I ever properly kissed — you know, the knee-trembling kind of kiss. He was older than me, and he knew a little more what he was doing. I still remember the smell of him. He smelled different — clean and . . . something else. He smelled prosperous."

"Was he rich then?"

"Lord, no. It may have seemed that way to me then. He was better off than my family and most of the people I'd grown up knowing. I don't mean that. His family ran a small building company in New Jersey. They were okay."

"How quickly did you get married?"

"I met him in 'forty-four, outside the cinema in Norwich. We'd been to see Cary Grant in *Arsenic and Old Lace* — the Sunday matinee. He had his uniform on. I always had a bit of a thing for a uniform. Still do, frankly. Watch me walk past a fire station sometime. My friend Joan had met his friend John before. They got talking, and so we did, too. We were big on foursomes. I liked his accent. I guess he saw something in me that he liked. I wasn't a bad-looking broad, in those days."

You could see that. Even at eighty-two years old, Violet was a handsome woman. She must have been really good-looking when she was younger.

"It went from there. You made a date. You met up. Always the four of us, Joan and John, Gus and me. That was about it, in those days. It wasn't as if you got to see a huge amount of each other. He was on the base. I was on the farm, and that was bloody hard work, I tell you. We weren't playing at it like Marie Antoinette. We wrote to each other. Nothing worth reading, I don't think."

"No long, poetic love letters?"

Violet smiled. "Not at all. More like notes that should have been conversations. You know — the basics about each other.

Getting-to-know-you stuff."

"Did your dad like him?"

"Who knows? Gus wrote to him, early on, asking permission to write to me, I think, but I don't think Dad ever bothered to reply to that. And he came out to the farm only once. They didn't talk much. I remember Gus saying he wasn't going to bother to ask him for his blessing on the two of us marrying. He said he didn't think it would honestly help much. I loved him for that."

"Wasn't your dad at your wedding?"

"No. He kept on working. Neither of us had anyone from our families there. That was how we wanted it. I didn't want my old life butting in on my new one. My friend Joan stood up for me. He had John. It was nineteen forty-six. They were shipping out. We had to fix it up fast. Raid everyone's clothing coupons to get a decent suit to wear. We didn't have a cake, or anything like that. Just a nice tea, in the fanciest hotel in Norwich, the four of us.

"I think Gus would have preferred to marry at his home, in New Jersey, and I know his mother was always sad she hadn't been there, but they wouldn't let you go, you know, unless you were actually married. No fiancées allowed. In case the blokes changed their minds, I suppose. John did.

321

He said he was going home to fix things up for Joan — back to Sacramento. We had such plans, Joan and I. We had no idea, really, how far Sacramento, California, was from Elizabeth, New Jersey. Who knew, then, how big this country was? Six months at the most, he swore. He promised to come back from California for Joan, but he never did. Poor Joan. She ended up marrying a milkman called Colin, in Coronation year. Not sure she ever got over it.

"But not me. I was married by then. Mrs. Gus Campbell. I was on my way. But hearts and flowers — not exactly. You'd be amazed how institutionalized the whole process was. I suppose it had to be, there were so many of us."

"How do you mean?"

"Organized. The men were mostly gone, by the time we got to go. We couldn't go privately. You couldn't fly, of course, in those days, and there were no ships. Except ships the government ran. Just to move us. The *Queen Mary,* the SS *Argentina* . . . I went on the *Queen Elizabeth.* It was a major palaver. Gus's family had to vouch for me — say they'd look after me, and all that. You had to have all your papers in order — birth certificate, marriage certificate. A ring and a prayer wasn't enough. You had to prove you were kosher, and that there was a real man waiting for you in New York. I had to go to London. I took the train on my own from Norwich — I'd never done such a thing before — to the U.S. embassy, to fill in all the forms and things. I'd only been once before — with my mother. She took us down for King George's coronation — me and my sisters. My dad was furious, but she said it was important. In my memory it was a colorful place — spick-and-span — and glamorous. It was really shocking to be there in 'forty-six. It seemed like everything was gray and broken and ruined.

"They gave us medicals and vaccinations. You could have felt quite offended, if you'd wanted. Years later I read about Ellis Island — about how it was for all the immigrants who'd gone before me — and what happened to us didn't seem too bad, but at the time . . . Well, you weren't used to being poked and prodded. I never have got used to it, frankly.

"Then there was an army camp. More physicals. It was quite comforting — there being so many others like you. I met a couple of girls from near home, and we hooked up. One was going to Texas. I don't remember where the other one was headed. We stuck together and had a laugh. Had my first cigarette at that camp."

"You don't smoke, Violet."

"Did, though. Forty years or so. Till it stopped being fun. All that gloom-and-doom talk."

"And then what?"

"Then we took the train to the ship. The *Queen Elizabeth*."

"As in the cruise ship?"

"Yes. Except it had been adapted for us. I never heard of a cruise ship where you slept ten to fifteen girls in the one room."

"Like a dorm of brides."

"Brides and kids. A lot of the girls were already pregnant or had babies by the time they got on those ships."

"I can't imagine what it must have been like."

"Noisy, excited. Not a scrap of privacy. Pretty disgusting, if you were seasick. Fortunately for me, I have the constitution of an ox — never even felt queasy once. Lots of the girls were nervous, not just seasick. I think there were more than a few second thoughts."

"Not you, though?"

"Not a one. I stood on that deck like Kate Winslet on the *Titanic,* with my arms wide open, willing it forward into my new life."

"What about your sisters?"

"Was I sorry I was leaving them behind? Not really. They'd both gone, by then, hadn't they? It was every girl for herself, once my poor mum died. And I didn't give my father a second thought. I don't suppose I gave Gus as many thoughts as I should have. I just couldn't wait to get there, and get on. A new life in a new country. I couldn't wait."

"Wait a minute. What did you say his name was? Gus what?"

"Gus Campbell."

"Not Wallace."

"No, not Wallace."

"So the Wallace is . . . ?"

"My second husband. But that's not for tonight. I'm parched now. And you've listened long enough. Maybe you should tell me some thing about you."

"It won't be remotely as interesting."

"It will be to me."

The power came on at 10:30 p.m. The glare of lights and the glow of televisions found them all in unfamiliar states. The residents of the building who'd been elsewhere when the blackout came started to make their way home.

Maria Piscatella resumed making chicken cacciatore and hoped Ernest hadn't been

325

stuck in a hot, airless subway car this whole time. Hunter Stern drained the bottle of red wine he'd had no business opening but had, in memory of the 2003 blackout and the best row he'd had in ages — the one he'd picked with Violet Wallace next door, a formidable and worthy opponent — and looked over his case notes for tomorrow's appointments. Todd and Greg, who'd made it home and resorted happily enough to the oldest diversion in the book, pulled on their Missoni robes and wandered into the kitchen, postcoitally ravenous. Jason Kramer grabbed the remote control for the television, flicking between an episode of *CSI* and CNN coverage of the power outage, grateful still that Kim and Avery were out on Long Island.

Eve dozed peacefully on Violet's sofa. As she walked softly around, blowing out candles, Violet looked at her from time to time and smiled. She didn't want to wake her. She liked having this girl here. It was strange, spending the evening in the twentieth century, in her past. She didn't remember the last time she'd spoken about her father, or thought about Gus.

Jackson sat on the sofa where he'd been all evening, trying to make sense of what had happened. Below him Madison and

326

Emily both lay in bed, each feeling humiliated and embarrassed, Emily berating
herself for believing that Jackson Grayling
the Third could be different, might be
special. The internal monologue of whether
or not to go up and see him had raged for
the first ninety minutes of the blackout. She
wished she hadn't listened to the voice that
sent her. She'd been right, from the beginning. Now, at least, she knew.

And Charlotte emerged from the elevator,
hot, tired, and stiff, but elated. She thought
she might have a plan now.

■ ■ ■ ■

AUGUST

■ ■ ■ ■

JACKSON

What was he doing? August in New York? This was a first. He should be out in the Hamptons now. Not here. He should be messing around with his friends, on Jet Skis and boats. Board shorts and Topsiders. Drinking beers and tequila shots, and eating lobster rolls. Building bonfires and making out with whichever pretty girl he ended up with at the end of the night, in whichever bed was nearest. Sleeping until noon, and not going to bed before dawn.

That was the pattern of his summers.

And what had been wrong with that? What was he doing here? Sweating in a button-down and chinos, listening to his mother complain about the heat of the city.

Martha was fanning herself furiously with a Spanish lace fan and debating whether to move tables. "There's more shade there. Shall we move?"

"Whatever."

"Thank God your father isn't here. He'd be in a foul temper. He likes his heat with an ocean breeze, and there isn't a puff of wind in this city today."

Exactly. That was why he'd asked for an audience with his mother. He knew that his father might be the head of the family but that his mother was the neck.

"You look nice." She stopped fanning for a moment and looked him up and down. "Very nice."

A Ralph Lauren pastel button-down shirt and chinos had been his mother's idea of a good look for him since he was two years old. He hadn't had to think too hard about what to put on today. He'd just had to shop for it; he hadn't owned either since she'd stopped shopping for him. Clean-shaven and neatly combed, too, he knew he was looking exactly the part of the dutiful son he wanted to convince her he was.

"This was a nice surprise, I must say, Trip. When you called, I thought you'd be calling from one of those trashy house shares you will insist on doing out in the Hamptons. I did not expect to see you in person. That was a very nice surprise. And looking so good, too."

But this wasn't about Martha. Was it all about Emily? He wasn't even sure of that

332

anymore. Something had changed. Something had shifted in him. Because he'd met Emily. She'd spun his world and the way he viewed it, and it was still spinning, and he wasn't as comfortable as he had been with how it looked. He wanted to see it, see himself, differently. He wanted Emily to see him differently. Not that he would tell his mother *any* of that, of course . . .

That meant a job.

It seemed Emily had changed everything for him — a woman he barely knew. In a way, Trip felt like he'd been hypnotized, and that Emily had been the one who snapped her fingers and woke him up. He'd been sleepwalking and now he was awake. Awake and alive. It was a mystery to him, but he felt powerless in the face of his feelings. Emily had no idea.

No idea at all what she'd done.

He needed his mother now.

CHARLOTTE

It was the hottest night of the summer — it had to be. Charlotte couldn't sleep. Romance novels usually sent her quickly enough into swooningly sweet dreams, but she wasn't reading romance novels anymore. She hadn't read one since the night she'd been trapped in the elevator with Che. The stack of titles she usually kept by her bed — new volumes and old favorites — had been moved to the floor by the bedside cabinet, replaced by her new reading material.

She'd started the next day. She'd thought of it in bed, and been too excited by the idea to sleep that night. She'd gone into work early to use the computer to google everything she wanted to know. What did people do before Google?

The Rosetta Stone program she'd ordered had arrived within the week. She'd chosen that method because it promised the quickest results. She'd checked out some books from the library, too. Conversational Spanish. An English-to-Spanish dictionary.

She'd learned some Spanish at school. She'd never been very good at it, nor especially interested, as a child. She'd have preferred to learn French. Even then, she'd dreamed of Paris, most romantic city in the world. But they didn't offer French at her high school. Just Spanish.

And some of it had come back quickly. She'd be able to order drinks and tapas, or book tickets on a ferry. Find the cathedral, and introduce her brother. All that useless high school stuff they taught you. What she needed was a bit different.

She knew that people who wanted to stop smoking or become more assertive or lose weight sometimes listened to hypnosis tapes overnight — that the messages entered their brain subconsciously while they slept. So she played her Rosetta Stone disks at night, through her headphones, for a while. She slept on her stomach, though, and they kept slipping forward and off her head, so she abandoned that. She wore headphones to and from work and on her long weekend walks — her one concession to this city's obsession with fitness — and while she did her ironing, repeating the words and phrases over and over again. She worried about her accent; she couldn't roll her *r*s, and she thought her *th* sound was all wrong. But lots of vocabulary came flooding back, and some of the grammar, too.

She had an almost friend, Samantha, at the library, who was married to an Ecuadorian and spoke fluent Spanish. Charlotte practiced on her sometimes, at lunchtimes, and wondered when she would be brave enough to speak in Spanish to Che.

It wasn't good enough just to start saying *Hola* and *Adiós* and *Cómo está usted,* though. That would come across as patronizing. She wanted to be able to really talk to him. She daydreamed of a moment when she'd come out of the elevator, or he'd hold the door open for her when she got home, and she'd just start speaking — a joke, or a humorous story — and he'd be amazed and delighted. She'd be funny, in Spanish.

Lovers did that. They were dedicated to their cause. All the great lovers of literature. Ali MacGraw was wrong. Or her script was. Love didn't mean never having to say you were sorry. What a ridiculous line that was. Only a man could have written that. She hadn't much direct experience, admittedly, but she'd had a father and a brother, and she'd watched, and read about a thousand couples over the years, and she knew that men just plain didn't like to say sorry. That was why Erich Segal wrote that nonsensical line. To get generations of men off the hook on the apology front. Love meant sacrifice and suffering and dedication. Lovers conquered. They overcame adversity. They moved mountains. They learned to speak Spanish.

The first time she saw Che after the power outage, she'd been disappointed to hear them revert to their old cordial relationship. There'd been no lingering glances. No accidental touch of his hand when he was handing over a package that had been delivered for her. Neither of them referred to the evening. And the next time, and the time after that, you almost couldn't tell that anything extraordinary had happened between them. But she knew differently. Each frustratingly mundane encounter strengthened her resolve. She would learn, and they would speak, and then, over the years, the night in the elevator would become the stuff of their own legend, told and retold, embellished, perhaps, but just as romantic for all that.

VIOLET

Up on the transformed roof, Eve and Violet sank gratefully onto the teak bench and took great gulps from the big glasses of lemonade they'd carried from Violet's apartment. The ice had quickly melted, but the drinks were still vaguely cool. It was still hot, although it was late in the afternoon now.

It had been hot all week. The newscasters kept telling them it was ten degrees above the seasonal norm, sounding smugly excited from their air-conditioned studios. Things were supposed to be cooling off now, but they showed no sign of doing so. It was hotter than July had been. Eve couldn't wait for the fall. The humidity was exhausting at the best of times. When you were pregnant, it was almost intolerable. Her ankles were swollen already; she hadn't expected things like that until much later. And the tiredness . . . It was debilitating. Some mornings, she never made it out of bed at all. And even if she did, exhaustion would sometimes strike without warning — while she was shopping or walking through the park or talking to Ed. Heavy, instant, extraordinary fatigue that demanded she stop whatever she was doing and curl up on her bed. Sleep would come immediately; she could feel it rolling over her like a wave. She was sleeping with just a sheet these days, it was so hot. The apartment had air conditioners — huge noisy machines that obliterated the views in all the rooms — but she hated their rattling, whirring din and switched them off. It seemed to irritate Ed; he came in every evening soaked in sweat from the subway, pulling at his tie and top button, exasperated at the heat in the apartment. But she couldn't have them on when she was home. And she was home a lot. Sleeping. She always woke up from these daytime slumbers hot and sweaty, usually with a headache. Ed went to Bed Bath & Beyond and bought old-fashioned fans. Quieter, but much less efficient — they stirred the sweltering air a little, but didn't really alleviate the problem.

It was a good thing he was away so much right now. She felt about as interesting as a carrot. She didn't want to talk to him when he came home at night, and she didn't want to share the sofa with him. She wanted to stretch out her full length and watch *CSI* without speaking. It was all she had the energy to do. His bulk in the bed beside her during the night made her hotter. She felt bad about it, and she hoped it would pass. Too often, when he was home, she was crabby or he was short with her. Five minutes in, and they were both irritated. He'd come home, after the blackout, contrite and apologetic. They had kissed and hugged, and peace had been restored, but neither of the causes of the row had fundamentally changed. She was still needy. He was still neglectful. She wanted more from him than he was giving. So she let a little part of her shut down, close off from him.

She concentrated on herself. And the bump. And the sleep . . .

Days could go by when Eve spoke to no one. She thought, sometimes, that she was forgetting how to make small talk. The other day, she'd been up on the roof, and Charlotte had been there. The two of them had sat awkwardly together for a short while.

Charlotte was listening to headphones, reading a book. It looked like a language tape. She'd stopped, embarrassed, when Eve had arrived, although Eve had protested that she shouldn't.

"Learning Spanish?" Eve had glanced at the book Charlotte was reading.

"Yes." Charlotte said it as though she'd been caught doing something wrong.

"Good for you. I was rubbish at languages at school. Never tried Spanish. We did French, German, and Latin for extra torture. I was crap at all three of them, I'm afraid. How's it going?"

So she'd tried, but the conversation had been stilted. Eve blamed herself.

As she was leaving, her tapes and books stuffed into her New York Public Library tote, Charlotte smiled at the rise of Eve's stomach behind the cotton blouse.

"You're having a baby, aren't you?" Charlotte said. "I hope you don't mind my asking."

"Not at all," Eve replied, grateful for a subject area.

"How is it?"

"Tiring, nauseating, a bit scary, wonderful. All of those."

"It sounds wonderful."

For a second, Eve wondered whether

Charlotte was being sarcastic, but decided that she didn't think so.

"I think it's the most fantastic thing."

"You'd like children yourself, someday?"

"Oh, yes. Two or three. I've always wanted them, you know?"

Eve nodded. Shrugged her shoulders. "Me, too." She hoped she didn't sound smug. If she'd offended Charlotte, she couldn't tell. Charlotte looked like she was daydreaming. And then she'd hurried off.

Violet had no truck with Eve's self-imposed hibernation. She showed up, invited or not, two or three times a week and dragged her off the sofa. She always came armed with a plan. They would have lunch at the Met and wander around the Baroque tapestry exhibit, or tea in the Bemelmans Bar at the Carlyle. Dim sum in Chinatown, or a cupcake at the Magnolia Bakery in the West Village. Eve came to expect her, and to look forward to Violet's coming.

Violet never seemed like a much older woman. Eve's early pregnancy slowed her down to the extent that Violet often seemed younger and fitter. They took cabs to and from wherever they went, Violet declaring that subway use was a pursuit of limited appeal, best enjoyed out of summer. And they spent many hours sitting in sidewalk cafés, drinking lemonade and talking.

Today they'd been to the River Club with an old friend of Violet's who lived in the vast, grand building all the way over on the East River. It was a club, but it was an apartment building, too; Eve could only imagine how grand those homes must be. But there was something gently dated about the whole place. It had been like going back in time, to the 1930s. They'd swum in the tiny art deco tiled pool, the older ladies wearing Esther Williams floral swim caps, changed in the small cubicles with chintz curtains, attendants fluttering around them, and had club sandwiches and iced tea, served by a waiter in a spotless white uniform, under umbrellas in the beautiful private garden. Violet's friend Cynthia had clearly been, in her heyday, a New York society scion, and Eve had listened, entranced, to her stream of gossip and scandal. She didn't know any of the characters involved, but Cynthia's telling was fascinating nonetheless. Eventually, though, she had dozed off as Violet and Cynthia talked, waking only when Cynthia gently touched her shoulder with one immaculately manicured hand. She'd been embarrassed and had begun apologizing, but Cynthia had raised a hand in imperious protest.

"Darling girl! I slept through all six of my pregnancies. And at least one of the conceptions, so far as I recall." She winked. "Nothing to apologize for."

They were home now. Eve shucked off her sandals and wiggled her hot toes against the decking. "I'm so glad we did this! It's like a little oasis in the urban jungle."

"Me, too. Feels like it was just for us, though, doesn't it?"

"I think we're the late afternoon crew. I know Todd and Gregory come out here late at night; they were talking about it in the elevator the other day. And I think Milena brings Rachael's kids out here in the mornings sometimes. I've heard them up here, playing."

"It's much lovelier than I ever thought it would be."

"We should have a party — a terrace christening."

"Great idea."

"Can we do it before this nice weather disappears?"

"Can't see why not. I think only the usual suspects will show up anyhow. Can't imagine the Stewarts gracing us with their presence. Or Arthur, unless he bursts in a with a pair of secateurs and deblooms all the flowers."

"Is he really all that bad?"

"Worse. I've no time for him at all."

"Has he ever been married?"

Violet laughed. "Good Lord, no. Pity the woman who fell for him. You'd have to be a masochist. No, Arthur Alexander is simply one of life's deeply unpleasant people."

Eve wondered if anyone was that black-and-white. It seemed to her that life was much grayer than it used to be; she was emphatic about much less these days. For some reason, she didn't believe Arthur Alexander was all bad.

Violet had moved on. "Better plan it for after Labor Day. Maybe the weekend after next?"

"It was fun today. Thanks for taking me. Cynthia's a hoot."

"She certainly is."

"Does she really have six children?"

"Five now. Lost a boy in Vietnam. And, at the last count, twelve grandchildren and a few greats, I think. A veritable tribe. Doubt she could name half of them — the greats, that is. I daresay she knows her own children."

Eve giggled. "That's terrible."

"There are compensations. She's not the sit-on-my-lap-and-I'll-read-you-a-story sort of granny. But she is the trust-fund, college-tuition-paid, mansion-on-Nantucket kind of granny. I expect that's been enough for them."

"Wow. Six children! I can't even imagine having that many."

"And always a brace of nannies. Cynthia wasn't nearly so hands-on as I expect you'll be. Too busy, and altogether too grand, bless her."

"How do you two come to be friends?"

"She was a client of my husband's. In the fifties and sixties. We used to go to 'dos.' Dinner dances, that sort of thing. We liked each other a lot. I think I was a novelty for her; she was born and bred in Manhattan society. I still remember the first time I met her. We were in line at the same do. Waldorf Astoria. In its heyday — when it was one of the very best hotels. I had the only cloth coat in the ladies' cloakroom, and a drugstore lipstick to reapply in the bathroom. Not because my husband wouldn't have bought me nice things. I think he would have got me anything I wanted, bless him. I just wasn't that way inclined. I carried on the way I always had before I married him. No furs, no Elizabeth Arden. That tickled her."

"We're talking second husband, I presume?"

Violet winked. "Have you been taking notes?"

"Well, it doesn't sound like she could have been a 'client' of Gus's. Gus had customers, right?"

She smiled. "She wasn't."

"But before you get to the second one, you've got to tell me about the first one. I haven't forgotten. We left you on the prow of the bride ship, listening to Céline Dion singing 'My Heart Will Go On.' "

Violet laughed. "Don't you have to take a nap, or make dinner for your poor neglected husband?"

"Neglected husband? That's rich! Nope. Ed's got a late meeting, with drinks. Won't be back for ages." Don't care if he is, she added, only to herself. I'd rather be with you right now. "And I feel strangely awake today. You've got time for a couple of decades, I'm thinking. I might just get you to the present day by the time this baby comes!"

"You remind me of me and my sisters, sitting around the radio listening to Saturday serials."

"I love listening to your stories."

"Bless you."

"Really. I do. I want to know about Gus. Please." Eve stuck out her bottom lip and looked at Violet sideways, from under her eyelashes. Violet smiled and slapped her friend's knee gently.

"All right, all right. Do you know, it sometimes seems to me that that time, the years of my first marriage, didn't even happen. It is so long ago, and I carry with me almost nothing of it. I wasn't even the same person. It's like it happened to someone else, you know?"

"He was waiting for you, though? When the ship docked?"

"He was waiting for me. So were his mother, his grandmother, and his three sisters."

"Blimey. That must have been pretty intimidating."

"Terrifying. They all spoke at once. More like screeched, actually. They had his New Jersey accent, only more so, and at a higher-pitched decibel level. It was pretty overwhelming."

"And Gus?"

Violet smiled. "Gus was different. Out of uniform, back on his home turf. A familiar refrain, I daresay."

"They're all a bit different, aren't they, once you take off your rose-colored spectacles."

Violet looked at her sharply, but when Eve

347

didn't add anything, she carried on. "You've got to remember, we hardly knew each other. Not really. I'm sure you don't want details, but suffice to say we'd had a wedding night, in Norwich, but that was it. And that had been pretty disastrous. Maybe disastrous is a bit harsh. But it hadn't given me a lot to live on, during the time apart and the voyage over. And I don't think I'd realized quite how it was going to be. I mean, I'd known we'd be living with his family, to begin with at least, but I imagined it would be short-term — that he'd be as keen as I was to get our own place. I wanted to have my own home — make my own rules. Do my own thing."

Eve nodded. She was remembering her beloved cottage and the incredibly intoxicating feeling of owning it, back at the beginning.

"That first night, we went back to Gus's parents' house. The rest of the family was all there — not just immediate. Gus seemed to have three hundred aunts and uncles and cousins, and they were all there — anxious to clap eyes on the English girl Gus had married. They meant well, I know, but it was far too much, too soon. My family had been so small and so different. We had never, ever talked about personal things.

Gus's lot were all nudge, nudge, wink, wink about us."

Eve squirmed with sympathy.

"Do you know, more than sixty years later, all I can remember about that first night — our first night in America and only our second as man and wife — is that the bed creaked and squeaked. All I could think as I lay under Gus was that everyone must be able to hear us. It was awful. I couldn't wait for it, for him, to be finished. I was totally mortified. I could barely face them the next morning."

"Not much of a honeymoon."

"Not much of a first year at all. It quickly became apparent that Gus was quite happy where he was, and he couldn't see why we'd want the expense and inconvenience of moving out into our own place when we were, so far as he was concerned, perfectly well set up where we were."

"Didn't you tell him?"

"Oh, I tried. But Gus had a way of talking you round. He said we'd move when we had a child, and since that didn't seem to be happening, he saw no reason to rush."

"What did you do?"

"Jockeyed for position with his mother. Played house in the one room, and played second fiddle to her in every other part of the home. She was a nice enough woman, I suppose. But it was pretty clear I wasn't expected to work, except and unless I wanted to make myself useful in the family business — the lumber yard, the hardware store. They all lived together and then worked together all day, and it didn't seem to bother any of them, being on top of each other all the time. And there wasn't a lot else to do. I had imagined, I guess, that I'd make friends easily enough, but that didn't happen either. They were a big family who had little need for outsiders, it seemed."

"What about his sisters?"

"They couldn't ever seem to stop treating me like an outsider. Not with hostility. Just with this sort of curiosity and carefulness that was very wearing. The town wasn't big. And although New York was pretty close, it wasn't somewhere they went often. I went myself, a few times, in the first months. I loved the city, it was so exotic to me then — unfamiliar in almost every way I could think of. Busy and exciting and a big adventure, you know. Gus hated New York. I could never persuade him to go in, on a Sunday or anything. They disapproved of my going in alone. If I suggested we try and see a show or go look at a museum or something, he looked at me like I was advocating dancing naked around Central Park. He was a small-town boy, my Gus. You couldn't tell, when he was back in Norwich. We thought all Americans were the same. You couldn't see. Mind you, I think I must have been one of the lucky ones. When I think about the girls on the ship — some of them off to Louisiana and Kentucky and Tennessee. I think I probably had it easy in comparison with them."

"It doesn't sound easy."

Violet shrugged, nodding. "I was pretty low. I was closer to the new life I'd dreamed of, but still far away. I'd escaped a home I wasn't happy in, for one I didn't feel I belonged in. I loved Gus, so far as I knew about love, but I'm pretty sure I wasn't in love with him, as they say. We hadn't a lot in common. And I came to be regarded as a bit of a failure, because I didn't get pregnant. All of Gus's sisters had their first babies in the first year of marriage, and that's what they expected of me. It got to be quite an elephant in the room, the fact that I wasn't."

"Poor you. That sounds really tough."

"I was cared for and comfortable. People had it much worse. But my goodness, I was lonely."

She was me, Eve thought suddenly. She

was me. This life is my life. She put one hand across her tummy, above where the baby was. This is different. This makes it different. This will make it okay.

"Did you ever think about leaving him?"

"Honestly? No. Never."

"I think I might have done."

"So might I, now. We were different then. You didn't do that. Divorce — that wasn't an option for so many of us. You stuck it out. You'd made your bed."

"But if that's how it was in the first year, it must have grown worse over time."

"Yes and no. In the third year, I got my own house. I guess everyone had gotten tired of waiting for the pregnancy that never came, and we moved out anyway. For the first time in my entire life, I was mistress of my own home, and that was what I had always wanted. It was small, just one and a half bedrooms, really, and it was only two streets from his mother's house. But it was ours. I was as proud as punch of that house — cleaned it from top to bottom almost every day — not that there was much else to do besides clean it, and cook in it. But it was still in Elizabeth, New Jersey. And I still shared it with Gus."

"Did you two fight, then?"

"God no! I'd have loved to fight. Believe

me, sometimes I tried to pick a fight any chance I got, just for some excitement. Fight, swing from the chandeliers. Gus didn't fight, at least not with me. And he sure as hell didn't want to swing from the chandeliers. That bit of our married life never really picked up much. He liked a quiet life and a quiet home. That drove me crazy. Actually, I think that's what he thought I was — crazy. One day, I'd just had enough. Enough of the boredom and the quiet, and the . . . the mediocrity of the whole sorry thing. I picked up his plate. Meat loaf and mashed potatoes with gravy. His mother taught me to make meat loaf first thing after I'd arrived, because it was Gus's favorite. We had meat loaf at least once a week, every damn week, and every time he ate it, he smiled at me and told me it was good — almost as good as the one his mother made. I just hurled the whole thing at the wall, right behind his head. It made the most fantastic crack when it hit. Meat loaf and gravy slid down the wall.

"Gus just pushed his chair back from the table and walked out of the house. Didn't come back for a couple of hours, until I'd cleared it all up. And he never mentioned it, not once. Never could clear it up entirely, mind you. There was a gravy stain on that wall for the rest of the time I lived there."

"You never talked about it?"

Violet shook her head. "Not directly. I think he thought I was crazy because I hadn't had a baby. I'm sure that's what his mother and his sisters told him. It made sense to them."

"But that wasn't it?"

"No. I was going crazy because I hadn't had a life. Not a baby. I most definitely didn't want one. I'd been tied down all my life. I saw a baby as just another millstone. I could feel time passing, and nothing was happening to me, and I couldn't stand it. It was like all that stuff I'd been through — that feeling I'd had on the boat all those months and then years ago — like it hadn't had anywhere to go. It was all still inside me, still waiting. In some ways, I think I was crazy, actually."

"So what happened in the end?"

"Gus died." Violet shrugged.

"Oh, my God! When?" Eve hadn't expected that.

"In nineteen sixty. November the sixteenth. Same day as Clark Gable."

"That's . . ." Eve was counting.

"Fourteen years after we married."

"That's a long time to be unhappy."

"Yes, it is."

"How did he die?"

"Heart attack."

"He was a bit young for that."

"Yes, he was. Far too young. I thought it might have been the meat loaf. But the doctor said there must always have been something wrong with his heart. He made it sound like Gus was a ticking time bomb."

"That's very sad."

"Gus's mum was the one who really broke my heart. She sat out on their porch for hours, although it was freezing cold, rocking on the swing. She wouldn't come inside. I sat with her for a while, and the whole time I was there she only said one thing to me. She said, 'No mother should outlive her child.' "

Eve rubbed her tummy a little again, and shuddered.

"Her grief, his mother's grief, was so much bigger than mine. It broke her."

"What did you do?"

Violet shrugged. "I sat up the whole night, after his funeral, staring at the gravy stain on the wall behind his chair, thinking. In fourteen years in that town I hadn't made a proper friend — not really. The wake was full of people, but there wasn't a single one there who knew me, who really knew me. It seemed obvious to me."

"You came to New York?"

She nodded. "I wasn't going to go back to Norwich, was I?" She smiled. "I grieved for my husband, don't think I didn't. I felt guilty, like I had about my mother. I felt that I hadn't saved him. Maybe if we'd have been happier at home — and he can't have been happy, even though he never said — he'd have been stronger. Maybe he was swallowing stuff all the time, pushing it under the carpet like I was.

"But I hadn't died. I was alive. This was my chance, and I had to take it. I sold the house, which had passed to me when he died. I used what was left over after funeral expenses and the mortgage and everything, and what we'd had in the bank — which was more than you might think, since we'd never spent much doing anything. Poor Gus. He'd waited and saved and planned. Then he died, before he'd done any of it. And I moved to Manhattan. I rented a fifth-floor walk-up, down on Fifty-eighth and Third. Poky but clean, with good neighbors. And I enrolled at a secretarial college just off Wall Street, downtown. I was thirty-one by then, much older than most of the girls there. But I was quicker than them. I was driven by those lost years. I had the highest WPM of my graduating class, and my shorthand wasn't half bad either. I had my pick of jobs. I think employers thought I was a good bet. Widow in her thirties. Unlikely to marry the first banker or lawyer who smiles twice at her and go off and have babies."

"Is that what you wanted?"

"I don't remember wanting it. I wanted to live. Being someone's daughter and someone's wife, that hadn't given me the life I wanted. I don't think I was in any hurry to get into all that again. Someone's mother would just have been another label."

"So which job did you take?"

"The one that paid the best. I had my eye on those apartment buildings on the Upper East Side. The ones with the white-gloved doormen and the big marble foyers. You know the kind." She winked at Eve.

"I went to work for a firm of accountants on Park Avenue. Johnson, Bell and Wallace, Partners."

"For a Mr. Wallace, I presume?" Eve was enthralled. She sat forward, her elbows on her knees, but that was uncomfortable, and so she leaned sideways on the sofa, toward Violet.

Violet pulled a shocked face. "Most definitely not for Mr. Wallace. I worked for Mr. Clarence Johnson. Five foot three, two hundred sixty pounds, wife and three children in a mock Tudor in Scarsdale."

"But there *was* a Mr. Wallace?" Eve giggled, bouncing on her toes a little.

Violet slapped her own thighs decisively and stood up. "Yes, there was. But Ed has to be heading home just about now. And I'm sure he wants his wife at home in the apartment, pouring him another gin and tonic and making his dinner. Not sitting here gasbagging with me."

Eve smiled. She hadn't realized the time. Violet would be shocked if she could see the inside of the Gallaghers' refrigerator. Making dinner for Ed, doubtless ravenous after a couple of martinis with his clients, was not even a possibility at this point, unless he wanted to eat chocolate chip cookie dough and split a blueberry yogurt. Violet was right. Mr. Wallace would have to keep, and she would have to brave the express aisle at the Food Emporium.

■ ■ ■ ■

SEPTEMBER

■ ■ ■ ■

THE ROOF TERRACE

Eve and Violet had done the work for the party, determined to celebrate the achievement of all involved before summer was over and the containers started looking bleak and dull. Eve had ordered some party platters — crudités and shrimp and guacamole with tortilla chips — from Fresh Direct, and Violet had bought the wine. They'd posted a notice in the lobby. Eve had taken a picture of the terrace and affixed it to the notice enticingly. She was almost excited . . .

Eve tapped her glass with a knife, bringing the crowd to order. She looked, again, for Ed. He'd promised he'd be here by six thirty, and it was six forty-five already. He'd promised. He never used to break promises he made. These days he seemed to toss the promises airily in her direction and forget them straightaway. She was looking for him, optimistic fool, but she knew she hadn't

361

really expected him to be here on time.

Violet cleared her throat. "Welcome, everyone. Welcome to our outdoor space! We did it!"

There was a slightly self-conscious ripple of applause and great big cheers from Eve and Todd.

"Many people have contributed, of course, to the pastoral vision of loveliness you see before you this evening. Thanks must go to the entire committee."

"And most especially to you, Violet. Without you, there'd have been no committee!"

"And no terrace in the first place!"

Violet raised her hand in protest. "No heckling, please." But she was smiling broadly. "Let's not argue about who should get the credit. Let's just be glad that we have such a wonderful space to come and just . . . be. We're unbelievably lucky to have that, in this city."

"Hear, hear," someone said.

"So let's raise a glass and christen the roof terrace. And here's to all who sit and enjoy her."

Glasses were raised. It was a gorgeous evening. Hot, but much less relentless than the heat in July and August had been. Theirs was a gentle breeze, and the beginnings of a crimson sunset as their backdrop.

Almost everyone had come, Eve realized. Funny how party invitations garnered a better response than work invitations. She didn't see Arthur Alexander *(Quelle surprise!)* but she had caught a glimpse of Blair Stewart and almost everyone else. She'd nudged Violet, who'd whispered waspishly that it was true then, what she'd heard — that Blair Stewart would go to the opening of an envelope. Blair hadn't stayed; she'd probably only come to see what they'd done and figure out what to complain to the board about. Which wouldn't get her far, since the board was all here, enjoying the terrace as it was supposed to be enjoyed.

Todd, flouting the no-white-after-Labor-Day rule in linen, and Greg, resplendent in seersucker, were holding court in the new wicker chairs, flanking Violet, who looked fabulous, wrapped in a gauzy, beaded shawl and still smiling.

Eve had had a lovely chat with Rachael. She wasn't anywhere near as intimidating as she'd once thought she was. She was lovely. She hadn't been around much in the summer; Violet had said something about a house in Connecticut. Same with Kim, who had told her herself, back in June, that she spent the summer out at Jason's family house on Long Island. Eve wondered whether she herself would be doing that next summer. She couldn't imagine leaving Ed on his own for that long. That would feel odd. Not that he'd mind, on current form. No one nagging him to get home for dinner. Or the very occasional special event that meant something to her. She was mad now. Her irritation of earlier had sprouted into full-blown anger. It was really . . . piggy of him not to get here. There'd better be some cast-iron excuse. Who was she kidding? There always was.

Rachael had brought Mia, in her pajamas. Her boys were watching the Mets, she said. She hadn't realized until tonight that Eve was pregnant, and she'd cooed and aahed obligingly when she'd found out, recommending her pediatrician and asking about Eve's hospital plans. Eve told her she was having a sonogram the following week.

"Will you find out the sex?"

"I think so. Ed wants to wait, but I don't think I can stand the suspense. Did you know? About your three?"

"The first two, no. David said there were very few surprises left in life, and this was one of them. But after two boys, I told him he could wait, if he wanted, but I was determined to know if she was a girl."

"Did you want a girl?"

"You shouldn't say so, I know, but yes! Three boys? Don't get me wrong, I adore my boys. But a little girl — well, we all want one, don't we?"

"I don't mind. Funnily enough, I think Ed would really like a girl. I don't mind, so long as it's healthy. That's a cliché, I know."

"Hey, it's a cliché because it's true. That's all that matters. You must tell me if it's a girl, though. I have boxes of the most beautiful baby clothes — gifts we got sent and things we bought for Mia. Some of it never even got worn! She grew like a weed, my little one. I'd put things away; two weeks later, I'd get them out and she'd be too big." She laughed, and kissed the top of Mia's head, and Eve felt a stab of envy, and excitement. That would be her, soon, with a soft, warm head to kiss.

But where the hell was Ed? This was the only thing she'd achieved since she got here, and the least he could do was turn up to help her celebrate. The truth was, she was a bit embarrassed. She knew Violet thought Ed was a bit neglectful and uninterested. She was still a bit embarrassed about the day of the blackout. She was more private than that. She'd shown Violet how upset she was, and she wasn't used to how that felt. And she wanted him to prove her wrong. This wasn't helping.

Todd had cornered her by the dips, putting an arm around her shoulder, like they'd been friends forever. His Acqua di Parma was a little overpowering. Pregnancy had made her sensitive to smells. She concentrated on trying not to lean back, away from him.

"So what did you do to Violet Wallace?"

"What do you mean?"

"I mean you've thawed the old girl out, well and truly. Don't get me wrong — I adore her, but then, I've always had a thing for eccentrics."

"Violet's not eccentric!"

"Oh, darling, she so is. I love it. All those candelabras, and always eating at the table, with good linens."

"Doesn't that just make her posh?"

"What–ev–er." Todd said it in his ghetto fabulous way, swinging his hips in a figure of eight. "I still love her. Up until lately, I think I was the only one. Well, Hunter Stern, but I think he just had the hots for her. Ugh. Wrinkly love." Todd wrinkled his nose. He was easily distracted. If he were under twelve, Eve thought, he'd be diagnosed with ADHD and put on Ritalin. Maybe Greg should start sprinkling some on his oatmeal.

"Why? Why do you think no one loved her?"

"Prickly. Frosty. Remote. To name but a few characteristics. Words I may or may not have heard bandied about —"

"That's nonsense. She's one of the kindest, sweetest, most interesting women I've ever met."

"Which brings me back to my question. What did you do? That softened her up?"

A guy in a suit appeared at the door. At first she thought it was Ed, began to smile in his direction, but this guy was shorter and slighter. She didn't recognize him.

For a moment, Emily didn't either. She did a double take when she realized it was Jackson. He was carrying a small wrought-iron table with a tiled top. He walked over to Violet and put it down in front of her. Violet and Todd stopped talking and smiled at him. Jackson spread his hands, gesturing at the table.

"Something for your garden. There are chairs, too — four of them. They're downstairs. I couldn't carry them."

"Jackson, that's beautiful!" Violet stood up and kissed him on both cheeks. "What a sweet boy you are! How thoughtful!"

Greg and Todd exchanged a raised eyebrow. Violet glared at them. "Isn't it, boys?"

They nodded.

"It's the least I could do, really. I haven't exactly been the most civic-minded resident . . ."

Emily watched the exchange from the other side of the roof. Charlotte nudged her.

"I'm going."

"Don't do that. Stay. Please."

"I can't, Charlotte. I don't want to be here if he's here. I feel, I feel humiliated. I'll see you later."

"You should at least find out what he's got to say about it. You haven't given him a chance to explain. That's not fair. To either of you. You wouldn't be so upset if you didn't care."

Emily kissed Charlotte quiet. Charlotte tugged at her hand, but Emily pulled it away, shaking her head. "I'm done. Bye-bye."

The elevator took ages. She pressed the button again and again, as though that might speed it up. Downstairs, Hunter Stern was unloading a week's worth of Fairway groceries, and he wasn't in any hurry.

Jackson had seen Emily the moment he'd stepped onto the terrace. Just like at the triathlon. She was a magnet for his eyes. He believed, after the race, after finding her in that crowd, that he could spot her anywhere. She looked gorgeous tonight. But when didn't she? She had her hair down. He hadn't seen it that way before. She was wearing a cotton sundress in a pale turquoise, and her shoulders gleamed golden in the early evening light. He saw her leave. He'd only come to see her. It was clumsy, he knew, and the table might have been over the top, but when he'd seen the notice in the foyer, announcing the opening garden party, he'd known she'd be there. She'd been avoiding him since the blackout. Madison Cavanagh, however, he couldn't seem to evade. Every time the damn elevator doors opened, there she was, alternately glowering at him and affecting not to notice him at all, even when there were just the two of them in the small space. He hadn't seen her here tonight, thank God.

He'd left Emily messages, but silence. He desperately wanted to explain. If he was resorting to the grand gesture, it was because he had no choice. Except to walk away, and that he couldn't do. Instead, he followed her.

He ran his finger around his collar. It was too hot for this getup. But he'd wanted Emily to see it.

At first, his father had been cynical, as Jackson had known he would be. That's why he'd gone to his mother first. By the time the two men had sat down across from each other in his father's study a couple of weeks ago, his mother had cajoled, petitioned, and eventually ordered that his father give him a fair hearing. She could tell he was really trying.

"So what's brought on this change of heart?"

"It isn't so much a change of heart, Dad. More a kind of distilling down of what I want into something I actually can have."

"I haven't a clue what you just said. That what they're teaching at Duke these days — psycho nonsense?"

Jackson bit his tongue. This sparring was nothing new.

"So Dad," he'd said, keeping his voice low-pitched and calm, "the question is, are you planning on keeping me here so that you can point out a few more of my failings, or are you going to do what you've been trying to do to me for years — find me a job?"

"Of course I'm going to help you, Trip. I'm your father. I'm merely trying to find out what your motive is. You've never shown so much as a flicker of interest up until this point. What is it? Afraid the cash cow is going to be withdrawn?"

Jackson stood up angrily. "Jesus," he whispered, alarmed by the room's acoustics. "That's a really shitty thing to say. Keep your stinking job. I don't need this —"

His father stood up and came around to his son's side of the desk. "No, no, I'm sorry." His father remained standing, one hand on Trip's arm. "I shouldn't have questioned your motives so closely. Sit, please. Sit down and let's talk."

"About the future, and not the past. That's my deal."

His father nodded silently.

And so Trip had a job. Of sorts. His father had found him something, apprenticing at his law firm. He said he'd move him every few months, so he could learn another part of his father's business. The stupid thing was, Trip liked it.

"You'll take over one day. You know that?"

Of course Trip knew. Hadn't he heard it for years? But it was pointless if he couldn't get Emily to notice him again, to like him again. It was for her, all of this.

She was standing by the elevator, pushing the button furiously, and she didn't look at him at first.

"Let me talk to you?"

The elevator was at 2.

"There's no need."

"There's every need. I want to explain. You haven't let me. Nothing happened that night."

"It doesn't matter to me whether it did or not."

3.

"I think it does."

"Don't flatter yourself, Jackson."

"Look, you were looking for me. Don't lie to yourself, Emily, even if you're lying to me. I know you were."

4.

"So?"

"So you saw something, and I know what it looked like. But that wasn't how it was. Madison showed up, and she threw herself at me, and once, I'll admit, I'd have gone for it. But not anymore. I didn't want Madison. I don't want anyone else. It's only you, Emily. I've been gone since the moment I saw you in the elevator all those months ago. Totally gone."

5.

Emily was staring at the floor.

6.

"I told her I wasn't interested. She was leaving, wasn't she, when you saw her?"

7.

"You've got to believe me, and you've got to give me a chance. You think you know me, you think you know who I am, but I don't know how you can. I don't even know myself anymore. Since I met you."

8.

The elevator was almost here. Jackson was desperate. He wanted to stand in front of the doors. She had to listen to him. She had to.

The doors of the elevator opened, and a tall man stepped out. Jackson thought he was the English guy. Ed something.

"Good evening."

"Hi."

Emily stepped into the elevator. Jackson didn't know whether to walk in and stand beside her. He didn't know what was in her infuriating, gorgeous, maddening head.

"You'd better come in here."

She knew nothing had happened between him and Madison. Really. She'd known very quickly. All those messages. His face. She didn't know what had happened that night between them, but she knew, with a certainty that took her by surprise, that it wasn't what she had initially suspected.

As the doors closed, she turned to him. The smallest smile played about her lips.

She leaned forward, her hands on his chest, and kissed him lightly on the lips. Then stood straight again, watching him.

This girl doesn't know what she wants, Jackson thought. For a second, he hesitated.

And then he kissed her back. Once, twice, his lips dry and soft on hers. She brought one hand up to the back of his neck and held him there for just a second. That was all he needed. He began to kiss her in earnest, pushing her back against the panels of the elevator.

He couldn't believe she was letting him kiss her. After all these months. He was almost afraid to touch her. Afraid to make a move, in case it woke her up, and she changed her mind. She was here, with him.

He was touching the skin on her arms and shoulders, the skin he'd wanted to touch for so long. It was as soft as he'd known it would be. The muscles beneath the surface were hard and defined. She smelled like baby powder and ozone and sunshine.

She had her eyes closed. He wished she'd open them. He wanted to see their extraordinary color looking back at him, giving him permission. He held her face in his hands, his fingers in her silky hair. Someone — was it him? — had pushed the button for Emily's floor. The doors opened and they fell into the foyer, and then through Emily's door. He almost pushed the bike off its wall hook trying to shove the door closed behind them.

God, he wanted her. But it had to be her decision. He had to wait.

She stopped. Not like when he'd stopped, with Madison. He knew she didn't want to. She made herself stop. A couple of times she pulled back, then grabbed him again, her mouth hungry against his, every inch of her pressed against him. Eventually she got serious about stopping and took two or three real steps back from him, her arms out in front of her to keep him away.

They were both out of breath and panting.

"What's wrong?"

"Nothing's wrong. I just don't want to go too fast."

"That's fine, Emily. That's fine." He held up his hands in surrender. "Whatever you want."

"I mean, I want to. It's not that. I really want to. But it's too soon, you know? I have to know I can trust you. I have to know you a little better all around. I mean, I don't know what you're like — not really. Like this — you're probably used to doing this. I'm not. I haven't had a lot of boyfriends.

Honestly. And I've never been the kind of girl who just jumps into bed with someone. I sound old-fashioned, probably. Maybe I am. But I just don't."

"I don't want you to be."

"Really?"

"Really. I want it to happen. God, yes. You may never know how much, Emily. But I want it to mean something when it does. I mean, if it does. I don't want to assume . . ."

She was smiling at him now. "You're nervous."

"Hell, yes." He rubbed his hair ruefully. "I'm more nervous than I've ever been in my life, for God's sake. Do you believe me now — what I said upstairs? This is new for me, Emily. Really new."

She did believe him. She believed him about Madison and she believed him now. At least, she really wanted to, and that was a big step for her. She smoothed her dress and pushed her hair back behind her ears.

"Look. It's early. Do you want to go out, do something? We could take a walk. See a movie. Get some dinner. Whatever you want. Let's do this right, yeah?"

She smiled gratefully. "That sounds good."

Out on the street, Emily slipped her hand into his. It felt like the most natural and wonderful thing in the world to him in that moment. Two people watched them as they walked to the corner and then disappeared. Jesus, taking Che's shift, who congratulated himself on being the person whose sage advice had brought these two beautiful young people together. And Madison, who had climbed out of a taxi in front of the building just as they were leaving.

They didn't see her, but she saw them.

EVE

Upstairs, Eve slammed her front door and went straight to the bathroom, slamming that door, too, for good measure. She put the plug in and began running a bath, pouring a big dollop of the bath stuff that smelled of lavender and was supposed to help you go to sleep. It would take more than lavender this evening. She was too cross to sleep.

Ed made a mug of tea and knocked tentatively on the door. She hadn't locked it.

"Can I come in?"

"I don't want to talk to you."

"Fine. I'm just bringing you tea."

He put the mug down on the side of the bath.

Eve was lying back with her eyes closed. He looked at her body. Her breasts were bigger, and the nipples had darkened. Her stomach was swollen, rising above the bubbles, and her belly button was stretching out a bit. She was, now, obviously pregnant.

And he was obviously a shit. At least, as far as she was concerned.

"I'm sorry, Eve."

"What for? For not bothering to show up at my party until it was almost over, or just for being in the doghouse now?"

"Both?"

She opened her eyes and looked at his face.

He smiled his winning smile. "Can I come in?"

"Fuck off. I'm cross."

"I'm coming in."

He pulled off the trousers from his suit and unbuttoned his shirt.

"There isn't room."

"There is."

He dipped one foot into the hot water and splashed her a little. "Are you sure this isn't too hot? The baby isn't supposed to take baths too hot."

"How do you know that?"

"Been reading my books."

She didn't know that. He must have read them while she slept.

He sat on the end, facing her. She looked at him expectantly.

He shrugged, his arms wide. "What? Whatever I say won't help, will it? You're not interested in the crucial call they hauled me back from the elevator to take, are you?"

"Is that true?" She narrowed her eyes at him.

"I swear."

He leaned over and kissed her knee. "I wanted to be there, Eve. I promise I did. I'm sorry. I am."

She didn't say anything.

"And I want to be forgiven."

She sighed. He dropped to his knees in the water and moved up until their faces were level. Water splashed out of the tub onto the floor. He nuzzled her damp neck, and she brought one hand up to the back of his head. His stomach grazed hers, though he kept all his weight on his hands and knees, careful not to lie on her.

"I never told you you could get in this bath."

"And you never told me I couldn't."

She didn't have the energy to be mad anymore. He'd been late to the party, and he shouldn't have been.

But she was tired of fighting. And he was here now . . .

RACHAEL

The morning that Rachael found out David was having an affair was perfectly normal, until that moment. It was Sunday, and Milena didn't work on the weekends, except the occasional Saturday night, and sometimes during the summers out in Connecticut. Rachael loved Milena, and she recognized how much easier she made their lives, but she loved it, too, when Milena wasn't there, and her children were all her own.

David had slept until eight, as he liked to do, but she'd been up since five thirty, as she always was. No alarm required — she just woke up. She'd run her six miles around the reservoir in the park, Coldplay blaring through her iPod, and been home before the children woke, to make pancakes, as she did every weekend. They had stumbled along the corridor at the sounds of the kitchen, tousled and sleepy but hungry. She had talked to them while they ate, nursing a mug of Earl Grey, and leaning against the breakfast bar. Jacob was starting West Side Soccer across town later; he was excited to get his uniform on and get down there. He had his mother's energy, Rachael recognized, and it would be good for him. Noah wanted to go and watch. David had said he would take them, and Mia had been promised her favorite morning — Barnes & Noble, to read picture books on the floor, followed by lunch with her mom. The boys were watching *SpongeBob,* making the most of their permitted weekend television hour, and Mia had crawled back up into bed with her father for a postpancake snooze. Rachael had stood leaning against the doorframe watching them for a moment. They were facing each other, Mia's little leg tucked under her, and her fingers fanned out on the pillow. Their profiles were the same; so were their dark curls.

It was always a bit hard, making the transition from country life in the summer back to city life and the approaching fall. This weekend would have been beautiful out there. It was still hot, but the humidity had disappeared completely. But life had revved up again. School and sports and obligations . . . It had been a lovely summer, though. David hadn't spent as much time up there as she'd wished he could, but they'd all made the most of the time they had had together. She was proud of her husband, and work was obviously going really well.

David forgot his BlackBerry. She'd let him

sleep a little longer than he should have, and the three boys had had to rush to get out of the house in time for soccer. It was unlike him to do that — to hurry and to forget things. Other women's husbands moaned about misplacing phones, keys, and wallets, but not David. Later she wondered for just a second whether he'd forgotten it on purpose. Whether on some deep level he'd wanted to be found out.

Rachael wasn't snooping. Why would she? He'd done or said nothing suspicious. Nothing was out of the ordinary, off routine. She had no reason to check up on him. If she was really honest, she'd never entertained, for a moment, the idea that he would need to cheat on her. When she first realized he'd gone without it, she put it down on the table beside her, sure that he'd be back within minutes to claim it. She and Mia were making clay animals. Mia was working on what she assured her mother was an elephant, and had instructed Rachael to get started on a lion, with a big mane. Rachael had just retrieved the garlic press, planning to squeeze clay through it. Mia was chattering delightedly. This was exactly the kind of thing she loved to do and only really got the chance to when her big brothers were elsewhere. They weren't great at the sit-down art projects, and Rachael and Milena had cleaned enough clay out of rugs and paint off walls to have learned the lesson some time ago. So the machine vibrated next to her as she fed the garlic press with clay. Instinctively she reached for it, assuming that it would be David, calling to check that the BlackBerry was at home, rather than in the hands of someone who'd found it on the street, or down the vinyl seat of a cab. He'd have borrowed the phone of one of the other dads on the soccer sideline. New message. She knew his password. It was *janomira* — the first two letters of each of their names, Jacob, Noah, Mia, and Rachael. She knew his password, she opened mail that came to the apartment addressed to him. She knew his social security number and his blood pressure and the pretax amount of his last bonus. He was her husband. She knew everything.

Except this. Rachael didn't know this. *call if you can. i miss you.* For a moment, confused, she assumed he'd written it. To her. Then realization dawned, and she felt instantly stupid that she could have thought that. Somebody was missing him. It wasn't Jacob or Noah or Mia, and it wasn't her. It was somebody who had no right. Beside her, Mia chattered on about elephants and their trunks and the lion's mane, and about how long it would take them to dry so she could paint them. Rachael kept pushing clay into the garlic press until Mia noticed and said she thought there was probably enough for a mane now.

She couldn't scream or rant, because Mia was there and David wasn't. She wished she were brave enough to press the green button and find out who was missing her husband, but she couldn't do it. She stared at the BlackBerry until her eyes lost their focus, and she tried to stop her brain and stop her heart from racing so fast. She missed beats, and she felt dizzy, a little breathless.

Mia was pulling on her sleeve, dressed in her raincoat and boots, though it was pretty hot and sunny outside (they were new, and pink, and she would wear them to bed given the opportunity), asking when they were going to Barnes & Noble. She was finished with the clay.

Rachael didn't even make her take off the wet-weather gear.

She tried to stay calm, as Mia sat contentedly on the floor of the bookstore, surrounded by a stack of picture books she'd collected from the tables and shelves. She tried to stop her brain from getting ahead of itself. She tried different scenarios. Versions in which the text was harmless, innocuous, a mistake. Meant for someone else. Sent in error. A stupid, stupid joke. The funny thing was, she knew.

The other funny thing was, if you'd asked her yesterday how she would react to something like this, she'd have sworn she'd be brave. She would have returned the call on the BlackBerry. She would have waited at home and confronted David. She'd have been loud and righteous and angry — at least at first.

She was none of those things.

She was terrified.

She couldn't bear the thought of going back to the apartment and seeing him.

When David came in after soccer, there was clay all over the table. Rachael never left a mess. He felt a flutter of panic — maybe Mia had hurt herself, maybe she'd had to run out to the ER, and that was why they hadn't cleaned up. There was no note. He saw his BlackBerry on the corner of the bookcase just inside the front door. He'd realized very soon after he and the boys had left that he'd forgotten it but knew he didn't have time to go back for it. He'd actually acknowledged to himself that he'd had more fun without it. He'd run up and down the sidelines with Noah and actually watched Jacob. He knew that if he'd had it with him, he'd have been "fiddling" with it, as Jake called it. He picked it up, wanting to call Rachael and find out what had happened. That's when he saw the text and the flutter of panic became a wind.

Stupid girl. Stupid, stupid girl. How could she have done that? She was never, ever supposed to do that. In rearranging his moral codes in order to justify the affair, David had told himself that at least he was completely honest with Stephanie. Stephanie knew there was a wife and three children, and that there were no weekends or holidays, and that there was absolutely no possibility of his leaving Rachael for her. He'd been clear about that from the beginning. He'd never said a single thing to her that he didn't mean. That meant he didn't have to feel bad about Stephanie, however bad he felt about Rachael. Stephanie knew the score. She was a volunteer. And she'd broken the rules.

What he didn't know was whether Rachael had seen the text. At least, he couldn't be sure, and that uncertainty was like an itch, all over his skin. Cold fear ran down his spine at the thought that she had. It would explain the mess, and the absence of a note. His finger shook on the keys of the Black-Berry, dialing her number. He was about to find out, he guessed.

The call went straight through to Rachael's voice mail, and David was lost for words. When he did speak, he kept his tone light but sounded silly to himself, like a children's television announcer, artificially high and jolly.

"It's me. We're back. Jake's got a great left foot, turns out. We were thinking of coming to meet you, if you don't mind boys at lunch. Give me a call, let me know where you are? Okay. Bye."

The boys were watching television again, and though he knew he should stop them, he was glad they were occupied.

He put himself in the far corner of the apartment, facing the wall, and dialed Stephanie. She answered immediately. "Hey, baby."

"You texted me. During the weekend." He sounded cold and angry, even to himself.

"I know. I'm sorry."

"Not as sorry as I am."

"Why? What's happened?"

"I don't know. I think Rachael might have seen it. I left my BlackBerry behind when I took the boys to soccer this morning."

"Oh, my God."

He was silent.

When Stephanie spoke, she sounded breathless. "I'm so sorry."

"Are you? Really?"

"Of course. You don't think I meant that to happen, do you?"

He didn't know anymore. He thought they'd had that straight. "She didn't call you? You haven't had any calls?"

"None. Not until you. Honestly."

That gave him hope. Rachael had balls. She was likely to have called the number, if she had seen the text.

By six o'clock, Rachael still wasn't home, and she hadn't called, and he was sure she had seen it. She was letting him stew.

He hadn't had a clue what to do with the boys all day. Rachael always organized weekends. They clamored to go swimming at Asphalt Green, or to take their scooters to the park, but he didn't want to be out when Rachael got home, and they were easily pacified by the unexpected luxury of a whole afternoon on the Wii. He fed them peanut butter and jelly sandwiches, without the vegetable crudités he knew they would normally have on the side, and let them dip Oreo cookies into their milk.

At some point, as he went through the

motions of the afternoon, he realized that, when it came to caring for his sons, he only really knew what he wasn't supposed to do. What was banned, what was controlled, what was prescribed. He didn't view them proactively at all. What could they do? What did they like to do?

When had that happened? When had his life become this complicated?

He had carefully and studiously avoided, up until this point, acknowledging the ridiculous cliché that he had become by beginning this affair, but sitting in the apartment waiting for Rachael, growing more afraid by the hour, it stared him right in his stupid face.

It had started at the beginning of the year. Not, at least, in the tawdriest of ways — at the office holiday party — but in January, when New York's gray, frozen winter still stretched out for another few months. Stephanie worked at the office — the executive assistant to an opposite number of his in another department. He'd first noticed her during a series of meetings over a deal last year. He remembered distinctly the surprise he'd felt when he registered an unfamiliar reaction. She was pretty but by no means beautiful. One of those New York women who really knew how to make the best out of what they have — always immaculate, ultra slim.

He had never so much as looked at another woman that way — not since college. Rachael had always been enough.

She'd made it happen, he thought, realizing how weak and cowardly he sounded, even inside his own head, as he voiced the thought. He was pretty sure none of it was his idea, not in the first place. In fact, he'd given her a wide berth after those meetings. He wasn't a fool. Not then, at least. She knew he was married, a father. She knew what she was doing. She'd made it very, very clear that she was his for the taking, and eventually he'd given in and taken her.

The first time had been easier than he might have imagined. They'd been at an off site, down at the Four Seasons at Battery Park. She'd flirted all day — during the coffee breaks, and across the table. They bumped into each other later, outside. She was smoking a cigarette, leaning against a tree. He'd gone out for some fresh air, thinking he might call Rachael, but realizing it was late — she'd be asleep already. No one else was around. She'd beckoned him over, and he'd stood with her while she finished the cigarette. He'd never smoked himself, never found it attractive in a woman, until that moment. He was transfixed by the shape her mouth made when she exhaled smoke. It was suddenly so overtly sexual. Following her inside, into the elevator, to the door of her room — it was almost like he was in a trance. He was someone else. She closed the door behind them and pulled his mouth down to hers before he had the chance to speak. And he just gave in. He let it happen to him. There was a moment — a second, before it was too late — when he could have stopped. He tried to conjure Rachael's face, but he couldn't. He tried to imagine his wife's breasts, as he stroked Stephanie's, but it was like he'd forgotten them. He hovered over Stephanie's naked body, feeling her breath, faintly smoky, on his skin, and . . . let it happen. He literally could not think about anything other than being inside her, and he didn't feel like himself again until later, after he came, and it was over. The first night, the first time, the alchemy made it happen. After that first time it got much, much easier.

It was sex, of course. Not that often and, frankly, not all that great. David was not the kind of cheating husband who found sneaking around and clandestine liaisons erotic. He wasn't, he reflected, a natural adulterer.

Actually he found keeping track of his lies exhausting. But his conscience bothered him less than he might have imagined. Stephanie had a good body, but so did Rachael. She still looked more or less like she always had — golden, taut, and pert — like the girl in the white bikini on the beach in St. Barts all those years ago. You couldn't tell she'd carried the three pregnancies. Stephanie was eager to please, and she had certainly had one or two new tricks, but neither did he have complaints about Rachael. He knew other guys who moaned that their wives went off sex after they had children, but not Rachael. It was, he supposed, regular, but still inventive, never perfunctory. And not always at his instigation. If he occasionally felt as though sex was something on Rachael's to-do list, somewhere between "book the babysitter" and "order sushi," at least they did it often, and well. David had a friend at the racquetball club whose wife had actually told him, after a martini or two, that she submitted to sex three times a week mainly because it burned up to 750 calories and was a good inner thigh firmer. It saved her a spinning class. Multitasking taken to a ridiculous level. Only in New York.

He had meant to stop it. At first, when it

had just been once or twice. That was a liaison, not an affair. Then after a few months. But when the summer had come, with its sudden promise of unfettered access to Stephanie, he reasoned it would keep until September. Rachael was away so much, up at the house with the kids. She was so focused on them. He gave them, all of them, every ounce of his energy and his love on the weekends. He allowed himself the ego boost and the easy release of Stephanie during the week. That July Fourth weekend, Stephanie had waited for him in the city. He'd taken the jitney, and then the cab, and found her waiting naked in bed for him, nothing else on her agenda all day except pleasuring him and being pleasured in return. She couldn't, apparently, get enough of him. There was something so simple about that. She had never once, until now, placed any demands on him. She'd asked for nothing from him, beyond what he gave her while they were alone. In September, he told himself, in September he'd finish it. He should have done it sooner.

In the increasingly rare moments when he was honest with himself, he knew what it was that drove him, again and again, into her bed. He knew why he was doing it. Because he believed he was better than

Stephanie. Smarter, and cleverer. More successful. Because when he was with her, he didn't have to try and be as good as she was. Because she thought he was fan-fucking-tastic.

He'd never wondered what was in it for her.

When Rachael finally came home, Mia was asleep on her shoulder. Over their daughter's head, she flashed him a look that insisted on silence. She spoke only to the boys at first, laying Mia down gently on the sofa while she asked about the soccer and the afternoon. Jacob asked where she'd been, and she told him she and Mia had been to the movies and out for ice cream, and that next weekend she'd take them wherever they wanted to go — the Natural History Museum, or to the park. David hovered in the background, waiting for her opening gambit. The waiting was sickening. She put the children to bed, sending each of them down the hallway, in their pajamas, to kiss him good night. Each child was a silent reproach. He heard her turn off the lights, say a last good night. But still she didn't come to him.

He couldn't stand it, in the end. He went in search of his wife in their bedroom. Ra-

chael was in their bed, fully clothed, facing
the wall, so he couldn't see her face. The
covers were pulled up high, and she was
clutching them to her.

"Rachael?"

She didn't answer.

"I want to explain. I want to apologize."

Still nothing.

"She's someone from work . . ." He didn't
know what else to say. It meant nothing, it's
over, I'm sorry. Even he knew they were all
empty, pointless words — the futile, foolish
lexicon of the cheat — and he couldn't
bring himself to say them out loud. She
didn't want that either, it seemed. Rachael
sat up without looking at him, and held up
her hand. "I don't want to hear any of that."

"What do you want?"

"I want you to go."

"Go where?" His voice trembled.

"I don't care, David. Just go. I don't want
you here. I just can't have you here now."
There was no rage in her voice. She sounded
tired.

Even through the fog of his guilt and fear
he felt indignation. This was his home. His
children were here.

"I don't want to go."

"That's too bad, David." She narrowed
her eyes at him. "I don't want any of this. I

didn't ask for any of this. You don't get to say what happens next. Did you honestly think you would? I think I'm entitled. I don't want to see you or to have to talk to you until I'm ready. Me, not you. Can you understand that? It's my choice."

He wished she would rage and rail. Or cry. This controlled, quiet Rachael was frightening.

"I'll pack a bag."

She got up and left the room without saying anything else. Once he'd thrown some stuff — he didn't concentrate on what — into a travel bag, he came back down the corridor to the living room. He didn't know quite where to go. Not to friends. His friends were their friends. It was impossible. He couldn't do that. A hotel? It seemed so surreal. Rachael sat in silence in the twilight, her hands folded in her lap. She didn't look at him when he came in, so he moved to stand in her line of vision. Holding his bag to his chest.

"What will you tell the children?"

She'd thought it through, while he was packing; that chilled him. "That you're on a business trip. You can call them in the morning if you want to."

"When should I tell them I'll be back?"

"Don't use them to try and make me

commit, David. That's low."

"I just want to know what to tell them. They're bound to ask, you know they are. I want to know what's in your head, Rachael."

She flashed him a look of pure disdain. "No, you don't, David. You really don't. You've had God knows how long to get your story straight. Don't expect me to help you now."

She didn't sleep that night, but she didn't cry until Milena arrived the next morning at eight a.m.

Milena had been with them since Jacob was a baby. Fifty years old, she lived across the river in Queens with her husband. Their two children, both married, lived nearby. She was fabulously calm and warm. Rachael didn't know which of them loved her more — the children or she herself. Milena had been a part of every trial and every triumph of the last six years. They'd hired her when Rachael was eight and a half months pregnant with Jacob. Almost as soon as they'd found her, Rachael relaxed, and went into labor, and Milena had been Jacob's third visitor in the hospital. She remembered lying back, watching Milena pick Jacob up so easily, murmuring Polish endearments to him, and feeling herself suffused with Millie's calm confidence. She was a little like a mother, actually. Sometimes a little more like a mother than her actual mother. It was Milena who bought her cabbage leaves when she had mastitis — twice — and got her through the agony. When Jacob had fallen in the playground in Central Park and split his forehead, it was Milena who had bundled them all into a cab, and Milena who had held Jacob down when they put the stitches in, without a local anesthetic, because the cut was too close to his eye to numb the area. Having Milena made Rachael's life possible. She knew she couldn't leave the children with someone who didn't love them. And Millie loved them. You only had to watch her with them to know that. She liked to think Millie loved her, too.

So when Milena walked in on Monday morning at eight, just as she did almost every day of every week when they were in the city, it was the most natural thing in the world for Rachael to burst into tears. If she was shocked, Milena gave no indication. She held her briefly, then patted her on the back and told her, not unkindly, not to cry in front of the children. She made her a cup of hot, sweet tea and made her lie on her bed while she finished getting Jacob and

Noah ready for school and preschool. Rachael curled up like a baby.

"Mama's not feeling well," she clucked.

"Has she got tummy ache?" Noah asked, his eyes wide. "Is she going to throw up?" His voice was full of horrified delight.

Milena ruffled his hair, and tsked at him. "No, she isn't. She needs peace, Noah. Come kiss her, and then she's going to have a rest here. I will take you to school this morning."

When she got back, she put Mia in front of her Baby Einstein DVD in the living room, and the strains of Beethoven floated down the hallway. Coming back to Rachael, with more tea, she perched on the edge of the bed and let Rachael sob in her arms for a few moments, murmuring gentle endearments into the top of her head. She pulled Kleenex from the box on the side table and handed them to Rachael.

"What's wrong, Rachael? Tell me what's happened."

"Oh, Millie. The worst thing. David. He's having an affair."

Even as she said it, she couldn't believe she'd become, overnight, that woman.

EVE

An old dog at last learning his new tricks, Ed had been on time for the sonogram, fetching plastic cups of water for her to drink so that she could fill her bladder. He'd held her hand as she lay on the bed, and the technician smeared the jelly on her. Eve looked down at the smooth, taut belly, and wondered when the stretch marks might start their march across her.

She wanted to know the sex of the baby, and Ed had relented. She wanted to enjoy imagining and daydreaming about a girl or a boy, and not just a baby. The baby didn't cooperate at first. The technician told her to get up and walk a few times around the room. The woman slipped out and was gone for ages.

"Do you think everything is all right?"

"Of course it is. You saw it, didn't you? The heartbeat. All those measurements she took — they were fine. She's gone for a cigarette, or a coffee, or something."

"Promise?" As if he could.

"Promise."

When the technician came back, and Eve lay back down, the baby rewarded their patience with a spread-eagled position. They didn't need to be told that she was a girl.

Eve looked up at Ed, who was squeezing her hand so hard it almost hurt, and saw that there were tears in his eyes.

"A girl. It's a girl." He took her face in his hands and kissed her hard, on the mouth. "You're growing me a girl!" He was laughing, and when he pulled back, he punched the air with his fist.

They began by agreeing not to tell anyone at all. When they came out of the doctor's office, they went straight into one of the expensive boutiques on Madison and bought a tiny pink jacket and socks that looked like black patent Mary Janes.

By the time they got back to the subway, where he was going south and she was heading north, he'd said he might tell John, in the office, who had four girls. And the first thing Eve did when she got upstairs to the apartment, after having a pee, was pick up the phone.

"Cath?"

"Sis? How are you?"

"It's a girl! We had a sonogram this morning. The baby's a girl!"

"That's wonderful!"

"I know. Do you know, I think I wanted a girl all along. I just didn't say so, because Ed already had, and that would have felt unfair on a boy, if we'd both said it."

"They can't hear in there, you know."

"They can actually. You're supposed to play them Bach and read them the classics and not fight and swear and things."

"Excuse me. My two listened to a lot of Pink Floyd. I read them bits from *Okay!* and Geoff and I had our very best rows when we were trying to build flat-pack nursery furniture. How I must have damaged them."

"Yes, well, it explains a lot, now that you mention it . . ."

"Up yours."

They both laughed. "You know what I mean. I didn't want to say out loud that I wanted a girl. Now I can, though. Because she is!"

"And Ed was pleased?"

"He cried. Actually got wet-eyed. Right there in the room, in front of the technician. I think it suddenly got very real for him, when he saw that."

"Ah, bless him."

"I wouldn't go that far."

"How is he? Still working the crazy hours?"

"Pretty much. I've given him the rest of the pregnancy. Then things have to change."

"Does he know that?"

"No. I mean, he makes promises until he's blue in the face. But no, I haven't issued any ultimatums. It's not my forte."

"You'd better get better at it, otherwise he'll carry on."

"I know."

"Is he working because he has to, or because he wants to?"

"Bit of both, I think. I mean, I think the long hours are part of the culture. England wasn't any different, really. But I think he's having a ball, too. I think he loves it."

"And you don't want to piss on his bonfire?"

"No. I will, mind you, once she's here. I'm not going to be a single parent."

"Good for you! So, everything else all right, with her, I mean?"

"Yeah. Think so. They had this amazing machine; it took a three-D picture of her. You can see the profile and everything. It's extraordinary."

"Fancy."

"I'll see if I can scan it and send it to you."

"Polly is obsessed. She'd love that."

"Bless her."

"She's got a list of names for you. Don't hold your breath. I know Britney is on it, and Hannah."

"Nothing wrong with Hannah."

"There is if you have to have Montana as a middle name. You got any ideas?"

"Lots. I want something cool. Ed wants classic. So there are two lists, basically."

"Tell him he can name your boys."

"Don't think he'll go for that."

"Oh, Eve, it's so exciting. I wish you were here, or I was there. I feel like I'm missing out. My first niece. I'm missing it all."

"We'll be home for Christmas, Cath. And you'll come out when she's born, won't you?"

"Try keeping me away."

"Why don't you bring Polly?"

"I don't think I'd get away with leaving her behind."

"And then we'll come home in the summer."

"It's not the same."

"I know. I miss you, too, Sis."

"You tell that husband of yours to take care of you. No heavy furniture, all that stuff."

"I'll tell him."

"Tell him I'll kick his arse if he doesn't look after you properly. I know where he lives."

"I'll tell him."

KIM

Jason was home, and she'd cooked dinner. She'd really been trying, lately. She'd felt a shift, after July Fourth — felt that she'd pushed Jason as close to the edge as she'd ever seen him, being nasty to Rachael at the party. Words exchanged that night, never used before, still burned in her ears and her heart. She had been frightened by the change. It seemed almost like he'd given up on her. He'd been so quiet, the weekends through August. So cautious and deliberate when he spoke to her, which wasn't often. He'd been friendly, without being warm. There'd been no intimacy between them, during the days or at night.

He'd concentrated all his efforts on Avery, and she'd responded, which was unfamiliar to Kim, who was more used to using Avery if not as a weapon, then as armor against him. Avery was hers, after all. But that had changed, too, during the late summer. Avery actually wanted her father, this new dad, who took a real interest in her and wanted to have fun all day. She wanted to go exploring in rock pools with him, and to sit on his shoulders in the surf and squeal with delight as the waves broke on his head and splashed her. For once, Kim was the outsider. She didn't like how that felt, and she'd come back to the city with a new, firmer resolve to try harder to include him or, bizarrely, to include herself.

She didn't know how much he had noticed at first. He'd had a lot of work in the first couple of weeks of September. And a lot of what she did, he wouldn't have known anyway.

She was forcing herself to do things she hadn't done before. She was leaving Avery with Esme for chunks of time in the mornings. How hard that had been. She'd joined a Pilates class, and she went three times a week. At first she'd hated everything about it. She'd hated leaving Avery, hated biting back the instructions she wanted to bark at Esme, ensuring that every minute of her absence was filled as she thought it should be. Hated Avery's not crying as she left. She'd hated the room full of happy, chatty women with unfeasibly tiny asses, and not being able to do the exercises so that she felt the way the instructor said she should feel.

Slowly, gradually, though, she was coming around. The instructor had known she was faking, and she'd knelt patiently beside Kim, explaining each move, and now she did feel it; she felt connected with her body and her muscles for the first time in a long time. You could see it, too, after a few weeks. At least she could see it, naked at home in front of the mirror. There was a new tightness across the midriff, and her shoulders were less hunched. She was aware of how she stood, how she looked. The hated pouch was smaller.

The freedom felt good, too. For the longest time, she had gone through life with a strict set of self-inflicted rules. Where could the stroller go? When was nap time for Avery? Was this the right thing to be doing? Now she could go where she wanted, whenever. She could have her toenails painted at twelve thirty, while Esme gave Avery lunch. She could shop for vegetables and fruits down at Whole Foods without having to let Avery count potatoes and steal grapes, and afterward, she could take the escalators to the second-floor stores and wander around J.Crew and Sephora, if that was what she wanted to do. Sit with a book in an armchair in Borders — an adult book, in the adult section. For ten minutes, or twenty. Or half an hour.

She ran into Eve one day, in Gymboree. Eve had two or three outfits in her hand. Kim wondered whether she'd mind being seen; the outfits were all definitely girly. But

Eve had beamed when she'd seen her, holding up the clothes, and whispering conspiratorially, "Guess what flavor, then!"

Eve knew nothing of Kim's struggle, and for the first time in a long time, Kim was happy to talk to someone about motherhood, and about Avery, without mentioning the assisted conception. It didn't matter. They talked while Eve paid, and then they wandered up the street together and even stopped for a Jamba Juice, chatting about their daughters. Eve seemed lit up from inside, and Kim felt light and easy.

The biggest revelation was how okay Avery was with this new mother, this new life. It made her dedication look and feel to her like martyrdom. Avery hadn't needed her to do what she had done. This child, the one who spent time away from her, with Esme and with Jason, and who turned a tiny bit golden in the warm September sunshine, and who talked, in the bath, about children she'd played with in the park with Esme, was lighter and easier and giggled more.

Kim could almost feel herself unclenching. Like she'd been holding herself taut and tense, for years — which, of course, was exactly what she had been doing — and was now, finally, starting to relax. The sky was not falling in because she wasn't the one who woke Avery up from every damn nap she ever took. Or because Esme let her have a Mister Softee ice cream from the truck on the corner of Seventy-sixth Street and Lex.

She actually liked Esme. She'd had no idea how lovely she really was. That made her feel ridiculous. Esme eventually felt brave enough, mystified but grateful at the change in her employer, to make a few suggestions about Avery. And Kim listened. It didn't automatically make her panic to relinquish control. What she had to force herself to do, at the beginning, driven by a creeping fear about Jason, became easier and more natural every day.

When they'd first been married, long before the dream of Avery turned into the nightmare of IVF, she'd cooked for Jason several times a week. Her office had been near Grand Central, where there was a spectacular market, manageably small, for commuters and harassed executives, but stocked with a huge variety of meat, fish, vegetables, and cheeses. It had become a ritual. Two or three nights, she'd stop off there on the way home to pick up fresh ingredients for dinner. She'd actually made things — marinades and sauces and even pasta, from scratch — in their small midtown kitchen, stuffed full of the aspirational appliances and gadgets they'd registered for at Williams-Sonoma before the wedding. Food had been their aphrodisiac and their foreplay, and her gift of love to him, and mealtimes had been elaborate and lengthy, with candles on the table, a bottle of wine, and a CD in the player. And they had talked. How they had talked.

Now she wanted to get back to that. She wanted to get back to those people they'd been before they'd gotten separated in the maze of their lives.

She hoped they weren't too lost.

JASON

He had noticed, of course. He'd noticed everything. The day she'd come back from the Hamptons, she'd been different. He'd been ready, after the summer, to talk about a divorce. He'd run the word around his head, tried it on. This wasn't a life. This wasn't how he wanted to spend the next twenty, thirty years. Maybe it was time to give up.

But then she started to make changes. At first the changes were small. She had her hair cut differently. She kissed him good-bye on the lips and not the cheek in the mornings, when he left for work, and she actually looked at him when she did. He thought she'd lost weight, not that she really needed to. Either that or she'd started holding herself differently.

The way she asked him if he'd be home for dinner was different, too. She always sounded hopeful. Now on the nights when he said yes, he'd come home to a fragrant apartment, full of the smell of a home-cooked meal. To a table laid for two. No CNN.

At first he was bewildered. He didn't know what to attribute this to. Jason had no game plan. His behavior wasn't deliberate or calculated, and so he didn't immediately see Kim's new leaf as a result of something he'd done or said, or not done or not said. In August he'd just been protecting himself. He didn't have the energy to battle with Kim anymore. It wasn't who he wanted to be. But the night of the July Fourth party at Rachael's, when he'd looked in on his wife and daughter, made him realize that he needed to have his own relationship with Avery. He couldn't rely on Kim to make Avery feel about him the way he wanted her to feel. Not warring with Kim was the by-product of concentrating his efforts on Avery, not the other way around.

If you'd asked him, that July night, whether his marriage stood a chance, he'd have told you no. He'd have said that he couldn't see a way through — that they were surviving on the memory of something that had once been good, and on the old promise of the people they had once been together but were no longer capable of being. The fear he'd felt that night was not of losing Kim. He'd come to believe he'd lost her years ago. It was of losing Avery, his daughter. Without ever really knowing her.

He was disconcerted a little by this Kim. He did a great job of quashing any excitement or hopefulness. He couldn't trust her. And he didn't know if she was just forcing herself.

So the dinners were eaten, but the conversations were stilted and awkward. In the old days they'd washed up together and usually gone straight to bed, if they could actually wait until they got out of the kitchen. Now he thanked her, almost formally, for the meals and insisted on doing the dishes alone, saying she deserved to put her feet up and watch TV.

He often thought, as he stood at the sink, staring into the windows of his neighbors, that if this marriage was a game of chess, then this was stalemate. He'd tried. He'd tried for a long, long time. He wasn't trying now. Not really. Kim was. Trouble was, he wasn't sure he wanted her to.

It was almost funny.

EMILY

The alarm clock buzzed once, twice. Emily reached over without opening her eyes and pushed the off button. But instead of swinging her legs out onto the wooden floor, she rolled over, her arm curling around Jackson's smooth, brown back. The running didn't seem quite so important these days. And the bike hadn't come down off the wall in a week. She was in a cocoon. They were. She remembered the rest of her life, in moments. She thought of her mom while she showered. And of Charlotte, listening to NPR while she dressed. At work, she made herself think about what she was doing. But there wasn't any food in the fridge, and she hadn't checked her bank balance in days. Everything, anything that wasn't Jackson was a distraction. An interference.

She opened her eyes and looked at his face as he slept. The clock behind him said 6:15 a.m. They didn't need to get up until 7:30. Jackson slept deeply, but when she moved away in her sleep, he pulled her back uncon-

413

sciously, tightening his grip around her waist, one hand possessively under her pajama top, against her breast.

Last night, they'd kissed and touched themselves drunk, and she'd almost had sex with him. She couldn't wait much longer. She didn't want to. All the pieces were almost in place. She wanted him, that much was beyond doubt, and he couldn't hide how badly he wanted her. She trusted him. Or at least she thought she was beginning to. She liked him. They talked for hours. And lay in silence for hours.

Emily had never felt like this before, and this guy, the guy in the bed with her — he was the last person she'd have ever guessed might do this to her.

But she liked how it felt.

CHARLOTTE

Che must be on holiday. She hadn't seen him for almost two weeks now. If she'd been braver, she'd have asked one of the others. Or the relief doorman. But she didn't know his name. And she was embarrassed to sound interested in Che's whereabouts.

She could have asked in Spanish. If she'd been brave enough. She'd been working really hard. She seemed to have a lot more time to herself lately. The garden was finished. Emily was busy with Jackson. She was happy for her friend, but she missed her. It was the story of her female friendships from high school and college all over again. She was all well and good until the next guy came along. Then she was easily dispensed with. Until the next heartbreak, when her services and sympathy were required again. It was a familiar pattern, and there was almost something comforting about it — the natural order was preserved. Emily wasn't unkind or anything. She was in love, that was all. And a romantic like Charlotte, who lived for that stuff, vicariously if necessary (and it always was), could hardly complain. It was just that they'd had fun, in the summer, the two of them. She missed Emily. Even Madison was in a strange mood lately — distracted and grouchy.

It was almost time. She was going to speak to him, as soon as he was back. She was going to ask him if he wanted to go out. Maybe for Halloween. Or to the Macy's Thanksgiving Day Parade. Maybe sooner. Maybe by the time of the parade, they'd already be going out together.

In her mind, the encounter the two of them had had in the elevator, the previous

July, had taken on qualities it hadn't entirely possessed at the time. He'd held her glance for just a little longer. His smile had been more intimate. Their conversation more insightful. She'd built it up, and if she knew, in her heart of hearts, that it wasn't all quite true, she also believed that soon it could be.

To Charlotte, a woman who had dwelt in a sort of fairyland for most of her adult life, this was already as real as it got.

■ ■ ■ ■

OCTOBER

■ ■ ■ ■

RACHAEL

Rachael hadn't seen David for three weeks. He'd been to see the children, three or four times during the week, and on the weekends. She'd made sure it was Milena he saw when he came to the apartment. At first she was too angry. Too afraid of showing him how colossally hurt she was. Then too humiliated.

So far, the children hadn't asked too many questions. Jacob was the only one who was likely to discern the difference between then and now. David had always traveled on business and worked his fair share of late nights. If Jacob had wondered, he'd asked Milena, either through some innate sense that Rachael didn't want to talk about it, or because it was Milena who happened to be around.

She knew she couldn't go on like this indefinitely. Late at night, alone in bed, she wondered if she was overreacting. She didn't even know the extent of what he'd done, did she? The details she'd found too abhorrent to know at the time now tortured her. She wanted to know everything. She needed to see him, but every time it seemed possible, that new cowardice she hadn't realized she possessed surfaced, and she couldn't.

In the end it was Milena who made her do it. Milena was the only person who knew. She hadn't been able to tell anyone else — not her friends, who were, anyway, mostly their friends; not people at work; and certainly not her mother or father. One evening, while she was folding laundry, Milena came and sat at the kitchen table with her.

"You need to talk to him, Rachael. You need to sort this out."

"I know. I don't know what to say to him."

"Let him talk. Then you'll know what to say. You need to give him the chance to explain to you. You need to know what's happened. You can't make any decisions about the future when you don't even know what he's done."

"Does it matter? Are there degrees? Isn't cheating cheating?"

Milena smiled and clicked her tongue. "Of course not. There are a thousand degrees, sweetheart. Sex, love, soul mates. Infidelity of the mind, of the heart, of the body parts. Most important is why. You need to know why."

"Are any of the degrees okay, Milena?"

"No, chicken. None of the degrees are okay. Nothing that hurts you, or risks hurting the children, is okay. But some things can be forgiven more easily than others. If you choose to."

Rachael wasn't sure that she could forgive any of it. Or whether forgiveness was something you could choose to bestow, but she knew Milena was right.

And so she agreed to meet him. Lunchtime, not evening. Neutral territory. A restaurant not too close to either of their offices, as quiet as she could make it. She told her assistant she wouldn't be back in the afternoon. She couldn't imagine being in any state to go back.

To be fair, David looked terrible, too. She hated the "rabbit in the headlights" look on his face. She wanted to slap him, and at the same time she wanted him to hold her. For so many years, it had been him. He'd been the cure and the antidote and the answer. She couldn't get used to the idea that he wasn't that person anymore.

They made brittle, polite small talk for the first five minutes. Took brief refuge in the subject of their children. It was surreal.

David took a sip of water. "Rachael. I'm sorry. I want to say that to you. That's what I want you to hear from me most of all."

"I'm sure you are." Her voice was shrill with sarcasm. She hadn't meant to begin that way, and under the table she squeezed her fingers into her palms. Don't be like that.

"Don't be like that," he implored. "Not sorry I got caught. Sorry I ever did anything to hurt you."

"What did you do, exactly, David? I think it's about time I knew what we were talking about, don't you?"

"I wanted to tell you straightaway, that first night."

"I wasn't ready to listen then. Now I have to be."

He took a deep breath. "Her name is Stephanie. She's someone at work. I mean, she works for the company — she's not in my department or anything. I don't see her from day to day, not in the normal run of things . . ." His voice faded away, but Rachael didn't interject.

"It started earlier this year."

"When?"

"January."

She raised her eyebrows. Longer than

she'd hoped.

"It's all been painfully obvious, I suppose, how much of a fucking idiot I've been. The overnights, and off sites in the spring. She never came to the apartment. She never met the children or anything like that."

"I never thought for a moment that she might have."

"She didn't."

If he wanted credit for that, he could forget it.

"And the summer?"

He'd been afraid she would ask.

"Yes, I saw her this summer. When you were away."

"Fourth of July weekend?" She was staring down at her cutlery.

He was afraid to lie anymore. "Yes."

She sighed. He saw the pain that last one inflicted, in her face.

"Do you love her?"

"No." His voice was scornful.

She raised an eyebrow at his tone. "Do you not love me?"

"No. I mean, yes. I love you. I still love you. I never stopped loving you. And our children."

"Don't bring our children into it. We're separate. Not at this moment. I can't bear to have you talk about them. But you've done this to them, as well, you know. Not just to me. To our family."

"I know."

She stared down at the tablecloth, past his head, trying not to cry.

"Rachael." He wanted to touch her hand, but he didn't dare.

"So why, David? Why would you do it?"

"Look, I can't say anything that's going to make this okay, can I?"

"No, you can't. But I need you to make me understand why. I mean, you must have an answer to that. You were the one who did it. You must know why."

"It's complicated."

"No, it isn't, David. It really isn't. I thought we were happy. I mean really happy. I've lain awake night after night since this happened, going over and over everything. I don't get it. Weren't you happy? Were you lying when you said you were?"

"No."

Again he felt the urge to take her hand, but when he reached across the table, she flinched from him, and she knocked her glass over. Water spilled all across the tablecloth and into her lap. She dabbed at herself with her napkin, waving the omnipresent waiter away. David saw that she had tears in her eyes and she was shaking. She wasn't wearing her wedding ring, and that alarmed him. There was a narrow white band of flesh on her finger where the ring had been for all those years. She'd never taken it off.

It seemed hopeless.

What was she hoping to hear? She didn't even know. "This isn't going to work. You don't have anything to tell me. You can't fix this, can you?" Rachael stood up.

"Please don't go."

"I can't stay."

"Stay. Talk to me."

"I've been talking, David. I'm the only one who's been talking."

He threw a twenty-dollar bill on the table and followed her out, feeling the eyes of the waiters and the other diners on him.

Outside, she was trying to hail a cab. It had started to rain.

"I was stupid to think you could say anything that would make a difference."

"What are you saying?"

A cab pulled up across the street, discharging passengers. Rachael ran across in front of the oncoming traffic and had climbed into the car before he had a chance to catch her. She couldn't look at him. He wanted to bang on the windows. He wanted to lie across the front of the car so the cabbie couldn't drive away. He wanted to scream. He did none of those things, and the car sped away as he stood aside, watching his wife disappear.

It was still raining the next day, in the late afternoon, when his secretary brought in a letter that had obviously been sent by courier. It was from Rachael's lawyer — the one her family had always used. He'd met the guy at his wedding. The man had pumped his hand and wished him luck. He'd uncapped beers for David at the July Fourth party in Southampton. Now he was asking for details of David's own lawyer. Rachael believed it was time, the letter said, to open a dialogue about the terms of a divorce settlement.

David hadn't seen Stephanie, except at work, since Rachael had found out about the affair. She had tried to speak to him right after the weekend, but he'd written a terse, brief email, telling her that Rachael knew about her and that she must understand he could have nothing more to do with her. He didn't miss her at all. Sex was the very last thing on his mind, and sex was really all they had had, so it didn't surprise him. He saw her a few days after he sent the email, in a sandwich shop near the office. She was with a coworker, several places ahead of him in line. He didn't stay. But it struck him for the first time how average-looking she was — how ordinary.

Rachael, by contrast, had never looked so lovely to him as when she walked into the restaurant on that rainy day. He knew people were looking at her. People always looked at Rachael. Her hair, which she battled so valiantly to smooth and tame, refused to comply in wet weather, and tendrils curled around her forehead and ears. It always took him back — that damp hair of hers. Back to the surf that morning a million years ago. Back to her beautiful exhausted head lying back on a pillow in the delivery suite after each of the children had been born. Back to Rachael, fresh from a thousand showers at home, swallowed by a vast terry robe, padding barefoot around the apartment. It took him back. She had looked tired and vulnerable, but her eyes were still huge, made a darker brown by the pallor.

He sat at his desk, facing outward, to the view up Lexington Avenue, with the letter in his hand, staring out, trying hard, he was surprised to find, not to cry. And wondering just what it was, deep within his psyche, that had led him to this act of extraordinary self-sabotage.

JASON

Kim had said something strange was going on next door. She hadn't spoken much about the Schulmans since the Fourth of July party. They were a hot-button topic, he supposed — for both of them, in different ways. But he'd raised it, this time. He hadn't seen David for weeks, and although it wasn't unusual for him to take business trips, they were usually brief. Jason couldn't remember the last time he'd seen him. Or large bundles of his dry cleaning, returned during the day and hung next to his own on the long rack in the doormen's closet. Or the five of them together, heading off for the park.

Kim said Esme had been talking, down in the basement, to the Schulmans' maid. Not Milena, who would never be so indiscreet. This was Padma, the girl who came in to clean and do laundry twice a week and didn't have the same degree of loyalty to and affection for her employer. They'd been in the basement laundry, apparently, Esme and Padma, folding washing, and Padma had remarked casually that her loads were down, with Mr. Schulman not being around. No damp gym clothes, no black and navy socks to match up. Esme had asked where he was, and Padma had raised her index finger to her lips, shushing and shaking her head. Mr. Schulman had moved out, she said.

Kim spoke nervously. She wasn't used to Esme sharing confidences with her; that part of their relationship was very new. She wasn't sure how Jason would react to the gossiping, either. She concentrated on not sounding excited or salacious about the story. She still remembered the tone of her own voice, that day at the beach. His face as he watched her speak.

"Moved out? When?"

"Last month, Esme said."

"And so what does that mean?"

Kim shrugged. "I don't know. I don't know if it's permanent."

"Have you seen much of Rachael, since the summer?"

"Hardly anything. You?"

"No."

Truth was, Kim didn't feel excited or salacious. It made her feel a bit sick. If perfect Rachael Schulman's perfect marriage could fall apart (and why else would David move out?), then hers was far from immune. She was doing what she could, but she wasn't getting far. Jason was still careful and remote and distant. Panic fluttered deep in her belly. She wondered whether the fear was of being without him or simply of being alone.

EVE

Eve's first Halloween was in full swing. She could have had no idea how huge an occasion it was for the city. There was a carnival atmosphere. Stores all up and down Lexington hung lanterns and fake cobwebs and gave away small packets of sweets. Restaurants dressed up their staff and offered special ghoulish menus. Everywhere was crowded, although it was pretty cold, and a school night. Children milled about, serious about the business of collecting their loot in plastic buckets. The building next door held a party in the foyer. All the kids on this block, and others around the neighborhood, went. The residents dressed up and hung decorations across their wooden paneling. They took turns manning the candy buckets. Someone had made a red punch that seemed somehow to smoke, and was filling orange plastic cups with a ladle.

Earlier in the week, there had been a list in the elevator where residents could sign up for trick or treat, with a time slot. Eve had written in "7A, 5–9 p.m." and bought party packs of candy at CVS, which she'd tipped into her biggest bowl. By six p.m. no one had rung the doorbell and she was curious to go outside, so she left the bowl on the table between their front door and the Piscatellas and called the elevator. Maria came out. Eve hadn't seen her for a couple of weeks, she realized. It seemed like that wouldn't happen, living so close. But it did.

Maria cooed and aahed at the bump. "You're really showing now, huh?"

Eve nodded and rubbed her stomach proudly. "Almost twenty weeks."

"You look beautiful. Can I touch it?"

"Go ahead. You can do whatever you like, if you say I look beautiful. To me, I just look fat."

Maria laid her two hands reverently on Eve's belly, letting them rest there for just a moment, as though it was good luck. Maybe it was an Italian thing. Eve didn't mind. Strangers on the subway — that was something else. The other day she'd had to change cars to escape the attentions of some nosy woman who asked more questions than the ob-gyn. But Maria was lovely.

"Nonsense. You modern girls — you're crazy. You want to put on ten pounds and

431

be back in your skinny jeans a week later. Relax, enjoy. Be a good home for your baby, Eve — that's all that matters." Maria always said the right thing. "Me, I was huge, with both of them. I ate pasta every day. Ernest fed me. He wanted big healthy bambini. Got them, too — nine pounds the first, the second almost ten. Still makes my eyes water, thinking of it."

Eve grimaced. That sounded vast.

Maria laughed. "Listen, one day for a lifetime. It's worth it, believe me."

"I know."

"So you're taking the little one out for her first Halloween, huh?"

"Mine, too. We don't have anything like this in England. We try, a bit, these days, but the effort seems a little pathetic in comparison to all this. The stores have been full of Halloween stuff for weeks now. I want to go and see what it's all about."

"It's crazy." Maria shook her hands above her head. "It'll be easier taking her now, when she's in there, than when she's a toddler, believe me. We lost my Bradley one year. My God. There's a whole street, over on the West Side — closes to traffic, every house decorated. People come from all over the city to trick-or-treat there — come early and stay late. It's a scene, I tell you. We lost him in the crush. Lost him! Can you believe? He was about four years old."

"How scary!"

"You don't know how scary. It was maybe five minutes, that's all. I remember I had Ariel in the stroller. I was running one way, Ernest the other. I thought I was going to die. Everyone looked the same. I remember he was wearing a little devil costume. Red cape, horns. There must have been a hundred little devils there that night, all in the exact same getup from Kmart. It was like hell."

"Where was he?"

"Sat on the step of one of the brownstones — counting his candy. That's my Bradley. Has to be organized. He was always that way, from a baby. You never had to yell at him about his homework, nothing. Ariel now — she was a different kettle of fish." She laughed at the recollection. "Easier now, believe me!"

KIM

Trick-or-treating was out of the question for Avery, even for this new Kim that she was working so hard on becoming. She hadn't gone cold turkey on the old Kim, and the old Kim was absolutely not into the

433

whole Halloween thing. Everything about the holiday brought out the old fears and doubts. The evening was fraught with danger, so far as Kim was concerned. It was dark, it was cold out, the streets were too crowded. Regular candy was bad for you. Adulterated candy could be fatal. Every year, didn't you read dreadful stories about apples with razor blades, and poisons injected into sour gums? In future years, there might be controlled experiences Avery could have — Halloween parties at school, at friends' houses. Kim might get over it and become one of the carefree Halloween mothers surrounding her this year. Until then, they just pretended it wasn't happening.

Kim didn't put candy out either. She didn't like strangers coming to the door. She had raised the point at the co-op's AGM the previous year: surely opening the building to nonresidents posed a security risk? But they had done it again this year. Kim had not signed the list, and she hoped no one would bother her. If Esme had been working, then maybe . . . If she knew what time Jason would be home from work, then maybe. But Esme had gone home, and Jason hadn't said when he'd be back.

She'd made a lamb tagine, finding the

recipe in an ancient pre-Avery cookbook, pages stuck together with years-old gravy, and its rich cumin fragrance filled the apartment. The couscous sat on the side in its bowl, waiting.

RACHAEL

"Come on. Come on. Come on." Rachael took a deep breath and tried to count to ten. At the Fifty-first Street stop on the 6 line, twenty people were trying to squeeze themselves into a subway car with room for only ten more. Manners and reserve went out the window as everyone squeezed and insinuated themselves into other people's personal space. One person was refusing to get off, though his bag and half his enormous ass were definitely not on the train. The doors sprang open again and again, and an announcement came from the front of the train, the driver as exasperated as the passengers, saying that the doors wouldn't close with objects in the way. The fat "object" in question pretended not to listen and kept leaning inward in the hope that someone might create the five or six inches necessary to let the rest of his backside on. Rachael silently cursed, and around her, people muttered and moaned.

Eventually a young guy pulled the buds from his iPod out of his ears and issued an authoritative profanity, and the doors were closed five seconds later, although the train didn't move for another fifteen. The more of a hurry you were in, the slower the train went; it was like the eleventh commandment, only handed down to the train drivers. Rachael had left work a few minutes later than normal; she'd been on a conference call to LA and hadn't been able to get them off the phone, since they were blissfully midafternoon. And the subway was slow. The revelers were already out in force — adults in costume, in the late afternoon. Didn't these people have jobs? Women in sexy nurse outfits. Men with vampire teeth and painted-on widow's peaks.

The kids would kill her. She'd promised to take them out trick-or-treating, and she was late.

Of the many things about David that made Rachael mad these days, this was one of the biggest. She hated that he'd made her feel so damn guilty about the kids. She'd never have wanted to be late for them, but it had never mattered so much before when she was. She felt compelled to be better and better than ever before — to get every single encounter and conversation and moment with them absolutely right, to make up for what was going so horribly wrong at home. And that was his fault, for God's sake. Not hers. She was angry every day, and she hated it. She was too angry to eat and too angry to sleep. It was making her feel ill.

So was this damn train. They had lurched into Sixty-eighth Street now — Hunter College. The car rearranged itself, exhaling briefly as passengers disembarked, then sucking in again as a new raft of young students got on.

Jason Kramer was suddenly six inches from her face, with his arm clutching the rail above her head. Which was the last thing she wanted to deal with right now. He'd taken his jacket off, and there was a small sweat patch in the armpit of his white shirt. He was always just a little too close, only this time it wasn't his fault. She fixed a smile as the train pulled out of the station at last.

"Jason! Hi!"

"Hi, Rachael."

"Crowded, huh?"

"Just a bit."

They elected not to talk further, just smiled and grimaced and rolled their eyes at each other like bad mime artists. At one point the train lurched, and Rachael was flung (so far as you could be flung in a car so crowded) into Jason. For the briefest second, she was sure that he put his head down on top of hers, where it had hit his chest, his cheek resting for just a moment against her hair, but just as quickly he moved back and laughed nervously. Next to them a couple of kids, she in skintight jeans and he in trousers so baggy they defied gravity, passed the time by kissing noisily, slurping at each other's wide-open mouths, oblivious to the discomfort their behavior generated around them.

It seemed to take forever to reach Seventy-seventh Street. Rachael and Jason spilled out of the car gratefully, swept along by the tide of people also rushing toward the light and the air of Lexington Avenue. Rachael thought about ducking into a store on some pretext, and thus losing Jason, but she was already late, so she resigned herself to walking the few blocks to the apartment with him. She walked as fast as she could in three-inch heels, talking a little too loudly about the weather, how mild it was for Halloween. How quickly it would be Thanksgiving. Anodyne, innocuous conversation, passing the blocks . . . Jason, however, was not to be distracted.

"Are you okay, Rachael?"

So he knew. The tone of his voice gave it

away. News passed through the building in the heating vents. Maids, doormen, porters. Who came, who went. How often you changed the sheets on your bed. What you threw away. They knew too much about you. No such thing as a secret in an apartment building. Not for long.

But it was precisely this pitying, concerned face, this inappropriately gentle voice, that Rachael had been hoping to avoid. Jason was her neighbor. He wasn't her friend. He knew nothing about her and David. Not really. She didn't want to be having this conversation with him.

"I'm fine, Jason. Really. Thanks for asking."

"I mean, I don't want to interfere, and it's none of my business —"

"No." So don't then, she thought.

"But, well, I'm really sorry to hear about . . . about you and David."

She didn't answer.

"And if there's anything, anything at all I can do for you, please, just let me know."

"That's very kind, Jason, really. But there's no need."

"Even if you just want to talk . . ."

If she did want to talk (and she really didn't), what on earth would make him

439

think he would be the person she'd want to talk to?

"Talk about what?"

She should have let it go, but he'd annoyed her now. He stuttered a little, she was glad to see.

"David. He's . . . left . . . he's gone . . . hasn't he? I mean, I . . ."

"I've asked him to move out. He's been having an affair, and I've asked him to give me some space."

He might as well know the truth. It couldn't be worse than whatever the rumors were. He wanted to talk? Well, then, let him talk . . .

But now Jason was strangely quiet.

"That's what you were getting at, isn't it? That's what everybody wants to know."

"I didn't mean . . ."

They were home now. Jason at least did her the courtesy of not talking in front of the doorman. Maybe this excruciating conversation was over. But he started again, once the elevator doors had closed. Standing just too close, as usual.

"I think he's a fool."

For a second she couldn't believe that's what he'd said. It was so staggeringly inappropriate. "Excuse me?"

Jason smiled shyly, but a blush was spreading across his cheeks. "I'm sorry, but I do. He's a fool if he's cheated on you, Rachael."

Rachael stared at her shoes and wondered how to reply. She was suddenly tearful. How dare he do that? Jason grabbed her hand and held it tightly between his own, clasped at his heart. The action of pulling her hand there turned her toward him, and her hip bone banged against his. It was a strange and awkward movement.

"Because you're so lovely. Who could possibly be better than you?"

He was trying to look into her eyes, but Rachael couldn't let him. This was ridiculous.

The elevator stopped on their floor, the doors opened, and the two of them stood staring at a miniature cop, a cowboy, and a Disney princess, who in turn stared back at them. Jason dropped Rachael's hand like it was molten hot and, at last, stepped back away from her.

"Hey, you guys! You look great!" His voice was too big and hearty for the small foyer, and the children shrank back.

"Fantastic!" Rachael didn't think she sounded normal either. "I love it. Mia, did Millie do your makeup? You look beautiful!" Mia had small pink circles drawn on each cheek and vivid blue on her eyelids.

Milena stood in the doorway to Rachael's apartment, eyeing Jason suspiciously.

Rachael spun around and narrowed her eyes at him, but her tone was light when she spoke.

"So, great to see you, Jason. Give our love to Kim and to Avery, won't you?"

Then she and Millie bustled the children back into the apartment, and she closed the door and leaned against it from the inside.

"What was that?"

"God knows, Millie. God knows."

Left alone on the landing, Jason felt exactly as stupid as he had acted just now. He didn't know what had come over him. What an idiot he was. He looked at his own front door and tried to refocus his mind on what was waiting for him on the other side.

What a mess.

VIOLET

Violet had gone walking with her, raising an eyebrow ever so slightly when Eve said that Ed was away overnight in Washington. Eve saw the eyebrow, but she ignored it. She was trying not to mind — all the overnight trips and late evenings in the office. He'd promised and she'd promised to believe that once the baby was here, he'd slow down a bit — be there for her and his child. He was bound to have to pull more than his weight at work this first year; he had to prove himself. That's what she told herself. Violet's wandering eyebrow wasn't going to get her started tonight.

They walked twenty or thirty blocks, watching the kids with their plastic pumpkins and the teenagers with their racy costumes. It was fun just to be outside on the street, watching.

Once they were tired, they went back to the building in a cab. Todd and Greg were on their way out, dressed as Morticia Addams and Uncle Fester. Todd looked uncannily good in a long black wig and stretch velvet. Greg just looked tolerant. They were going to a party, they said, then down to the Village for the annual parade. Violet had put jacket potatoes in the oven before they went out, and she served them split, loaded with butter and baked beans she'd warmed in the microwave. With just the addition of a humble sausage, she'd added, it would have been the perfect autumnal supper. Violet still missed sausages, after all these years. Especially in the autumn. Baked beans, the only ones that tasted right, you could get in most supermarkets these days — in the weird eclectic selection they labeled as English. Branston Pickle, Marmite, baked beans, Yorkshire tea, and lemon puff biscuits. They always had lemon puff biscuits in the English section, even though Eve couldn't remember the last time she'd seen one in England. The eighties, she thought. But sausages were a constant source of disappointment to both the expats — the novice and the old hand.

They ate the feast on their laps on the sofa (Eve reflecting briefly that her lap's days were definitely numbered), and when she'd put her plate down, Eve rubbed her tummy. "There you go, baby. You may have an American passport, but you'll also have a taste for English food if Violet and I have anything to do with it."

"No peanut butter and jelly sandwiches in your future then?"

Eve wrinkled her nose in distaste. "Not even if they start calling it jam."

Violet handed her a cup of tea. Always a cup, at Violet's. She eschewed mugs absolutely.

Eve curled up in her favorite spot on Violet's sofa.

"So, Violet Wallace. I'm ready to hear about Mr. Wallace."

Violet winked. "Isn't this a night for scary stories and spooky tales?"

"I've always preferred a romance myself. This one is a romance, right?"

Violet sat down. "You're incorrigible."

"Come on, you have to tell me. You know you want to. You can't leave me hanging . . ."

"All right, all right . . . Mr. Wallace. Steadman Wallace. He was the youngest partner at the firm, but he was ten years older than me. In his early forties when I joined the firm, just after I graduated. I didn't have much to do with him at first. Not for a long time, really. I was still learning my job, and there was a lot of new information to take in. I enrolled in a few evening courses in basic accountancy — not because I wanted to train as one but just because I wanted to be better at the job I had. Believe it or not, I actually found it pretty interesting. Well, some of it, anyway.

"Mr. Johnson was a sweetheart really, looking back. He was good to me. I enjoyed going to work. I was happier than I'd ever been. I think of them as my Mary Tyler Moore years. Everything I earned was mine, and every decision about my life was mine, too. I moved into a fourth-floor one-bedroom flat in a brand-new condo just off Fifth Avenue, south of the Guggenheim. I loved that place. It was just a rental, but it felt more like mine than anywhere I'd ever lived before, if that makes sense. It was pretty small but perfectly formed, and I had a park view from the front windows.

"I got to know some of my neighbors, and there were a few of us — single girls. I was older than most of them, of course, but I quite liked that role. I was a bit of a house mother; that's where I did most of my listening. Broken hearts — all of that, you know? And I explored. Like I'd wanted to all those years earlier when I'd gotten off the boat. I got to know the city like the back of my hand. It was relatively safe then; it wasn't until the seventies and eighties that there were big no-go areas. This was nineteen sixty-two, before the world went crazy, you know? I went everywhere. I did the walking of my life — miles and miles. I think I saw every painting and sculpture there was to see."

"It sounds amazing."

"It was. I had friends if I wanted company, but quite often I was fine on my own. You know how bossy I am; I loved pleasing myself. I'd never done it before. I'd gone from my parents' house to Gus's parents' house, and then to Gus's house. I'd never had my own money, my own space. It was . . . extraordinary."

"Yeah, yeah! Get to the Mr. Wallace part, will you?"

Violet laughed. "You said you wanted romance. I'm trying to explain to you that those years — between husbands, if you will — those were when I had a romance with myself, sort of. I honestly wasn't looking for a man. I think I thought at that point that I'd spend the rest of my life on my own. And I thought that was okay."

"Until Mr. Wallace made his move . . ."

Violet laughed. "If you'd ever met him, you'd know how hilarious it is to describe him that way. Steadman didn't have 'moves,' as you so charmingly call them."

"So tell me." The baby kicked. It was a very new feeling — only in the last week or so.

"I'm getting there. Mr. Johnson retired in, I think, nineteen sixty-five, when I'd been with the firm two or three years. Around the same time, Steadman's secretary, Mary, went off to have a baby. That was it, in those days. No maternity leave. She was gone, off to the suburbs, never to be seen again. So it made sense for me to transfer to Steadman. I don't think I was even all that pleased about it. I'd been happy with Mr. Johnson. We'd found a great way to work together, and I wasn't sure I wanted to change. I told myself I'd give it a few months."

"And that's when it started."

"Not exactly. It was a really, really slow burn, Steadman and me. With Gus I had the palpitations early on, and they petered out. With Steadman they took a while to start, but they lasted much longer. I know you want to hear about thunderbolts and violins and roses, but it really wasn't like that. Do you know what really happened? The truth? We got to know each other — first at work, then, as time went on, outside of work — and we liked each other. Really got to know each other. We liked each other very much. We were great friends. For the longest time.

"I showed him the city I loved, and he showed me his. Steadman loved opera and classical music — things I'd never really been exposed to. He took me to Carnegie Hall and other places. And I started to love it, too. He taught me about fine food and good wine. We were different, he and I, and I was excited to see things through his eyes. I think I was just . . . ready. I wouldn't have been, after Gus. I needed that time on my own."

"What about him? A guy in his forties, right? Was there ever a Mrs. Wallace?"

"Not before me. He'd been shy. And serious. And hadn't really known where to look."

"And then there you were?"

"I suppose."

"So what made things change between you?"

Violet paused. "A starry night, a supreme soprano, and a gin martini."

"And you said there was no romance in this story."

"I never said that." Violet's eyes were sparkling. She went over to a chest of drawers and pulled out a photograph, looking at it herself, then passing it to Eve. Steadman. In a dinner jacket, his hair slicked back. He was tall and slender. He looked a bit matinee idol, in black-and-white. He had thick-rimmed glasses on, and a shy smile, and one of those faces that seems to belong to another time.

"It was November. Crisp and cold and bright. We'd been to see *La Bohème.* I'd never seen it live before, although Steadman had played me the sound track. It came to the Met in the fall and Steadman got tickets. I couldn't believe the voices. Especially the soprano — Mimi. Her name was Mirella Freni, and she was . . . exquisite. I was . . . moved, I suppose. There was a gin martini, in the bar in the intermission. And there were stars — I'm sure there were — on the walk home. Brighter than I ever remembered seeing them before. Brighter than seemed possible in the city. And he kissed me. He just kissed me. Afterwards he said he'd been wanting to do it forever, but he'd never been brave enough or sure at all that I would be receptive. But something aligned, that night, something just a little bit magical, I suppose. He stopped suddenly, on the sidewalk, outside an antiques store on Madison, and spun around to face me. Then he just took hold of the tops of my arms, tightly, and kissed me."

"And?" Eve's hands were clasped together. "And . . . ?"

"Were you shocked? You must have been. All that time."

"Yes and no. I was, at first, I suppose. But almost immediately — I can't explain it adequately — it seemed like exactly the right thing."

"That's lovely."

"It was, rather." Violet stared into the middle distance for a moment, one finger gently stroking Steadman's cheek in the picture in her hand.

"And that was it?"

"Pretty much. Steadman was old-fashioned. He seemed to set about romanc-

ing me properly, after that. Flowers. Can-
dlelit dinners. The odd passionate clinch
outside my front door, but nothing more.
He wasn't like that. I'd have happily abandoned convention at that point, but Steadman wanted to wait until we were married.

"So it seemed a good idea to get on with
that, as you can imagine. He went down on
one knee, with a Tiffany box." Violet stuck
out her hand, and Eve took it and looked at
the aquamarine and diamond platinum ring
as though she hadn't seen it a hundred
times before.

"It's beautiful."

"Isn't it? He chose exactly what I'd have
chosen for myself. I'd never had an engagement ring before. I hadn't been engaged, in
the traditional sense; it was all so perfunctory and fast and practical with Gus."

"Did Steadman know about Gus?"

"Of course. I couldn't have kept that kind
of thing a secret from him."

"And he didn't mind?"

"What would that have achieved? We both
wanted to move forward. We were excited
about a life together — a new life. Looking
backwards would have been pointless. So I
was a widow, and he was a forty-five-year-
old virgin. Who cared? What mattered was

that we'd found each other. We were so happy."

She looked happy, Eve reflected, just talking about him. Her features had softened, and her eyes were sparkling.

"What kind of wedding did you have?"

"Small. We got married on a Friday, the following May, down at City Hall. We had two people from the office as witnesses, and lunch, just the two of us, at the St. Regis. With champagne. And a night in a suite there, too, but I shall draw a discreet veil over that, except to say, if you'll permit, that that was a wedding night . . ." Just for a moment, the young woman she had been passed across her face, flushed and excited. She went back to the drawer. "I think I have a photograph of us, here. I wore a lilac suit with a pillbox hat. Here we go." She handed Eve a picture of the two of them. "It was a wonderful day. We took the train to Niagara Falls for our honeymoon. I had a new valise from Macy's. I still have it. And a trousseau. Steadman insisted I shop for new clothes. He said I deserved to feel like a bride. He worried that I'd missed out on all the traditional trimmings — the big white dress, the church, all of that. I told him I didn't give a damn. I told him that this, all of this, everything about it, was perfect.

"And I meant it. He was perfect to me. I didn't know that was possible."

Eve thought about Ed. Was he perfect to her? She might have thought so once. She loved him, very much. She never doubted that — at least she never had before. But perfection? That seemed impossible.

She wondered why Violet kept the photographs hidden away in a drawer. One day, she'd ask.

ARTHUR

Arthur Alexander hadn't enjoyed much in recent years. Not a whole lot in his entire life, truthfully. *Benny Hill* reruns on television. Shamed politicians and fallen idols. Anything with heavy cream, preferably pie. That was probably his downfall — the heavy cream. But he may just have enjoyed the ironic, dark humor of dying on Halloween. It was too quick, of course. It did feel like they always said it did — like an elephant sitting on your chest. He'd had the ache down his arm for a couple of days, and been breathless walking back from the store, but at his age neither the aches nor the sensation of breathlessness were unusual, and he thought nothing of them. He'd been tired, too, but what was new? He was always tired.

It sometimes amazed him how much. But he supposed that actually he was more tired *of* life than tired by it these days.

He wouldn't have gone to the doctor, even if he had linked the symptoms. He hated doctors, and now he had no insurance, so doctors pretty much hated him, too. He couldn't remember the last time he'd been. And God forbid that they should hook him up to those monitors and poke and prod at him with their instruments of torture, telling him to stop eating the heavy cream. He was ready to go. He'd been ready for a long time.

If Arthur could have changed anything about his death, short of hastening it by twenty years, he might have chosen to sign up for trick-or-treating in the building, when the sign went up in the elevator last week — although he never had, in all the years he'd lived here — and then he might have died with his door open, slumped in his wing-backed leather armchair, the ultimate trick for the neighborhood's children. That might have made him smile. But he hadn't seen the list. No one came that night to trick-or-treat. Five days later, the porter told the super that Arthur hadn't left garbage in the service entrance all week. The doorman, prompted, added that he hadn't checked his mail either. He wasn't on vacation. Arthur hadn't been on vacation for years. In the end, it was Todd and Greg, on their way out to walk Ulysses, who told Mr. Gonzalez he really should check on him. They went with him, to make sure he did, leaving Ulysses tied to the awning pole. They knocked for ten minutes, calling his name through the door, then let themselves in with the master set of keys and found him.

Hardly any of his neighbors had noticed his absence. Just the two men he'd spent years avoiding. To them, to the other residents, he'd been an old curmudgeon. An irritable, grumpy old man, homophobic and rude, cantankerous and unkempt. They didn't know anything about him. Eve's hunch had been right, though she never knew it. It wasn't their fault. He'd chosen it that way. They didn't know that he'd once wanted to be a doctor himself, that he'd had to put his studies on hold in 1942 when he was called up. They couldn't imagine that he'd been engaged, before the war, to a plump girl with deep blue eyes called Nancy, a girl who couldn't or wouldn't wait for him and married his younger cousin before he came back, and that he hadn't been able to trust anyone fully since. If they had known that Arthur had been in the 42nd Infantry Division during the war, one of the units that marched into Dachau in April 1945, might they have treated him differently — made excuses for his behavior, recognized that a man cannot see those things without being profoundly changed forever? Probably not. New York was full of refugees and survivors. Of that war, and a hundred others. It was possible that descendants of the few Jews that Arthur had liberated during those spring days over sixty years ago were living in the buildings that surrounded his home — on his own block, maybe. Arthur had never been to a Veterans Day parade, never worn his medals. He wasn't proud of himself. He was ashamed of himself, and of everyone else.

He hadn't seen good in the world since that morning, and death, when it came, quick and painful, was more of a relief than anything else.

EMILY

Charlotte and Emily had been out for Thai food. Trip had wanted to spend the evening with her; he'd been invited to a party in Brooklyn, and he'd wanted to take her with him. She hadn't met any of his friends yet.

They were still in the phase where they were enough for each other — where they didn't want to share. She wasn't eager.

She said she'd feel like Barbra Streisand did with Robert Redford's friends in *The Way We Were.* Out of place and gauche. "You're all blue bloods, I bet."

"Absolutely. American royalty. They'd hate you, you're right. I'm ashamed of you, in fact. Don't come."

"Are you using reverse psychology on me?"

"Maybe. Listen, you crazy girl. My friends are not some homogenized group of cloned Duke graduates, you know." He paused. "Okay. Maybe they are. All the more reason for you to come — freak them out a bit. Besides, I want to show you off. They'll all love your ass. Can't a guy brag?"

"You can brag all you want. I'll give you a picture to show them. I'm going out with Charlotte. I haven't seen her for ages."

"Can we at least meet up later?"

"Won't you be drunk?"

"Not if I have a reason not to be."

"Okay. I'll be your sobriety cause. Come see me when you get back. I'm bound to be home before you."

"Should I bring my toothbrush?"

"Don't push your luck."

They still hadn't had sex. There'd been an extraordinary amount of kissing and touching and almost everything else, but they'd never made love. It was almost killing him. It wasn't the sex that he wanted most — although he wanted that in the worst way. He wanted to sleep with her. Just sleep. He didn't quite recognize the person he was when he just lay still with her warm, soft body in his arms, fitting so perfectly against his, her chest rising and falling peacefully, in perfect rhythm with his own quiet breathing. There was a stillness about him in those moments that was new, and wonderful, and addictive like no drug he'd tried.

He told himself it had only been six weeks. He'd never actually been with a girl for that long without having sex, and in fact there had only been a few he'd stayed with for that long. He knew she was into him, too. It was the same damn will and single-mindedness she was showing that got her through a triathlon.

What he wouldn't have admitted to anyone was that he liked it. It felt . . . special. This was a good time. He was up by seven thirty — an hour he'd seldom seen in his old life — every weekday. Showered, dressed. They had breakfast together — usually in her apartment. They rode the subway together. They talked, the whole time. She told him about her childhood in Oregon. About the men in her mother's life. That made sense of her, to some extent. He told her some, but not all, of his family stuff. She made him honest.

He didn't want to go to the party without her. But if he knew he could see her when he got back, he would go.

Charlotte and Emily were walking back through the revelers, their arms linked together. They'd met Eve and Violet on the way out earlier, stopping to admire Eve's bump.

"Do you want kids?" Emily had asked Charlotte later, after they'd ordered.

"I'd love to have some. Didn't she look gorgeous? And happy?"

Emily nodded. She had.

"Not on my own, but I'd want them with someone I loved. What about you?"

"I didn't use to think so."

"But now?"

"I don't know. It wasn't in my plans, for the longest time."

"But things change, right?"

"Things change, I suppose. They could change, anyway. Look at me now. With a boyfriend."

"Is that what he is?"

Emily's eyes sparkled. "I think so. I mean, we haven't . . . it isn't . . . we're not what you'd call serious, not yet."

"You mean you haven't made love?"

"No. We haven't. Do you think that's weird?"

Charlotte raised an eyebrow. "Me?"

Emily squeezed her hand. "Sorry."

"No need. That's love for you. It changes things."

"Who said anything about love?"

"Your face said everything about it."

Emily broke into a wide grin. "Did it?"

"Yes, it did. That big dopey grin you're wearing right now, for example, speaks volumes."

"How's the Spanish?"

"You're changing the subject."

"No, I'm not. The subject is love, right?"

"So you are changing it. I'm so far away from that, it isn't funny. Or maybe it is. I'm what you call infatuated. Whole different ball game."

"Only difference between you and me, Charlotte, is that I took the leap of faith."

"I love you for saying that, but you and I both know that the list of differences between you and me is a hell of a lot longer than that. Besides, I can't take a leap of faith; he's on vacation. I haven't seen him for days. Weeks."

"So when he gets back?"

"Funnily enough, I was making myself a promise about that just the other day."

Emily made her believe it might be possible. She loved her for that. Emily might just give her the courage she needed.

It had been mild for the end of October, earlier in the evening, but when they came out of the restaurant's warm interior, the cold air hit them. It had to have dropped ten degrees. They bundled into their coats and each other and walked fast toward home, stomping their boots hard against the pavement to keep their toes warm.

"I'm going to ask when he's coming back."

"Don't you dare!"

"Why not? It's me asking. Not you. Perfectly normal small talk. Then you'll know."

"Hey, Jesus." Jesus had the collar on his jacket up when he opened the door to let them in. "Thanks. Cold out there."

He nodded, rubbing his hands together. Emily hadn't realized how late it was. Maybe Jackson was already back. Charlotte had pushed the call button for the elevator.

Emily glared at her. "So, Jesus. We were wondering — when is Che going to be back from vacation?"

461

"Che isn't on vacation, miss."

"What do you mean?"

"He left. He's moved to Florida. You didn't know?"

"No. We didn't know."

"He said he'd had enough New York winters. Nothing to keep him here, he said. So he went south. Like the birds." Jesus laughed at his own joke, making a bird by linking his two thumbs together and waggling his fingers at them.

"Pájaro." Charlotte's voice was small.

"Sí. Sí. Pájaro." Jesus was still laughing.

"Spanish for bird," Charlotte said.

As Emily watched, her heart aching, her friend seemed to shrink a little. She pushed her face down inside her scarf.

"God, Charlotte. I'm sorry." She pushed her into the elevator.

"You'd no idea he was planning to leave?"

"No. You heard Jesus. There was nothing to keep him here."

"Charlotte."

"I waited too long."

Emily didn't know whether Charlotte had waited too long or not. She didn't know whether there had ever been anything more between them than there was between Che and any other resident. Charlotte lived in a dream most of the time, and it was possible there hadn't been. It didn't matter now. It had been real to her, and now it was gone.

She needed to get Charlotte upstairs and into her apartment. She looked horribly as though she might cry and Emily wanted her to be able to do that freely and in private.

"Wait — wait. Hang on a second. I want to go up."

Jesus pushed the door open button. It was Madison. In the most extraordinary costume. Her tiny breasts were spilling out of the top of a black PVC corset, which topped a skirt made of what seemed to be a spider's web. It was so short that you could see her underwear, and so sheer that the whole shape of her was unmistakable. She looked unbelievably sexy, in the smuttiest way. She had a girlfriend with her, in a red PVC devil getup. You could smell the alcohol before they even stepped into the elevator. The devil had a run in her red fishnets.

"You two calling it a night already?"

Emily answered for both of them, leaning into Charlotte protectively. "Think so."

"We're just back for a pit stop. We're between parties, aren't we, Tanya?" The other girl nodded. "Don't you just love Halloween?"

"Best night of the year."

If Madison had caught Emily's heavy

irony, she didn't say so. Charlotte was staring at the floor.

"So how are things going with you and Trip?" She rolled the *r* of his name, drawing it out suggestively.

"Fine. Great, actually. Thanks." Emily hadn't known Madison even knew they were seeing each other.

"I'm glad. He's a good-looking bastard, that one. And he's good, too, if you know what I mean."

Tanya giggled.

"Isn't he, Emily? Let's face it — not marriage material. Although all that lovely money would be nice. You do know he's stinking rich, right, Emily? Course you do. Smart girl like you. Rich as . . . who is it?"

"Bill Gates," Tanya volunteered, hiccuping.

"I was gonna say some Greek guy. But you get the idea, no? And he's great in the sack. That doesn't hurt, huh? While you're waiting for Mr. Right, he's a pretty good Mr. Ooh Yeah Right There." She writhed as she said it. "Not a bad way to pass the time in a blackout, hey, Emily?"

Madison and Tanya tumbled out at the second floor and disappeared into Madison's apartment without another word. Loud rock music filtered through the door while Charlotte fumbled in her purse for her key.

"I guess that'll be tricks for us then, not treats this year." Charlotte smiled, but it was hard work.

When Jackson got home a couple of hours later, no one was answering — not at Emily's or at Charlotte's. He went down and checked with Jesus that they were home safely, then went back and knocked again on Emily's door. He tried the handle but it was locked. He guessed they'd had too much to drink or something. Gave up and went to bed, frustrated and disgruntled. But not before he'd strung the red rose he'd brought home for her through Emily's door knocker. A girl should have a treat on Halloween. Even if it wasn't the treat he'd hoped to be giving her.

Emily stayed with Charlotte that night. Charlotte cried for a long time, lying with her head in Emily's lap, wrapped in her chenille bathrobe. She wasn't crying for Che, she said, so much as for the idea of him. Around two in the morning she'd laughed a little, through her tears, and said she was crying, too, for all the hours she'd wasted on the Spanish lessons, and Emily laughed back, though she wanted to cry, and said Charlotte would have to concentrate on Hispanics in general from now on.

Eventually, Charlotte climbed into bed and fell into a headachy, exhausted sleep, having handed Emily a pillow and a blanket for the sofa. Emily knew she didn't want to go upstairs, didn't want to face Jackson tonight.

Emily asked her if it was true, about Madison and Jackson. Not that night she'd seen them together, but before that. And Charlotte answered, honestly, that she didn't know. "I thought you knew him better than that by now. Why would you listen to Madison Cavanagh? She was drunk. She's jealous. Why would you believe her?"

It was the same question Jackson would have asked. She didn't have an answer. Maybe because she wanted to. Maybe because it was easier. Maybe because it was a good excuse to push him away.

"I don't get you," Charlotte had said. "You've been so happy. It doesn't make sense, letting some idiot like Madison put you off."

"Maybe I've been a fool."

"Why would you say that? You've done everything right. You haven't jumped into bed with him. You've gotten to know each other. You like him, Emily. I know you do."

"That doesn't mean he's right for me, does it?"

Charlotte shrugged her shoulders, exasperated. "Is this because your mother is coming for Thanksgiving?"

"No. Why? Why would you ask me that? What's that got to do with it?"

"You tell me. You're the one finding excuses to dump him. Are you afraid she'll disapprove or something?"

Emily didn't know.

The next morning, when she went back to her place to change for work, she found the rose in her door, a little wilted but still beautiful. She put it to her nose as she filled a tall glass with water. There was an ache in her chest. In the bathroom, she ran the water until it was steaming, and when she heard the phone ring, she climbed in and shut the shower door, letting the hot water sting her skin.

■ ■ ■ ■

November

■ ■ ■ ■

EMILY

Emily's mother was a slight, almost wiry woman, stronger than men a hundred pounds heavier than she was. She wore mom jeans and a little too much makeup, and her earrings were always just on the wrong side of tasteful. But Emily loved her.

She went out to LaGuardia to meet her, and when her mother appeared in the crowd at the baggage claim, let herself be enfolded in her arms and in the scent of her childhood.

"*Kochanie, kochanie.* Let me look at you." She held Emily's face between her hands and kissed each cheek, then stood back and gave her an appraising stare. "Still beautiful, still too thin."

Emily had bought the airline ticket online. Her mother would stay for Thanksgiving and into December. She'd never been to New York in the winter before, and she was excited to see the tree at Rockefeller Plaza and to skate at the Wollman Rink. Emily had been afraid her mother wouldn't let her pay her fare, but her mother had accepted graciously. She supposed it was tradition. Her mother had raised her, and now that Emily could, there was honor in letting her daughter take care of her a little. The new apartment made a slightly longer visit an option now. Emily would give Mama her bed and sleep on a blow-up mattress she'd borrowed from Charlotte, in the living room. Easier, too, now that Jackson was no longer on the scene. She'd tell her mother; she never kept secrets from her. She'd never really had secrets worth keeping. But she'd rather tell her the story in the past tense, without her mom's having to meet him.

She didn't wait long. On her mother's first day, she took her into the NBC studios, signing her in at security, giving her a tour. When Matt Lauer came out of his dressing room as they walked past, she thought her mother might faint with pride and excitement. Afterward they ate out. Emily had made reservations for the two of them at an upmarket steak house in midtown, and she ordered them each a glass of champagne. Her mother's delight made her glow from within.

And the story of Jackson Grayling III

poured out, over a fourteen-ounce New York strip with a side of baked potato.

"You make him sound like a boy you wouldn't give the time of day to. Surely he could not be this bad, if you went out with him for a while."

"You wouldn't have approved, Mama," Emily concluded.

She raised her hand. "It is not for me to approve or disapprove, *kochanie.* It is your life. All I have ever hoped for is for you to be happy, and for you to maybe learn just a little from some of my mistakes. Not too much — no mother can ask that for her child. Just a little. And happiness. That most of all."

"That's what I mean, Mama. I don't think I would have been happy with him."

"But you were. Even if only for a while." Emily shook her head, and her mother reached across the table to take her hand. "You may be wrong, my girl — about him, about me. Have I made you so afraid to trust?"

"It wasn't your fault."

"What happens to us is not our fault, no. What we do about it — that is always our fault."

Emily didn't know whether she was talking about herself or Emily or Jackson. Or all of them.

EVE

Eve was shopping in Whole Foods when the pains started. They weren't dramatic, stabbing pains at first: they were more like nasty period pains — low and growly and persistent. It took her a while to realize that they were coming and going. She was concentrating on her shopping. This was her first Thanksgiving dinner, and many of the components were a mystery to her. She was pretty sure she couldn't bring herself to make sweet potatoes with grilled marshmallows on top, but she was going to have a damn good stab at the rest — cranberry sauce, the lot. Pecan pie for dessert. Violet was coming. She'd thought about inviting Rachael and the kids, too, feeling shy at her own presumptuousness, but Rachael was taking them away for the holidays — she'd been talking about it for a couple of weeks now — somewhere hot. With a whole turkey for just the three of them, Eve reasoned they'd be eating turkey sandwiches for weeks, but those little boneless breast joints and turkey crowns seemed so sad and apologetic, she couldn't bear to buy one. It was odd, all this turkey-drama in November.

They'd be doing it all again in December when they went home for Christmas. She couldn't wait. Christmas at Cath's. All the familiar decorations and tastes and sounds. After Mum died, it had felt like there'd never be another proper Christmas, but now this new one had replaced the old one, and she loved it. Noisy children running around close to hysteria. Geoff's parents, and the neighbors from the lane drinking eggnog. Midnight mass at St. Thomas's on Christmas Eve. A seasonable unreasonably early start, with stockings at the end of the bed. The men disappearing to the pub in the morning, the minute the peeling of brussels sprouts and carrots was mentioned. She was excited to be heavily pregnant in the midst of it all. Being great with child was so . . . appropriate. She'd bought a velvet dress from A Pea in the Pod for Christmas day — the perfect Nativity-play blue, and stretchy as hell. She was just about okay to fly there and back, the doctor said, just after New Year's, with a note from him. The baby wasn't coming until the beginning of March.

Poor old Polly had just had her appendix out. Cath had called that morning. Polly had woken them all up in the middle of the night, howling with pain and throwing up all over the place. It was about to rupture,

Cath said; the doctors didn't know why she hadn't been in agony for hours earlier. Cath had sounded drained and exhausted, and almost weepy, which was unusual for her. Geoff was looking after George, she said, and she was sleeping on a mattress-type arrangement in the children's ward. "Backache, heartache, and tummy ache" was how she described herself.

"She'll be fine," Eve had reassured her.

"Of course she'll be fine. This is regular kid stuff. I know that. Unless she gets eaten alive by MRSA or something horrid like that. It's just that she looks so small and bloody vulnerable lying in that big bed, with a great drip hanging out of her arm. It makes you realize, that's all. How lucky you are, and how bad things could get."

"You sound like me, not like you."

"God forbid. I'm all right. I just need to get her home and have a bloody big whisky and a bear hug from Geoff."

The plan was to release Polly the day after Thanksgiving, providing everything was going well. Eve had gone straight down Fifth Avenue and bought a card that played a Hannah Montana song, and a bear she'd "built" at the Build-A-Bear workshop, recording her own voice singing get well wishes onto a small machine that had been sewn into her bear along with a heart and two pounds of fiber stuffing. By Christmas, Polly would be back to her old self, appendixless but otherwise relatively unchanged, except for the dramatic story she would have to share. Eve had had appendicitis when she was fifteen. She still remembered how much it had hurt.

Once they were back, in January, after her picture-perfect Christmas, she planned to seriously nest. The spare bedroom needed babifying. It was currently painted a green that definitely erred on the side of sludgy; she had something far brighter in mind. Custard, maybe. She couldn't decide whether to go with the bright primaries they had at this great baby store on Madison, or with soft pink and lace. The book said babies responded to strong colors. But she wanted it to be pretty, too. She wanted a rocking chair, with a soft, downy cushion to lean your head against while you rocked. And a mobile that played "Clair de Lune."

Not so long ago, the months had loomed ahead of her, empty and lonely. Now she was afraid there wouldn't be enough time.

The supermarket was horribly crowded. And no one here seemed especially thankful. Wasn't that always the way? Tempers were short, and lines were long at the meat counter and the checkout. Some poor sod had the job of marshaling the battalions, standing way back past the soup and salad section with a sandwich board on, advertising himself as the end of the line, so that optimistic fools who had made their way to the cash registers had to retrace their steps, moaning and griping, past the thirty or forty people already in front of them. A Seinfeld-like voice came over the PA every five minutes, apologizing for the fact that deliveries were not guaranteed in four hours today, occasioning more tutting and muttered swearing. The Pilgrim fathers would not have approved. Eve found the end of the line and took her place, leaning forward on the handle of her cart and rubbing the small of her back with the other hand. People glanced at her nervously, and she smiled at them reassuringly. This damn bump was too big. People routinely thought she was farther along than she actually was. And right now they were clearly anxious that a full-term woman's water would break in the checkout line two days before Thanksgiving, slowing down their own progress.

The regular nature of the pains she was experiencing had occurred to Eve only as she neared the end of her journey up and down the aisles. She had been spooning olives into a plastic tub. Funny, she hadn't liked olives much, before she got pregnant. Must be something to do with the salt, she figured, this craving she had now. She had looked at her watch, trying to remember how long they'd been happening. *What to Expect When You're Expecting* said they were Braxton Hicks, practice contractions, and that they were perfectly normal. She didn't remember reading that they happened this early, but then she hadn't committed the whole book to memory. There were whole chapters she hadn't quite been brave enough to read yet. She'd grown accustomed, over the last few months, to her body doing weird things it didn't used to do. The heartburn, the sudden bursts of energy or exhaustion. Since the baby started moving, she'd felt even stranger. It was wonderful, yes, but it was kooky, too. She tried to imagine the faint flutterings and pulsings as tiny feet and hands, but they still didn't seem real.

She still felt okay when she got to the front of the line and paid for her shopping, thanking the gods once again for the $5.95 home delivery, four-hour window or not, and went upstairs to one of her favorite places — the Bouchon Bakery, on the third floor — for a cool drink and a sit-down. It was there that the pains got just a little stronger (so that she had to stand still by the milk and sugar station and steady herself with her hand, just while they lasted) and just a little closer together (twice between ordering her lemonade and paying for it, although the service was always a little slow), and she began to worry seriously. Sitting down without the distractions of the supermarket forced her to concentrate, and she instinctively felt this was not right. Eve made three calls on her cell phone, taking deep breaths and willing herself to stay calm. She called the ob-gyn, she called Ed, and she called Violet. The receptionist at the ob-gyn put her through right away. They told her to come straight in. She had hoped they would sound relaxed, say it was nothing to worry about — overexertion, perfectly normal. Send her home to watch Ellen DeGeneres. She'd heard no smile in the voice that told her to take a cab. At Ed's office, one of the secretaries, who all sounded the same, answered his direct line and said he was in a meeting and did Eve want her to interrupt him? She sounded as though this would be, in her opinion, unreasonable. Eve said no, she'd call back. Not to worry. Violet answered on the second ring. She must have been sitting in her armchair, next to the table where she kept the only phone in the apartment.

"I think something's wrong, Violet. I think I'm in labor."

"Where are you?"

"I'm at Columbus Circle. The doctor said to come in."

"Give me the address."

Eve did.

"I'll be there in fifteen minutes. Unless you want me to come and get you first?"

"No. I'll get a cab. There are always loads outside. That'll be quicker."

"All right then. I'll see you very soon, Eve. Hold on. It's all going to be fine."

"Thank you. Thank you, Violet."

Outside, the sun shone bright, but the air was very cold, and it stung Eve's face as she rushed to where the cabs usually pulled in. Five or six groups huddled on the pavement, arms out, waiting for cabs to swing around from Broadway. Eve wanted to scream. She pushed against the heavy revolving glass door, and as she did, fluid began to trickle down her leg, and her tights were wet. A sob rose in her throat. She half ran, ungainly and slow, to the edge of the street, where a woman in a turquoise tailored overcoat and high-heeled boots was waiting, one arm outstretched, the other cradling her cell phone to her ear.

"Please. I need to take a cab. Your cab."

The woman looked her up and down, then lowered her hand, and turned away without a break in her conversation, giving up the cab but not one ounce of human kindness.

In the end they couldn't stop it. In the twenty-first century, in the Western world, in a city known for its medical expertise, in a hospital better equipped than almost any other, with all the drugs and all the knowledge, they couldn't stop it. They couldn't stop the contractions. Eve was in full-blown labor, at twenty-seven weeks, and they couldn't do anything at all about it.

Violet called Ed. Eve told her the number, and Violet went out into the hall and used a pay phone. This time his secretary put the call straight through, and Violet heard mild panic in his voice.

"Violet?"

There was no time for preamble. "Ed, you need to come down to the hospital. As quickly as you can. Eve's gone into labor."

"But it's too soon."

"I know it is. The doctors are trying to stop it. I'm sure they can. I'm sure they'll help her." She wasn't — she'd seen glances exchanged between the doctors and nurses, glances she knew and was grateful that Eve, focused on her pain and her fear, had missed — but it was what he needed to hear. "But she needs you. I'll stay until you get here."

He barely even said good-bye. Or thank you. The line went dead.

When he arrived, they told them there was nothing that they could do. Eve was going to deliver their child today. Far, far too early. She refused an epidural. She wanted to feel every single thing. There wasn't really time anyway. The baby came fast, once the futile efforts to stop her from coming failed. A different team of doctors. A different room. They wheeled her to delivery. She thought how excited she should be now.

The long, long wait would have been over. First babies were often late, weren't they? The baby might have been a day or two, even a week late. She might have been pacing the floors at home, taking long afternoon walks in the weak March sunshine, trying to get things started. Ed might have made his chicken curry — the famously vile and pungent one he'd existed on at college — made her eat it, hoping the curry powder would work its magic on her. When something worked — even if it was just the passage of time, and nothing to do with the walks or the curry — and things started, they'd have checked her packed bag. Called Cath, to put her on standby. Debated when labor was established enough to take a cab the few blocks to the hospital. Ed would have wanted to go early. She'd have wanted to stay at home longer. Cath had been sent home, with her first baby — told that she was only half a centimeter dilated, that there was no bed for her. She'd felt humiliated and embarrassed. Eve wouldn't have wanted to risk that. The doorman would have wished them luck, as he hailed them a cab. The cabbie would have driven slowly and carefully, telling them in broken English the story of his own wife, and his own first child's arrival.

This was all wrong. She felt only pain and terror. They wanted to help with the pain, but Eve would take nothing. Twice she threw up, retching violently into the kidney dishes they handed her. It hurt, but she wanted to feel all of it. They had nothing that could help with the terror. Ed was ashen and quiet. Shocked. He was supposed to be making jokes and taking photographs.

When Ed arrived, Violet had slipped away, kissing her once on the forehead and squeezing her hand. Eve wished she hadn't gone. Violet might have been able to calm her down, she might have been able to keep talking. Ed wasn't any good at this. She remembered him joking about how great he'd be.

They didn't need to tell Eve when she was fully dilated and ready to push. Her body knew. She had never felt a physical sensation as intense as the desire to propel her baby out, but at the same time her mind screamed and railed against the waves. This last part didn't hurt, not really. The baby wasn't big enough, she realized, missing the pain she had read about. She slithered out in a last rush of fluid, and Eve fell back against the gurney, her body shuddering in shock. There was no cry, and the staff converging between her legs worked quietly and rapidly. The baby was lifted away, held not like a baby but like a thing. She could only see the top of its head, blue and mottled. There'd been a heartbeat, all through the short labor.

They'd put a monitor around her stomach, and she'd watched the screen beside the bed. There'd been a heartbeat. The baby was born alive, she was almost sure of it. Ed's head hung down; she couldn't see his eyes. He was holding her hand, but it felt at that moment as though she were entirely alone, and everything was happening very slowly, and very far away.

"Is it . . . is she alive?"

For a moment no one answered her, and she wondered if they had heard. Then a nurse bent over so their faces were close. Her eyebrows were drawn on, thick and unnaturally dark.

"Yes. She's alive. They're working on her now, Eve. They're good doctors. The best. You've got to trust them now." Why wasn't Ed asking? Why wasn't he checking? Why wasn't he fighting . . . ?

No euphoria. No laughter. No husband's triumphant kiss, wet with tears of relief and joy.

And then she was gone, wheeled through the double doors by a team of white-coated doctors.

"We're taking the baby to the NICU, Eve. Okay?"

No. It wasn't okay. It wasn't okay at all. Eve wanted her baby. "Go with her, Ed."

"I should stay with you."

"I want you to go with her. Please. Go with her. She shouldn't be alone." She shouldn't die alone, she thought.

Ed wiped his eyes with the back of his hand and stood up. He couldn't let go of her hand, and he pulled her arm out to its full length before he released her fingers. She didn't watch him as he left. In the time

486

after he went, as her placenta was delivered, and she was tidied up before they took her back to a room somewhere else, she never took her eyes off the clock on the wall behind the nurse's head. Counting the minutes without news, and wondering what was happening to her little girl.

The baby was born at 5:37 p.m. two days before Thanksgiving. She weighed 1 pound 2 ounces. Before either of her parents touched or held her, she was laid, spread-eagled, in an incubator, naked but for a diaper so small it wouldn't fit a doll. It looked as though she should be cold; it went against the instincts of everyone except the NICU nurses to see a baby so vulnerable and uncovered. But she lay on a radiant heat pad that warmed her from beneath. She was mottled and pale and her veins looked like a blue cobweb spun across her. Her breathing was controlled by a ventilator, because her lungs weren't developed enough to breathe on their own, and although the nurses assured her parents that the machine was gentle — especially designed for infants this small and weak — it still looked medieval to them, forcing her tiny chest to heave up and down, so fast it made you want to pant just watching her. She was jaundiced, so a light shone on her translucent skin all the time, and she wore a minuscule mask to protect her eyes. Ed might have nicknamed her Zorro. If he hadn't been made so utterly sad and broken by watching her lying there.

Her parents learned a new and terrible lexicon overnight. Things to fear. It was a long, strange list. Unspellable and unpronounceable. Apnea. Hyperbilirubinanemia. Anemia. Respiratory distress syndrome. Intraventricular hemorrhage.

Her eyes were vulnerable to blindness. She didn't have enough surfactant on her lungs' surfaces. She didn't have enough red blood cells, and her body was too immature to provide them. Her kidneys, bowels, and liver were not as developed as they should have been. Nothing was. But she had fingernails. Pretty, shell pink, perfectly round fingernails.

There were things they knew. They knew that the first three days were the most dangerous time, but that this journey could take months, and have repercussions that would last for years.

And they had numbers in their heads. Numbers that they never stopped thinking about for even a second: 40 to 50 percent. Their baby had a 40 to 50 percent chance of survival. Ed worked with numbers and odds and percentages every day of his life, but none, not even in the most important deals, had reverberated around his brain in this way.

And there were things they could only guess at. They called her Hope. What else could they have called her? Hope had not been on the long lists that Eve had made as she lay on the sofa throughout the summer, except maybe as a middle name, but it was the only name either of them could come up with in the hours after her birth. They couldn't remember what was on the lists. The lists belonged to a different time, a different birth, a different baby. And as they looked at Hope, through the transparent plastic of her new home, they held each other and they tried to be thankful.

KIM

Big family holidays had been making Jason sad for years now. Big family holidays called for big families. Long trestle tables full of chaos. People talking over each other, and handing around dishes piled with food, and laughing.

Theirs was nothing like that. He was an only child. Kim was an only child. Now Avery was, too. His parents were gone now.

489

And Kim's. They were orphans, much sooner than they might have expected to be. Orphans without aunts and uncles and cousins. Life wasn't like an episode of *Friends.* People spent Thanksgiving with their families, not their friends. It was just the three of them for Thanksgiving this year, as it had been every year for the last three. There was no one else. Kim's father had been with them four years ago. But his advanced dementia had meant, by then, that he barely knew in whose home he was eating Thanksgiving dinner, dull-eyed, slack-jawed, and spitting potato with every mouthful. He'd died quietly in the three weeks or so between Thanksgiving and Christmas, and Jason had felt a little ashamed of the relief he felt when he realized he wouldn't be having his Christmas dinner spat at him, too, or be introducing himself every five minutes in his own home.

It had always felt forced. Even when they were happy together. They were always too noisy, as though they were trying to sound like more of a crowd. Too cheerful.

Jason finished work on Wednesday night and headed home, heavy-hearted, for the four-day weekend. At least Rachael was away. Kim had said she'd flown to the Bahamas on Wednesday morning, very early, with the children. He couldn't face her — hadn't been able to since Halloween, when he'd made such a prize idiot of himself, and he'd seen that look on her face.

Neither Kim nor Avery came to the door when he got home. The apartment was quiet. He didn't smell dinner, and he realized he'd grown used to it, in the last couple of months. He felt suddenly hungry, deprived of this sensory stimulation, and he wandered into the kitchen. Kim wasn't there. The surfaces were all clean and ordered. Avery's wooden high chair was neatly folded against the wall. He looked at his watch to confirm that he was home at the usual time. He was. He opened the refrigerator, but there was almost nothing in it — some leftover meat loaf from last night, a half-eaten macaroni and cheese that was almost certainly Avery's. No turkey, no vegetables, no pie. Nothing that constituted, so far as he could see, preparation for tomorrow's little, obligatory feast.

They must be out. Maybe they were shopping for food now, although God knows why you'd leave it so late in the day. The supermarket would be a war zone at this point.

Loosening his tie, a little pleased at the solitude, he wandered down to the bedroom he and Kim shared. She was there, sitting in the armchair next to the bed, in the dark, staring out at the lights of the city.

"Kim?"

She didn't answer.

"Are you okay? Where's Avery?"

"She's gone home with Esme."

"Since when?"

"Since Esme took her this afternoon."

"For how long?"

"I've got to go and pick her up in the morning, before Esme leaves for her sister's in Philadelphia. I'll pick up Avery and drive Esme to the train station."

"Why?"

"Because she's taking the train to Philadelphia."

"Don't be stupid, Kim. Why is Avery at Esme's? You know perfectly well what I mean."

She turned to look at him.

"She's with Esme because I didn't want her here when we had the conversation we're about to have."

Now he saw a suitcase by the chair. The suitcases were kept on the highest shelf in the closet. Smallest ones inside the bigger ones. This was a medium-sized one.

"What's with the suitcase?" Whose things were in the case? he wondered. Was she throwing him out or leaving him? He felt calmer than he thought he would have. This had been coming, coming for a long time. He just didn't know what "this" was yet.

Jason took his jacket off, and his shoes, and sat down on the edge of the bed.

"Can't you even look at me?"

He swung around, but he couldn't bring his eyes up to hers.

"Jason? Please?"

He switched on a lamp and looked at his wife. Kim had been crying. Her eyes were red-rimmed and swollen. He felt a dull ache begin in his chest, and realized that it hurt him to see her hurt.

"We can't keep on like this, Jason. It isn't working. We're not working. It isn't fair to any of us — you, me, or Avery — to keep limping on like this. For how long? How long could you keep going like this, Jason? Another year, two, five? How much more of your life do you want to waste this way? Because I don't want to waste any more. I'm done."

She got up and walked to the window, hugging herself.

"I know it began with me. I know I changed. When we couldn't get pregnant. I know you lost your wife when that happened. For a long, long time. After Avery came, too. I will never completely understand what happened to me, and I will always, always feel to blame for it. Always feel guilty about it. But I can't undo it or erase it. The only thing I can do is move forward.

"I've been trying. I've been trying for months now. I got frightened, back in the summer. For the first time — and I can't really believe it was the first time, I'd been pushing you away for so long — I thought you might leave me. And it scared the hell out of me. I didn't know if it was just the thought of being left alone or whether it was you. I'd let things get so bad that I didn't know if I loved you at all anymore. And so I thought about it, Jason. I really, really thought about it. About you and me — us. And all the years. The good ones and the bad ones.

"I realized I could handle being alone. I'd been functioning like a single parent for years, after all. Shutting you out. But I couldn't handle being without you. But you won't let me back in, Jason. I've been trying for months. You know it. Trying to get back in. Either you're punishing me. Or you can't forgive me. Or you just don't love me anymore. You have to tell me which it is. It's your turn to think, Jason. To really think."

She came back toward him. He thought

she might touch him, but she stopped short of that, hovering beside him. Her voice was quieter now, like her nerve was deserting her. "For weeks I've been afraid of what might happen if I said this to you. But I can't do it anymore. I can't keep trying and keep wondering what you're thinking. I need to know now. If you don't love me, I don't blame you. If you can't forgive me, I don't think I blame you for that either. But if you're punishing me, you have to stop now. Enough. Enough." She raised her hands in a gesture of surrender. Her eyes implored him.

"So whose stuff is in the suitcase?"

She sighed deeply. "Mine. And Avery's. We're driving down to Washington tomorrow. We're going to stay with Sue. My old college friend."

"So you're leaving me?"

"I'm not 'leaving' you, Jason. It's just for a few days. I just want you to have space to think. And when I get back, I want you to tell me what you want to do."

"And Avery?"

"I've been using Avery as a weapon for long enough. That all stops. Whatever you decide, she's your daughter, and you're her father, and I won't do anything, ever again, to interfere with that. You're allowed to separate us, in your head, I mean. You don't have to have me to have Avery. I'm not hiding behind her."

"But she'd live with you?"

She saw him wince. Her voice trembled a little when she replied. "I hope so. I can't imagine a life without seeing her every day, Jason."

Nor could he. The ache had spread, radiating out through his whole chest, and up into his throat.

She picked up the case.

"You're going now?"

Kim nodded. "I have to. You don't have to answer me tonight. I've had days to think about what I wanted to say to you, and now I've just hit you with it all. We've forgotten how to talk to each other. You have no idea how to respond to me, do you?"

She was right. He couldn't form a complete sentence, even in his own head. He didn't want her to go like this, but he could see that she had to.

"I'm sorry," he said.

"I'm sorry, too. I'm so, so very sorry, Jason."

She started to leave the room, and he stood up from the bed as she passed, pulling her into him. They stood for a minute, their arms tight around each other, without speaking. He couldn't remember when he'd last held her that way. Then he released her, and she continued to the doorway.

Without turning around, she said, very softly, "I wish I could go back and change it all," and then she was gone, and Jason was alone.

RACHAEL

Rachael was thankful. Thankful for the gentle breeze that made eighty-eight degrees comfortable, thankful for the children's club, thankful for the room service menu. At this moment, Jacob and Noah were working on their serves with the tennis pro, and Mia was making a princess tiara and wings in the shade with the battalion of smiling nannies that had carried her away after breakfast. And Rachael was eating the most delicious lobster roll on her balcony, washed down with her second glass of crisp, cold pinot grigio.

God, her mother had been right. This was absolutely the right thing to have done. Spending Thanksgiving with David was still an untenable suggestion to her. Spending it with her family out on Long Island, as was the tradition, would simply have drawn attention, for her and for the children, to the

David-shaped hole in the family. Her mother had practically made the booking herself. Granted, she hadn't referred to David at all — acting as though he were on a business trip and Rachael and the children needed a temporary diversion. But she'd gone online (Rachael was always slightly surprised at how her mother had embraced the Internet; she researched and shopped and downloaded endless photographs) and found this break. Five nights at the Four Seasons, Great Exuma, in the Bahamas. Normally, it wouldn't have been Rachael's thing. Too vanilla. Too many women in Lilly Pulitzer shift dresses and men in pastel-colored Ralph Lauren polo shirts. Too WASPY, too preppy. This was not her tribe. That was working for the whole experience so far. It made no difference to the children — the nuances and subtleties of the socio-economics escaped them entirely — but it protected her from unwanted "friendly" advances around the pool and at the break-fast buffet. She wore her wide-brimmed sun hat and fashionably huge sunglasses and a certain unapproachable air. She'd never been the type to make friends with other couples on vacation; that was fine for children but smacked to her, in adults, of a certain uneasiness with each other's company. What did she know, though, hey? Being the wife of a man who cheated was a new and uncomfortable role for Rachael, and it was making her question so much about herself that she was exhausted just by thinking.

The journey had been hellish. Traveling at Thanksgiving was for the certifiably insane, or those with their own private jets, of which there were several in the small airport at Great Exuma. Foul weather had delayed the plane at LaGuardia, making at least a small dent in the four-hour layover in Miami. Mia had been horribly and suddenly sick on the small plane that had brought them to the islands, and had lain listless and smelly on her lap while Jacob and Noah fought over their DS games in the seats behind, garnering fierce looks from the other passengers, all of whom appeared to be dressed in lime green and sugar pink. She felt like she'd been through a wringer by the time the transfer Town Car deposited them at the entrance to the resort, and she had managed only to smile weakly at the friendly girl serving fruit punch and to follow the bellboy to their room like a refugee seeking shelter.

The mood of the children had miraculously changed. The maid had spelled out each of their names in small, colored sponges around the edge of the bathtub, a real crowd pleaser, and there was a small beach bag for each of them in the closet, containing a bucket and spade. They had torn off their foul tempers with their travel clothes and wrecked the carefully packed suitcases searching for board shorts and a bikini. Rachael had followed them meekly to the pool, sinking gratefully onto the nearest sun lounger. She didn't remember ever feeling so tired. Rachael didn't "do" tired. Up at five. Still up at midnight. That was her modus operandi. It seemed to her, lying there, that maybe it had all caught up with her at last. After all those years, all those missing hours of sleep seemed to be demanding to be taken right now. She leaned her head back and closed her eyes, just for a minute. She must have fallen asleep and was awoken perhaps ten minutes later by the loud splash of Noah, without water wings, falling in at the deep end. The lifeguard got to him before she had even stood up and returned him to her, spluttering and indignant, with a kind smile. Rachael felt the disapproving stares of her fellow sunbathers burn into her more searingly than the sun could ever do. Some people's faces reflected pity at her — the exhausted single mother, kids out of control.

This was how it would be, if she didn't take David back, went ahead with this divorce. This is how it would always be. She felt old.

Things didn't seem so grim the next morning as the bright sunshine woke them. All four of them had slept, miraculously and simultaneously, for twelve uninterrupted hours, and the sleep had worked its magic.

David emailed her constantly. He'd been doing it since the day they'd had lunch in October. She'd called her mother when she got home that day, and told her. She'd expected her to brush it away, but her mom had surprised her. Her reaction was fierce and furious. She knew too many women, she said, who'd turned a blind eye to one transgression, only to find themselves the victims of serial cheats and liars. It was her mother who'd suggested the lawyer's letter.

"Darling," she'd said. "I'm not saying you'll go through with it. But you've got to start strong, if you plan on staying. You've got to put the absolute fear of God into him. If you're going to move past it, it has to be on your terms. Completely. And if you're not, you need to be protected."

Her mother had called the lawyer. She'd driven in and stayed for a week, lavishing attention on her grandchildren and love on Rachael. Rachael didn't remember a time, actually, when her mother had been more gentle or attentive. It was like she was sick, and her mother had come to nurse her. And she *had* been sick. Physically ill with the stress of it. In all the time that she was there, Rachael's mother never once offered an opinion on what she should do long-term. She never asked for details or castigated David. She and Milena just took over the running of the home and the care of the children and let her concentrate on work, where she was sure things were sliding because she was so damn preoccupied, and on figuring out what to do next.

Her copy of the letter her lawyer sent to David had shocked her almost as much as it had shocked him, although she had instructed that it be drafted and sent.

And then the emails had started.

At first they made her angry. He hadn't been able to articulate things to her in the restaurant, when he'd had days and weeks to think about it, and now she was expected to wade through paragraphs of explanation and apology and remorse via the computer. She'd wanted a grand gesture so badly that day; it wasn't until the email traffic started that she'd realized that. She'd wanted him to do something or say something that would give her a place to start to move forward from. He hadn't come close.

Millie had told her, at the beginning of November, after Halloween, that she had to start being there when he came to see the children. It wasn't right, Millie said, that the children never saw their parents together.

Being with David in front of the children was peculiarly painful. It was the dreadful combination of the habitual and normal with the new and strange. Mia still hadn't noticed, despite everything, but the boys knew things weren't as they should be. Jacob had started looking at her strangely when he spoke about his father, trying to gauge her reaction, and Noah had stopped sleeping through the night, something he'd been doing since he was three months old. Most nights now, Rachael would be awakened at two or three a.m. by the sound of his feet, padding into her room, and the feel of his compact, warm body sliding in under the duvet next to her. She knew she should take him back to his bed, but she couldn't. He comforted her, just with the shape of him. He made the bed smaller.

She hadn't expected to still be this angry. She was sad and confused and frightened for their futures.

But often she was just mad. Rage bubbled deep in her stomach. How dare he do this? To her, to them. To himself, for God's sake.

She knew he was staying with an old college friend, in a loft down near Bleecker. Sometimes the emails he sent came with a lighter tone — an attempt at humor in the bleakness, she supposed. He wrote about doing his laundry, and his inability to ever have cereal and fresh milk in the apartment at the same time. She saw flashes of the humor she had lived with and loved for so long. But really, they were sad.

At other times he wrote a stream of consciousness about why he thought he had done what he'd done. Initially, those emails made her maddest of all. She wasn't his shrink. But she read them, because she couldn't not read them. He wrote reams about his mother, and about how he had never felt good enough for her, and how he had never really believed himself to be good enough for Rachael. He wrote about her mother. About the way she'd been with him, in the beginning, as if that began to explain it to her. She thought all night about that one. About the two of them at college, as newlyweds, building their careers, putting together a home. Why hadn't he felt like he was good enough? What had she ever, ever done to make him feel that way?

She missed him, too. Physically — the very presence of him. She missed him every day, in the spaces of their home, and the faces of their children.

But nearly three months after he'd blown their world apart, she was no nearer, lying on a beach in the Bahamas, or sitting at a desk in midtown, or lying in a bed full of memories uptown, to knowing whether she wanted him back or not.

JASON

Jason ate Chinese on Thanksgiving, from a grotty little noodle bar on sixty-seventh. He would have stayed in, but there was no food. He thought the fresh air of the walk might do him some good — shake him out of the funk he was in. He felt like he'd had a tension headache for days. His eyes were red and sore. He was the only Caucasian in the restaurant, and the only person alone. For a few moments, after he walked in, the noise of chatter stopped, and everyone stared at him, like in a western, when a stranger comes into the saloon. For a ghastly moment he wondered whether he'd inadvertently stumbled into a private party. But then a waitress gestured frantically for him to sit at the table in the window, and once his Tiger beer and plate of noodles had been delivered, he was forgotten. He chewed each mouthful far more than usual and stared at the hygiene certificates on the wall.

Afterward, he wandered slowly back to the apartment, past restaurant windows, feeling like a pauper in a Victorian melodrama. Families. Families everywhere. He wondered what his wife and child were doing.

He was too tired to sleep. Eventually, at around three a.m., he went to the medicine chest in the bathroom in search of something that would knock him out for a few hours. He squinted at the labels on the bottles, almost all of them pediatric. Tinctures for dry coughs and runny noses and creams for burns and cuts, medicated bandages and allergy capsules. Right at the back, he found a homeopathic sleep remedy Kim must have bought at some point. Only one sheet of pills was left in the box. As he pulled it out, he saw, behind it, a pink ovulation testing kit. It had to be years old. He remembered her buying them; she'd come home with the first one really early on in their quest to get pregnant. He'd laughed at her as she studied the leaflet, pretending to be offended that she was attempting to assist his virility and her fecundity. He'd said it was a waste of money — that they didn't need it.

What a time of innocence that had been.

CHARLOTTE

It was almost too cold in the park today to walk. The air stung Charlotte's cheeks and made her eyes water. She was walking into the wind. Veering left, she cut down behind the Delacorte Theater, past the puppet theater. Only the dog walkers were out, besides her. The usual Sunday parade of strollers and toddlers and smooching couples had been driven into the wine bars and Starbucks, where the heating blasted out. She'd grabbed a venti decaf latte as she passed by but didn't stay in the warm cacophony. She loved the park when it was like this — practically deserted. She couldn't conceive of the Central Park of a few years ago — a dangerous no-go area for a woman. She was never afraid here. She was free here. This was her thinking time. For weeks now, she'd been thinking about Che, and what the incident had meant. She almost laughed out loud at herself — "incident." Hardly. One exchange in an elevator on a hot night. Weird how hot New York had been just a few months ago. The severity of each season made the others before it seem like folklore. The night it was so hot the power failed, and she sat on the floor of the elevator with a man she barely knew but who had been the romantic lead in her daydreams since the first time she'd seen him.

It hadn't been the ending she'd imagined for herself. It hadn't even had an ending, she realized, any more than it had had a beginning, not really.

He was in Florida. She was here. She'd never see him again. The sadness she had felt the night she found out he'd gone, the tears she'd shed in Emily's lap weren't shed for Che but for herself. And what she'd lost hadn't been Che. It had been the ability to hide behind foolish dreams.

Strangely, it wasn't so awful on the other side of that imagination as she had always feared. At least what she had felt had been real, even if the relationship hadn't. It had been muddled with the pages of her novels, perhaps, but not entirely fictional. She would always believe there had been something behind his eyes that night. Something just for her. And it hadn't been strong or compelling enough for him to want to do something about it. And it wasn't real enough for her to do anything about it. There would be no dramatic flight to Florida, no using her new Spanish to trawl through the Hispanic community there trying to find him. No falling into each other's arms, weeping with gratitude that the gods had allowed them to be reunited. None of that crap. But there had been something.

On a bench south of the puppet theater she spotted the old woman she sometimes saw in the park. The one with the leather corset and the gray plait and the big, military-style backpack. The lady who lived here in the park and sometimes ate lunch early on a Sunday morning at the Boathouse.

Whom had she loved? Whom had she dreamed about? Whom did she dream about still?

The woman made her wonder if everyone felt like she did. Whether, for everyone, the search for love, for a partner, for the other half that made you whole was the rhyme and the reason and the song. She was so separate, this woman. So alone. But was it by choice? Sometimes the set of her shoulders, the slightly imperious way she looked at people who were staring at her made Charlotte think so.

Did she envy that? No.

Today something made her, for the first time, walk straight up to the woman where she sat on the bench and proffer her the undrunk coffee. Maybe it was the cold weather. Maybe it was a test.

"Would you like this? I haven't drunk it. It's still hot."

The woman nodded but didn't speak, and she didn't look at Charlotte when she took the white cup, or say thank you after she took the first long sip from the lid. Charlotte felt shy then, standing there, waiting for God knows what. She sidled away, sticking her hands in the pockets of her quilted coat. She'd gone maybe fifteen feet when the woman called to her. "Thanks." One word, said loud, in a deep, husky voice.

Charlotte nodded briefly but kept on walking. She knew she didn't ever want to be that way. To keep fifteen feet between herself and the rest of the world.

■ ■ ■ ■

DECEMBER

■ ■ ■ ■

RACHAEL

Jacob was in bed with her again. Rachael woke up at five a.m. with his warm shape pressed into her back, forcing her to the edge of the mattress. Most nights now it was one or other of the boys — sometimes both. Only Mia — too young to realize what was happening — slept on, as she always had, oblivious and peaceful. This was the third time this week. Rachael turned around and moved him, as gently as she could, back into the middle of the bed. He stirred, and she put her arm around him, stroking his chest and murmuring to him. It was too early. Mia would be up at six, clambering in and demanding a cuddle.

Her early starts were a thing of the past. She hadn't run in the morning since she'd asked David to leave. She couldn't leave the kids alone, and there was no one else at home. In fact, she struggled to leave the bed herself. Her energy levels were in her boots.

Her mother said she was worried. Rachael knew she phoned Milena, when she was at work, to talk about her. Mom attributed permanent exhaustion and a lack of interest in life to depression and thought a doctor and a pill were the fix Rachael needed. Rachael, in turn, attributed her mother's diagnosis to a woeful disconnection with reality. She was permanently exhausted because she never stopped, and her lack of interest in life (for which read refusal to drive out to Southampton every weekend) was simply an unwillingness to spend time with her mother. She needed to concentrate on the kids. She couldn't worry about herself. Jacob's teacher had called last week. She'd asked if everything was okay at home. Jacob's concentration was off, she said.

She'd taken them to Connecticut a few times, although opening up the house made her sad, and she couldn't lay the fire. David always did that. She'd sat back on her ankles for ages, building the damn thing the way she thought she'd seen him do it a hundred times. Once it was lit, she couldn't figure out why the house was filling with smoke. It was Jacob, in the end, who told her she hadn't opened the flue. He must have been watching more closely.

It was him that she was watching closely.

This bed hopping wasn't all. There was the stuff with school. Even at home Jacob was quiet and there was a new neediness she hadn't seen in him before. He followed her around the apartment when she was home. He seemed always to need to be with her, almost touching her. She shouldn't allow the bed thing, she knew. But she couldn't turn him away. Besides, his presence was a comfort to her, too.

He was stirring again. In the light from the hallway, she saw him open his eyes. She smiled and stroked his cheek.

"Hey, baby, it's early. Go back to sleep."

He yawned and curled up again, resting his cheek in his hand. But his eyes were still open.

"Is Daddy coming home, Mommy?"

It was a direct question, the first one really that she couldn't avoid answering. Noah and Mia asked for David but were, thus far, happily mollified with an answer about the weekend or next Wednesday evening. She guessed their sense of time was different. It had been more than three months. Jacob was starting to get it. She knew exactly what Jacob meant, and she knew, too, that she had to answer.

"I don't know, darling." She didn't. Her mother acted like it was already over. It made her wonder if she'd ever believed in her and David — whether she'd just been pretending, all these years. You couldn't give a second chance to a man who'd cheat, she said. Once a cheater . . .

Milena said the opposite. She said a family was a hell of a thing to destroy. But she said something, folding laundry one day — staying later than she was supposed to, because she knew that Rachael was drowning — something Rachael kept coming back to. She said that Rachael had to forgive him, had to really, truly forgive him, if they were going to give it another try. That was what kept her awake — wondering if she could.

"But who has to decide? You or Daddy?" Jacob's question — naïve but so, so insightful — threw her.

"I do."

"Why?"

"Because I have to choose for all of us. Whether we should all live together again or not."

"I want to choose for myself."

"I know, sweetie. I know. But you can't."

Jacob shook his head. "I choose that Daddy comes home. I know that's what Noah and Mia would choose, too. You can ask them if you want, but I know. We choose that Daddy comes home."

Her heart ached.

"And Daddy, too. Daddy wants to come home."

"He told you that?"

"No. He doesn't talk about any of that stuff. Not to us. But I know."

She kissed his forehead.

"We used to be all happy, all together, all of us. Now it's not as good. It was better when Daddy lived here, too."

"Sweetheart, I know that all sounds easy. But grown-ups are different. It's more complicated than you know."

"It isn't. It's easy. You just have to say it's okay for him to come home, Mommy."

She squeezed him tight.

"Please. Please, say it's okay. I want my daddy to come home."

His little shoulders heaved in a dry sob, and Rachael's heart broke all over again.

JASON

Kim had come back. He'd arrived home from work, and they were there. He'd seen Avery's furry pink Crocs in the hallway as soon as he'd opened the door, and he felt immediately giddy with relief. They were back.

He stood on the threshold of the living

room. Avery was sitting cross-legged on the rug, doing her favorite fifty states puzzle. As she put each state in, she said its name, although she was still too young to read them. "Kentucky. Georgia. North Dakota." She'd done that puzzle a thousand times. She knew most of them by heart. He watched her until she faltered on a piece, then he dropped down to his knees and crawled to where she was.

"That's Maine. Remember? Show me where it goes."

"Daddy!"

Avery dropped the Pine Tree State and threw her baby arms around her father's neck. Jason held her tightly, burying his nose into her, breathing in her familiar smell.

"You're tickling me, Daddy. And I . . . can't . . . breathe . . ." Avery was giggling and trying to pull away.

"You call that tickling?"

He laid her tiny body across his lap, and tickled under her arms and across her tummy.

Avery kicked and squealed with delight. "Stop it. Stop it!"

Jason kissed the bare skin exposed by the wriggling, and sat her up in front of the puzzle again. "Okay. I'll stop. If you show me where Maine goes."

She dropped it into place with a triumphant flourish.

"Clever girl."

"I missed you, Daddy."

"I missed you, too, Avery."

"Can we get bikes? Mimi and Bruce have bikes. Mimi let me ride hers, but it was too big. I fell off. Look!" She proudly showed her father a scabby knee. "Can we get bikes, Daddy?"

"What did Mommy say?"

"She said we'd ask you."

Jason laughed. "She did, did she?"

"I did." Kim was in the doorway, leaning against the frame, her arms folded around her. How long had she been watching? She was nibbling her lip nervously.

Jason kissed the top of Avery's head and stood up. Avery went back to her puzzle, absorbed by Florida and Washington.

"Hi."

"Hi."

It was his turn to talk. He knew that. So much had spilled out of Kim, the night she'd left last week. He'd barely said a word. She'd gone to let him think, and he'd done nothing else. And now it was his turn to talk.

"Glass of wine?"

They went into the kitchen, and he un-corked a bottle of red from the rack.

"How was Sue?"

"She was good. Avery had a ball with Mimi."

"She rode a bike."

"You should have seen her. She loved it. There's no fear in her."

He nodded.

"She must get that from you." Kim shrugged.

Jason shook his head. "I wouldn't say that. I'm pretty terrified right now."

He handed her a glass. They sat at the table, on opposite sides, facing each other.

"You said if you could go back, you'd change it all."

"Did I?"

He nodded. "I'd change lots of it. I'd change the parts that we wasted, not being good to each other. But there are lots of times I wouldn't change a second. When you left, I lay down on our bed, and I thought about you, and I thought for all the time you were gone, about all of it, and by the end of it, those were the only parts I could think about — the times when I wouldn't change a second. They were the moments, the days, the months and years I couldn't get out of my head." He looked at her. "Even to a dolt like me, that said something."

"What did it say?"

"That I didn't want to lose you. Not lose this. Not lose Avery. Any of this. You. I don't want to lose you, Kim."

Her eyes filled with tears. "Jason."

"I'm not done. There's more I want to say."

She nodded.

"I was complicit in what happened. I let you get the way you got. I was afraid, and I was a coward. I should have fought you. Kept you with me. I just let you go. And then I became this sort of broken, self-pitying idiot. Who could love that?"

"I could. I do. I love you." Kim reached across the table and took his hand.

"And I love you. Things need to change. We both need to change. Mostly, I think, we need to get back to being good to each other. What were those vows we took? I meant them when I said them. I think you did, too. We just lost them along the way. Love, honor, cherish, respect. I want to get them back."

"That's what I want, too." She kissed his hand with dry lips, where it lay on top of hers, and he stroked her hair.

Avery ran in. "I finished the puzzle! Come

see!" She pulled at their hands, clasped on the table. It broke the moment. A single tear rolled down Kim's cheek, and she brushed it away with her index finger, sniffing.

"Why are you crying, Mommy?" Avery brushed her mother's cheek.

"I'm happy, honey. That's all."

Avery snorted at Kim's foolishness. "When you're happy you laugh, Mommy. You don't cry. Crying is when you're sad."

RACHAEL

David rang the doorbell. In his own home. The one bag he'd left with in September had expanded over the time he'd been away to two suitcases, a suit carrier, and a cardboard box. He barely had time to put them down before the children flew at him.

It was an unbelievably poignant thing — his ringing the doorbell. But also, to Rachael, an indication that he understood where she was in all this. He'd heard her.

The children were a huge buffer. That wouldn't last, she knew. The children would go — to bed and to school, and then off into life. She didn't think that far ahead; she couldn't think much past today. She'd spent so long thinking that she would be with David forever, looking into a future in which he was a fixed mark. How complacent that seemed now. How arrogant, somehow. It had been hard, really hard, learning to view the future differently. She hoped he would be there. But she didn't count on it. Not anymore. She knew she never would again.

She'd called him, a few nights after she'd held a sobbing Jacob in her arms, listening to him beg for his father. They'd met at a bar near the apartment. She'd needed to explain.

"Do you want to come home, David?"

"More than anything in the world."

"Will you tell me why?"

"Because I love you. All of you. Because I miss you all more than I can even begin to express. Because nothing works without you."

"Me? Or the kids?"

"I can't separate you. You, the kids. You're my family. My life."

"I can't separate you either. You, the kids. It's the same for me, David. If it was just me, I don't know. I don't honestly know if I could get past this."

He nodded.

"But it isn't just me. That's why we have to try, isn't it? Because it isn't just about us."

David didn't speak. He didn't dare.

"So, look, David. Here's how it is. The kids are a given. They love you, they miss you, they want you home."

"And you?"

"I love you. I always have. I miss you, too. Part of me wants you home so badly I can't think straight. I've had a long time to figure this out. I've been so angry with you for most of it. Angry that you would do this. To me and to us. Leave me to pick up the pieces. Make me choose. So angry that you'd put me in that position. I'm too tired to be angry now. I have to forgive you. I'm still not really sure whether I'm really ready to forgive you, or just too tired to be that mad anymore."

Again, he nodded.

"But this forgiveness thing — I've figured it out. I've broken it down. I have to forgive you twice. The first is for what you did. I think I can do that. The second is much harder. I have to forgive you for blaming me for what you did. Those emails — all those emails. They were about why you did it. They were about your mother and me and not measuring up. Like I pushed you into the arms of someone who would make you feel good about yourself. Because I wasn't doing that. That's just bullshit, David. It's just an excuse. You're just a guy who had an affair, because he could get away with it. Because he'd been married a few years, and he wanted to try something different. You've told yourself this stuff to make yourself feel better about what you did. And I want you to stop doing that. I want you to take the blame. You did this, David. Just you. You have to own that. This is all pointless if you can't do that.

"I could let you come back, but I couldn't forgive you — for that part. And it wouldn't work. That's what you've got to work on. That's where my trust has been most damaged. Do you understand what I'm saying to you?"

"I think so."

"Because I don't want to let you back in, let the kids have you back, if we aren't going to give it a real shot. I don't want to put any of us through that."

She laid her hands on the table, resting her case. She was relieved to have said it. David reached for her hand, but she pulled it away, flinching as though he'd scalded her. He had to speak first. He had to say the right thing.

When he spoke his voice trembled with emotion.

"I swear to you, Rachael . . . I swear to

you that if you give me a second chance, if you let me come back to you all, I will never, never, never hurt you again." He was crying now, and a big part of Rachael wanted to just put her arms around him, but she couldn't. Not yet.

She put her hand back on the table, and this time, when David laid his own across it, she didn't pull it away. She let it lie there, on hers.

Later, at home, Millie's eyes filled with tears when Rachael told her. Her mother would have to wait. Millie hugged Rachael and told her she'd done the right thing, and told her everything would be okay. And Rachael almost believed her. She wanted to, more than anything.

Mia's favorite book right now was *The Three Little Pigs*. She had to have it read to her every night, or she refused to get into bed. She liked the huffing and the puffing and the blowing down. That night, as she read it again (or rather, recited it, having committed it to memory a while ago), Rachael realized that she had once believed she lived in a house of bricks, but actually it had been straw. Beautiful straw, perhaps, but still easily blown. Maybe everyone did, before the wolves came. Maybe the real challenge was realizing that you had to rebuild with bricks, and figuring out how.

And so here he was, her husband, the father of her children. Home.

Jacob was crying again, silent tears rolling down his cheeks. "Are you staying?" He said it twice, as though he hadn't believed it the first time. The four of them hugged in the hallway, and then Jacob reached out for Rachael and pulled her into the embrace. David's arm went around her waist, so tentatively, where once it would have been possessive and knowing. She laid her head on his shoulder, with Jacob and Noah and Mia wriggling below them, Mia's arms around her legs.

And exhaled.

EVE

For Eve, life had changed beyond all recognition. She hadn't slept a night in her own bed since Hope was born. She hadn't shopped for food or cooked or wandered around Banana Republic or had her nails done. She could barely remember a time when her world didn't revolve around the NICU. She'd been green, at the beginning. But now she knew. She knew her way around the ward, and the quickest way to the coffee shop. She knew most of the nurses by name and which doctors were sympathetic, which businesslike and dispassionate. She slept fitfully on the uncomfortable cot in the family unit and made tea, using tea bags Violet brought in for her, from the boiling tap in the kitchen also reserved for parents. She learned to wash her hair and body in the large sink.

All of this she learned by osmosis. The only thing she thought about, first thing in the morning, all day and all night, last thing before she fell asleep, was Hope. She studied the charts. She asked to have every tiny thing explained and defined to her. She knew what all of it meant. Knowledge wasn't power here, but it was the only thing she could do. Once in a while she saw new faces. A baby would be promoted out of the NICU, and a new one would come. She couldn't empathize. She didn't have anything spare. She had never been so focused about anything in her life.

But Hope's hemorrhage came later than they usually did. The usual timetable had been writ large on the seventy-two-hour list, that dreadful first day when they'd sat with the pediatrician and been given their list of things to fear. They might have dared whisper, if you'd asked them, that they were out of those particular dark and frightening woods by then. They'd moved on to different lists. It was December 16, in the late afternoon. Hope was three weeks old.

Ed was working. He'd started going back, for a few hours here and there, a couple of days before. Eve had encouraged him. They didn't both need to be there, she said. She was the one who had to pump milk, and he was the one with a job, so it made sense. She knew he was relieved to be gone for a while each day. God knows she would have been. She couldn't leave.

Earlier that day, she'd been talking to one of the nurses — Deidre — who'd started talking about the future, just a little bit forward from now, about a world where Eve would go home at night to sleep, come back in the day.

Violet had been in at lunchtime. She'd brought a bag from Eve's apartment, with some clean underwear and a change of clothes. After she'd changed, they'd walked around the block — the first fresh air Eve had had in two days. It was always a surprise, when she left the hospital, to see that the world was unchanged. Everyone was doing what everyone always did. The Thanksgiving decorations had given way to Christmas, and everything was festooned in red and green. Everyone else looked normal.

"Hope will still be here for Christmas."

Violet looked at her, and then smiled. "Of course. It's only nine days."

"It'll be a strange Christmas."

"I've had a few of those myself."

"Where will you be?"

"At home. As usual."

"Will you come in? See us?"

"I will. Of course. Hope's first Christmas."

She said it with such conviction, Eve wanted to hug her. Hope's first Christmas. Who cared that she'd spend it spread-eagled in the incubator? There were going to be more — so many more. The story of Hope's first Christmas was going to become part of their family legend — told and retold under the tree every year. Told so often that it didn't even sound, anymore, as scary as it had actually been.

That day, after her talk with Deidre and her walk with Violet, Eve began to look, for the first time since Hope had been born, forward beyond the next hour, the next night. Forward further than that. This might be all right. She told herself she had a feeling. For the first time. So it was real, not something she made herself feel because everyone rattled on about the power of positive thinking as though it were a wonder drug. A real feeling of optimism for Hope's future. She almost rang Ed to tell him, but told herself to wait, he'd be back at six p.m.

Violet clenched her fists in the back of the cab that took her home. She was tired — more tired than she remembered being for a long time. She hoped she was right. She hoped that preaching optimism about Hope was the right thing to do.

It happened at four p.m. She was sitting right there. Hope didn't move. Hope didn't look any different. The machines told them. She had suffered a massive bleed into her brain. Painless, swift, and life-threatening. Of all the bumps and troughs of the last three weeks, this was the biggest. Their faces told her, but she knew it anyway.

Deidre asked if she wanted her to call Ed — get him back sooner. It was four forty-five. Eve said no, that she was going to pump some milk. Pumping meant privacy, and privacy meant she could cry alone. She'd done a lot of crying since . . . since it had happened, but she'd never really grown used to crying in front of all of them.

She didn't know how to tell him that this had happened. She didn't even want to say it out loud.

When Charlotte answered the quiet knock on her door, she wasn't sure whom she was expecting. Madison never came these days, and she had barely seen Emily since her mother had been over. Maybe it was the porter with some dry cleaning. She didn't expect Jackson.

She still wasn't quite used to Jackson looking the way he did. She'd never seen much in him, when Madison had gone on about him, or even when he and Emily had been together. But up close, in her doorway, clean-shaven and well dressed, he looked good.

"Hi."

This had to be about Emily. She smiled, stood back, and ushered him in.

"I've come about Emily."

Well done, Inspector Poirot. A guy like Jackson Grayling did not knock on the door of a woman like Charlotte Murphy to talk about Charlotte Murphy. There was always an Emily in the wings.

"Sit, please."

Jackson sat. Charlotte took the chair opposite.

"I thought you might know what the hell is going on."

Charlotte shrugged, unwilling to betray a confidence.

"You know, I guess, that she isn't seeing me anymore."

She nodded. "Yeah, I heard. I'm sorry. For what it's worth."

"Do you know why?"

"Specifically?"

"Specifically, generally, instinctively. I'll take whatever you've got, Charlotte. Because, frankly, I'm a mess, and I need to understand it."

"I'm not sure I understand it myself, Jackson."

"What has she said?"

"Not much that makes sense. She's scared, I think. I don't know if you know much about her background, all of that?"

"Some."

"Well anyway, it seems to me that she has serious trust issues. She'd rather be alone than take risks, I think."

"But it was going brilliantly. That's the part I don't understand. It was like flicking a switch. Do you know what happened?"

Charlotte couldn't lie. His distress seemed utterly genuine to her, and she had never agreed with Emily in the first place. So she told him about Halloween. About Madison

Cavanagh and her stupid drunken insinuations.

Jackson shook his head incredulously. "But we'd sorted all that out."

"I know. And I don't think, for what it's worth, that she actually believed her. It was a peg to hang all her anxiety on. The way you started out — all the grand gestures. Your background. The girls . . . all of it. She was overwhelmed, I think."

Jackson rubbed his temple. "But none of that matters. None of it."

"I know." If she were braver, Charlotte might have touched his shoulder.

He sat for a moment.

"Do you think it's all over then?"

A slow smile broke across Charlotte's face. "Hell, no! If you're giving up that easily, Jackson, you aren't who I think you might be. I've watched you, over these last months. People don't see me, I'm that kind of girl." Jackson opened his mouth to protest politely, but she stopped him with a hand. "They don't. And I'm okay with that. I don't want to be noticed by everyone." Just someone. "But I see everything. And I see you. If you want her, fight for her."

Old habits died hard and slowly. The rest of the line, memorized from several readings of a Harlequin Romance about a medieval princess with purple eyes was "Fight with every last breath in you, and every last drop of blood. Fight with all that you have. Fight." She didn't give the whole quote, of course.

But Jackson got the picture.

ED

Violet went to the hospital each day. They knew her now, in the NICU. In the absence of other family, she seemed to have been granted grandparent privileges. She had grown familiar with the process. You took off your jewelry, washed your hands thoroughly, then slathered yourself in that ghastly Purell stuff. Then you could go in, admitted to the locked unit. There were six or seven babies who'd been there even before Hope. She recognized their parents, and they would nod and smile at each other, gently, but they didn't speak. Everyone was on their own in the NICU. It wasn't a race or a competition. You couldn't judge your baby's progress alongside another's. A lower birth weight, a shorter gestation — there weren't any rules. It was just a lottery. They were all on their own.

Eve seldom left. She went home to shower and change her clothes every two or three days. She took short walks in the blocks around the hospital. Picked up lattes from Oren's Roast and sandwiches from the deli. She phoned Cath. She pumped milk — enough milk for five babies. It was literally the only proactive thing she could do for Hope — fill bottles that she couldn't even feed her, so that the nurses could drip the milk into her — and she did it like a woman possessed. Her milk had come in fast and furious. She hated her body, she told Violet, for getting this right when it had so failed Hope inside her. And she sat beside Hope's incubator, waiting for doctors and nurses to come and update her. It was a long day. Boring, exhausting, as stressful as anything Violet could imagine, uncomfortable and frightening. So Violet went every day, to do what she could. Sometimes she sat with Hope while Eve took a walk. Sometimes they walked together. Violet knew fully how much she was needed here, and though she would have done anything in her power to have changed the course of events that had led her here, she was glad to be useful.

This particular evening, just hours after she and Eve had talked about Christmas, she saw Ed sitting on one of the chairs in the entrance, with his head in his hands. She sat down beside him and touched his shoulder.

"Ed."

He turned to face her, ashen. "Hope's taken a turn for the worse. The very worst."

Violet put a hand to her throat. "Oh no, the poor thing. What's happened?"

"She's had a massive brain bleed."

Violet caught her breath. She thought she knew what that meant. "My God! What are the doctors saying?"

He shook his head. "It doesn't look good. They haven't said, they won't know for a while, but we were told, back at the beginning, that this was the biggest thing she'd face."

"I thought the danger time for that had passed."

"So did we. We'd started to believe we were out of the woods."

"I know. Eve was talking like that, the last time I saw her."

Ed smiled a grim, tight smile. "Too soon. We let ourselves believe it too soon."

"Where is Eve?"

"She's in the hot room, with Hope."

"And you're out here?"

Ed's eyes filled with tears. "I came to call Cath."

He hadn't been on the phone.

"Then I just couldn't go back. I can't do

it, Violet. I can't sit there in that gruesome room, just waiting. I can't keep sitting there. I can't fix it. There isn't a damn thing I can do. I've never felt so utterly helpless in my life."

"You can be with Eve."

"I don't even know if she knows I'm there or not half the time. She's so focused on Hope. And so tired."

"Of course she's tired. You're both exhausted."

"She doesn't need me."

"Of course she does. Listen, Ed. Forgive me if I'm speaking out of turn. But you don't have a choice. This has all begun, and I wish to God it had happened differently. But it didn't. You're in it, and you're in it till the end now, whatever the outcome is. You can't walk away, from either of them — Eve or Hope. Eve does need you. Like she's never, ever needed you before." She's needed you all along, Violet thought. You've been the one not seeing.

Ed sniffed angrily. "It's not bloody fair."

"No, it's not. It's shitty, Ed. Shitty and awful. But you need to pull yourself together and be Eve's husband. You need to be Hope's father. Even if it is the last chance you'll get. You'll regret it forever, if you let them both down. Believe me." She stood up and gave him one last pat on the shoulder. "Are you coming?"

EVE

Hope died at eleven a.m. on December 19. At ten fifteen the nurses unhooked her from all the tubes and machines that she'd been attached to since she'd been born, took her out of the incubator, and wrapped her in blankets. Ed and Eve sat side by side on the large striped sofa in the Family Room and waited. The Family Room. It seemed a cruel name. She and Ed couldn't feel like a family, after today. The staff had tried to make it as normal and unhospital-like as they could; there were fabric blinds at the windows, and boxes of toys and books for siblings. There was a big television in the corner, with a plaque attached to it announcing which wealthy New Yorkers had donated it to the ward. But it wasn't normal. There was nothing remotely normal about today, Eve thought. Today my baby is going to die. It's over.

They'd told them the night before that there was nothing else they could do or try. That Ed and Eve needed to sign papers and agree to the suspension of treatment, the withdrawal of the life support that was keeping Hope alive, filling her lungs with the only air she'd ever known, and moving the blood around her tiny body. Deidre held her hand tightly. They explained, kindly and gently, that it was only the machines. There was nothing of the person that Hope might have been, or become, left in that body. They would stop them — they needed to do that. Unplug and unhook and undo everything. And that it would only take a few minutes after that for her to slip away. Eve hated those words, even as she nodded, even as she signed. Slip away. Hope was going to die. Not slip away or pass. Die. Be gone forever.

When she woke up the next morning, the morning after they had signed, she found it hard to breathe. She wanted to die with her. It was as simple and as clear and as real as that. She wanted to die with Hope. She lay in bed, refusing to open her eyes and acknowledge that morning had come, and listened to Ed making tea in the kitchen. When he brought it to her, she smiled weakly at him, waiting to see what he would say. He kissed her cheek but didn't speak. The night before, he hadn't held her. They'd lain in the bed, side by side, each one lost in their own thoughts. She wanted to reach out for him, but she couldn't. She felt utterly alone in her grief. In the bathroom, Ed put the radio on while he was shaving. She pushed past him and switched it off angrily. She couldn't bear to listen to the sounds of a normal day, not today, and she hated him a little because he could.

"I'm sorry," he said. "I didn't think."

Of course he didn't. She meant to push back past him, but he caught her and held her, her arms rigid at her sides at first. They stood like that for ages, the hot tap still running, shaving cream in her hair.

And now they were here in the Family Room, waiting to stop being a family before they had ever really started. She'd read about families who took their children to the chapel to die. Or out to the park. That sounded nice. But she couldn't. She was totally dependent on their help at this point. The nurses, and the doctors, and the machines. Even though there was nothing more they could do for Hope, she couldn't take her away. She had to stay here.

After she brought Hope in, Deidre left. "I'll be right outside if you need me."

If Hope was breathing at all, her breath was shallow and gentle, in sharp contrast to the big jerky movements her chest had made on a ventilator. Here, close to death, she looked more like a real live baby than she ever had before. Like a very small, perfect, healthy baby. Eve caught a sob in her throat. She didn't want Hope to see her crying, although Hope's eyes were closed, and they always, always would be.

Beside her, Ed shook a little, and she knew he was crying, but she couldn't comfort him, not yet. This time was for Hope. On the way, in the cab, Eve hadn't known what she would say, or if she would say anything. But now, with Hope in her arms, she felt the sudden, urgent impulse to talk to her. She told her, in a gentle whisper, all the while stroking her tiny fingers, how much she loved her. How no baby could ever have been more wanted or more loved or more beautiful. That for the rest of Eve's life, she would love her and remember her and miss her. She told her that she was sorry she hadn't been able to do better. Carry her longer, help her more, fix it. She looked at Ed, in case he wanted to say something. His face was contorted with suppressed sobs.

"I can't," was all he managed.

Eve kissed Hope once, very gently, on her lips. Hope smelled just like a baby. Of Johnson's shampoo and baby soap and powder. It was the smell that broke her at last, and she began to cry.

Afterward it seemed like the hour and the

day and life itself stretched out in front of them, completely empty. They were drained and exhausted but incapable of sleep. They signed more papers, and they left the NICU for the last time. Eve had been here every day, all day, since Hope was born, and she couldn't imagine not coming here. This small room had become her entire universe, and she would be lost without it, she knew. Everything else had faded into the background.

At home, the apartment felt alien. Violet had left a card with a short note, and a raspberry pie Eve adored from the coffee shop on Lexington, on the bench outside the door. She didn't know. Eve didn't begin to know how to tell her. She thought of Maria, off with Ernest and the kids on their Christmas cruise. Eight islands in eight days. She imagined what Maria would say, how her face would look, when she came home and discovered what had happened.

"Are you going to call Cath?"

"I don't think I can."

"I'll call."

Cath had left two messages since Tuesday, and Eve hadn't had the energy to call back. Hadn't had the words.

As soon as she heard Ed say Cath's name,

though, she reached for the receiver, and he handed it to her.

"Eve?" She could hear the fear in Cath's voice.

"She's gone."

"Oh, my God." Cath burst into tears, and the sound of her sister's sobs made Eve cry again. For long minutes the two of them cried into the phone without saying much at all. Eve remembered the day Mum had died. They'd been together then, not separated by thousands of miles, but the crying had been the same. She had a clear memory of Cath's tears and dribble and snot soaking her school shirt as they held each other in the time before Cath remembered that she was the big girl, the one who must do the looking after and the comforting.

Cath remembered again now. "I'll come."

"No." Eve shook her head.

"Why not?"

"You can't. Polly still needs you, they all need you. It's almost Christmas. Flights cost a fortune. Besides, there's nothing to do here. That's the stupid thing. It's all done."

"There's everything. What if I need to see you? What about a funeral?"

"We don't want one."

"What do you mean?"

"I can't do it, Cath. I can't do the church

thing — the impossibly tiny white coffin. I just can't do it."

Cath's tone was gentle. "Ssh. Ssh. I understand." A pause. "What are you going to do?"

"They'll cremate her. We can have the ashes. I want to bring her home."

"Of course. When?"

"I don't know. Soon."

"Okay. I love you, Sis. I'm not going to say it's all going to be all right, because I know it isn't. I don't really know what to say. Except that I love you. Come home. Come home so we can see you and cuddle you and then we'll figure it all out, okay?"

Eve couldn't talk anymore, through the tears and the exhaustion. She gave the phone to Ed, who held her hand as he and Cath whispered to each other. Eve knew Cath was asking questions. Was she sleeping? Was she eating? Had the doctor given her something? Trying to take care of her.

And she knew it was helpful for Ed to have Cath to talk to, and she was grateful for that at least, because she didn't know how to help him herself.

It was Ed who called Violet, too. He called her the next day, from the office. He'd wanted to stay at home, but Eve was insistent that he should go in. He'd missed too much time, she said, already. There was, surprisingly, nothing to do today. She had wrapped herself in her bathrobe and was sitting on the sofa under the window when he left, staring out at the city. She'd switched on the television, not caring what the channel was. She wanted the voices to stop her from thinking. It was QVC. They were selling last-minute Christmas presents. He'd kissed her proffered cheek, and she'd smiled at him, but there was nothing of her in the smile. She'd barely said three words. Ed ached. He ached to help her, and for her to want to help him. He felt like he was failing, because he couldn't make it so that the two of them could grieve for Hope together. He was supposed to be able to fix that. And he couldn't. He couldn't reach her.

He'd left the front door to the apartment open, and Violet let herself in. Eve barely looked at her. Violet kissed the top of her head, gently. "No need to tell me. I called the hospital last night. And I spoke to Ed."

Eve closed her eyes, and a single tear ran down her cheek.

"I'm making us some tea."

In the kitchen, Violet put the kettle on the gas and tidied what little mess they'd left while she waited for it to boil. The refrigerator was almost completely empty, she noticed, looking for milk. It was like they'd been away on a long holiday. The work surfaces were dusty.

For a while she didn't talk. She just sat. Eve was grateful for that. She couldn't think of anything that even Violet might say that would help. She was glad she was there, though. For ages, the two of them sat and the city swirled around them — helicopters overhead, cranes on the building site a few blocks over, taxis honking their horns. The thick gray sky was full of snow, although it hadn't started falling yet. You could smell snow, Eve reflected. This was only her first winter, and already she knew when it would fall. She would never see snow again, she knew, without thinking of Hope.

And then Violet took a deep breath and started to talk to her.

"Catherine. My little girl was called Catherine."

Eve was instantly riveted. She turned her head from the window to Violet. She'd never seen so much feeling on the old lady's face, pain suddenly etched into the deep lines that ran across her forehead and into the corners of her eyes.

"She died in December, too. Almost this time. Almost forty years ago."

"Violet. I didn't know."

"How could you have done, my love? I never talk about her."

"She was yours and Steadman's?"

Violet nodded. "She was ours. Our Christmas miracle. I was thirty-eight when we married. I'd never fallen pregnant with Gus's child, so I just assumed I couldn't. We didn't have this modern sense of entitlement about it, in those days. If you didn't get pregnant, you lived with it; there was no choice. I thought it must be me, but it must have been Gus who had the problem. How he would have hated not being able to blame that on me. And thirty-eight used to be old, you know, for having babies. In those days.

"I'd told Steadman I couldn't have children. I didn't want to keep anything from him, like I said. He laughed. I remember that. He said I was more than enough for him. That he'd reached a point where he had given up on ever having what we had, and that it was everything, having it. He said he'd probably be jealous if he had to share me with someone else. But he wasn't, in the end. I never thought he would be, actually. When I missed a period, then another, I honestly thought it was the change, coming early. I was forty-one years old. I couldn't believe it when the doctor told me I was pregnant. I think at that moment I was happier than I had ever been. I'd given up. I don't think I realized until that second how sad that had made me.

"Catherine was born at home — in my apartment downstairs — the week before Christmas, in nineteen seventy-one. That was a Christmas. It snowed as if to order. One of those huge dumps that bring the city to a standstill. The kind that doesn't just go gray and brown in one day — the kind that stays white and powdery and perfect, in the trees, and on the rooftops. Steadman decorated a tree, just a little one, while Catherine and I slept. We'd never had one, when it was just the two of us. It seemed silly. But he said Catherine had to have one. He carried it home from the corner of Park. It was such a pretty tree. It was such a happy Christmas."

"I can't imagine ever having a happy Christmas again." Eve's voice sounded raspy.

"Of course you can't. And you won't. Not a perfectly happy one. This will always be a part of you now."

"Violet?"

It seemed almost as if Violet had forgotten Eve was there. The two women looked at each other.

"Violet. What happened to Catherine?"

Violet shook her head. "The Christmas she was five, Steadman took her out without me. We hardly ever did that. We liked to be together. You hear women talking about 'me' time these days. I don't remember ever wanting that, whatever it is. We went everywhere together. The carousel in Central Park, the Bronx Zoo. She adored the boats, and lunch at the Boathouse, and the Alice in Wonderland sculpture. She loved to go to the Met and the Museum of Natural History. And the Statue of Liberty. You used to be able to climb up into the crown, you know, before nine eleven. Catherine climbed those stairs when she was four years old. All the way up.

"This particular year — nineteen seventy-six — the two of them went out to buy my Christmas present. I didn't need anything. I never knew what it was they'd been planning. They'd been conspiring, the two of them. Catherine had this idea, they said. Steadman had bought tickets to the Radio City Music Hall Christmas show. She'd seen it with me, the year before, when he'd been at the office Christmas party, and she'd been at him since September to take her; she wanted him to see it. They were going to make a day of it. I didn't mind. I had wrapping to do, and a few secrets of my own. And I loved to see them both together. Catherine was all dressed up. She had a beautiful Liberty print corduroy pinafore dress. Steadman had bought it for her. He spoiled her. He'd waited fifty years for her, and he spoiled her rotten . . . Except she wasn't spoiled really. She was a lovely, smiley, beautiful little girl.

"I still remember waiting out in my hallway with them for the elevator. Catherine always pushed the button; woe betide anyone who got there first. They knew her in the building. Everyone used to let her push . . ."

It seemed to Eve that the air in this room, the air between the two women, was thick with misery — old, new, all the same. It frightened her, how vital and fresh and real Violet's grief was, at that moment. This would never, never go away.

Violet's voice trailed off, and she looked down at her hands, folded in her lap. When she spoke again, her voice was completely different. She sounded almost rehearsed, like a news announcer. Maybe that was the only way she could say the words.

"Steadman and Catherine were hit by a car that afternoon. Crossing the street on Sixth Avenue."

"Oh, my God."

"The driver wasn't drunk, and he wasn't speeding or driving recklessly. He was an ordinary man on a regular day. I daresay it was the worst day of his life, too, though I never had any sympathy to spare for him, I'm afraid. It was just a stupid, unlucky, awful accident. They were both taken to Lenox Hill by ambulance. That's where they were when I got the call. They told me to hurry, and so I knew. There was no moment when I thought it might be broken bones or concussions. I knew from the start, from the voice, that it was very bad.

"And it was. Steadman died first, at about seven that night. He'd hit his head. On the car, on the street — I never knew, really. I don't think he ever stood a chance. He'd taken the brunt of the force, you see. I like to think he had a split second, and that he'd put himself in harm's way, trying to save her. He would have wanted to do that. I hope he never knew he'd failed. Catherine died in surgery, early the next morning. Her organs had been damaged. They couldn't repair them, and she died on the table. Seven hours. For seven hours, they were both alive, and I was there with them both. Neither of them ever spoke to me or looked at me again. They were both unconscious the whole time. I felt torn in two. I stayed with Catherine. I knew that was what Steadman would have wanted. I wasn't with him when he died, because I was with her, before they took her up to surgery. But I wasn't with her either, in the end. I was sitting outside in the corridor, waiting. It was cold; it was almost Christmas. I couldn't bear to think of them lying on the cold pavement. Not even for a minute, waiting for the ambulance. You'd think in those seven hours I'd have said good-bye — at least to one of them. But I couldn't. I wasn't ready. I didn't want to believe that I had to."

Violet stood up and moved to the sofa where Eve sat. Eve took her hand and held it between her own, gently.

"I'm so sorry, Violet."

"And I'm sorry, too. For you and for Ed, and for Hope."

Eve squeezed her hand.

"I haven't been where you are, Eve. I wouldn't presume to tell you how you're feeling. I had my Catherine for five extraordinary years. You didn't have Hope for five weeks. Even if you had, everyone's pain is different, and I wouldn't dream of telling you I know how you feel. But I need you to know that I do understand. I do understand. And if that helps you, even a little, then that's what I want knowing to do for you."

She could see that Eve was listening. Eve. This lovely creature she'd known for less than a year but had already come to care for so much. The girl who'd sat curled up on her sofa and listened to her stories. Who'd let her be a tour guide around this extraordinary city, and who'd reminded her of that extraordinariness, excited and wide-eyed like she herself had been in 1947, more than sixty years ago.

Eve. Just a few years younger than Catherine would have been. They would have looked nothing alike. Eve's voluptuous blond prettiness would never have been Catherine's. Catherine was dark and wiry, like Steadman. Violet had seen pictures of Steadman's mother as a young woman — formal, staged photographs taken at the turn of the century, when she was taking in sewing on the Lower East Side. She thought Catherine would have looked just like her.

Violet had never pretended Eve was her daughter. She'd never imagined herself in the role of Hope's grandmother. She was too much of a realist for that. But Eve's coming into her life had been both the most wonderful and the most painful thing that had happened to her for a long, long time.

In a sense, Eve had brought her back to

life. She'd been shying away from feeling things for years.

Eve's pain echoed through her in lots of different ways. She remembered like it was yesterday how it felt to lose Catherine. She didn't have to remember it, even. It was there, every day. Knowing Eve made her mourn the adult Catherine had never been, the mother she had never become, the generations that would not be because she had died.

But there was something else.

She'd thought she was doing the right thing, shutting herself off from the world. Not physically — she'd never done that. For decades she'd been living in the world, in this world. She had friends, she had commitments, she had hobbies and interests; she had a life. But she never again, after Catherine and Steadman died, gave herself away to any of it. She never let anyone in. She never loved another person again.

She wasn't supposed to love people. She'd loved her mother, Kathleen, and she'd died. That had written the blueprint for her adult life. She'd loved Gus, in her way, and her love had done nothing good for him. And Steadman, and Catherine. She'd loved them all, and it didn't work. In some ways she saw herself as Adam's daughter more than she might ever have imagined. She saw it now, here, in Eve's apartment, on this snowy day, for what it was — perhaps for the first time.

It was a wasted life. Full in almost every way except the one way that counted.

She didn't want that for Eve. Suddenly, that mattered more than anything else.

EMILY

The office Christmas party was still in full swing, not due to reach its zenith for another couple of hours, but Emily had left early. Her feet, in the four-inch heels she had risked because they went so well with her midnight blue satin party dress, hurt. And she wasn't feeling festive. She missed her mom, she missed Jackson. Suddenly (standing in the middle of a crowd of people intent on drinking the free punch dry and singing Christmas-lite pop songs around an electric piano) the sofa, an episode of *Friends,* and a footbath sounded like heaven on earth.

The new doorman, Jose, held the door open for her and then said something about a package waiting for her. He handed her a box with the label of a Polish deli in Little Poland, across the Williamsburg Bridge in

556

Greenpoint. Impressed that her mother had found such a place, and suddenly reminded how ravenous she was, having eschewed the lukewarm seafood buffet at the party, Emily sank gratefully onto the bench in the foyer, kicked off her shoes, and opened the box. Nestled on shredded tissue were a dozen or so *pierniki,* the gingerbread biscuits of her Polish childhood Christmases. They'd always been homemade; she remembered cutting them out of the spicy dough as a small child. These were beautiful — still homemade, but uniformly so — exquisitely iced snowflakes and trees. She took a bite from one, the merest nibble at the corner — they were too pretty to eat — and read the card. How clever her mother was.

They were from Jackson. The card said simply, "Thought these might make you smile. Jackson xx."

He was right.

That wasn't all. She put the lid back on the box and rode the elevator to her floor. Hanging on a hook on her door was a *pajaki.* How did he know what this would do to her? It had to have been a lucky guess. These were the tastes and adornments of her childhood Christmases. The mobile was brightly colored — red and green and pink and gold. She hadn't seen one since she was a girl. Even her mother didn't have one anymore; the one Emily remembered had long ago been torn and shredded beyond recognition. His message was clear.

Emily leaned against the wall of the hallway, her hand across her mouth and her eyes full of tears, thinking of Jackson in his neon Emily T-shirt at the triathlon. And of him carrying the table onto the roof terrace for Violet. The rose — her Halloween treat. Charlotte's face swam in her mind, reading the Yeats poem back to her, her eyes imploring.

She pushed the up button on the elevator, still clutching her box of *pierniki.* She left her shoes under the *pajaki* in the hall.

He didn't answer. She rang a few times, then took the elevator down to the lobby, in search of Jose.

"Where is Mr. Grayling? He's not home?"

"He's gone now, for the holidays, Miss Emily."

"Gone?"

"To his parents. I don't know where. He took a suitcase, though. And left the keys for the maid to get in . . ."

She was having the weirdest déjà vu, remembering Charlotte on Halloween. Florida. He'd gone to Florida, too. Everyone flew south. He'd left the gifts, and he'd gone.

Disappointment kicked her in the solar plexus.

KIM

Kim couldn't remember a better Christmas. She wanted to capture every minute of it. She wanted to put it all in a snow globe and shake it up every day so she could watch the three of them. They'd never been on Long Island for Christmas before, but she didn't know why not. It was the perfect place to be.

It was cold. Freezing cold. They'd been to the beach in the morning, and even in hats and scarves, with Avery so bundled in her fleece balaclava that only her eyes were visible, the sea air stung them. Their eyelashes froze. The three of them had run on the frozen sand for a few minutes, Kim and Jason swinging Avery between them. In the far distance they could see someone walking a dog, but everywhere else it was deserted, like they were the only three people in the world.

Avery tilted at the waves, screaming with fear as the white foam touched the toes of her snow boots, and running backward to escape. A couple of times, Jason swept her up just before she fell, and threw her in the air. He had a brief flashback to the summer. Remembered watching the other families on the beach reproaching him with their joy. Was that so recent?

The first couple of weeks after Kim had come back from Washington had been odd. They were a little like strangers — careful and thoughtful and considerate with each other. A little unnatural. They hadn't bickered over anything trivial and domestic, and they hadn't made love. It didn't feel right yet.

One morning in mid-December, Avery had spilled her orange juice at breakfast time and begun wailing inconsolably. Jason had snapped at her, irritated by the splash of sticky liquid onto his suede brogues, and Kim had snapped back that it was his fault, that he'd put the glass too near her. They both stopped, momentarily horrified, and waited to see what happened. And it was okay. Nothing happened.

And then the Gallaghers' baby had died. Kim had heard from Todd, their neighbor. She hadn't known Eve well, and Ed hardly at all. But she was devastated for them. Stories like that brought all the pain of her own struggle to have a child, the dreadful precarious vulnerability of it all, back into the forefront of her mind. That night, holding each other close in their bed seemed, for the first time, completely natural. And then they were kissing and touching each other, and he was moving inside her, and it was familiar and new at the same time. Afterward they both slept, wrapped tightly up in each other.

They were home.

CHARLOTTE

On a week's holiday, Charlotte was working double shifts at the soup kitchen. They upped the capacity at the holidays. No one was turned away this week. Breakfast, lunch, dinner. There was a sort of mobile hospital in the back, where the homeless could see a podiatrist or a dentist. And a big Goodwill, for new clothes. Some company promoting a new laundry detergent had set up a temporary laundromat where people could wash the clothes they already had, and there were hot showers, razors. Men and women walked through the doors looking close to death, and sometimes, within a couple of hours, Charlotte would see them sitting at a table in a sweater like her grandfather would wear, hair damp and clean and combed back, eating hot soup. It was her own Christmas miracle, and it was slightly addictive. Staying home seemed pointless. Selfish even. She could do so much here.

Even the damn Spanish was useful. Emily had laughed when she told her. Said something about the karma fairy at work. They would come and find Charlotte sometimes, when a Hispanic with little or no English showed up. And Charlotte would talk to them. Find out what they needed, and help them find it. It was, she realized, the language of love. Not how she had imagined speaking it, but more potent and more powerful.

Charlotte was no fool. She knew what was going on. She knew she'd climbed out of herself, moved away from the person she'd been, and become this new person. She just hadn't known, all those years when that was what she had longed for, that it was so easily achieved. If she stayed in this new skin long enough, the old skin would shrivel and dry up and go away. Charlotte could feel it.

It was Charlotte who told Jackson where Emily was going on New Year's Eve. What time she'd be leaving. She could feel that, too. Those two needed a shove in the right direction.

And she was the woman to do it.

EMILY

Emily stood on the steps of the building, cursing the snow. She had three-inch heels on, and they were fabric. She was already late, and there would be no cabs to be had, this being New Year's Eve. If she went back upstairs and got snow boots, she'd be even later, and then she'd have to figure out what to do with them. Damn it. It was a sign. She hadn't wanted to go to the damn party anyway. She had wanted to stay home. She'd allowed herself to get talked into it by someone who lived a block north — someone she didn't know well — and now she wasn't even there. The friend had called earlier and said she'd meet Emily there, she was getting dressed at a friend's house. The whole thing was a disaster. If she hadn't paid $250 for the ticket, and if she hadn't promised the girls from work, she'd go back upstairs and change into sweats, watch movies on demand, and eat ice cream. New Year's Eve was for kids and for lovers. And she wasn't either one of those.

And then Trip was there, coming out of the elevator doors. In that bizarre way that New York apartment buildings had of spitting out the people you wanted to see most, or least. Fabric shoes forgotten, Emily almost leaped out of the building and started heading down the sidewalk toward the subway, pulling her collar up against the snow.

She hadn't seen him since he'd left the Christmas presents. If he'd been there that night, she'd have flung herself into his arms and never left. But a week had subdued her reaction, and she was cautious again.

"Emily, Emily. Wait." He caught up with her, and ran in front of her.

"I don't want to do this now, Trip. Go back inside. Or go out. Go wherever you were going and leave me alone, will you?"

"I can't do that, Emily."

"You can. There's nothing here for you."

"There's everything. I've changed everything for you."

"I never asked you to do that."

"I wanted to do that. For you, for me. For us."

"I'm not your therapist, Trip."

He grabbed her shoulders. "No. You're my future, Emily. You're what I want. I love you. Listen to me. I changed because, when I met you, I saw the life I could have, the life I wanted. You made me want to be something. To be more than I've been . . . different. You made me want to be the sort of person who would deserve you. I love you. *I love you!*"

He was almost shouting by the end. A couple passing on the other side of the street stopped and looked at them. Raul was leaning out under the awning.

Emily looked at him. Snow was settling in his hair and on his eyebrows. His eyes, his lovely eyes, were pleading with her, and her resistance melted while everything around her froze.

"I love you, too." She said it quietly, almost to herself.

"You what?" He laughed. "I almost didn't hear you. Raul sure as hell didn't. Say it again, Em?"

"*I love you!* Are you happy now? I love you, you idiot. And my feet are freezing."

He picked her up and swung her around, once, twice. And then he carried her back inside, past Raul, who winked at them. "Someone around here is going to have a Happy New Year, huh?"

"The very happiest, Raul, the very, very happiest."

■ ■ ■ ■

JANUARY

■ ■ ■ ■

Eve

Christmas had been strange. They'd ignored it entirely. No gifts, no tree, no turkey. No *It's a Wonderful Life.* No carols from the King's College choirboys. Ed had made a beef curry. Violet had brought a fruit crumble. After lunch the three of them had walked through Central Park, from the boat pond up to the north end of the reservoir and beyond, as far as the Lasker Rink, the skating rink no one except New Yorkers knew about — up in the one hundreds.

It was freezing, but they didn't mind. It meant the park was quiet. They didn't talk much while they walked. Eve kept her arm linked through Violet's and tried not to think. She kept her face up and into the cold wind until her eyes stung. Violet took her to Steadman's bench — the one she'd bought in remembrance of him. They sat there for a while, until it got too cold.

That night, for the first time since Hope

had died, she let Ed hold her in their bed. He'd learned, over these last few weeks, to stay on his side. But that night, just before he'd fallen asleep, she'd rolled into him, one foot pushing in between his, and he'd turned and spooned her, and she'd put her arms over his as they curled around her, pulling him closely into her, squeezing him tightly. The feel of her stomach, deflated and empty and jellylike, made him so sad he wanted to cry, but he didn't let himself. He just held her and was glad to be allowed to. It had been so long, and he had missed her so much.

The next morning, they were still entwined when he woke up. They had both slept so deeply, they had barely moved. He kissed the side of her neck to see if she was awake.

Then he spoke to her, soft and gentle in her ear.

"Do you want me to take you home?"

She turned over slowly and lay, her face inches from his, her eyes staring intently into his.

"What do you mean?"

"Take you home. For good. Leave here."

She'd thought of little else since Hope died. At first, she'd wanted to bolt immediately. She'd wanted to drive from the funeral home, where they'd picked up the pitifully small urn, signing for it like it was a UPS package, straight to the airport. To get on the first flight back.

All through Christmas it had been there. The elephant in the room. Ed hadn't raised it. Nor had she. But it sat in the middle of every room and every conversation.

Only Violet had asked, one evening. Ed had been out, picking up milk and bread. Neither of them had been able to shop more than a meal or even a snack ahead since they left the hospital. There was no room in them for lists about anything. Ed went out every day and came back with a bag from Gristedes that never seemed to contain the ingredients for more than one meal.

"You'll go home?" Not so much a question. Her voice was uncharacteristically small when she spoke.

Eve rubbed her sleeve across her eyes. Even when she wasn't crying, they prickled and itched and were always red.

"You didn't."

"I didn't have anyone to go home to."

"That isn't why, though, is it?"

Violet looked at her quizzically. How did this slip of a girl know so much?

"No."

"Did you stay because Steadman and

Catherine were here?"

Violet shook her head slowly. "I don't believe in that. Steadman and Catherine are here." She lay her palm across her heart. "They are where I am."

"Why, then?"

"I didn't want to give up."

"Would going back be giving up?"

"I don't mean you. Please don't think I mean you." Violet smiled. "I suppose I'm more American than I thought I was. It's rubbed off on me, after all these years. I think it already had by the time Gus died. And that's why I didn't go home then. I thought it was pride. But maybe it was something else, even then."

Eve didn't understand. "What do you mean?"

"I mean I just felt I had to move forward. Not backward. Overcome. Pioneer spirit, I guess you'd call it. Go west, young man."

"So Ed and I should move to LA?" Eve was joking, and Violet almost laughed. "And you're the Unsinkable Molly Brown?"

"Something like that."

Ed had come back then, with deli ham and a baguette and a piece of Brie that wouldn't be ripe for ten days.

And now Ed was offering her an escape. He'd take her home. Home. Ed sat up now, pulling the sheet up on his chest. When he spoke again, he was deliberate and slow, his hands clasped in his lap.

"All my life I've been pushing, Eve. I've let it get in the way. I let that happen here, worse than before. I didn't just lose Hope here. I lost you. I ignored it because I wanted it to be different. You weren't happy. And instead of trying to fix that or even acknowledging it, I just pretended it wasn't so. And I'm sorry for that. And I want to make it right. I want us to go home. For all sorts of reasons, but mostly because I want my Evie back."

He stroked her cheek, felt it wet with tears.

"I don't know if that can ever happen, wherever we are."

"Not exactly the same — we'll never be exactly the same again. I know that. Hope happened, and I don't ever want to forget that she did. But I need you to know, to believe, that you are the most important thing in the world to me, Evie. More important than a job, or a home. You're my home. I'm not just me. I'm half of us. It has to work for both of us, otherwise it can't work for either."

"What if home didn't work for the you part of us?"

"I'll make it work. I was happy there

573

before this all came up. Work-wise. I'll get another job."

"So you'd do that? For me?"

"For us. I'd do it in a heartbeat. I'm only sorry it's taken me so long to say so. That we've had to go through all this for me to say so."

Eve burst into tears. She felt like a huge dark cloud had just been lifted from her. She could go home.

She pulled Ed's face down to hers and kissed him, more passionately than she had in weeks. He responded slowly, confused. They kissed for a couple of minutes. Longer than it would normally have taken for him to put a hand on her breast, or to pull her hips in to feel him responding to her. Each instinctively knew it was too soon for that. But they both felt the huge relief along with the beginnings of arousal. Something had shifted and, in moving, had given them a glimpse of their future.

She pulled away first, though she kept a hand on the side of his face.

"I don't want to go home. I mean I do. For a while. I need to see my sister, and be at home. For a while. I need to take some time."

"Sure. I know . . ."

She put her finger to her lips to quiet him.

"But only for a while. I want us to come back, Ed. I want us to make it work here. I want us to fix ourselves, fix each other — here. Where it all went most wrong. If we can fix it here, do you see, we'll be unbreakable. And I want us to be unbreakable, Ed. I want us to be stronger than we've ever been before."

VIOLET

Violet had suspected, from the moment Hope had died, that they'd go. It was the right thing for them to do, to go home. Eve was right — there was nothing here for them now. They would heal faster and better at home. Among the things that were familiar to them, and the people who knew them best. She worried for Eve and Ed. All the balances that had existed in their marriage had shifted when they moved here, and Hope's death had exacerbated that. They needed to go home. She saw it clearly.

But it hurt her. As much as anything had in years and years. She would never see Eve again. For a while, maybe, Eve would call. Write. Then there would be Christmas cards for a few years after that. They would always share Christmas, in their hearts. They had both lost a child at Christmas, and each would think of the other, unconsciously, forever. She knew that. But Eve and Ed would have more children. Their names would appear on the Christmas cards — children she had never met and would never know. With lots of love from Ed, Eve, Emily, Hannah, Theo . . . Those children would never replace Hope, but they would make it better. The pain would recede, so long as they let it, and New York would become just a chapter in the book of their long lives together. And Violet a person who helped them, then.

She was more than eighty years old. She would never fly to England again, she knew. Why would Eve come here? This good-bye was real, and final. And very soon the door would close and she would be alone again. Not long after that — not long in real terms — she would die.

She couldn't wish she hadn't met Eve though. In some ways it seemed to Violet that Eve had helped her more than the other way around.

They'd sat here in this apartment so often, together, the two of them. Talking, always talking. Eve had pulled Violet's stories out of her and listened to them like a child, and Violet had woven them around her like a shawl. Today she had no words. Ed was downstairs, lifting bags into a cab and making arrangements with the super. The rest of their things would be collected and shipped soon. The lease wouldn't be up until March, but money didn't matter now as much as Eve did, and Ed knew that, and Violet was glad. She liked him, but she didn't think he'd put Eve first as often as he should have while they were here. It had taken something catastrophic, like this, to make him see straight.

Eve had lost weight, and it made her look really young. The bulge of the pregnancy looked odd against her skinny arms and legs, her gaunt face. She was huddled into a sweater that was now too big for her, and the neckline hung slackly around her shoulders. Or it might have been Ed's. She still had dark and puffy circles under her eyes, red from crying, and she was crying now.

Violet's own eyes filled, and she pulled Eve into her arms, squeezing her tight, planting kisses on the top of her head. Neither of them spoke for a moment, and it was Violet who ended the embrace, gently pushing Eve away and holding her by both shoulders.

"I'm coming back, Violet. We're coming back. We talked about it."

Violet's knees felt weak.

"Is that what you want? It's not Ed."

"No." Eve smiled, a real, broad beam, the first Violet had seen in a long time. The eyes were red, but the smile was real.

"He said he'd go. He said he'd give it all up. It was me, Violet. It was me. And you. It was what you said to me."

Violet didn't exactly remember. She'd said so many things.

Eve squeezed the top of her arm.

"You didn't sink. You floated. I'm going to float. I'm going forward. I'm going to stay."

The women hugged. For a long time.

"I'm glad, lovely. I'm so glad." That was all Violet said, and she muttered it, almost inaudibly, into Eve's hair as she held her.

"Go on now. Ed's waiting."

"I'm going to miss you, Violet. So much."

"And I you, my sweet girl. But I'll be here, waiting."

"I could never say thank you enough . . . for what you did for us."

"No thanks required. You be happy, Eve. You. Be. Happy."

Eve nodded silently, pursing her lips. She didn't believe, yet, that it was possible. It was too soon.

Violet reached past her and pushed the button, and below, the elevator creaked into action. She pushed an envelope into Eve's hand.

"Read this later."

The elevator arrived, and the doors opened. Eve backed into it, still holding Violet's hand.

Violet pulled it away gently and waved, blowing a gentle kiss in Eve's direction with the other hand, forcing a bright smile that would make it easier for both of them.

Back inside, once Eve had gone, Violet blew her nose hard, put on her glasses, and rifled through her CD collection until she found the disk she wanted. Once she'd put *La Bohème* (the 1965 Met recording) in the machine and pressed play, she poured herself a large glass of sloe gin. Then she took Steadman's picture, the one she'd shown Eve, out of the drawer where she'd kept it, and the others, for far too long, and stood it against the candelabra on the sideboard, where the lamp shone brightly on it. She rested one finger on Steadman's cheek for a moment. Then she sat down, rested her head against the back of the chair, and closed her eyes, losing herself once more in the soaring aria, and in the memory of that night so long ago.

EVE

The flight was full. The captain had just announced a flight time of six hours and twenty minutes. There was a good tailwind, he said. Doors were cross-checked. In the aisle, a stewardess stood wearing a life vest, while on the screen in the headrest of the seat in front of her, a jaunty cartoon steward informed her how to fit her own oxygen mask before she attempted to fit that of a child traveling with her. Yeah, right.

Eve pulled her seat belt out from under her bottom. Her arm brushed the pocket of her sweater and she remembered Violet's card. She'd cried most of the way from the apartment to JFK, lying on Ed's lap. She cried everywhere these days, with impunity. She sometimes wondered how long it would take for normal social sensibilities to kick in again and stop her from doing it.

She'd cried in the departure lounge, aware of, but not caring about the mild disturbance her emotions were causing her fellow passengers. She'd watched the Hasidic Jews reading the Torah and bobbing at the plane through the plate glass window. Which seemed incongruous, since the Virgin plane sported its usual scantily clad Vargas girl and was named Gloria.

She'd automatically taken the glass of champagne proffered on boarding, but she hadn't drunk it. The stewardess had shrugged sympathetically when she'd taken the full glass away.

Ed was reading the *In Flight* magazine, looking to see which films were playing, with one hand on her knee. He was better at doing the normal stuff than she was. At first she'd found it strange and suspicious. But she understood now. It wasn't strange or suspicious. It was how Ed got through it.

She pulled Violet's card out and opened it. The lavender ink transported her back to their first meeting, the spring before, on the roof terrace. To the lady in the lilac suit and pillbox hat in the picture.

It wasn't a long note.

My dearest Eve,

You have thanked me, often, these last weeks. It is I who should thank you. You brought an old lady back to life, inside. You gave me back my memories and reminded me of the great love I have had in my life. And it is I who am grateful.

Don't let what has happened to you make you who you are as you go on, Eve. Let it be a part of you, but not everything. There is more life and more love in you than that.

"Do not go where the path may lead. Go instead where there is no path and leave a trail . . ."

With all my love,
Violet xxx

Ed leaned over. "Violet?"

Eve smiled weakly and nodded.

"She is a wise old bird, that one."

"She is indeed."

Eve looked at Ed, then pulled his face down to hers and kissed him lightly on the lips. He laid his nose against hers and brought his forehead to lean against hers.

"Are we going to be okay, Eve?"

She put her hand on the back of his neck and stroked his hair.

"We're going to be okay."

NINE P.M.

Since it was built in 1912, there had been 107 different surnames on the mailboxes in the mail room of the building. People had come and gone, married and divorced, been born and died. An apartment changed hands on average twice a year, although in this particular building, turnover happened mainly in the rentals on the lower floors.

As in a long-running play on Broadway,

the set stayed largely the same, but the cast moved on from time to time and was replaced. The board met, once a month, and discussed riser replacement and pigeons on the parapets. They interviewed potential new owners, poring over their financial statements and references; they squabbled with the management company and mollified people who complained about the noise and their faulty heating and the renovations happening above their heads.

The Gallaghers' apartment was quiet and dark. Ed had packed everything they'd bought for the baby, bought for Hope, into cardboard boxes. The boxes were in the wire storage bin in the basement, next to others they'd never unpacked. Things Eve had brought from England all those months ago and realized she didn't have room for. They were marked with thick red pen — "Kitchen," "Ed's ski stuff." Ed hadn't written anything on Hope's boxes.

The refrigerator was empty, except for a few jars of tomato sauce and relish. There were some clothes, hanging in the closets, and shampoo and shower gel still left in the shower and by the bath.

The city had left its mark on Eve and Ed. Deep red welts across their marriage and their dreams for their future. But the Gallaghers had left no mark on the city, except those few things they left behind in the apartment. A few boxes in the basement and chairs on a roof terrace in the east seventies. A name in the records at the coroner's office. But nothing much.

Perhaps no one ever did.

But they'd come back. They would heal and they would mourn and they would come back. To start again. This wasn't the end of the story they would write here in New York, against the backdrop of buildings and smoke and steam rising from subways. This was just the chapter of silence, and quiet, and stillness in the melee. The apartment would wait for them. So would Violet. And so would the city.

A sorority sister of Madison Cavanagh's, Clara Morton, had bought Arthur Alexander's apartment on the third floor. For a bargain. The walls were nicotine-stained yellow, the kitchen units had been there since the 1950s, and the whole place smelled of urine. She and Madison were testing paint colors on the grubby walls, before the contractors moved in next week. Clara worked for New York's top fashion PR firm and prided herself on her sense of color. Strips of turquoise and aqua blue adorned the living room, with a vivid coral in the adjacent kitchen, where there would eventually be a wall of glossy lacquered units with stainless steel tops. The kitchen would never get dirty, because Clara would never cook. She barely ever ate. They'd opened all the windows to combat the stench, and icy cold air blew in at them, so they still wore their coats.

Madison didn't know Arthur had died in the apartment — she'd never taken any notice of the old man when he was alive — but even if she had known, she wouldn't have told Clara. People were funny about that stuff, and it might have put her off. And this was her idea in the first place. She was done with Charlotte Murphy, frump that she was. She'd only been being nice to her in the first place. And as for Emily and Jackson — let them have each other. She had buried the rejection deep. Not just Jackson — Emily and Charlotte, too. Since Halloween, Charlotte had frozen her out completely. She remembered being with them in the elevator, but she struggled to recall what had been said. Whatever it was, she'd been drunk. And she was probably only joking. No, she didn't need it. She was a gorgeous girl, with a killer body and great style. She could do better than the lot of them.

Clara would be a breath of fresh air —
someone decent to have fun with at last.

In 5B, Todd and Gregory, Ulysses between
them on the rug, curled up with big glasses
of cabernet sauvignon to watch *Infamous* on
HBO. They were supposed to be at a reading in Barnes & Noble at Union Square; a
friend of Todd's had just published a guide
to shopping for interiors in the city. But it
was too cold, and they were too tired. Greg
had been in surgery for most of the day and
had canceled before he got home. Todd
didn't want to go without him. And since
said author was more of a frenemy than a
genuine friend, neither felt guilty. They'd
both seen the movie before, in the theater,
so they were half chatting, half watching.
Greg sighed, rubbing his eyes.

"Tough one?" Todd asked, his arm around
Greg's neck.

"Long one." Greg nodded. "They saved
the kid I was working on, though. You
wouldn't have bet on it, when we went into
surgery this morning. I thought we were
looking at an organ donor."

"But he's all right?"

"He'll be fine."

"I love that you do that."

"Do what?"

"Save lives. Change lives."

Greg smiled at him. He knew that. Todd had his very own kind of white coat syndrome. He always had.

"Of course, I do, too. People seriously underestimate the psychological effect of fringe on a drape, you know."

Greg picked up a cushion and playfully banged Todd in the chest with it. "Shut up. Truman Capote is about to hear the verdict. This is the best part . . ."

Above them, Rachael sat at her desk, checking emails. Beyond her, in the sitting room, David sat reading. It was just like it always had been. Except that it wasn't, at all. Everything was different.

She'd known it wasn't going to work. Almost right away. The shift in their bedrock had been too great; the crevasse between them was too wide.

She'd done it for Jacob and Noah and Mia. She'd done it for herself. She'd done it out of pride and shame and fear — that new feeling that had become horribly familiar over the last few months.

She'd believed she could make it work. She'd believed she could do what Milena had talked about. If she hadn't, she would never have put them all through it.

But she was wrong.

In a while, he'd come over to her at the desk and kiss the top of her head, and she would resist the impulse to flinch, to tell him he no longer had the right. He would tell her it was too late to be working. Lead her down the corridor to their bedroom. His eagerness to make amends was almost embarrassing. She'd let him make love to her, maybe. He was trying to do it as often as they had done before, as though that was a measure of success, of how the two of them had recovered from his infidelity. He'd be attentive, and thorough. And she'd lie there. Thinking that this life — the life they had now — was sepia. The color was gone. It had seeped away.

She told herself that the children were okay. And that because they were okay, it had to be okay for her, too. But she wondered how long she could do it for . . .

Across the hall Kim leaned against the doorframe of Avery's room, watching her daughter sleep by the light from the hall, as she so often had. But like next door, now everything was different here. Jason was cooking a late supper, and the delicious scent of grilled lamb wafted down the corridor. One of Avery's legs was sticking out of the blankets, but Kim knew that if she tucked it away, the fix would last two minutes. She'd already done it twice tonight.

Last night Avery had woken up, distressed by a nightmare, in the small hours, and they'd taken her into their bed with them. Kim couldn't help but think of the times when she'd used Avery as a human shield against Jason. Not now. They'd lain, heads resting on their elbows, facing each other, smiling. She was surprised at how mushy the pair of them were. They'd never been like this — not even in the early days when they couldn't get enough of each other. Getting each other back had done that. The outside world had receded and life was just about the three of them.

For just a moment, for the first time ever, as they lay there, Kim had thought about another baby. Not about the shots and the hospital visits and the endless roller coaster of excitement and disappointment. About another baby lying here between them. It was a thought she never believed she would have. This . . . this whole thing was something she never believed she would have. No hurry. They had all of their lives . . .

Outside, it had stopped snowing. The plows

589

were hard at work on the streets, and doormen up and down the blocks were shovel-
ing their stretches of sidewalk and mopping
their snowy marble floors. Hunter Stern's
last patient took the elevator with Jackson
and Emily, on their way to dinner, and
reflected that a relationship like this one
was what she needed — not this two-
hundred-dollar-per-hour therapy that her
insurance wouldn't cover and her parents
didn't know she had. This couple, young
and handsome, fizzed with chemistry and
affection, holding hands, and standing so
closely together their bodies touched all the
way down, her head on his shoulder. Why
couldn't she have that?

That was what Charlotte used to think.
Now, making her way home from the subway, bundled against the cold, she saw them
walking toward her. They didn't notice her
from so far away; they were absorbed in
each other. Jackson was saying something,
and Emily was laughing. And she thought
to herself, One day I will have that.

ACKNOWLEDGMENTS

I would like to thank Trish Todd, and everyone at Touchstone, for their belief in this book and for their tremendous hard work. I feel in safe hands. I am also grateful to my agent, Jonathan Lloyd at Curtis Brown in London, for his support, his humor, and his brilliant team.

My husband, David; my daughters, Tallulah and Ottilie; and my parents, David and Sandy Noble, deserve thanks in this book, as they do in every one, for everything that they do for me.

And finally, I'd like to thank my friends — the old ones, back in England, who visit and write and call and email, and the new ones in New York, who have made my time here such fun.

READING GROUP GUIDE
THE GIRL NEXT DOOR

FOR DISCUSSION

1. Violet and Eve become close friends over the course of the book. In fact, Violet is one of Eve's only friends in New York. What do you think Violet and Eve are looking for in each other? How does their friendship develop into more of a mother-daughter relationship? What do they share in common besides their British roots?

2. Until motivated, independent Emily comes along, Jackson is aimless and not particularly concerned that his life is going nowhere. Can Emily be credited for the changes that he makes? Who else in this book is saved by someone they love or motivated to be someone better?

3. When we first meet her, Charlotte is at a point in her life when she fantasizes about

what she wants but never acts upon it. How does her fantasy of her relationship with the doorman force her back into reality? Does she ultimately grow up?

4. Eve's solution to her loneliness (and to Ed's new workaholic schedule) is to have a baby. How does she think having a baby will change her relationship with her husband and make her happier? Are her expectations met? Discuss whether you think Eve made this decision for the right reasons.

5. The Kramers' and the Schulmans' marriages begin to fall apart around the same time. How does each couple deal with their marital problems differently, both in public and in private? Why do you think the Kramers pulled through, even though they appeared to be worse off?

6. In spite of living in such close quarters, the residents of the building are very private, interacting only in the elevators and the halls and taking great pains to mask their problems. David Schulman's secrets tear his marriage apart, and the Kramers' secrets nearly do the same. Emily hides from Jackson after the blackout

misunderstanding. How do these secrets, although often meant to be protective, end up hurting the characters?

7. At the end of the book, Eve and Ed fly back to London. Do you think they will ever live in New York again? Where will the other characters be in five years? Still in New York, or not?

8. Elizabeth Noble chooses a Ralph Waldo Emerson quote for the book's epigraph: "Do not go where the path may lead. Go instead where there is no path and leave a trail. . . ." Discuss the relevance of this quotation for the main characters. Who is forging a new trail and why is it so important to do so in life?

9. What significance do you think the title *The Girl Next Door* holds? Who do you think the title refers to? What did you think the title meant when you first picked up the book? How did reading the book change the title's meaning for you?

10. New York is a powerful place for many people. How does each character connect with the city? How are they drawn into it? Do you have a relationship with New

York? Even if you've never been there, do you feel you know it through books and movies?

A CONVERSATION WITH ELIZABETH NOBLE

Have you always wanted to be a writer? Do you come from a family with artistic ambitions?

I desperately wanted to be a lawyer when I was young. A British barrister. I always wrote, though — short stories and poetry. I typed my first novella on a children's typewriter I got for Christmas, during the summer holidays when I was about twelve. I'd have made a lousy lawyer, I suspect; and by the time I went to university in 1987, I'd changed my mind, and studied English literature. As an adult, *The Reading Group,* my first novel, was absolutely the first thing I'd written. I'm the only writer in the family — my brother is a teacher, my sister is a midwife, Dad was a banker, and Mum a nurse. I'm lucky in that it's a family where everyone's dreams and ambitions are supported and celebrated equally.

Like Eve, you also moved to New York City from England. Tell us about your

experience being new to the city. What advice would you give Eve? How similar are Eve's experiences to your own?

When I first came to New York, I fell in love with the sights, sounds, and speed of the city. Then the honeymoon ended, and I became exhausted by trying to keep up with everything. I found it hard to make friends and felt awkward and lonely, just like Eve. I'd never presume to give her advice. What worked for me was remembering who I was, caring less about pleasing everyone else, and getting on with having a fantastic adventure in this incredible city. Eventually, things slotted into place. I'll always be English, and I'll go home eventually; but while I'm here, I'm going to make the most of it!

How much of an influence does your life have in your writing? Were any of the characters inspired by your friends or neighbors? Which character in *The Girl Next Door* do you relate to the most, or find yourself most similar to?

I imagine it is pretty obvious that Eve is the character in *The Girl Next Door* I most relate to. Many of Eve's feelings of loneliness and alienation — and just generally feeling all wrong in her new home — came directly from my own process of adjusting. But I'm a little bit Charlotte, too, in some respects; and I'd love to be a venerable, wise older lady like Violet.

Your earlier book, *Things I Want My Daughters to Know,* uses letters to provide structure. How did the idea of an apartment building help you to structure this novel?

Having an apartment building at the core of *The Girl Next Door* is helpful in that it provides a reason for all these disparate characters to meet and interact, just like real life does. This is the first time I've had a place almost be a character in a novel. Structure is vital in a novel — it's a little like having a recipe to follow in a kitchen — and for me it helps keep me focused and my story tight.

This is your fifth book. How have you developed as a writer since you first started out? Do you feel that your work has changed significantly or developed in a different direction than you may have originally intended?

I hope so! I think I have more confidence in my own voice and faith in my abilities (although there are always dreadful patches of self-doubt and loathing during the writing process!). One change I have tried hard to instigate is my early tendency to resolve too neatly and a slight compulsion to happy endings. Life is messier than that, and I have tried to make my conclusions a little less tidy to reflect that.

Which of your books gave you the greatest trouble to write? And which gave the greatest pleasure or pride?

The Reading Group was the hardest — you've no confidence, no real idea of what you're doing, because it's the first one. I had sold it to my UK publisher on the strength of 50 pages, and the next 550 came hard. *Alphabet Weekends* was undoubtedly the most fun to write: The pleasure in constructing a love story when you essentially knew the outcome very early on but just wanting to revel in the journey, was immense. I am inordinately proud of *Things I Want My Daughters to Know,* possibly because it is the most personal to me. I am probably always most obsessed, though, with whichever novel I am currently writing.

How do you work? Do you put ideas down immediately or do you walk around with them for a while, letting them incubate? Who reads your writing first? Do you have any superstitions about writing?

My editor is always the first person to read a new book, and I'm notoriously unwilling to share anything at all until I'm finished. I write in a frustratingly disjointed way and tinker all the way through, adding bits to the middle long after I'm happy with the ending, so I only really want someone to read the end result. This requires trust by the spadeful from anyone who edits me. I'm not remotely superstitious about it, and as a working mother with two young daughters, I can't afford to have too many rituals or pretensions either!

Who are your literary influences and what are you reading right now?

By my bed right now, I have Penny Vincenzi's new novel, *The Best of Times*. Penny is a friend — we met on a book tour about five years ago — and I love her stories; *The*

Guernsey Literary and Potato Peel Pie Society, because everyone is raving about it; Candace Bushnell's *One Fifth Avenue,* because I wanted to see how she wrote New York, and Michael Connelly's *The Scarecrow,* because he's so darn good! I read mostly fiction, but across the whole spectrum, and I usually have two or three books on the go at the same time. I'm not sure about literary influences, but I adore Anita Shreve and Armistead Maupin.

Are you working on anything new? Will any of the characters from *The Girl Next Door* make an appearance in an upcoming novel?

I am working on two new novels (a first for me — it is interesting to switch from one to the other!) The first is a love story set back in the UK. The second is a sequel to *The Girl Next Door* in which several characters are reprised, most particularly Rachael and Charlotte. . . .

The employees of Thorndike Press hope you have enjoyed this Large Print book. All our Thorndike, Wheeler, and Kennebec Large Print titles are designed for easy reading, and all our books are made to last. Other Thorndike Press Large Print books are available at your library, through selected bookstores, or directly from us.

For information about titles, please call:
(800) 223-1244

or visit our Web site at:
http://gale.cengage.com/thorndike

To share your comments, please write:

Publisher
Thorndike Press
10 Water St., Suite 310
Waterville, ME 04901